Jean Rover

Touch the Sky

Copyright © 2021 by Jean Rover
Blue Agate Press
Salem, Oregon

ISBN: 978-0-9967130-2-3 (Blue Agate Press)

Library of Congress control number: 2021916436

Cover art: Josh Huhn, In House Graphics
Manufactured in the United States of America

For Henry, Elizabeth, Jack, Terry
And especially
Tyler Andrew Rover

AUTHOR'S NOTE

So where do stories come from? In 1998, a small boy actually did go missing while on an outing to find a Christmas tree with his father and paternal grandfather. That boy was never found. What happened to him is a mystery. After reading media accounts of this very touching and heartbreaking story, my mind began to play *what if this, what if that?* While inspired by real events, *Touch the Sky* is a work of fiction. All characters, places, organizations, and events are fictional, and any resemblance to actual persons living or dead, events, or locales is entirely coincidental.

CHAPTER 1

Big Bat Wilderness 2009
The boy whimpered, but could barely move. His eyelids fluttered; then opened. The dim room lit only by a small, open fire appeared fuzzy and dreamlike. He blinked his eyes and tried to focus. Orange light bounced off dark walls and he smelled wood smoke. An ember popped. Where were his clothes?

"Mama?" His voice shook.

A man, bundled in rough clothing, came out of the shadows. Tall with a weathered face and feral eyes, he smelled musty, like old straw. On the wall behind him, his giant shadow swayed to the rhythm of the dancing flames.

"Where am I?"

The stranger grinned, lit a cigarette, and took a long drag.

"Where's my mom?"

He crumpled the empty Camel package before tossing it into the fire. "You're here, kid."

"Here?" The boy's eyes had adjusted to the faint light. There were no windows in the room, crowded with unfamiliar things. Swaddled in some kind of heavy cover, he shivered. "I'm cold."

The stranger pushed him closer to the fire and piled on more wood.

"I want to go home," he pleaded.
Outside the icy wind howled. Driving snow battered trees.

CHAPTER 2

Five weeks earlier

Cally Benson heard her father's labored footsteps on the stairs. He cleared his throat, making a loud, flemmy *herrhemm* which sounded like a barista frothing milk for a latte, and shuffled toward the bathroom. Once the toilet flushed, he whistled several bars of "On Top of Old Smokey" as he worked to "fix himself up."

She felt her chest tighten. Normally, Cally loved mornings in her cozy farmhouse kitchen with its yellow walls and blue gingham curtains. But since her father's arrival two weeks ago, things had gotten tense. She sucked in her breath, placed her palms together, and shot a nervous glance at the ceiling. *Please make this morning be peaceful.*

After filling a mug with black coffee, she turned on the oven of her electric range and laid out strips of bacon on the broiler so the grease would drain. Pancakes would be just the thing for a snowy morning. She mixed the batter, poured it onto the griddle pan, and waited for the lacy bubbles to pop.

Pete, her husband, stamped his boots on the porch. He quickly closed the door against a blast of wind. "That's serious snow out there." After tossing the morning paper onto the table, he brushed flakes off his wool hat and heavy jacket before hanging them on the coat rack, then ran both hands over his curly, light-brown hair as if to wake it up. Traces of snow melted off his waffle-sole boots, leaving puddles on the kitchen floor.

Cally felt him nuzzle the back of her neck, rubbing his cold face in her shoulder-length dark hair. She turned and gave his cheek a quick peck. "You're cold, like ice. Better have some coffee."

Another strong gust of wind slammed snowflakes against the kitchen window, shaking the shutters causing them to make sloppy, staccato sounds. Thankful for her warm jeans, Cally zipped up the blue fleece jacket she wore over a thin sweatshirt. She used to throw on her winter bathrobe and then dress after her eight-year-old son, Cody, left for school. Now with her dad on board, she made an extra effort to look presentable.

She slipped a stack of pancakes onto a flowered breakfast plate. "Hot off the griddle," she said.

Pete warmed himself briefly by their small wood-burning stove, got coffee, and settled down at the table with his pancakes and the paper.

A loud gargle escaped through the bathroom's thin walls. Water ran into the basin at a fierce pace. Soon, the door banged shut. Sam entered the kitchen and yawned a long *Arhhhhh*. "It's colder than a well-digger's ass in the Yukon," he blurted, the belt of his jeans hitched up high around his belly. He scratched his ribs.

"Did you sleep okay, Dad?"

Sam looked tired and older than his sixty-eight years. His pink scalp showed through his thinning, ruffled white hair, and lines around his mouth reached his chin. The frown marks between his still-dark eyebrows seemed deeper this morning.

"Had to take my Advil. Dang arthritis is actin' up." He grabbed a paper napkin from the plastic holder on the counter and blew his nose with a loud honk. When he finished, he pulled open the tiny door on the wood stove and tossed it in. "There's nothin' like wood heat to warm up a house. Back in Montana, it got us through lotsa cold winters, let me tell you." He pulled back the kitchen chair, scraping it against the tile floor, and seated himself.

The *screeeeech* of the chair legs made Cally clench her teeth.

"You wouldn't have trouble sleeping if you didn't doze in front of the TV and then hit the sack at midnight," Pete growled from behind the sports page.

Cally winced. Her father's aging ears required a deafening TV volume, which was a sore point with Pete. He also claimed Sam's loud snoring bounced off Big Bat Mountain and shook squirrels out of trees.

Pete had never warmed up to Sam, a hardheaded, retired truck driver, who liked to get his nose wet in pints of beer. Like an old, rusty pipe wrench, once Sam locked onto an idea, he'd never let go.

Cally's mother had died in August, causing Sam to fall into a deep depression and engage in bouts of heavy drinking. Pete had reluctantly agreed to let Sam stay with them in Forest Lake. It wouldn't be forever, Cally had assured him. Just until her dad got his feet on the ground.

She set a plate of pancakes in front of Sam. He reached for the butter, smeared on gobs, and drowned the cakes in maple syrup. "Your mother always made good flapjacks." Sam rubbed his hands together over his plate and took a bite. "The first thing a smart trucker learns out on the road," he said with his mouth full, "is where to find a damn good hasher. Why, I remember—"

Pete pushed his chair back and stood. "Is there any more coffee?"

Cally could see Pete's cup didn't need refilling. He was just trying to avoid another one of Sam's repetitious, convoluted road stories. She glanced at the clock and stepped into the hallway. "Cody," she called up the stairs to her young son. "You need to get moving. Cody, are you—"

The phone rang.

"I'll get that," Pete said, visibly relieved.

Cally set a platter of bacon on the table near her father's plate.

Cody sauntered into the kitchen. A clump of his brown hair stood on end, and his large, dark eyes looked sleepy. He plopped his thin body down in a chair.

"Hi, buddy," Sam said as Cally brought Cody the pancake that she'd kept warm in the oven.

"Here's the syrup, buddy," said Sam. "I left some for ya."

Cody wrinkled his nose. He reached for the Jif and coated his pancake with a thick layer.

Cally screwed the lid back on the jar. "Cody would spread peanut butter on the walls of his room if we let him." She returned it to the fridge.

Sam winked. "You better be careful with that stuff. It'll make your mouth stick shut."

Pete cradled the receiver between his ear and shoulder. "Let me write the location down." He hung up the phone. "We got another sick deer over by the lake." His blue eyes turned serious. "I'll have to go out there and take tissue samples. That makes number three."

Cally and Pete had grown up in Montana, graduated from Montana State, and married after their senior year. They settled in Bozeman, where Pete worked as a field wildlife biologist. Four years ago, they'd moved to Forest Lake, a quiet community of about 500 located at the edge of southern Oregon near the California border when Pete had taken a similar job with the State of Oregon.

"What's wrong with 'em?" Sam asked. He wiped syrup from his chin with a napkin.

"We think it may be adenovirus. It's a highly contagious disease, but we still haven't got definite results back from the lab. The one we found over by Hadley's Lake Store was a young deer with a plastic bag in its stomach."

"Benny said the deer ate caramel corn, and it stuck in her throat," said Cody, his dark eyes sad.

"Eat your breakfast, hon." Cally gave Pete a nervous look. Cody's penchant for fantasy continually frustrated his dad.

Cody took a bite of the bacon he held in his fingers. "Benny says —"

"People shouldn't feed the deer," Pete interrupted sternly. "And quit with that Benny stuff."

Startled by his father's tone, Cody swung back against his chair, his eyes locked on the table.

Pete turned toward Sam. "When it gets cold, folks think they have to leave food and water out for the deer. These makeshift feeding stations cause the disease to spread. It's like people with the flu sharing a water glass. We've posted signs, but apparently, some of 'em can't read." He took a final, hurried swallow of coffee. "I'll have to contact Deputy Blake again and have him meet me at the lake."

"Why call a deputy sheriff?" Sam asked.

"Blake will have to shoot the deer. He's always willing to help, and he lives here in Forest Lake. That makes it convenient."

"No! Don't let them do that," Cody pleaded.

"We don't have a lot of choice, son."

"But—"

"Hope that virus don't reduce the deer population," Sam said, "or we won't be able to hunt next year." He stifled a small burp with his hand.

Pete rolled his eyes at Cally. While he enjoyed hiking and fishing, he never hunted. And, he didn't particularly like hunters. In his opinion, they seemed more interested in beer parties than foraging for food. When the underbrush was dry, the careless ones started forest fires.

Sam grinned at Cody. "Hey buddy, wanna go deer huntin' with me next season?"

Cody pushed his food around on his plate. He gave his mother a sideways look.

"Cody is too young," Pete shot back. "He's only eight."

Sam shook his head. "Hell, I taught Cally to shoot a gun when she was ten."

"We don't have guns in this house," Pete said, his voice rising.

Cally slipped another pancake onto Sam's plate, hoping more food would fill his mouth and end the conversation.

Sam wasn't letting go. "Cody's a country boy." He drenched the cake in syrup and glanced at Cally. "You can't shelter a country boy."

"Let's change the subject," Cally said.

"Dad, can I have a dog?" Cody asked.

Cally pressed her index finger to her lips. "Now isn't a good time to bring that up."

"You said to change the subject. Why can't—"

"Cody, we've talked about that a thousand times," Pete interrupted. "A dog is a lot of responsibility."

"Every boy should have a dog," Sam said.

Pete glared at him.

"Brittany has a dog," Cody said.

"It's out of the question," Pete said, crossing his arms, "until we quit getting calls from your teacher."

"It's a Cocker Spaniel puppy. They named it Bowser. Brittany said Bowser has a brother who needs a home. Mom, can we—"

Pete slammed his hand on the table. The lid on the sugar bowl rattled. "Cody, what did I just say?"

Cody hung his head.

Cally smoothed the hair on her son's head. *Pete is too hard on Cody. He's never going to be an outdoorsy kid.* "You'll need to dress warm, honey. It's snowing outside and it's windy. The school bus may be running slow."

"Wear those good Snobuster boots I bought ya, buddy," Sam said.

Pete pulled on his heavy jacket. "I've got to be going, too." He sighed and gave Cally a hurried kiss. "Remember what I told you, Cody," he said before heading out.

Cally adjusted the straps on her son's sturdy boots and fastened his hooded jacket. Cody pulled away. "I can do it, Mom." When he reached for his backpack, *The Goblet of Fire* tumbled to the floor.

Cally picked it up, slapping it against her open hand. "I told you, you can't take your Harry Potter book to school." She looked at Sam. "He reads it in class instead of doing his work."

"Aw, Mom," Cody whined. "I need it."

"You can read the book at home. Remember what Dad said. We don't want another call from your teacher."

"I don't like Miss Brackston." He folded his small arms in front of his chest just like Pete did when he made up his mind about something.

"Listen." Cally pointed her finger at him. "You need to settle down and do what your teacher says."

Sam broke into snorting laughter. "I never liked my teacher, neither. We used to tape her desk drawer shut when she wasn't lookin'. Boy did that make the ol' bag mad."

Cody giggled.

Cally narrowed her eyes. "Dad . . . stop."

Cody heaved the backpack over his thin shoulders, and Cally gave him a hug.

"Be sure to stay in the bus shelter until the school bus comes," she said, holding the door open. "You don't want to end up sick for the holidays."

Cally watched Cody make his way down the porch steps. She could hear his boots crunch the snow. She brought her coffee to the table and took a bite of Cody's half-eaten, peanut butter-smeared pancake.

"For God's sake, put some meat on that kid," Sam said. "He eats like a bird."

Cally sipped her coffee, set the cup down, and leaned back in her chair. "I'm worried about Cody. He's having problems at school."

Sam waved his hand in the air. "Aw, boys will be boys."

"His teacher says he has trouble focusing . . . like maybe he's hyperactive."

Sam leaned his chin on his hand. "There were no hyperactive kids when I was in school. You gotta quit coddlin' the boy."

"He's a bright kid, but he gets distracted."

"Give him responsibilities, somethin' to do. A dog would be perfect for starters, or maybe a horse." He scratched his stomach.

"His teacher suggested a therapist in Klamath Falls, but Pete thinks it's just a stage that he'll outgrow. We don't want to put him on medication."

"Pills? Specialists? Holy shit. Before I'd drug a kid, I'd put a basketball hoop up in the barn. You aren't usin' it for nothing. Pete needs to spend more time with him."

"Pete tries, but he just ends up getting mad. Cody's got quite an imagination. He likes to read and draw."

"Draw? That's girly stuff. What the hell does he draw?"

"Well, lately it's bugs—spiders, nice grasshoppers, and, uh, ladybugs."

Sam's eyes widened. He rubbed the side of his face.

"They're quite good, actually," Cally said, defending her son. "The ladybugs, I mean, and . . . he . . . names them."

"Ladybugs, with names?"

"He's almost got a whole . . . um . . . family." She cleared her throat. "He's a very talented little boy."

"Kee-rist," Sam groaned. He looked like someone who'd just hit his thumb with a hammer.

CHAPTER 3

Deputy Sheriff Ken Blake made his rounds Monday morning in his Jeep Cherokee equipped with four-wheel drive and snow tires. Aside from shooting a sick deer last week with Pete Benson, the territory he covered—a large portion of remote Klamath County—was in a deep yawn. Ken smiled to himself. Forest Lake and its environs were like that most of the time, not counting the occasional scuffles at Benders, a tatty bar and grill out on the highway that ran east of town.

Around 10:00 a.m., Ken headed toward the grade school, parked his Jeep by the playground, and watched groups of bundled-up kids bounding out for recess. Last Friday, he'd responded to a call from Principal Cora Everson. A teacher had reported a suspicious vehicle with a scruffy-looking middle-aged man sitting in it, parked near the playground. He'd been saying something to several younger children, but when the teacher approached, he sped away. Cora was leery because the teacher had seen that car there before. She'd described it as a dirty maroon station wagon. No one knew the make or had gotten a license plate number.

Ken was concerned because a young boy had recently gone missing near Grants Pass. Although that was a good 100 miles away, he knew that perps on the run could show up anywhere.

Little Darrel Petersen was round-eyed and excited to be talking to a cop in uniform. "The man wanted to know how to get to the highway and find the Big Bat," he said when Ken had interviewed him last week.

"Yeah," said Lotty Davis, fidgeting, her voice coming out soft. "He was lost. That's all."

Darrel stared at the black Glock pistol hanging on Ken's duty belt. "Is that real?"

"You betcha," Ken said, amused.

Darrel wrinkled his freckled nose. His two front teeth were missing. "You ever shoot anybody?"

Ken stifled a chuckle. He loved talking to kids. He folded his arms and mustered up his drill-sergeant voice. "Guns are serious business. Never play with guns. And don't ever be talking to strangers."

Ken had assured Cora that he would include the school on his rounds, especially when the kids played outdoors. He also agreed to visit the school and talk about safety.

After the bell rang and the kids returned to class, Ken drove out to the highway toward Hadley's Lake Store to follow up on a report of a theft of clothes and canned goods. In spite of heavy snow that had fallen the previous week, the road was plowed and sanded, leaving dirty piles of snow mounded on each side of the highway.

He found Amos Hadley, the storeowner, pacing outside wearing a dark wool mackinaw. Wisps of white hair crept from under the red knit cap covering his balding head and hung over his ears.

"They sprung the locks," Amos blurted.

The Hadley family had owned the store for as long as Ken could remember. It now stayed open in the winter to cater to skiers, since there wasn't a ski lodge on or near Big Bat Mountain. The Big Bat, as locals called it, had one central round peak, and smaller pointed ones on each side that made it resemble a bat in flight.

Hadley's was a good place to purchase last-minute groceries, sundries, camping supplies, and fishing tackle. New items included freshly brewed Starbucks coffee, pre-made sandwiches, and some apparel. Except for an extensive remodeling which expanded the back and west side, the look of the storefront had changed little since he and Jim Fallingwater were young sprouts stopping in to buy ice cream.

"I tell you this guy was a real pro," Amos said. "Never thought he'd break in here with my double lock there on the back door."

Ken dusted the lock for fingerprints, doubting he'd find anything. Over the last few years, the store had been a frequent burglary target. It was isolated, and it took time for law enforcement to respond. There had been more thefts reported at the lake cabins, too. Most were vacant in the winter, although skiers now rented a few.

Inside, Amos had a warm fire going in his small, black wood-burning stove. The rich aroma of freshly brewed coffee lingered in the air. Amos took off his hat and hung his coat on the wall pegs by the front door.

"Did you check the cash register?" Ken asked. "Any money missing?"

"That's the heck of it. This guy springs two locks on the back door and doesn't touch the till. I don't leave that much in it, just a few dollars to make change in the mornin'." He pulled the drawer open with a veined hand blotched with liver spots.

"The things I figure is missing is the food, an Alpine ski jacket, a couple of blankets, a water bottle. Dammit Ken, that bastard cleaned me all out of my Camel cigarettes. Shit, and all the canned beans. He made a real dent in my soup, too."

"You oughta install a camera," Ken said.

Amos wasn't listening. His lower lip trembled, and his usually sallow face was red. "And men's socks. He took socks. That's how I know it was a guy. Damn people, come up here and act like a bunch of hoodlums. Who'd steal a ski jacket except some goddamned skier?"

"C'mon, Amos, those folks are your customers. Since they discovered the Big Bat's powdery snow, your business has been humming. Folks in town say that's how you got that brand new Silverado you've been driving all over the county."

Amos glared, pursed his lips, and swallowed. His Adam's apple went up and down. "Who the hell do they think they are? I heard they took over Ben Hothan's barn and had themselves a beer party. Now if that don't beat all. Damn snobs."

"The thief didn't take any cash, and it doesn't make sense that skiers would steal all those canned goods for a short stay," Ken said.

"Dammit, you gotta do something about this." Amos's eyes narrowed. His cheek twitched. "There's gonna be more people comin' here after Thanksgiving to get in some skiin' over the long weekend. More will be comin' in after Christmas for the winter holiday. The motel in town is booked full, you know. I want some protection out here."

Ken gave Amos a hard look. The old guy seemed to be blaming him for the burglary. "You gotta meet us halfway. Install a camera and an alarm. Post some signs."

"Those idiots probably can't read. I'm gonna bring in my huntin' rifle. Spend a few nights up here."

"That's the last thing you should do," Ken warned.

"I pay good taxes for protection. Dammit anyway."

"I told Pete Benson I'd drive out to the lake area," Ken said, "to make sure folks aren't leaving food out for the deer.

While I'm out there, I'll check and see if anyone saw anything unusual. Guess you heard about the deer?"

"Yeah, damn people don't have a lick of sense."

It was almost noon, so Ken bought a roast beef sandwich from the cooler, a bag of chips, a package of cashews, and coffee. Once he turned into a customer, Amos seemed to breathe easier.

"How's Lydia these days?" he asked as he made change.

"Still teaching sixth grade. She's got her heart set on starting a small library in town this summer."

"A library? Where?"

"Don't know. But we've got a lot of used books piling up in the basement. Lauren is helping her."

"Your girl almost all growed up now?"

"She's a junior in high school."

Amos stared as if his mind were miles away, but only for a moment. Back to business, he jerked open a notebook and started making a list of the stolen items. Ken left him muttering to himself about needing to see his insurance agent.

***

Fog hanging over the lake obscured any view of the Big Bat. The trees in the distance looked like they'd been sprinkled with powdered sugar.

Ken sipped his coffee as he drove around the cabins. Periodically he stopped to inspect back doors and windows. There were no signs of forced entry, and he didn't spot any containers that would entice deer.

Most of the people who'd come for weekend skiing were gone. Only one cabin appeared occupied, but there was no vehicle parked out front. A short woman about Ken's age, somewhere in her mid-forties, answered the door.

She seemed startled to see the tall, dark-haired deputy standing on her porch. "Has something happened?" Her eyes, wide behind red-rimmed glasses, moved from the badge on his brown coat to the brim of his matching campaign hat.

He didn't want to alarm her. "No ma'am. I'm just checking for food left out for deer. We had to shoot a sick one up here last week. People feeding them makes the illness spread."

She looked relieved but puzzled. "We've been here about five days. We haven't even seen any deer," she said. "My husband and kids are out taking a last run on the mountain."

That explained the absence of a vehicle. Ken looked past her and glimpsed a cardboard box on the table and an open suitcase on the couch. "We also had a theft down at Hadley's Store," he said casually. "You seen anyone who looked odd — like they weren't here for recreation?"

"No. Nothing like that at all. As soon as my husband and sons return, we're going home to Eugene."

"You have a good day, ma'am. Sorry to have bothered you." Ken tipped his hat.

"I'm glad to see they have law enforcement up here at the lake." She smiled and shut the door. He could hear her locking it.

By the time Ken got back to the highway, it was two o'clock. Maybe it was the stop at Hadley's or the eerie way the clouds moved in the darkening sky. Or, maybe it was because the place where he'd shot the sick deer the week before was the same place where years ago they'd found Christie Jenkins' body. Instead of heading back to town, Ken drove farther up the road toward Hawk Canyon.

The old logging roads weren't passable in winter, so Ken pulled off to the side where he could see Cooper's Hawk River cutting through the canyon, the foggy west side of the Big Bat barely discernable. His growling stomach reminded him he was hungry. He unwrapped his sandwich, took a big bite, and washed it down with a swig of cold coffee before tearing into the bag of barbecue chips.

As he ate, he stared at the shrouded mountain. He and Fallingwater had romped out there. Jim, a full-blooded Modoc Indian, had pretended to be Captain Jack, the legendary chief of the Modoc tribe. Jim would wage war against the cavalry, which was usually just Ken. He'd take off whooping, and Ken would follow in hot pursuit with a toy cap gun yelling, "Captain Jack, you're surrounded. Give yourself up." The cavalry rarely caught Jim because he was clever and more familiar with the trails and caves.

Ken hadn't talked with old Mo in ages. Mo used to take them on camping trips, hiking deep into the forest along steep, winding trails. Mo, like Jim, was Modoc, and the only father figure Jim had known. Jim's own father, an abusive drunk, had died of a heart attack when Jim was twelve.

Ken shifted his gaze north. It was over there, somewhere in the gloomy distance that he and Jim had become blood brothers. It'd been right after they'd seen an old western movie in which a cowboy and Indian chief cut their fingers and mingled their blood. The boys had snuck off with one of Mo's old hunting knives, gashed their index fingers, and vowed to be friends forever. Then Jim had grown up and gotten involved with that Christie Jenkins—a one-sided, tragic affair ending in her murder.

Ken munched the last of the cashews. Every time Christie's mother, Myra, now a stout woman with faded reddish hair and deep frown lines on her forehead, crossed his path, she shot cold stares at him. Once she passed, he felt her daggers lingering in his spine.

"Christie would never have married that Indian," Myra hisses to anyone who'll listen. "And that nincompoop of a deputy . . . He cheated us. We never got justice."

Floyd, Christie's father, carried his bitterness close to the surface. He ran the gas station, and since it was the only one in town, Ken couldn't avoid going there. A short, thick man who always dressed in blue coveralls and a brown baseball cap, Floyd was polite enough. But when Ken tried to make small talk, Floyd just said, "Yep, Yep," and busied himself pumping gas. When he was done, he'd hand Ken the receipt, look down at the asphalt, and mutter, "Okay, now."

That was it.

Ken understood their pain. He had a daughter, too, but there wasn't a damn thing he could do about the past.

He crumpled the cellophane packaging from his lunch and stuffed it into a paper sack he carried for trash. The wind gusted and a few icy flakes fell. Periodically, it slammed the snow against the windows of his Jeep. He saw a vague resemblance to Jim in the eerie clouds, first a head, transforming into a face. Images flashed in his mind of their two bleeding fingers and then of Christie's red hair and all that blood in the grass.

He couldn't help himself. He pulled a wool cap out of the glove compartment, jumped out of the Jeep, and stood overlooking the canyon. The chilly wind penetrated his coat and icy sleet bit his face. "Captain Jack," he yelled. His voice boomed across the white wilderness.

"Jack, Jack, Jack," the cold mountain echoed back.

"Captain Jack," Ken shouted again. "I will *never* forget."

CHAPTER 4

Friday, December 4

A heavy morning rain finally dislodged the downspout by the Bensons' kitchen. Water drummed down the side of the house and splattered into a muddy puddle. Through a steamy window, Cally saw Sam climbing off his ladder. He had ventured out during a break in the rain, only to be caught in a cold, windy downpour.

"Kee-rist, it's soupy out there," Sam grumbled when he came inside and pulled off his dripping rain gear. "It's like a tall horse pissing in a goddamn bowl. First snow, then this goddamn rain."

Cally tossed him a kitchen towel to dry his face.

Sam worked the towel over his wet cheeks and rubbed it hard against his scalp. "You can get whatever you want for weather in this state if you wait long enough."

"I made you some fresh coffee." Cally filled a mug and brought it to the kitchen table.

"That blasted pipe is wore clear through at the elbow." Sam took a long drink from the cup and held it with both hands, warming his fingers. "I told Dottie I'd come by the café and measure for her ailing shelves. While I'm in town, I'm gonna stop in at the hardware store and get a new elbow for the pipe. Might as well kill two birds with one stone."

Cally smiled to herself as Sam hurried off to clean up. She was happy that Dottie, who she knew had turned sixty-two over the summer, but looked years younger, had taken a liking to Sam. Ever since he'd started having lunch at her café, she'd been hiring him to do odd jobs. First it had been a leaky faucet in the restroom, then a loose tile in the kitchen. Those small jobs had made Sam feel needed. Besides, the work got him out of the house and tired him out so he went to bed earlier, which pleased Pete.

"I'll catch lunch in town," Sam said, beaming as he came back into the kitchen. He'd changed clothes and carefully combed what still qualified as a full head of hair.

Cally detected the woodsy scent of the aftershave that he usually used on Sundays. *Dad is still a handsome man.*

Sam left whistling.

Cally folded the last towel from the dryer and scraped the lint trap clean, glad for some time alone. With Thanksgiving over, the radio station now played round-the-clock carols and she hummed along. After dinner, she'd ask Pete to haul the Christmas lights down from the attic and test the bulbs. Maybe on Saturday they could drive into Klamath Falls for some serious shopping.

She shelved the towels and started a batch of sugar cookies. She'd broken two eggs into the mixing bowl and was reaching for the vanilla, when the phone rang. The holiday spirit that had welled in her body evaporated, and a small shiver of dread, then anger, jolted her. Cody was in trouble.

Again.

How many times did they have to tell him? The last thing she needed to do on a Friday afternoon was drive through heavy rain to face an angry teacher.

The office secretary tapped on the wooden door with the frosted pane that said "PRINCIPAL," then ushered Cally in.

Principal Cora Everson sat behind her desk. She glanced at her watch. "Hello, Mrs. Benson. We've been waiting for you." She was a big woman with short, steel-gray hair that framed her large, moon-shaped face. She motioned to a chair in front of the desk next to Eula Brackston, Cody's teacher.

"Sorry I'm late. I was baking cookies. I . . . uh . . . skipped lunch."

Both women looked glum.

"I hardly know where to start," said Miss Brackston, a short, middle-aged woman, whose appearance never changed. Every time Cally saw her, she wore a denim skirt and those clunky, brown leather boots. "We were doing long division. Cody finished his lesson early, so he started drawing deer." A pencil resting on her right ear stuck out of her close-cropped, curly dark hair.

"My husband is a wildlife biologist. He's been dealing with some sick deer lately . . . one had to be shot. Cody has been very upset about that," Cally explained.

"I always give additional problems, so the kids who finish early can earn extra credit," Miss Brackston replied, as if Cally hadn't offered an explanation. "Instead, Cody was drawing." She handed several pages to Cally, like a prosecutor offering evidence to the court.

Cally looked at a pencil drawing of a doe, with a fawn standing next to a clump of grass surrounded by trees. An Indian boy stood in the background. The doe's face was especially well done. The proportions and shading on the fawn were almost perfect. Under different circumstances, she would have displayed the artwork on the fridge. "Well, if he finished the required work . . ."

"The *rules* are that students do the extra problems," Miss Brackston said. "Those are the rules." Her eyes widened behind the dark-framed glasses that rested on her tiny, ruddy nose.

"He prays for them at night," Cally said.

"Prays for whom?"

"The deer."

The teacher and principal exchanged looks.

"When I asked him why he was drawing," Miss Brackston continued, "he said he ran out of notebook paper." She crossed her legs. "However, when I checked his desk, he had enough in there to paper a wall." Her foot bobbed in the air.

Cally remembered the hundred-sheet, wide-line pack of paper she'd bought after Thanksgiving at Tillden's Grocery.

"He said he didn't like long division," Miss Brackston went on. "Said it wasn't necessary, that he could get the answers faster with a calculator. He . . . uh . . . insisted I was wasting his time."

Cally grinned. *You're wasting my time.* Pete muttered those exact words whenever he got impatient. "His father lets him play . . . use his calculator."

"I explained that it was important to learn how you actually got the answers." Miss Brackston's left eyebrow shot up. "Then, when we moved on to the next subject—spelling—I caught Cody drawing again. He said he already knew how to spell those words, and that someone named Benny asked him to draw deer." She paused and glanced at the principal.

"Mrs. Benson, there is *no* Benny in the classroom," Mrs. Everson said. Her fresh, red lipstick accented the tiny lines surrounding her lips.

Cally swallowed hard. Her face got warm. She knew Benny did not exist.

"When children live in a dream world that has nothing to do with reality, it's generally a sign of low self-esteem," Mrs. Everson continued.

Cally looked down at her lap, noticing a spot of flour on her thigh. "Well, that's good, isn't it?" she managed to say. "I mean that he already knew the words."

"He's *required* to do the exercises. So I made him spend recess at his desk . . . doing the exercises." Miss Brackston tilted her head backwards whenever she wanted to stress a point. "I took away his deer pictures, thinking that would be the end of it. Well, when the kids were standing in the lunch line—it was extra-long today because we were serving hot dogs and potato salad—Cody kicked the boy in front of him."

"He kicked someone?" Cally sat up in her chair. "That doesn't sound like Cody."

"Artie Bradshaw," Mrs. Everson said. "We had to put Cody in timeout."

Cally crossed her arms. She stared at the pencil jutting out of Miss Brackston's hair. Artie Bradshaw was a name she knew well.

"He said Artie called him a name," Miss Brackston said, "but that's no—"

"We've tried to teach Cody to ignore those kinds of taunts," Cally said. "As you know, Artie tends to bully Cody. The other day, he grabbed his hat and tossed it out of the bus window. I believe I called you about that."

"It's normal to want to defend your child, Mrs. Benson." Miss Brackston tipped her head again and stared at Cally's laced arms.

"We never did find the hat," Cally said lamely. For some reason, she felt like she was always speaking to Miss Brackston's nostrils. When the teacher looked away, Cally casually unhooked her arms.

"These things happen," Mrs. Everson said.

Cally tried to bring the conversation back to the bully. "As I recall, this Artie is a pretty big kid."

"The appropriate behavior is for the child to tell the teacher," Miss Brackston said.

Cally bristled at her condescending tone. The other thing she knew about Artie was that his father owned the drug store and was on the school board.

"What *exactly* did Artie say to Cody?" She gave the principal a level look.

Mrs. Everson ignored the question. "Cody is a bright boy," she said. "He understands the work, but he sort of keeps to himself . . . lives in his own world."

"Couldn't you give him something more challenging to do?" Cally asked.

"Mrs. Benson, you don't seem to understand." Mrs. Everson sounded annoyed. "Cody doesn't follow instructions and doesn't appear to respect authority. Kicking another student is unacceptable." She tapped her pen on the desk. "Restlessness, inattention, not finishing work, acting before thinking of the consequences—these could be symptoms of ADHD or some variation of it. Of course, these disorders occur on a spectrum of severity." She smiled. "All kids are different. I'm not suggesting Cody's case is extreme, but we need to determine if he actually has attention deficits, or if something else is going on. These things are very treatable if you get the child into the right hands."

"And what exactly are the symptoms for bullying?" Cally asked.

"Obviously something isn't right," Miss Brackston added, her head tipped up again.

Cally clenched her hands. What was this woman implying? "Cody is a very sensitive child. He—"

"I understand Eula has talked to you about these problems before—in fact, on several occasions." Mrs. Everson glanced at the open file on her desk and tapped her pen against something written there.

Not good at reading upside down, Cally nodded meekly. Eula Brackston's smug smile offended her.

"We intend to recommend an evaluation," Miss Brackston said. She pulled the pencil from behind her ear and stabbed the air to emphasize her point. "The district has a good psychologist."

"A psychologist! You don't have my permission to do that." Cally brushed the flour from her thigh in two brisk motions, not caring whether they noticed. "I need to talk with my husband."

The principal's face turned steely. Her eyes moved from Cally's face to her brown sweatshirt and stopped at the frayed hole in her faded jeans. She stared at it for a moment and then looked her directly in the eyes. "Of course, you can discuss this with your husband. Obviously, we'd want parental consent. There's a whole procedure we follow once we decide to make such an assessment. A psychologist may or may not be part of the evaluation team. It depends on the child."

Cally's mind flooded. *A psychologist for my little boy?* She could see Mrs. Everson's red lips moving but was too distraught to comprehend—something about a consent form, questionnaires, a team, a detailed report, and a whole bunch of acronyms. *Won't that stigma follow him for years?*

"That takes time." Mrs. Everson was saying when Cally tuned back in. "Once we get a handle on the problem, we can design a plan for him." She stood up behind her desk, indicating the meeting was over.

***

Miss Brackston agreed to dismiss Cody early since their meeting broke up a little after 2:00 p.m. Cally found him hunched over on a bench in the hallway outside his classroom wearing his coat and boots. His backpack was on the floor. Sitting there, he looked like an abandoned puppy. He glanced up but quickly shifted his eyes back to the floor.

She clenched her purse. "Let's go." Cody quietly followed her.

"Did you eat lunch?" she asked when they were in the car, remembering Mrs. Everson said Cody had spent time in detention. "They said today was hotdogs."

"No."

"Wouldn't they let you?"

"I wasn't hungry."

"Honey, you have to eat something."

"I'm not hungry."

"Well, I am."

Cally drove to the Dairy Queen. "Let's go in. I don't feel like sitting out here in the rain." She got out and slammed the door. Inside, she ordered two hamburgers, fries, and soft drinks. Once she'd filled two cups with Pepsi, she led Cody to a table in a far corner. The lunch crowd had long gone, leaving only a couple of other people in the restaurant.

"Okay, young man, what do you have to say for yourself?"

Cody scrunched down. He didn't answer.

Cally struggled to keep calm. She turned her head from side to side, trying to get the kink out of her neck and ward off a headache. "Well?"

"Mom, am I bad?" He sounded like a patient asking the doctor if it were true he had cancer.

His question startled Cally. She stared at her son—small, pale, and so precious. "Did they say you were?"

Cody stared at the table.

They did, Cally thought. Someone did. "No, honey." She sighed. Her voice softened. "But you need to listen to what your teacher says and try hard to follow instructions. We've talked about this before, haven't we?"

Cody tore the paper off the end of his straw.

"Cody, did you hear what I said?"

"Uh-huh." He blew through the straw, causing the wrapper to fly over Cally's shoulder and crash against the back of the booth seat.

"Bombs away!" He giggled.

"Cody!" Cally grabbed his chin. "I'm talking to you."

"I know, Mom." He plunked the straw into his cola.

"Your teacher said you kicked Artie Bradshaw."

Cody made a face. "He called me a name."

"What did he call you?"

"What?"

"I said, what did Artie call you?"

"A fruit loop."

"Did you tell the teacher?"

Cody ran his fingers over the small vase of artificial flowers on the table. "These aren't real, Mom."

She moved the vase to the side. "Cody, I asked you a question. Did you tell your teacher?"

"About what?"

"Cody!"

"Nope."

"Why not?"

The young man behind the counter called their number. Cally jumped up, retrieved the tray of food, and unloaded it onto the table. Cody clapped his hands and began swinging his feet. "Yummy," he said. He lifted his hamburger with both hands, taking a big bite.

Cally waited. "Didn't we tell you to talk to your teacher when something like this happens?"

Cody chewed, swallowed, and set down his burger. "Artie said I played with girls." He clenched his small fists. The remark obviously referred to his friendship with Brittany and maybe a lot more, but then they were only eight-year-olds.

"Mrs. Everson said that if you get in trouble one more time, she'll—."

"Brittany said Artie is a big dope."

"You know who she is, don't you?"

"Brittany?"

"You know I mean Mrs. Everson."

"The principal."

"She showed me these." Cally took the folded deer drawings out of her coat pocket and set them on the table.

"Hey, those are mine." He reached and pulled them to his side of the table giving Cally a sheepish look. "I did all the problems, Mom."

"Miss Brackston said the rules are that you do *additional* problems for extra credit."

"I don't need extra credit. I got them all right. I always get them right."

"Cody, those are the *rules*." Cally sipped her soft drink. Her throat was dry, and she hoped the caffeine would give her a lift. "You can't just go off and do what you want to do."

A flustered look crossed his face.

"Do you hear me?"

His lips trembled but made no sound.

What she said sounded stupid. The rules. The rules. Sometimes rules made little sense. Is that really what she wanted—a child who blindly followed rules? Suddenly, she was angry with herself. She hadn't done a good job defending Cody to those women. Sure, they had a point. Cody had been out of order in the classroom, but he wasn't a bad boy. He also wasn't a burly farm kid. They were overlooking the fact that he was an intelligent child who didn't respond well to their cookie-cutter education system. He was smart. Gifted even. He read at an advanced level. For an eight-year-old, he had exceptional artistic talent. You'd think educators would get excited about working with a bright kid.

That was the problem with a small town school—it had limited resources. She took a deep breath and exhaled slowly. If they lived in Portland, there would be more options for Cody. That thought stirred up other old wounds. She had never wanted to move to Forest Lake. Sure, the air was clean, and they were a few miles from a beautiful lake. They could hike, camp, and picnic in the wonderful outdoors, but there was a lot wrong with the place, too. Small towns were in-bred, too churchy, isolated, and populated with rednecks. On the surface, they appeared friendly, caring, and rock-solid until you lifted the rock and discovered all the creepy crawly things living in the darkness underneath.

She'd grown up in a remote, rural part of Eastern Montana, but until she'd attended college in Bozeman, she hadn't known another world existed. She'd been so naïve and backward. She certainly didn't want that for Cody. Pete insisted Forest Lake was a good place to raise a family. She agreed, but some days it seemed like she'd been buried alive. She would have liked to use her college degree, maybe teach school. Now it was a long trip to Klamath Falls if they needed something more than just the basics, and there were no real educational choices for Cody.

"I had to draw them," Cody said in a wee voice, bringing her back to the situation at hand.

"Why?"

"Benny thought it was a good idea."

She rubbed the base of her neck and wished she'd brought the Tylenol bottle along. "Cody, we both know Benny doesn't exist. He's just an imaginary friend."

Cally couldn't remember exactly when Benny had emerged, but it seemed like it was soon after they'd moved to Forest Lake. They'd bought Cody, then four-years-old, a kid's cowboy outfit, complete with hat, boots, and water pistol. One day he came in from the backyard and brought Benny with him for lunch. Cody had said he was an Indian boy and that he whispered secrets. When he was younger, Cally had thought it was cute and harmless and went along with the cowboy suit. She'd even set a place for Benny at the table. But Cody should be outgrowing this imaginary nonsense. Boys his age were already playing soccer, baseball, and getting interested in the outside world.

"You're a big boy now, and you need to make real friends. Friends like Brittany are okay, but you should play with the boys in your room."

"Benny is fun," Cody insisted. "And he *likes* me."

"He's not real, Cody." She slapped the table with her hand.

Startled, Cody quit eating.

She instantly felt bad. "Eat, honey."

What did she have to do to get through to this kid? The principal was right. She needed help. Pete just got angry and thought the louder he talked, the more Cody would get it, but it wasn't working. "Are there some boys in your class you'd like to invite over?"

Cody shrugged his shoulders.

"What about Mark who lives up the road? He seems like a nice boy."

"He doesn't want to play with me."

"Why not?"

"I don't know, Mom."

She watched him squeeze the plastic ketchup bottle and drown his fries. She and Pete had tried so hard to conceive this child. After a ruptured uterus and the emergency C-section, the doctor had said it would be her last pregnancy. The doctor was sorry. The nurses were sorry. They were all so sorry, but it changed nothing.

"All Mark wants to do is jump on the trampoline and shoot spit wads," Cody said.

"Don't you like the trampoline?"

"Sometimes. Mark doesn't do it right. He pushes and bumps into me."

"Cody," she said, trying to be positive. "These drawings are really good. Did you have a picture to look at?"

"No. Benny lives with the deer. They saved his life once."

"Cody!" she said sharply.

"They're his friends. He said we should make more signs so Dad could put them up and people wouldn't hurt the deer anymore." Cody took a big bite of his hamburger.

Cally watched him chew. "Cody," she said finally. "You've got to promise me that you'll listen to Miss Brackston and do what she asks. When you're in the classroom, the teacher rules. Understand?"

"I don't like Miss Brackston."

"Cody, what did I just say to you?"

"She eats nails."

"What?"

"Miss Brackston eats nails. Brittany said she puts nails in her Cheerios instead of bananas. That's why she's so grumpy." He was eating his fries with his fingers, getting ketchup on his hands and his chin. Cally pulled some extra napkins from the holder and handed them to him.

"That's enough of that."

"Okay."

"Okay, what?"

"Okay, I promise."

"And, if Artie or someone else picks on you . . . calls you names, takes anything of yours, you go to Miss Brackston and tell her . . . and you tell us."

"Okay."

"You're a good artist, Cody."

He looked up at her and grinned.

"Maybe this summer you can take drawing lessons. Would you like that?"

"Yeah." His whole face lit up.

"But only if there is no more trouble at school." Surely, she could find someone who could teach a kid about art—even if it meant driving to Klamath Falls on a weekend. There must be computer art programs.

"I'm sorry you had to come to school, Mom."

"I know, honey, but you still have to explain this to your dad."

"Uh-huh."

"He's not going to be happy when he hears about today."

His thin body stiffened. "Uh-huh." He shrugged his shoulders and swung his legs back and forth under the table.

"Cody, honey . . ."

"Now what, Mom?"

"I love you."

"Okay."

"I just wanted you to know that."

"I love you, too."

The rain fell in heavy streams again, pounding the parking lot asphalt in an angry tirade. She watched an older couple dash to their car.

She wasn't totally clueless. She had read about children struggling with behavioral problems and more on the Internet when Miss Brackston had first brought it up. She, and especially Pete, had been in denial. Now they were moving into reality.

She could see that it was all there—restlessness, trouble focusing, daydreaming about imaginary friends. She needed to talk with Pete. She needed her mother. She needed her Tylenol. God, she needed something.

CHAPTER 5

December 4, Friday night
After dinner, Ken Blake settled back on the comfortable living room couch with a cup of coffee, watching the evening news. He'd already traded his duty belt and uniform for jeans and a sweatshirt and had propped his feet on the ottoman when the picture of the young boy who'd gone missing over by Grants Pass flashed on the screen. While his wife, Lydia, and teenaged daughter, Lauren, happily sorted books donated for Lydia's summer library project in the kitchen, the distraught mother made a tearful plea for the return of her son.

He clicked off the remote and headed toward the kitchen. "So, do you have a date for the Candy Cane Dance?" he heard Lydia ask.

"What's this about a dance?" Ken said, setting his empty coffee mug on the counter. The musty odor of old books competed with the lingering smell of the pork chops they'd had for dinner.

Lydia's brown eyes peered at him over blue-framed reading glasses. Her layered honey-blond hair, parted on the side, ended just below her chin line. She hadn't changed out of the gray turtleneck sweater and tailored slacks she'd worn to her sixth-grade teaching job.

"Katy and I are just going to hang out," said Lauren. She was a younger version of her mother except for her nose. It was narrow like Ken's at the bridge until the rounded tip mirrored Lydia again. "You can dance or just stand around and eat, which is what most of the guys will do." She screwed up her face.

No longer listening, Ken picked up a copy of *Ivy and Bean* from the pile of children's books and stared at it. "The mother of that young boy who's gone missing over by Grants Pass was on the news. It's a helluva thing to have happen, especially with Christmas coming on."

"There's a kid missing?" Lauren's eyes widened. "Freaky." She twisted the end of her bright blond ponytail.

"The boy is in second grade. He got off the school bus in a rural area, south of Grants Pass on Tuesday. Nobody saw anything. He was gone in the blink of an eye."

"Maybe he didn't want to go home, so he took off," Lauren said. "It could happen."

"It's considered an abduction. This kid is not the kind that would run away. The FBI has joined the county sheriff's office in the search."

"The FBI, wow," Lauren said. "Maybe he got hurt and fell in some ditch. Did they check that out?"

"They went over everything with a fine-tooth comb." Ken waved the book back and forth. "It makes me wonder. You know, about that report from the grade school that a suspicious vehicle was parked there."

"What's the latest on that?" Lydia asked.

"We have nothing to go on."

"There was a creepy guy near the grade school?" Lauren cupped her hands over her mouth.

"The kids said he asked for directions. No one got a license number, and I have no real description."

"He's never come back that I know of," Lydia said. "Surely they'll find the Grants Pass boy. There's got to be an explanation."

"The first forty-eight hours are critical," Ken said. "They're already into the fourth day. The FBI has some profilers joining the search. That says it's serious." He looked at his beautiful daughter, standing there in faded jeans with holes at the knees, sneakers, and a green turtleneck sweater. In two months, she'd turn sixteen—sweet sixteen, bubbly, a good student, eager to get her driver's license. It seemed like yesterday he'd taught her to ride a bicycle. "You be careful at school. Maybe I should go to that dance."

"Oh, Dad," Lauren wailed. "Like the last thing I need is to have my father, the cop, hanging there."

"It might be a good idea. I'll be driving you, anyway."

"Mom," Lauren pleaded. "I'll just die. I can't wait till I'm sixteen and get my license."

"You'd *scare* the kids," Lydia said. "Grants Pass is quite a ways from here."

"Another odd thing," Ken went on. "Someone broke into Hadley's Lake Store."

"There've been burglaries out there before," Lydia pointed out. "Especially since we're seeing more tourists in the area."

"True. Strange that he didn't touch the till—just took food and clothing. That's what's weird."

"Dad, you're creepin' me out."

"Maybe someone needed food," Lydia said. "The holidays are rough for some folks. Not that that's any excuse for stealing." She paused and smiled at Ken. "You'll be happy to know we finally found a place for our library project."

Ken frowned and tossed the children's book back on the pile. "I thought you were setting up in the church basement."

"Pastor Rick wasn't crazy about that and, frankly, neither was I. Tillie has offered us the empty space over by his grocery store—the one that used to be the old shoe-repair shop. He believes a library is a great idea."

Lauren smirked. "And he hopes people will pick up a loaf of bread while their kids are getting books."

Lydia's eyes fluttered. "Now who said that?"

"Rich Tillden. He said his dad thinks the library will suck people into his store."

"Harrumph," Lydia muttered. "Well anyway, it's just perfect. We get more visibility, and the big glass windows have all kinds of display possibilities. Children who read over the summer months have a leg-up at the start of the school year."

Ken nodded. "I've been meaning to tell you. Dottie has a donation jar at her café for your library. When I stopped in for lunch today, she'd already collected fifty dollars."

"God bless Dottie. I've been thinking about asking the Woman's Club to hold a rummage sale. Maybe she'd like to join in."

Ken pointed to Lauren's holey jeans. "You're not going to wear *those* things to the dance are you?"

Lauren gave her dad an exasperated *What planet are you on?* look, followed by an eye roll.

"Your mother and I went to a few dances at the high school. Only back then we wore real clothes," he teased.

"Yeah, Dad. I've seen your high school yearbook. B-o-o-r-r-ring. Mom's name should've been 'Barbie.' They could've just stuck you two on top of a wedding cake. They still could, except for your buzz cut. I don't know why cops think they have to do that to their hair."

Ken touched the side of his head. "What's wrong with my hair?"

Lauren put her hands on her hips. "You look like a drill sergeant."

"Long hair is a grab handle in a fight and the correct term, young lady, is 'police officers,' not 'cops'."

Lydia winked at Lauren. "His high-and-tight hairdo adds to his cop aura."

Lauren laughed. "Like he needs one. *Nothing* happens in Forest Lake."

Lydia pulled some paperbacks from the box and tossed them aside. "My rough count says we have about three hundred so far. My goal for this summer is one thousand." She glanced at Lauren who was giggling. "What's so funny?"

"Jeez, Mom, that's more books than people in Forest Lake."

"So they read more than one. Why don't you guys help me move these books to the basement. Then we can celebrate our new library with hot chocolate and macaroons."

Ken hefted an armload. Lydia's irresistible coconut macaroons—a sure sign Christmas was just around the corner. He pictured the missing boy's tearful mother. *God, I hope that kid makes it home.*

CHAPTER 6

December 4, Friday night

Early December darkness quickly dimmed the view from the Bensons' kitchen window. The rain had stopped, and it was turning colder. Dinner—grocery store pizza and salad—was somber and quiet until Sam pulled out his crumpled, white handkerchief and blew into it with such force it sounded like a dying sea lion. Cally jumped. Pete looked disgusted. Cody picked at his pizza, pulling off pieces of pepperoni, ignoring his salad.

In between noisy bites, Sam's hand jabbed the air as he explained in detail how gutter systems worked. "The hardware store had just the part I needed, and I found some fine wood there for Dottie's shelves. She—"

"Can I be excused?" Cody gave his mother a pleading look.

"We...uh...had a late lunch," Cally said, as she nodded at Cody. "Actually, I'm not that hungry either."

He slid off his chair and scampered up to his room.

"Dottie thought my shelves—"

Pete tossed his napkin on his plate, pushed back his chair, and headed for the staircase. The scraping chair made Cally flinch. *Why can't men ever pick up a chair?* She tapped her fingers on the table and glanced at Sam. He shook his head.

Cally busied herself clearing the dishes. She had rinsed the last one and started the dishwasher when she heard Pete's heavy boots on the wooden stairs.

He headed straight to the fridge. "It's so damn hard to get through to him." Pete popped open a can of Bud Light. "I grounded him. No TV. No computer games. Zip. I finish saying that, and he asks if he can have a dog. A goddamn dog. What the hell is wrong with him?" He plopped down on a kitchen chair and tipped the can to his lips.

"I told you, he has trouble focusing," Cally said over the hum of the dishwasher. "His teacher wants to refer him to a team of specialists to formally evaluate him."

"A whole team?" Sam gasped. "For one little kid?"

"Apparently there's a big convoluted procedure they follow these days to evaluate kids they suspect are hyperactive, have attention deficits, or whatever. The evaluation is part of that."

Pete held his head. "An evaluation for acting up at school? That's bullshit." He slapped the table.

"It's a major over-reaction." She looked at Sam. "I've made an appointment with Dr. Maloney, our pediatrician, so we'll have our own evaluation. The problem is, we can't get in until after Christmas."

"That long?" Sam whistled. "I didn't know there were that many sick folks around here."

"It's the cold and flu season, Dad. And I guess the doc is taking some holiday time off."

"What kind of a kid do we have?" Pete suddenly blurted. "Why can't he get with it?"

Cally raised her hand to shush him. Every muscle in her body tightened. "There's nothing wrong with our boy," she said in a high, tense voice. "I'm sure Dr. Maloney will verify that. He's always been supportive of Cody. I'm not going to let those two old biddies steamroll us."

"I thought when I had a son, we'd go camping, fishing, play sports—all those things fathers and sons do."

Here we go again. Cally drew a long breath. "He's a creative little boy. There's not much available for a kid like Cody in Forest Lake. Look at these."

Sam examined the deer drawings she laid on the table. "At least he's off ladybugs."

"If we lived in Portland, we could enroll him in art school or something."

Pete's mouth tightened into a thin line. He took another swallow of beer. "Let's not get on that saw again. We've gone over that a hundred times."

"I think his teacher is clueless. Unfortunately, there's only one third grade class in the whole school." Her eyes widened. She looked at Pete. Maybe we should try to home-school him?"

Pete made a face. "That won't solve anything. He needs to ditch all that pretend stuff and learn how to get along with people. *Real* people."

"Thank God it's Friday," Sam said. "That'll give us a few days for this thing to blow over, and the kid can have a fresh start next week."

"We can only hope," Pete grumbled.

"It seems damn unfair to me," Sam said. "That other kid that called him a name was the one that started it."

"We don't care who started it," Pete said.

"It's not just about that other kid, Dad," Cally explained. "Cody wasn't following instructions in class, and he was drawing. Other times, he's been reading."

Sam missed the finer points of Cally's explanation. "I'd rather have a kid that can defend himself than some whiny crybaby. If it was me, I woulda slugged that other kid."

"What would that solve?" Cally demanded. She couldn't imagine her son in a real fight with husky Artie whose freckled, chubby face always wore a smirk. Besides, Artie was actually older, having failed the second grade. "Burt Bradshaw owns the drugstore, and he's on the school board. He's also very vocal about how the school should be run."

"What's that got to do with anything?" Sam asked. "I don't give a rat's ass who his ol' man is. Some bloated, big-shot asshole."

"Artie pushes the daddy thing for all it's worth," Cally said.

"The kid spends too much time in his room. He needs to do more outside stuff. I told Dottie I'd get her a Christmas tree for the café. I might as well get one for the house, too."

Pete's jaw clenched. "What's Dottie got to do with this? You seem to spend a lot of time at the café lately."

Sam's shoulders shifted downward. His face colored slightly.

"Pete, let it go." Cally knew what Pete was thinking. If Sam hooked up with Dottie, he'd be around for a long time.

"Hell, you can buy a tree for a few bucks in the grocery store lot."

"Pete . . ."

Sam cleared his throat. "Why don't I take Cody with me to help get the trees?"

"Nope," Pete said. "I grounded him."

"There's nothin' like gettin' out and cuttin' your own. I used to take my kids out. Remember, Cally?"

"Those were wonderful times. We'd come in from the cold, and Mom would make us hot chocolate and popcorn."

Sam beamed. "They say there's places over by the Big Bat where you can cut your own. We wouldn't be gone very long. Cody could—"

"No." Pete shook his head several times.

Hands on her hips, Cally's voice rose. "What do *you* suggest?"

Sam looked at Pete and then Cally. "Hell, we can get one for the school, too. If Cody got to pick out the school tree, he'd feel a little pride. It could go a helluva long way to impress them other kids. That would show that fat ass, Artie. Huh?"

Cally's face lit up. "I like it. Miss Brackston did say Cody has low self-esteem."

"I don't know," Pete said.

"It might be good for him," Cally insisted.

"You gotta teach a country boy what it means to be a man," Sam went on. "How can you earn a livin' drawin' junk?"

"Dad . . ."

"I don't know what the hell to do for that kid." Pete tipped his beer can to gulp the last drops. "I'm talking to him, his head goes up and down. Then he asks if he can have a goddamned dog. I got mad. I made him cry. He . . . he said he hated me." He crumpled the can in his hand.

Cally rubbed his shoulder. "Kids say those things, honey. It doesn't mean anything."

"That's one sad little feller you got upstairs," Sam said. "We wouldn't be gone long, Pete. Hell, it's Christmas."

Pete leaned his elbows on the table, his chin in his hands. "Okay, Sam," he finally said. He sat up and slapped his thighs. "You guys get the trees, then come back home. But that's all you do." He gave Cally a pleading look. "Nothing more."

CHAPTER 7

December 5, Saturday

Sitting at the kitchen table, Sam watched Cally's mouth move, but he was only partially listening.

"Pete's out warming up the car. Make sure Cody wears his snow gear. Don't stay out there too long," Cally instructed, before they headed out for their all-day shopping spree in Klamath Falls. "I put potato salad and ham sandwiches in the fridge for lunch."

"Yep, yep," Sam grumbled, irked by her drill-sergeant tone. He pulled out his pocketknife and cleaned under his fingernails.

"We won't be back until after dinner. There are crackers and a can of vegetable soup on the counter for you guys. All you have to do is add water and heat it up. That should hold you for a while."

"Uh-huh." He was on his third nail.

"And leave our tree outside. No sense bringing it in right away."

He snorted. "Wasn't planning to."

"Okay, then. We're off."

Once the door closed, he looked at the sorry can of soup on the counter. "*Pfft*," he muttered, snapped the knife shut, and scratched himself. "Soup is for sick people." He and Cody would eat lunch at Dottie's Café. Besides, he needed to measure the place where she planned to put her tree. And Dottie, well just being around her, made his heart swell.

***

The café was humming with jovial chitchat. Folks had come to town for the annual holiday raffle at the Mercantile and were now enjoying cheeseburgers with Dottie's famous wedge fries, chef's salad, and apple pie or wobbly, red Jell-O topped with whipped cream and green candy sprinkles.

Amid the clinking silverware and cheerful banter, Dottie smoothed her short pageboy, which got its ashy-blond tint from drug store Clairol kits. She grabbed the carafe and happily poured coffee, listening to chatter about who had won her "on-the-house" pancake breakfast and the other raffle prizes—a free haircut, frozen turkeys, and that new five-speed blender. Guy Lucas, they said, had nabbed the grand prize of a flat-screen TV. He was so excited, he'd skipped lunch and rushed home to hook it up.

When Dottie spotted Sam and Cody, she hurried over and personally took their orders. Sam chuckled after Cody asked for a peanut-butter-and-jelly sandwich. "You gotta order something that's on the menu," he said.

Dottie insisted she could whip up his request. She brought Sam a mug of coffee and a root beer for Cody.

The plastic Santa clock hanging on the wall above the counter chortled "Ho, Ho, Ho," and its turned-up nose blinked red. Surprised, Cody tossed his head back and giggled, his small hands drumming the table. Dottie returned a few minutes later with a PB&J "bunwich" with fries on the side for Cody and a cheeseburger and fries for Sam.

"I'm sure lookin' forward to having a tree this year," Dottie gushed. "There's nothin' like the smell of fresh fir boughs to punch up a room and get folks in the holiday mood." Hoping romance was still possible for a wrinkly, sensible-shoed gal like her, she kissed Sam on the cheek, causing him to blush.

She gave Cody a big hug and patted his back. "It's so nice that you're helpin' your grandpa. And getting a tree for the school, well that's super."

Cody's dark eyes beamed. "I get to help cut it."

"I know you'll do a good job." She promised hot chocolate and gingerbread cookies when they returned. She winked at Sam. "I may have to crack open a bottle of wine."

She looked down at Cody. "Say, I hear you're a great little artist. Would you like to make some of the decorations?"

"Yeah. Cool." Cody's face lit up like a Christmas light. "I know how to make a three-dimensional star."

"Well, that settles it." She rang up their bill. "Be sure to bundle up out there," she called as they went out the door. "It can get mighty cold up at the mountain."

***

They got to the Big Bat wilderness area a little after two. Sam told Cody they'd have to make it quick because it started to get dark at four. Cody climbed into his insulated red snowsuit, firmly fastened the strap of his black wool bomber hat, and pulled on mittens. Sam grabbed a small chainsaw from the pickup toolbox and handed Cody a hatchet. Their boots crunched snow as they ventured into the vast stillness. Evergreen trees of all sizes stretched as far as they could see, some with snow clinging to boughs. Sam inhaled the woodsy scent of the winter forest, the cold air stinging his eyes. As they walked, he explained what made a good Yule tree. "We want a full one that's got lots of branches. No gaps."

Cody ran ahead, circling back and forth in the snow, his arms outstretched like a bird looking for a landing space.

"Come back here. Don't run with a hatchet in your hand," Sam cautioned.

"Can we make a snowman, Grandpa?" He wiped his runny nose on his sleeve.

"We're out here to get trees, not play around," Sam scolded. Cody's lower lip protruded into a pout. Sam changed the subject. "Did you know that the average six-foot Christmas tree takes six years to grow?"

"Wow!" Cody twirled around. "These trees are almost as old as me."

"Some of 'em could take as long as fifteen years to reach their height. There's trees in these woods that's hundreds of years old."

"That's a lot of birthdays, Grandpa."

"You tell the age of a tree by cutting it down and counting the rings in its trunk," Sam said.

"Maybe trees have secrets, Grandpa. Maybe when their branches wave in the wind, they're talking to each other."

"C'mon now." Sam's forehead furrowed. "Let's not talk nonsense. Trees don't say nothin'. They take in carbon dioxide and let off oxygen. They make the air you breathe."

Cody stared at the trees in front of him. He took several deep breaths and exhaled frosty clouds. "Maybe some of those knot holes are really gigantic nostrils."

"Trees have roots. They don't have mouths, and they sure as hell don't have noses. Now come on." He suddenly stopped in front of a frilly green fir tree with a straight trunk and full boughs. "What about this one for the livin' room?"

Cody shrugged his shoulders. "I guess so."

Sam partially felled the tree with the chain saw, but he let Cody finish the job with his hatchet, so he could say he helped cut it. "Once you fell a good tree, you don't want it dryin' up in the house." He explained how to cut the trunk on an angle, so the tree could readily drink water. "We do that before we put it up."

"Does a tree stop breathing when it's cut?" Cody asked.

"If you make a proper cut, you don't end up with needles all over the floor," Sam said.

They walked farther into the forest, searching for a tree for Cody's school. Sam questioned him about size. Cody wasn't sure. "How's this one?" Sam asked.

"Look Grandpa! There's a rabbit." Cody ran to the snow bank where it scurried away, then ran back.

"Didn't I just tell you not to run when you're slingin' a hatchet?" His words had little effect.

"Where do deer go when it gets cold?" Cody wondered. "Hey, I think that's Benny ducking behind a tree."

"Benny who?"

"My friend . . . Benny."

"There's no one out here but us, buddy."

"I thought I saw him over there."

"Do you know which country had the first Christmas tree?" Sam asked, trying to get him back on track.

"Nope." Cody said in a low voice. His dark eyes scanned the wooded area.

"Well, it was Germany, hundreds of years ago."

"It's starting to snow, Grandpa." Cody stuck his tongue out to catch the swirling flakes. The wind began to kick up and blew the snowflakes in their faces. Cody said he was cold. Then he had to pee.

"Find a bush, and do your business," Sam told him. When he finally returned, Sam said, "Come on. We're burning daylight."

"How much longer?" Cody whined.

Sam ignored the question. "Out in the wilderness, it's hard to gauge a tree's height. Trees look smaller in wide-open spaces. That's why we gotta know the space we're tryin' to fill."

Cody wasn't listening. He whooped like an Indian and nicked nearby trees with his tomahawk.

"Don't do that!"

"I'm hungry."

"You just ate."

"I left my M&M's in the pickup."

"We'll be having cookies at Dottie's. C'mon now, buddy. Let's find a good tree for your school."

Cody hung his head. He kicked at the snow. He mentioned the candy three more times.

Sam took a deep breath, but it didn't help. His patience splintered. "Dad-blast it! Go on back to the pickup and have your M&M's. Once you get there, that's that. Just follow our footprints and wait for me there. You hear?"

He had forgotten to ask Cody whether the school tree was for his classroom or the main lobby area. He glanced over his shoulder only to spot Cody's red-clad figure scurrying away in the distance. "Shit," he groused, "might as well be pissin' in the wind." The safest bet, he decided, was a medium-size one, which he felled with his saw.

He wanted Dottie's tree to be extra special, perfect even. He remembered the kiss on his cheek and the springy freshness of her perfume. Even in the cold, it awakened something deep inside and made his blood surge. He hadn't felt that way in a long, long time. Then there was her promise of wine and that inviting wink. Maybe things in Forest Lake were going to turn out after all. He wandered farther into the wilderness, until he finally found what he thought was the right tree for Dottie. He would drag it back to the pickup and get Cody to help him with the others. Then they'd hit the road. "Damn kid," he muttered as he slung the saw over his shoulder and gripped the tree trunk. He hadn't expected Cody to lose interest so quickly. "Kids these days all need a good hiding."

Sam reached the pickup around four, but Cody wasn't there. He called but got no answer. "Dang it. Now where the hell is he?" They were already running late, and Dottie was expecting them. "Cody!" he shouted angrily.

He carefully loaded Dottie's tree into the pickup. "This one's a beaut." He grinned and gave the green boughs a tender pat. He was sure Dottie would be pleased. Maybe he'd get another kiss. "Cody," he yelled again. "Come on, dammit. Let's get moving."

He hunted for Cody's footprints in the snow, but there were none. Even at the turnout, fresh snow had filled in their tracks. "Cody!" he yelled. "It's time for cookies." He climbed up the embankment, expecting Cody to pop out from behind a bush or a tree, but the boy was nowhere. Sam loped back up the hill. Still no Cody. *Maybe he went off chasing another rabbit.* He slogged up one snow bank after another. *Maybe I should get the other trees by myself.* "Cody! Goddammit, he's got to be here somewhere," he grumbled.

Except for the wind, there was only a strange stillness and more blowing snow. There were no other vehicles parked in the turnout.

He was alone.

Tired, Sam rubbed his neck. His back ached. He took a deep breath, squared his shoulders, and squinted into snow, which was now thicker and falling faster. The dark, brooding sky blotting the light made it difficult to see. He was enough of an outdoorsman to know time was running out. His gut turned scared. His knees began to shake.

He jerked the flashlight from the glove compartment and again started a desperate search. "Cody! Cody!" Now, he was screaming. *Maybe Cody ran and tripped on that goddamn hatchet. Maybe he's hurt.* His heart pounded. His stomach churned battery acid. He should have taken the hatchet away. After each frantic call, he stopped to listen for a response, but there was nothing, just the cold wind blowing snowflakes into his hot face.

In the shadowy darkness, his eyes spotted the shape of a boy, but it turned out to be a small tree bobbing in the wind. He hurried toward a huddled form only to discover it was a boulder. He blindly trudged back to the pickup. He was breathing hard. He had to think. He didn't own a cell phone. *Maybe I should drive to the Lake Store and call Pete. But what if Cody showed up and thought I'd left without him?* He stood paralyzed, not knowing what to do. His tense eyes spotted headlights coming down the highway. He ran into the road, frantically waving his arms. It was a red 4x4 Jeep with skis on top. "Help me! Please help me," he begged out of breath. "I can't find my grandson. Please . . . please."

CHAPTER 8

Deputy Sheriff Ken Blake found Sam frightened and pacing in front of his pickup. By then it was dark and around six o'clock. Ken peppered him with questions. "Where had they been? How far had they gone into the woods? When had it started snowing? Why had he sent the boy back alone? How long had it been since Sam had last seen Cody?"

Sam choked out answers. He was cold, his face raw from the wind and snow. He said he felt dizzy and asked Ken to call Pete. "Pete's familiar with the area. Pete can find him."

"He's a little boy," Ken said. "A few minutes can seem like hours to kids. Maybe he got worried and tried to find you again." They briefly tried to retrace the steps, calling out to Cody, but there was nothing but snow and darkness. Ken hoped to calm Sam down so he could get more facts out of him. "He could've gotten out of the pickup. Some good citizen, worried about a small boy all alone out here may have driven him to town."

Sam squinted into the falling snow. "I . . . I told that kid to stay put. He wouldn't go with strangers."

"Are you sure he made it back to the pickup?"

"I told him to follow our tracks."

"He may never have made it, Sam. The snow probably covered your tracks."

"He musta made it. The candy's gone." Sam insisted.

"He could've wandered off course."

Sam shuddered. "Please call Pete. Please."

Because of the darkness, the blowing snow, and Cody's age, Ken wasted no more time looking for Cody or trying to get details from Sam. He radioed a missing person's report to dispatch. "Name: Cody Andrew Benson. A young Caucasian male, Date of birth, February 14, 2001, eight years old. Approximate height: 4 feet 5 inches, approximate weight: eighty pounds. Brown hair, straight; dark-brown eyes. Last seen wearing a red snowsuit, black bomber hat, and boots."

"Oh, God," Sam gasped when he heard those words, *last seen*. He held his head in his hands. The reality of the situation hit him hard, as if someone had dropped a boulder on his head. "Oh, my dear God, please call Pete."

"Has anyone reported a lost boy?" Ken said into his radio, which crackled and sputtered. "Okay, then let's broadcast the known details to the state police, other agencies, hospitals."

"He musta got back here," Sam said several times, his voice disjointed like the garbled sounds coming from Ken's radio. "There are no M&M's in the pickup. I checked every corner." But Sam couldn't be sure the candy was ever there. "Cody said he left them in the truck. I know that's what he said."

Ken pulled up the Bensons' vehicle information on his computer. He contacted dispatch again and asked the voice coming from the radio to find the parents. "They were Christmas shopping in the Klamath Falls area. We believe they're on their way home to Forest Lake. Let me know when you find them."

***

After a long day of shopping, a weary Pete and Cally stopped to eat at a local restaurant. They had settled on a shiny, new bicycle complete with helmet, for Cody and a new tool belt for Sam. They had just started eating when a wide-eyed waitress interrupted their meal. "It's the police," she whispered. "They want to speak to you."

By the time the Bensons chained up and arrived at the turnout, it was eight o'clock and snowing hard. A search-and-rescue team was already on the scene with plans to comb the area throughout the night.

Standing together under a blue tent erected by the rescue squad, Sam tried to explain what had happened, but Pete's eyes turned icy. "Why the hell did you let him walk back by himself?"

"We wasn't that far from the road. He wanted to go. I didn't think—"

"You didn't think!" Pete's face flushed. "He's only eight years old, for Christ's sake."

Sam flinched at the anger in Pete's voice. "He's a country boy. It's a straight shot out."

"Cody has no experience in the outdoors." Cally's voice quivered. The wind whipped the walls of the tent. "We've got to find him," she pleaded to Ken. "He's been out there . . . for what . . . six hours?"

Pete glared at Sam. His jaw tightened, his shoulders tensed, and his hands doubled into hard fists. Ken quickly put his arm around Pete. "Anger isn't going to help. We need to find the boy."

"Yeah." Pete's voice was a soft mutter. His shoulders sagged.

"We're doing everything we can," Ken said. "We'll continue the search throughout the night until we find him."

He introduced them to Carl Hathaway, the search-team leader, who showed them a topographical map of the area.

"Helicopters will be on the scene tomorrow once we get a break in the snow," Hathaway explained.

"There's no candy in the truck. I know he made it," Sam rambled. "It's not there."

Pete turned away. His hand rubbed the base of his neck. "We're in a helluva fix if all we got to go on is candy."

"I told him to follow our tracks. I told him," Sam pleaded to Cally.

"He's not thinking clear," Ken said. "He's been out in the cold too long. Take him into that trailer over there so he can warm up. If we can get him to calm down, we might get some valuable details that could help."

Volunteers staffing the trailer offered Sam some hot chicken broth and crackers. He took two swallows, but couldn't eat. The cracker stuck in his throat. He started to cough. A nice woman brought him a cup of coffee.

Cally didn't remember giving Cody any M&M's, but she kept small packages of the candy in the cupboard for school lunches and snacking.

Still, Sam insisted that Cody had said he'd left the candy in the truck. "He mentioned it gobs of times. There's no candy there now." He wanted Cally to look, but ice had sealed the door on his pickup, and several inches of snow covered the lone tree lying in the back.

CHAPTER 9

That night

Volunteers built a huge bonfire at the turnout, hoping Cody would see it and come toward the light. They brought in a small RV trailer, so Pete and Cally could remain close. Sam also stayed on the scene in a donated camper.

After several hours of searching in the darkness for his son, Pete finally returned to the trailer to rest. He lay awake on the small couch, his hands behind his head, staring at the ceiling. He couldn't sleep. He couldn't talk. He wanted nothing to do with Sam. "Just keep him the hell away from me," he snarled. Both Pete and Cally remained fully clothed, ready in case they received word about Cody.

Cally sat upright at the small dinette, staring out the window to make sure the fire kept burning. It was still snowing, and the temperature had dipped below freezing. She noticed movement by the dark trees and suddenly saw Cody coming out of the woods. He was shivering and so cold, he could barely speak. *Mom,* he cried. *Help me!* She scrambled to find her boots, but someone had moved them. She was going out there anyway, even in her stocking feet. Her body jerked up, and she realized she had dozed off. The comforter covering her had fallen away. She saw that Pete was gone, leaving just the dent in the pillow where his head had lain. She rearranged the comforter around her. If she could get this cold inside the trailer, what must it be like for Cody out there in the open?

She looked out the window and saw Pete helping to fuel the bonfire. A shower of fiery sparks shot into the sky. Against the glow of orange flames, she could see the black forest and snow still steadily falling. The wind brought the smell of smoke to the trailer and caused the flames to bow and flare. It howled and lashed snow against the metal walls and bent the treetops into eerie, ghostly shapes. Why didn't the damn snow stop?

Her anger with Sam would surge and fade. Of course he hadn't meant for this to happen. He was probably awake in the camper, but she couldn't go to him. He should not have let Cody out of his sight. Her son had no experience in the wilderness. Then she got angry with herself. She knew it was hard to keep Cody focused. She should have cautioned Sam. *I did, didn't I?* Her mind reviewed the conversation they had on Friday night. Then again, it was a stretch to think Sam would have understood Cody's problems. She wasn't even sure she did. But they didn't know for sure. They had never tested Cody. They just didn't know. She should have listened to Pete. He'd been against the tree outing from the start. She should not have tried to convince him. She should have left well enough alone.

Cally cradled her knees in her arms and rocked back and forth. She should be doing something to help, but what? Whenever she stepped outside, cold wind cut right through her clothing. The search-team leader had cautioned her about complicating the search. "Conditions out here, ma'am, are treacherous. I know ya want to help, but we already got a lost boy. We don't have time to be searching for other lost folks. It's best to leave the terrain to experienced searchers. You'll know what we know. I promise you."

They were good people. This would turn out all right, wouldn't it? They would spend Christmas together like they always did. Cody couldn't have gone far. Maybe he fell. Maybe he was hurt. *Oh, God,* she prayed into the snowy night. *Please help us find him. Please make him be okay. Please. Please. Please.*

Once they found Cody, she would make sure this never happened again. She would work with him. She would get him the help he needed no matter what. Her arms ached for her son. He was out there somewhere in that black coldness. Alone. Afraid. She could hear him crying in the wind as it howled, rattled the trailer, and made the snowflakes ping against the wall. The numbness in her body gave way to tears. They glistened in her eyes, spilled over the rims, and trickled down her face. What good were tears? She was glad Pete wasn't there to see her crying. But then, why shouldn't she cry? She was Cody's mother. She had a right to cry. Finally, her body loosened into deep, uncontrollable sobs.

***

Day one

At daybreak on Sunday, searchers renewed their efforts. Heavy snow still fell and continued until mid-morning. The search party swelled in numbers as hundreds, including the National Guard, came to search for Cody with snowmobiles, helicopters, and dogs. With a break in the weather, the searchers scoured the remote, rugged terrain, sometimes going over areas two or three times. They were able to pinpoint the area Sam had traveled by locating the other two trees he'd cut. They even identified some Cody had nicked with the hatchet, but found no sign of the boy. They fanned out from there, going deeper into the heavily wooded area, where they trudged through thigh-high snow. In some spots, fierce winds had whipped up drifts as high as six feet.

The story hit the news Sunday morning. Camera crews swarmed on tiny Forest Lake and the Big Bat. One by one, television stations and newspapers from Southern Oregon, Eugene, Portland, and Northern California sent crews and reporters. The story had all the elements of a seasonal drama—a small boy in search of the perfect Christmas tree for his school was lost.

Ken was with Cally during the first interviews. "We have a trained rescue squad combing the region," he said. "We are doing everything possible to find Cody. Time is of the essence. We'd like to talk to anyone who was in the area and may have seen the boy."

Cally scraped her dark hair back into a ponytail to keep it from blowing into her face. She wore no makeup; her eyes were red and puffy. She looked directly into the camera. "I'm not leaving the mountain without my son," she said emphatically. "We remain very hopeful." She asked for everyone's prayers. Her eyes teared up each time the TV reporters closed their reports with a description of Cody.

***

In the trailer, Ken briefed Cally and Pete over a lunch of tuna sandwiches and stale coffee in paper cups. For Ken, this was always the tough part. Families wanted hope, but he felt it was important to lay out the facts, just like a doctor when discussing a fatal illness with a patient.

Pete scowled. He pushed away his half-eaten sandwich. "I just don't know why in the hell Sam let Cody go off by himself." He shook his head several times. "I just can't get past that."

"I know things are tense between you two," Ken said. "I don't think Sam realized how far they'd gone. We've tried to piece together a timeline. As near as we can tell, they arrived a little after two o'clock. They cut a tree for your home. They were looking for one for the school when Sam sent Cody to the pickup. The second tree Sam felled is about a mile into the wilderness area. Then he went in farther to get a tree for the café."

"They were that far in?" Cally's jaw dropped. She hadn't touched her sandwich.

"Cody started back. It was snowing lightly at first, and then it picked up," Ken continued. "The snow most likely covered their tracks. Cody probably wandered off in another direction. Or, being a kid, he may have been distracted by something . . . a squirrel, a deer."

"The damned ol' fool was moonstruck," Pete croaked. His voice was hoarse from repeatedly yelling his son's name.

"If Sam had headed back immediately, he may have been able to locate Cody. But I would guess some time passed before he cut that third tree." Ken glanced at Pete. "Maybe forty-five minutes."

"Jesus Christ!" Pete blurted. He shook his head several times.

Cally gave Pete a cautious look. "Weren't there other people out hunting for trees?"

"Sam said he thought there were at least two other vehicles in the turnout when they arrived. He never actually saw the people," Ken said. "My guess is those folks started earlier and left the area before the snow began."

"When we left for Klamath Falls Saturday morning, we had no idea Sam was going to take Cody to town for lunch," Pete said.

Ken tried to keep the discussion on track. "We're trying to locate those folks to see if they saw the boy."

"Dad probably got to talking at the café, like he always does, and forgot about the time," Cally added.

"Hell, he planned this whole goddamn thing around Dottie . . ." Pete rubbed his neck like it hurt.

"It's not uncommon for this to happen," Ken interrupted. "People concentrating on trees don't realize how far they've wandered. I don't have to tell you that out there, everything looks the same. There are no bearings for reference points. We've had cases in the past where folks were fifty feet away from their car but couldn't find it when the weather turned sour. It can be difficult for adults, let alone a child."

"How . . . how long can he survive out there?" Cally asked. She folded her arms, gripping her body as if she dreaded the answer.

"It's difficult to say." Ken weighed his words carefully. "At least Cody is dressed warm. If he found a shelter of some type, like huddling next to a fallen tree or in a cavern or gully, it could help. Generally, the first forty-eight hours are critical."

"I see." She took a small sip of coffee and stared past the men.

***

Pastor Rick arrived in the afternoon to pray with Cally and Sam. Pete was not there. He had rejoined the ground searchers. A member of the congregation drove the minister to the mountain in his chained-up four-wheel-drive vehicle. They brought food, toiletries, a change of clothing, warm hats, wool scarves, and cards and notes from well-wishers. Pastor Rick prayed for Cody's safe return and for more favorable weather. "Be strong. Pull together. Get through this," he said. He hugged Cally and shook Sam's hand.

Sam clung to Cally as they watched the two men leave. "I just never meant for this to happen. I thought he'd be okay."

"Deputy Blake said you were a mile into the woods. What in God's name were you thinking?"

Sam's face looked ashen and tired. He didn't respond. He tightened his grip.

She pulled away. "That's quite a ways for a small boy to go by himself. Cody has no experience in the outdoors. None."

Sam closed his eyes as if expecting a blow. "The police interviewed me. Made me feel like a criminal."

"They talked to us, too. They're just trying to get information to help. Pete is going to let them into the house again so they can get"—she swallowed hard before finishing—"more scent samples. . . his DNA . . . and pictures."

"They asked me if I'd been drinkin.' I don't know why they had to bring that up. I haven't had a drop —"

"It will be all right once we find Cody."

"Did you tell them about … you know … the drinkin'?"

"No."

"They wanted to know about the hatchet. Where it was . . . the last time I'd seen it. Stuff like that. Why, if he was going back to the truck, did he need to take it?"

"Why did he take it?"

"I didn't need it. I had my saw. I only gave it to him so he could feel like he was helpin.'"

"But when he left, he had it with him?"

"I told him not to run with it a dozen times, probably."

"So, he had the hatchet?"

"He was playing Indian…hacking things with the hatchet …whooping … he thought he saw a friend."

"A friend? There was somebody else out there . . . that he knew?"

"I never saw nobody. There was nobody near us. The kid imagines things."

"Oh, no," Cally gasped. Playing Indian. Benny. He could have romped off course with his imaginary friend. That had happened before, only Cody had been much younger. They had found him, lost and crying in a neighbor's cornfield. Then again, maybe somebody else had been out there.

"They kept asking, 'Why did you send him back?'"

"Who did?"

"Those officers. I never sent him back. He wanted to go."

"That's probably because you were the last person to see him."

"I never harmed that kid. He couldn't of gone that far. He's got to be right under our noses."

***

Day two

With a break in the weather Monday morning, the search effort expanded. After low-lying clouds lifted, the helicopter again took off scanning the terrain using an infrared search and track system.

In the afternoon, a volunteer drove Sam to the hospital in Klamath Falls. He had joined the search but ended up suffering from exhaustion and heart palpitations.

The rescue team reported that they found an M&M wrapper, empty chip bags, snow goggles, and a glove. They discovered the candy wrapper about a mile and a half up Cooper's Hawk Highway. Ken told reporters it was unlikely that Cody could have wandered that far, but he sent it to the lab for DNA testing. The other items did not belong to Cody. There was no evidence the boy had actually reached the highway.

Searchers located a makeshift shelter of fir branches next to a large boulder, not far from where Sam had cut the first tree. They hoped that Cody had used his hatchet to build it, but tracker dogs could not detect his scent. They never found Cody's hatchet but speculated that it—and possibly the boy—could be under the very deep layers of new snow.

***

Back in Forest Lake, Principal Cora Everson cancelled morning classes so that counselors from Klamath Falls could help the anxious children, especially Cody's classmates. Ken agreed to drive back to town to reassure the schoolchildren at a hastily organized assembly in the school cafeteria. Word spread quickly throughout town about the early afternoon meeting.

When Ken arrived, he found the room packed with kids, concerned parents, teachers, and townspeople. Adults stood against the walls and some of the kids sat on the floor. Not used to public speaking, Ken was nervous, and he hadn't expected that many people.

As he approached the microphone, he spotted Lydia sitting next to Dottie. Lydia gave him a reassuring smile. Ken cleared his throat and proceeded to describe the search area. He covered rescue techniques including the roles of the search dogs, snowmobiles, and helicopters. "Cody was on a special mission, getting a tree for his school, but got lost." The room filled with applause. He explained how they believed Cody had gotten off-track. Some children cried. Brittany Bolin clung to her mother and buried her face in Mrs. Bolin's chest. A small boy in the front row eyed Ken's badge. His little arm shot up. "You have a question?" Ken asked.

"Um, um, when you find Cody, will . . . um . . . he be in trouble?" A low, sympathetic *ooh* rippled through the crowd.

"Cody has done nothing wrong, and there is no one to blame. He will absolutely *not* be in trouble. It's very easy to get lost when it snows out in the wild. Sometimes you can't see your hand when it's just a foot out in front of your face. That's why it's so important to stay close to your parents whenever you go to the mountain."

People wanted to know what they could do to help. Ken asked them to pray for Cody and his family and for a break in the weather. Several high school boys who had taken wilderness training volunteered to assist in the search. Ken said he would consult with search officials to see whether that was okay.

"You are all good people, and I know you want to help. But I have to ask you to stay away. The weather at this point is unpredictable. Oregon State Police have set up a roadblock and only authorized personnel are allowed into the area."

Dottie had no desire to put up the tree Sam had cut for her. After consulting with the principal and counselors, she and Lydia decided to give it to the school. Mrs. Everson announced this decision at the assembly and said they would call it "Cody's Tree." The children could decorate it with yellow ribbons and handmade paper ornaments containing prayers or well-wishes for Cody and his family. This, she said, would help alleviate tension and give the children something positive to do. She gave a nervous smile. "And my, won't he be surprised when he comes home and sees our fine tree all dressed up in his honor."

Ken agreed to have the tree delivered as soon as possible. Outside the school, he discovered Brittany and her mother waiting for him. "Please find Cody," Brittany said shyly.

"We're doing everything we can, honey," Ken assured her, but in his heart, he knew time was running out.

"When you find Cody, will you give him this?" She held up a small brown paper bag. Ken squatted down so he could be at eye level. "It's a dog collar. He said he was going to get a dog like mine." Brittany's eyes blinked. "His name is Bowser." She fidgeted. "It's red and has a bell."

"This is very thoughtful and very nice of you." Ken said.

Brittany wiped her eyes on her sleeve. "I'll be sure and give this to the Bensons and tell them it's for Cody. When we find him, you will be the first person I'll call."

After Brittany and her mother headed for their car, Ken waited for Lydia. Something made him turn around. He looked into Myra Jenkins's cold, blue-eyed stare. She had been at the assembly, too.

Ken nodded a greeting. Myra just stood there, her head tilted back, peering down her nose. In the afternoon light, she seemed older than he remembered, and there was more white hair showing through the various shades of orange. She scowled, suddenly turned, and hurried away.

He was relieved to see Lydia coming his way. She put her arms around him, gave him a big hug, and walked with him to his Jeep. "You look tired. I know this is tearing at your heart."

"It's going to be another long night."

"Be careful up there."

"We're shorthanded. Some of the key people from K-Falls are out with the flu. They're asking me to do more."

"But you've got a full rescue squad?"

"Yeah. No problem there. It's just the administrative things. I'm having to deal with the press, brief the family, coordinate with the rescue team, worry about what's going on in the rest of the county, the whole Maryann. I'm not complaining, I just would like to find that boy. Alive. It would mean so much."

"We're all hoping for that, Ken."

"Myra Jenkins was here giving me her ol' evil eye."

"You're a good officer, Ken Blake. Don't you ever forget that." She brushed her forehead against his.

"I won't be able to drive Lauren to her dance."

"Don't you even worry about that."

"They say the weather could get really bad on the Big Bat. If heavy snow reaches Forest Lake, I'd prefer she not go."

"We'll deal with that, honey." She kissed him on the lips. "Take it easy," she shouted, and waved as he drove off.

In the late afternoon, eerie clouds surrounded the Big Bat. Falling snow swirled in the biting wind. The crucial forty-eight-hour period had passed. Nighttime temperatures again dipped below freezing. Ken and the search squad sadly agreed that Cody could not survive long under these conditions.

***

The Cody Benson story gained national attention. The networks, CNN, and Fox News had crews on the scene.

"This is not a kid who has any experience in the wilderness," Ken told reporters. "It's Christmas. Miracles can happen."

Reporters and camera crews stayed at the Forest Lake Motor Lodge; they ate breakfast and sometimes lunch at Dottie's Café. With time on their hands, they tried to capture the flavor of the small town, talking to Dottie's customers, Cody's classmates, and Eula Brackston, his teacher. At the school, television reporters used the Christmas tree as a backdrop and occasionally read one of the notes the children had hung on it. They continually tried to characterize Cody. The Associated Press quoted Miss Brackston as stating that Cody was hyperactive and had attention deficit disorder. One TV station labeled him autistic. It cut to an interview with a New York child psychologist, who said Cody could have Asperger's syndrome, a type of autism in which kids have difficulty in social situations. "Kids with these kinds of disabilities," he said, "might hide from the searchers because they are afraid, think they did something wrong, and don't understand that they are lost." Back at the mountain, reporters peppered Cally with questions about Cody's behavior. Under siege, she retreated to the trailer.

Ken called a press conference and asked the media to respect the needs and feelings of the family. "There's no reason to believe Cody is hiding," Ken said emphatically. "When someone gets lost under these circumstances, he could suffer from the effects of hypothermia, dehydration, and frostbite. Kids, especially young ones like Cody, can get so hypothermic they can't even call for help."

Tina Williams, a TV journalist, with long blond hair and heavy eye makeup, angled for a scoop. "There are reports that Cody could be a runaway," she shouted through bright red lips. "Some of his friends say he had problems at school. What do you know about that?"

Ken called those reports ridiculous. "Cody is a good kid who was out looking for the perfect Christmas tree just like hundreds of other kids this time of the year."

"Was he in a fight at school?" Tina persisted.

Ken ignored her, checked his watch, and terminated the press conference.

Later, Tina and a cameraman waited for Cally to emerge from her trailer. She shoved the microphone in Cally's face. "Have you considered the possibility that Cody could be a runaway? Some kids say he was in trouble at school."

Cally took a step back, then stopped and held her ground. "Cody was loved, and like any child, had some problems." She could smell Tina's musky, vanilla perfume.

Tina pressed on. "But it's true he was having problems?"

"He was excited about getting a tree for his school. Cody was not the kind of child who'd run away."

"Do you wish you had gotten him the dog he wanted?"

"A dog? What dog?"

"Apparently, your son told some of the children he was getting a dog."

"I believe with all my heart that we're going to find Cody, and I'm not leaving without him." Cally turned and went back into the trailer.

"Was your father drinking the day Cody went missing?" Tina shouted after her. Cally slammed the door, a scowl on her face.

When the story ran on TV, several viewers contacted the station and offered to donate a dog.

Back at camp, Pete swore when he heard that some reporters had tried to paint Cody as a problem child. His sore throat ached. His voice was a raspy whisper. He could only croak complaints to Ken and the search team leader. "They're not helping this situation one damn bit. They shouldn't be allowed in the search area."

Cally fumed at the school and the people who gave any information to the news media about Cody's behavioral problems. It added insult to injury and was just plain mean. "Once we find Cody, I'm going to have a word with Cora Everson, and I plan to bring a lawyer." She blew her nose and wiped her eyes.

Pete wanted Ken to order the press off the mountain. "They're vermin in a feeding frenzy, looking for raw meat."

"Believe me I know this is stressful, but when a kid goes missing, we need all the help we can get," Ken explained. "We still need to locate those other folks who were parked at the turnout. Maybe they can help."

He assured the Bensons that he would speak to Tina Williams. He caught up with her near the command post, where she stood sipping a cup of coffee. "Listen, you need to lay off of the family. They've lost their son, and if that isn't enough, you're making them angry."

"Are you saying you're giving up on the search?" She was suddenly in reporter mode.

"What I'm saying is that if you don't back off, you'll have to leave," he growled.

"What do you know about the grandfather? Was he sober when he took the boy out there?"

"He's not involved."

"They say they found an empty bottle in his pickup."

"That's news to me."

She flashed a coy smile, revealing the small space between her front teeth. She took another sip of coffee, sending a puff of steam into the cold air. "You're hot, did you know that?" Her mouth parted slightly, and her eyelashes fluttered. She stepped closer.

Ken's face flushed. He touched the brim of his hat and moved back just as a whiff of her strong perfume hit his nose. Then his eyes locked with hers. "You're a sharp cookie. You understand what I'm saying? Don't harass the family. I won't warn you again."

As he turned, he heard Tina mutter, "Thank you Mr. Big." It almost sounded like she blew him a muffled raspberry.

Ken walked away. He had bigger fish to fry.

***

Day three

On Tuesday afternoon, excitement surged like electricity through the base camp. The search team had found a child's boot. After hours of waiting and pacing, Cally knew instantly when she saw it that it wasn't Cody's. Her son had worn the new snow boots Sam had purchased for him. Still, she clutched the child's boot, hugging it close to her chest. In some strange way, it bolstered her hope. If the boot had been Cody's, it would mean he was out there in his bare feet. Her grasp loosened when she learned weather forecasters predicted an even more powerful storm for the area, bringing high wind and more snow. On top of that, Ken reported that his department had located the people who had parked in the turnout when Sam and Cody arrived. Neither party could remember seeing an older man with a young boy.

That night in the small trailer, Cally dreamed of Cody again.

"Mom, I'm hungry." His outstretched arms reached for her. "My toes are black. They hurt."

Someone else was with him—an Indian boy. "Benny," Cally cried, looking into the chestnut-colored face. "Thank God, you're real."

Benny tried to tell her something, but she couldn't make out the words. Tears streaked his face.

"What is it, Benny? Speak louder. Why are you crying? Where's Cody?"

The Indian boy pointed to something, but she couldn't see what it was. Then she heard sobbing, and saw blood on the snow.

"Did he hurt himself?" she asked. "Did he run and fall on the hatchet?" She tried to move toward the weeping sounds, but her body froze.

"I'm coming!" she said aloud.

In the darkness of the trailer, she heard Pete crying. In all their years together, he'd never cried. Not like that. She got up from the small sofa, walked to the rear, climbed into the narrow bed with him, and cradled him in her arms. They didn't speak. The fierce wind whined and rattled the trailer. In her heart, she knew it was over.

***

Day four

Weather forecasters used the word "blizzard" to describe the storm they expected to hit the area Wednesday evening. With regret, the Klamath County Sheriff's Department called off the search, saying it could not risk the lives of the search team and the volunteers. They asked everyone to leave the mountain.

That morning an emotional Ken, along with a tearful Pete and Cally, met with everyone who had helped search for Cody.

"I know we're all heartbroken over these circumstances," Ken said, "but you guys did an excellent job. I promise you we'll be back here again"—he paused for a few seconds to avoid choking up—"when it's safe to do so, and we'll keep searching for little Cody until we have some resolution." He nodded at Pete and stepped back.

"We want to thank every . . ." Pete's already hoarse voice cracked. He swallowed to avoid crying. "We . . ." he started again, held his breath, swallowed again, and looked down. "My son . . ." He shook his head.

"It's okay," Ken whispered.

Cally reached for Pete; the two clung to each other and cried softly. Finally, Cally turned toward the group, her cheeks wet. "We can't thank you enough . . . each and every one of you." Her voice trembled. "This is not our final goodbye to Cody. We will hang onto every shred of hope . . . until we find him."

There was nothing left to do.

Touch the Sky

CHAPTER 10

The time spent on the mountain in the cold, cramped RV pinched hard like an unrelenting vise but had at least offered hope. Now, after four days at home, Cally felt rudderless, sinking under waves of grief. She sat in the rocking chair, moving back and forth, listening to its springs squeak and to the clock tick. The turbulence inside tortured her. The emptiness was indescribable; so was the fear. Drained and exhausted but too wound up to sleep, time stopped and despair ruled.

The sounds of buzzing helicopters, people getting excited over tiny clues and the daily briefings from the search team or Deputy Blake faded away. Anticipation had vanished, leaving just the huge pile of cards, notes, and gifts on the kitchen table. Some came from strangers as far away as Maine, who had followed the Cody Benson story on TV and who wanted, in some small way, to do something, to shine a ray of light on a bleak situation.

Brittany's gift, the small brown bag with the dog collar, sat on the coffee table next to more cards. Why had Cody told her he was getting a dog? They never actually agreed that he could have a pet, but none of that mattered now. He probably had an imaginary one, just like he had an imaginary everything else. Cally took the collar out of the bag and fastened it around the neck of a fluffy brown teddy bear, one of several stuffed animals people had left under the Christmas tree at school. She patted its head and hugged it as if it were a baby. Poor little Cody. She missed his crazy stories, his precious imagination, the way his small, white hand grasped a pencil and his little tongue perched on his lip as he drew.

Pete was on leave from his job until sometime in January. Although he'd seen a doctor, he still didn't feel well. Exposure had turned his face the color of a lobster; he had a deep cough that got worse at night, and severe laryngitis. He spent most of the time in bed clutching a heating pad to his chest.

Now, after restless nights on the couch, Cally was the one that rose early to start the fire in the kitchen stove and make coffee. A sullen Sam said very little and quickly departed for breakfast at Dottie's Café. It was his way of avoiding Pete. The two no longer spoke. Sam never returned until late at night. Cally thought she smelled alcohol on his breath.

Cody's presence was everywhere. His Harry Potter books lay scattered on the coffee table. A pair of his worn shoes peeked out from under the base of the coat rack. Every time she opened the fridge, that big, half-empty jar of Jif peanut butter stared back at her. She hated those packages of M&M's in the cupboard which she counted repeatedly to determine whether Cody had taken some. How could she be certain? The fruitless counting always ended in tears.

Sometimes she'd go into Cody's room and sit on his bed. It seemed different in there—strangely peaceful, calm. She could almost feel his spirit. A pair of his socks lay on the floor. The Christmas bike, with a yellow ribbon on the handlebars, stood in the center, waiting. The teddy bear with the dog collar sat on the bike seat. Cody would like that. She could see a ghostly version of him laughing and clapping his hands.

Where are you, my little man? How quickly things had changed. A few days ago, she'd anticipated a joyful Christmas with her family—all of them. Cody would be marking the days off on the holiday calendar he always made for the fridge. "Eleven days to go," he would happily chirp. Now there was nothing. Why . . . why . . . why had she let him go? Her father had meant well, but failed them. She should not have let him take her little boy. What if Pete never came around?

She picked up the teddy bear, giving it a tender squeeze, but almost dropped it when the doorbell rang—four aggressive bursts followed by loud, impatient knocking. Most of the well-wishers who stopped by to offer prayers, condolences, or food were not that eager. Maybe they'd found Cody. She dashed down the stairs and flung open the door.

"How do you feel about the decision to stop the search?" asked Tina Williams, microphone in hand, a wool hat covering her blond hair, and a sly smile on her red lips. A cameraman stood behind her. She stared at the teddy bear Cally clutched in her arms.

The words hit like steel daggers. The camera pointed directly at her. She wanted to shove Tina off the porch, but the camera's intrusive eye stopped her. She clung to the brown bear and swallowed, struggling to find the right words for Cody's sake. "We . . . uh . . . want to thank all the volunteers, neighbors, and friends —"

"You said you weren't leaving the mountain without your son," Tina prompted.

". . . kind people all . . . who helped look for Cody . . . or helped in other ways . . . and . . . who continue to help . . . like with these animals." She held up the bear, and her voice trailed away. "Uh . . . I'll never be able to thank them enough. Cody was a special little boy, and he will live in our hearts forever."

"What do you plan to do next?"

"When the weather permits, we'll return to the mountain —"

"To search for the remains?"

"To find our *son*." Cally's anger surged. "Please *do not* refer to Cody as remains. We intend to bring our son home." She stepped back to close the door.

Tina didn't back off. "Are you planning a memorial service?"

Cally slammed the door shut. Through the window, she saw Tina using their house as a backdrop for her report. Her ears perked to those awful words: "Tina Williams, News Channel 14, reporting from Forest Lake, Oregon."

Cally collapsed against the wall, wrapped her arms around the teddy bear, slid to the floor, and bent her head over her knees. The sickening scent of Tina's perfume lingered in the air. Her heart pounded. Her head hurt. She realized when speaking about Cody, she had actually said *was*.

Jean Rover

CHAPTER 11

"Ken!" Mo flashed his chestnut smile and leaned on his walking stick like an aging tree whose roots had loosened. With his left hand, he waved Ken inside. "Welcome to my lodge." His dark eyes sparkled above the aquiline nose in a face so deeply lined it could have been used for a dish rack. At seventy-five, he wore his once black hair which had turned steel gray, tied back in a sparse braid with a colorful red ribbon worked into the weave.

Ken had not visited the tiny house since all that trouble over Jim Fallingwater long ago. Everything seemed familiar, like taking a step back in time, except more worn and cluttered as if it missed Mo's deceased wife's loving hands. Her real name had been Claudia, and she had died fifteen years ago. Ken had always liked her. A stout, cheerful Kalapooyian woman, Mo had affectionately called her Happy Face. Childless, they'd considered Jim Fallingwater a son and were heartbroken over what'd happened. People claimed grief was what really killed Claudia.

Without her, the house's cream walls had grown dingy, and in one corner the ceiling paint cracked and peeled. A gray wool blanket lay crumpled next to a pillow with a scrunched-up heating pad on the faded-brown couch. An assortment of squat, amber prescription containers, a Kleenex box, a glass of water, and a piece of half-eaten toast covered the metal TV tray that stood beside the couch. A little wood stove with bouncing yellow flames visible through its small door warmed the room.

Mo snapped off the TV, which sat on a wooden stand with a large picture of Happy Face on top and a hodgepodge of magazines on the shelf below.

Ken seated himself in a brown leather recliner with a tear in the arm. He removed his heavy jacket and tossed it over the back of the chair. He loosened his collar. "I guess I'm not used to wood heat."

"There's nothin' like a good fire." Mo placed one hand on the small of his back. "Slipped in the kitchen. Now my back is grumbling. Shameful." His dark eyes lingered on Ken's badge.

"I see you can still chop wood," Ken pointed to a box of kindling, which looked like a collection of giant matchsticks.

"Stevie, a boy at the ranch across the road, comes and lends a hand. He helps me with chopping. He gets the wood in. Helps with the yard, too. I pay."

Mo offered Ken some coffee and used his walking stick to go into the small kitchen. The house smelled of bacon and potatoes. Ken glimpsed the untidy counters. Bottles, jars, cans, spoons, packages of crackers and cereal covered every inch. Two cardboard boxes of canned goods were stacked against a wall. An empty breakfast dish was still on the dark wood-grained Formica table—the same table he and Jim had sat at when they'd come back from an outing on the mountain with Mo. Happy Face had always served them generous scoops of raspberry ripple ice cream—her favorite—in green soup bowls.

A large, black cat with golden eyes the size of grapes crouched on the table, busy licking the dish. It looked up and spotted Ken, then it dashed out the pet door. Mo laughed. "Magic'll be back when he gets hungry. He's a good mouser, but he doesn't eat 'em."

Ken politely sipped his coffee, which tasted like it had been in Mo's big aluminum pot for several hours.

Mo pushed the blanket out of the way and lowered himself gingerly onto the sofa. He stared at Ken's duty belt. "What brings you here?" his voice serious. "It's been a long time."

"The boy lost on the Big Bat," Ken said.

Mo nodded, his face sad. Then he looked away, his eyes suddenly distant, as if he'd gone back to another time.

"The wind and snow were so bad up there, we . . . we couldn't recover him," Ken continued.

"The old man should not have sent the little boy back in the snow." Mo's dark eyes flashed anger.

"It was an apparent lapse in judgment. We think the boy had some disabilities, too. Attention deficits, you know—just an all-around sad situation."

"Yes, yes, sad. Real sad."

"Come spring, we're gonna make an all-out effort to find the . . . remains."

Mo's eyes narrowed. "People need to respect Bat Mountain."

"There's no one that knows more about that area than you." Ken leaned forward. "I thought you might help with the search. I mean, if you're feeling better, and if we provided you with some assistance."

"Hmmm." Mo pulled a cigarette from the package in his shirt pocket and lit up. "Hopeless. Very hopeless." He blew out smoke. "I don't guess the boy could of survived out there very long."

Ken eyed Mo's walking stick. "You wouldn't actually have to participate in the search. Just be there . . . sort of directing . . . giving us ideas."

"I don't know." Mo's brow wrinkled. He coughed thick and hard. "I don't go out there much anymore. Many ravines in that area. Weather is bad."

"We've got some time," Ken assured him.

"The boy couldn't of gotten far. He's somewhere close . . . under snow."

"Yeah. That's my theory. We won't be going out again until about March."

"Many gullies . . . many." Mo seemed to have already gone to the mountain.

"Then we'll hit it again with a full-blown search. If we find something, it'll give the family closure." Ken's throat tightened. "If not, I guess we'll move on." He gripped his coffee cup.

"Full search?" Mo turned his head toward the window. "Sounds like you have lotsa help." He stared at the icy rain. "The sky weeps for the little lost one."

"It's the hardest thing I ever had to do, to tell the parents that the search is over."

"Yes. Yes." The wind slammed sleet against the window. "This rain will make the highway slick as snot."

"I mean . . . you know . . . to tell them their son had frozen to death." Ken finished his thought. He placed his cup down on a small end table covered with white rings. "What do you say?"

"Foolish people don't understand the way it is. He shouldn't have let the little boy go on alone."

"Cody was their only child . . . I can still see that look of unendurable pain in their eyes . . . when they realized it was over."

"Yes. Yes. Very sad." Mo coughed again. "Their only son. May the warm winds of heaven blow softly on their souls."

"It's a helluva thing to happen just before Christmas."

"Yes, yes, hellish thing." Mo rubbed the small of his back like a child trying to avoid gym class.

"Sorry about your back," Ken said. He didn't want to pressure him into helping, but he knew Mo, in his younger days, had been the kind of man who could slip away for months and wander deep into the Big Bat Wilderness where he spent long nights by a flaming campfire carving Indian wood spirits.

Mo looked beyond Ken. He set his cigarette down on an ashtray heaped with butts. A piece of wood popped in the stove, making the flames dance higher. Mo's face broke into a wide smile. "When spring comes, I will help look."

***

Except for the little plastic trees on the tables and the Santa clock, there were no other Christmas decorations at Dottie's Café. Instead, a fluffy yellow bow hung on the back of each chair. A yellow ribbon ran along the full length of the counter. There was so much yellow ribbon strung throughout Forest Lake that the Mercantile was all out. A new shipment wasn't expected until next week.

Barber Bill set down his gooey hamburger lunch and wiped his hands on the paper napkin. "It's just about now that kid woulda come in for a haircut."

"He took a swipe at Artie at school," said Burt Bradshaw, the pharmacist. A big, heavyset man with small hands, he cut his meatloaf into tiny pieces with a fork. "Can you believe that? I mean, Artie's a pretty big kid." Burt looked a lot like Artie except he was bald, had a small mustache, and his cheeks were not as rosy. "Just boys' stuff, I guess."

"I read in the papers the kid had some problems, but he was always a nice, polite boy when he came in with the dad for a haircut."

"We haven't seen a blizzard on the Big Bat the likes of that one in twenty years," said Ed Bartley, who ran the feed store. "Next step I hear is they're gonna wait until the snows melt up there and then look for what's left of him."

"That's sad stuff for the family to hear with Christmas coming on and all. Real sad stuff," said Bill.

"I'd hate to be the grandfather. You gotta watch kids." Burt eagerly attacked a generous side of mac and cheese. "Don't know why that kid thought he could take on Artie."

"We were hoping this story woulda had a happy ending," Ed said. "I'm kinda anxious to hear what the sheriff has to say."

Dottie stood behind the counter with the carafe that always seemed to be an extension of her right hand. "You fellas need more coffee?" Burt raised his cup. He ordered more bread. Bill worked on his hamburger.

The bell on the door jingled. In strode a confident Tina Williams, notebook in hand, her musky-vanilla perfume competing with the smell of fries. She looked around and took the empty seat in the center of the counter between the men.

"Don't sit there," said Bill from his seat on the right. "That's the sheriff's seat. He always sits there."

"You mean the deputy, don't you?" said Tina.

The barber let it drop.

Dottie filled their cups.

Tina ordered a tuna sandwich and black coffee "I understand the grandfather and the boy ate lunch here before heading out," she said.

"Yes," said Dottie.

"Was he sober?"

"He was fine. They were both fine." She gave Tina a hard look.

"People say they've seen him around town drunk."

Dottie said nothing. She filled a white mug with coffee and pushed it toward Tina.

"If you see him, I'd like to talk with him."

"I'll let him know." Dottie moved away quickly. Sam, she knew, was upstairs in the apartment resting on the bed. He was heartbroken.

The bell on the door jingled again, and Ken walked in. All the talking stopped.

"Thought I might find you here," he said to Tina.

Tina swirled to face him. "Anything new?"

"No, nothing, but I need to have a word with you."

"I guess I'm sitting in *your* seat," she said. She wiggled her buttocks on the stool, making it squeak.

"Be my guest."

"Thank you. I will."

"Maybe we could step outside for a moment."

"I'm right in the middle of lunch."

"Okay."

All eyes were on Ken. The clinking of silverware against plates stopped. Suddenly, the Santa Claus clock struck twelve noon. "Ho, Ho, Ho," it chimed. Its nose blinked twelve times.

Tina rolled her eyes. "I guess that's the day's excitement around here."

"Quit sneaking up on the Bensons," Ken said in his police officer's voice.

"I don't sneak up."

"They're grieving. Can you understand that?"

"I'm just doing my job."

"One more complaint, and I'll slap a restraining order on you."

"Freedom of the press must be a foreign concept in Forest Lake?" She smiled sweetly.

"I'm asking you nicely."

"I'm answering you nicely."

"Cody was their only child. *Stay* off their property."

"Can I get you anything, Ken?" Dottie interrupted. She glared at Tina.

"No. I need to get to headquarters for a meeting. Thanks, Dottie." Ken jabbed his finger in Tina's face. "Remember what I said." Then he went out the door.

Tina swiveled on the counter stool. "He's got a cute butt." She laughed and took a gratifying bite out of her sandwich. "I just love cops with cute buns." She winked at Bill, who blushed and suddenly stared at the counter.

Burt and Ed exchanged looks. "The price of feed jumped again," Ed finally said, but his friends continued eating quietly. "Can you believe that—a whole dollar?"

***

Cally gripped the steering wheel hard as she passed houses lit up with strings of twinkling Christmas lights. The Winthrops had gone all out again, expecting to win the town's decorating contest. They'd strung small white lights on all their shrubs. A lighted reindeer stood in the front lawn, and a big, inflated Santa waved and bounced on the roof. The merriment all seemed wrong to her now.

She came to town during the darkness of the dinner hour to avoid people. Of course, they meant well. Everyone was sorry. They were all sorry, but when they asked about Cody or hugged her, it made the pain surge in her chest so she couldn't breathe, let alone talk. The other reason she wanted to avoid people was the purplish-green bruise on the side of her chin where Pete had hit her. It had happened when she'd heard arguing and swearing in the kitchen and had stepped in the middle of a fight between Pete and Sam.

"Just get the hell out," Pete croaked.

Sam stood near the door with a duffel bag, his face ashen.

"Dad, where are you going?" she shouted.

"I'm going to stay at Dottie's for a while. Then I'm gonna head back to Montana." His lips trembled. He looked at Pete. "I told that kid to stay put. He didn't listen."

Pete's eyes narrowed. "Didn't listen . . . he was only eight years old for Christ sakes."

"He wanted to go back, I —"

"One of the last things my son said to me was 'I hate you.' I'll never, *never* have a chance to make that right. Never!" Pete rasped. He lunged at Sam.

Cally jumped in between them. Pete's fist clipped the side of Cally's face. He was instantly sorry. Sam slammed the door and was gone.

"You son of a bitch!" Pete yelled at the closed door, his voice sounding like a cat hiss. He grasped the top of a kitchen chair to steady himself as he broke into a deep phlegm-laden coughing spell.

The next morning Cally had driven Pete to the hospital emergency room. After a series of tests, they'd admitted and treated him for pneumonia, releasing him after three days with a bottle of antibiotics and a vaporizer.

Now that Pete was back home, Cally needed to get a few things at Tillden's Grocery — canned soup, cheese, some bread, milk, maybe crackers, and lemon and honey for Pete's continually sore throat. Then she just wanted to escape.

Annoying Christmas carols played over the store's sound system. Shelves bulged with candy and cookies. Decorations were everywhere. A few more days and the damned holiday madness would be over.

Cally spotted Miss Brackston, Cody's teacher, staring at an assortment of beer and wine, so she headed toward the bread aisle and watched her from a safe distance. A short woman, Miss Brackston stood on her tiptoes in those brown leather boots she always wore, her nose thrust upward. She grabbed two bottles of wine from the top shelf. She looked to each side before slipping them into her basket. Cally was sure Miss Brackston was the one who had shot her mouth off to the media about Cody's troubles at school. One day, she would meet that little lump and have her say. But right then, she had no desire to listen to that woman offer her condolences as she surveyed Cally's bruise.

Cally was reaching for a loaf of bread when that familiar, musky-vanilla perfume crept into the air. She looked up, startled to see Tina standing in front of her cart. "Oh, no!" she blurted. She clutched the loaf close to her chest "Get away from me. I have nothing more to say to you."

Tina blocked the grocery cart. "I need to talk to you." Her voice softened. "I think there's something you should know."

"I'm calling the police. Didn't Deputy Blake speak with you?" Cally pushed her cart, but Tina stopped it with one hand. "Now, look —"

"Mrs. Benson, I was doing research, and I went through the Klamath County police blotter, checking for details. I found this. You need to read it." She thrust a piece of paper in Cally's face.

Cally pushed her hand away. "I said, get away from me." She swiftly turned her cart in the opposite direction.

"Wait! There was someone else on the mountain the day your son went missing. I have proof."

Cally turned to face Tina. "What did you say?"

"I said someone else was there. And Blake knew about it. Here, you've got to read this." She held out the paper.

"What is this?" Cally cautiously reached for the paper Tina flapped.

"Read it. Just read it."

On Monday December 7, 2009, Deputy Ken Blake received a telephone call from Henry Clifford of Newton, California in reference to a suspicious person in the area of Cooper's Hawk Highway on the afternoon of Saturday, December 5. Clifford stated that he saw a white male struggling with a small boy. Because of the heavy snow in the area, Clifford could not provide a clear description of the suspicious person or the vehicle. At one point, Clifford said he thought the vehicle was a pickup. He later said it might have been a station wagon. He did not get a license plate number. He said he didn't immediately report the incident because he thought it probably was a father struggling with his own child, but then he saw Deputy Blake on TV. Clifford said the suspicious person was wearing dark clothing, but could not describe what the child was wearing. No further information is available.

Cally bit her lower lip. Her hand shook. "You're saying . . . someone else was there?"

"Not just someone—a suspicious someone. The day your son went missing."

Cally read the paragraph again. She looked up at Tina.

"It means your son could have been abducted."

"Abducted?"

"Read that carefully. Clifford, the witness, saw a man struggling with a boy on December 5, the day Cody disappeared. I'm planning to do a story on this."

"You mean somebody—"

"The question you should be asking, Mrs. Benson, is why Deputy Blake let this drop. Why didn't he jump on this? Why didn't he report this immediately to the State Police or the FBI? Why is this just some footnote in a police blotter? Why wasn't an Amber Alert issued? I'm going to dig into this. I need your help."

Still wary, Cally asked, "Can I keep this? I want my husband to read it."

"Sure, it's a copy."

Cally glanced at the paragraph again, hugging the loaf of bread.

"You probably heard that there's a boy missing from the Grants Pass area—Randy Wilkes. He got off the school bus, and they never heard from him again. He disappeared just a few days before Cody."

"Yes. I remember reading about that. I . . . I think I have a letter from the family expressing sympathy."

"I've done some digging. I found out the Forest Lake Grade School reported that a suspicious character was parked by the playground and was talking to the children."

"I know nothing about that."

"Blake investigated and even interviewed some of the kids about the stranger."

"A stranger ... at the school?"

"Connect the dots, Mrs. ... may I call you Cally?"

"Why not."

"A boy is missing. A stranger loiters near the grade school. Then someone sees a guy struggling with a boy on the mountain the same day Cody disappears into thin air, just like that." She snapped her fingers in front of Cally's face.

Suddenly, Cally flashed on something Sam had said ... that Cody thought he saw someone…a friend…Benny… somebody. Sam said he hadn't seen anybody, but perhaps Cody had. "Maybe…it could be. My Dad said Cody thought he saw someone…he's a friendly little boy…maybe —"

"It's not maybe" Tina interrupted. "A witness *saw something.* It makes you wonder what planet Blake is on."

The animosity Cally felt toward Tina began a cautious thaw.

Tina stared at her. "What happened to your face? That's quite a bruise you've got there."

Cally touched the sore spot on her chin. "Oh, I . . . accidentally slipped on the stairs . . . and hit the banister. The phone was ringing. I hurried. I thought it might be about Cody. I mean . . . I don't know what I'm doing these days. It's . . . so hard."

"I can imagine," Tina said. "I'm planning to light a fire under the state police. You know, Cally, if someone abducted Cody, he could still be alive. I'll be in touch." She turned and scurried away.

Cally had squeezed the loaf of bread she held so hard it now had a waist in the middle. She tossed it in her basket, took another from the shelf, and pushed her cart down the aisle. *Still alive? Did she say still alive?*

CHAPTER 12

On Christmas Eve, Tina Williams stood in front of the darkened Forest Lake Grade School waiting for the cameras to roll. She wore a blue knit cap and jacket that set off her small blue eyes and cherry lips. Except for Tillden's Grocery and a few skiers at the Forest Lake Motor Lodge, the town was dead. People huddled in their snug homes or had already departed for somewhere else. A smug look on her face, Tina shifted her weight from one foot to the other. She bit the inside of her lip, anxious to be the first with the story. Her persistent digging had paid off; her timing was perfect. The macho pretty-boy reporters from the big networks had already left and were drowning themselves in eggnog. Her editor was happy. He'd even talked about changing her stringer status to regular reporter. Her soon-to-be-released bombshell gave her the power to set a whole town on edge and to force Mr. Big Britches Blake to swallow humble pie with his Christmas dinner.

Back at Channel 14, the weatherman finished his forecast, and the anchors joked about seeing movement at the North Pole. Then the station cut to Tina with late-breaking news. She gripped the microphone and looked directly into the camera. "State police are chasing a new lead that eight-year-old Cody

Andrew Benson, who disappeared while hunting for a Christmas tree with his grandfather, may have been abducted.

"The Forest Lake boy was last seen by his grandfather, who sent him back to their pickup parked in a turnout along Cooper's Hawk Highway. Because of heavy snow, investigators do not know whether Cody ever reached the pickup.

"However, police are now following up on a report that a witness saw a boy struggling with an adult male along the highway near the area where Cody Benson was reported missing. The recent abduction of a seven-year-old Grants Pass boy has fueled questions about a possible connection in the two cases."

A split-screen shot of Randy Wilkes and Cody with sweet smiles, the kind small boys make when they find presents under a Christmas tree, flashed on the screen. Randy had a curly head of rusty hair and blue eyes. Cody's dark-brown hair hung over his forehead, emphasizing his large, soulful eyes.

"We've also learned local school officials reported that a stranger in a maroon station wagon was spotted twice, parked near the Forest Lake Grade School just days before Cody Benson disappeared."

The station cut to footage of a somber Cally and Pete sitting on their living room sofa. Only Cally spoke. "My Dad said Cody told him that he thought he saw someone in the woods. Now, we hear all this other stuff. We just have to wonder why . . . why, under these circumstances, an Amber Alert—or some other bulletin—was not issued."

The station cut back to Tina. A cold wind rustled her blond curls.

"While details are still sketchy, state police are appealing to the public for any information about this case. We contacted the local sheriff's office, but they declined to comment. Tina Williams, News Channel 14, reporting live from Forest Lake, Oregon."

***

Shirley Mitchell had just replenished the chocolate kisses in the candy dish when this news flashed across her TV screen. "My goodness," she said. Her daughter, Mandy, and three children, were down from Washington. Tomorrow after breakfast, Mandy planned to drive to Eugene so the kids could spend Christmas Day with their father and his new wife.

"Did ya hear that, Mandy? They're sayin' that Benson boy could've been abducted. An abduction, in Forest Lake!" Her chubby hands removed the foil from a piece of candy. "Imagine that."

"You mean a kidnapping?" Mandy had come in from the kitchen with a damp dishtowel in her hands and sat on the arm of the sofa. "That doesn't happen here."

"Well, you be careful driving back. Don't you stop at any of those rest areas. You never know who could be lurkin' in those stalls. And call me when you get to Eugene." Shirley popped a chocolate candy into her mouth, letting it melt on her tongue.

***

Sam Lightener and Dottie Johnston watched the news in her small apartment above the café. Sam stretched out on the couch. Dottie sat at the end near his feet. They were enjoying beer and a spread of chips, dip, and cheese. Besides the flickering TV, the only other light came from a big red candle on the coffee table.

"Abducted!" Sam immediately sat up. "Did I hear that right?"

"That's what the gal said."

"Son of a bitch."

"Did Cody tell you he saw someone out there?"

"Yeah, I remember that . . . I never saw nobody. Cody was always makin' stuff up. That was just *one* of his problems. There was no one there—that I could see."

"Maybe you got distracted. I mean, with getting the trees."

"Goddamnit. I don't know how many times I have to say It." Sam's face suddenly reddened. "I never *sent* that kid back to the truck." His voice got louder. "He wanted to go." He took a swallow of beer and then another long one. "You'd think my own daughter woulda called me with this kinda news. But no, I have to find out about it over the TV. That's a helluva thing to hear on Christmas Eve."

***

"Wouldn't surprise me one damn bit if that guy was holed up somewhere near the Bat,"said Amos Hadley, watching the report with his wife, Mildred.

"You think it's true? That there's some nut loose?"she asked.

"Could be he's the one that's been stealin' stuff from the store," Amos said

Mildred put down the package she was wrapping, got up, and locked the door. "I wonder why Deputy Blake's not saying nothin'?" Mildred rubbed her swollen, arthritic knuckles.

Amos shook his head. "Aw, that guy. He can be as thick as a ditch. He hasn't done squat about the burglaries, either. Just comes out. Tells me to install a camera. Jesus. But who the hell would take a whole supply of beans and soup except some dirt bag?"

***

Ken Blake angrily switched off the TV. He and his family were about to leave for a Christmas Eve service at the church. "That little vamp never contacted me for any comment," he muttered to Lydia.

Lydia pulled her coat on. "Maybe she will. Things get crazy and complicated during the holiday."

"An Amber Alert. What the hell is she talking about? There has to be *evidence* of abduction and something to go on. The kid

106

couldn't have walked out that far. I went on what Sam said. Now she's got the Bensons all upset. I can't figure her out."

"Figure who out?" asked Lauren coming in from the kitchen, her face bright, her long blond hair hanging in waves past her shoulders.

"It's just cop stuff," said Lydia. She patted Ken's back. "Let it go, honey. It's Christmas Eve."

***

On Christmas morning, other news media picked up Tina's report. The newspaper ran a small story, attributed to Channel 14, on its front page. One local radio station repeated the story but offered no new details. The rest played Christmas carols.

On their way to tiny churches, parents clutched their children's hands a little tighter. "Too bad Dottie's is closed," said Donna Shaw, the wife of the tow truck operator, leaning forward on the front of her pew to talk with her neighbor. "Herb usually stops in there to get all the lowdown. He's seen that girl on TV hanging around there."

***

"At church they said a bad man took Cody," Brittany Bolin said to her mother, Sue, as she placed forks on the table for Christmas dinner.

"We don't know for sure, honey," Sue said.

"Does that mean he's not dead?"

Sue, surprised by her daughter's question, avoided the answer. She didn't think Brittany thought of Cody as being dead, but she knew that abducted children usually ended up that way, hours after they went missing. If Cody had to die, she hoped it was from hypothermia.

"We have to leave it in God's hands." She set out the cranberry relish. "It's always good to pray no matter what the circumstances."

Brittany squatted on the floor, her arms around Bowser's neck. She folded her small, plump fingers and closed her dark eyes. Bowser licked her face and nuzzled her brown curls.

Her mother smiled. "You know," she said once Brittany opened her eyes, "after we carve the turkey, I think you should pick out a special piece for Bowser to thank him for praying with you."

"I sure hope God heard us."

Sue stopped arranging the carrots and olives to bend down and hug her little daughter tightly. "Don't ever talk to strangers," she whispered.

***

The day after Christmas, people in Forest Lake sat glued to their TV sets, waiting for the evening news and the latest update. Some ate their holiday leftovers off TV trays so they wouldn't miss it. They were not disappointed. After a commercial on stomach acid, the news anchor cut to Tina, who stood in front of the motor lodge, sporting a red, Channel 14 baseball cap and matching jacket.

"The Bensons have criticized Deputy Sheriff Ken Blake for failure to adequately follow up on a report that a witness saw a man struggling with a small boy a few miles from the area where their son, Cody Andrew Benson, went missing."

The camera cut to Pete, whose voice had improved. "So much time has gone by. Whoever took Cody could be out of the country by now." His voice cracked. "We're devastated to hear a witness saw something and nothing was done. It's an unforgivable oversight. Just unforgivable." He shook his head and looked down.

"State and county investigators are appealing to the public for help," Tina continued. "They are especially seeking information about a maroon station wagon possibly seen in Forest Lake, a few days before Cody Benson disappeared."

The camera shifted to Detective Frank Lane, a state police spokesperson. "At this point, we don't know if the witness really has credible information, but we haven't ruled out foul play," he said.

"The sheriff's office continues to believe Cody froze to death in the snow," Tina said. The camera cut to a Tina interview with Ken. His unflattering close-up filled the screen. The tag below identified him as Deputy Sheriff Ken Blake. "We're not saying that it's not at all possible, I mean about the abduction, but I think it's very remote. Everything so far indicates Cody succumbed to the cold."

"Why wasn't an Amber Alert put out?" Tina asked.

Ken looked uncomfortable. The question seemed to catch him by surprise. "We interviewed the grandfather. Everything points to a little boy lost in a snowstorm."

"But when the witness contacted you about seeing a boy struggling with a man on the highway, why didn't you follow up on that?"

"That location was several miles away. Cody couldn't have gotten that far up the highway, and I had absolutely *nothing* to go on," he said. "A lot of people travel on Cooper's Hawk Highway during the ski season. Time was of the essence. We wanted to find a lost little boy before he succumbed to the elements. It's natural for the Bensons to cling to any possibility that their son might still be alive."

Tina frowned at him. She stepped closer into his personal space.

Ken didn't back up, even though his stomach churned. "We're still working this case." Tina was trying to intimidate him and make him the villain. He kept an even tone, but he could feel his face flush. "While the formal search has been discontinued at this point, we'll be taking search dogs and a crew back to the Big Bat as soon as the snow recedes enough to make it safe, perhaps as early as March."

The camera cut back to Lane. "This is a suspended case, and we won't close it until we resolve it," he said.

"In the meantime," Tina concluded, "the Benson family still clings to the hope that Cody is out there somewhere. Tina Williams, News Channel 14, Forest Lake, Oregon."

Like a fire in the dry underbrush, the story raged on. It developed national legs. The Bensons appeared via satellite on *The Today Show*, pleading for whoever took Cody to return him. They even got a call from Anderson Cooper, who aired their story in prime time on CNN.

Noted TV personality Nora Case of *Case Law*, a legal-analysis cable show, picked up the story and devoted several programs to it. "It's been six weeks, and where is little Cody Benson?" Case asked night after night, her intense green eyes staring into the camera. "Had the cops acted on the tip, this sweet little boy might be safely home with his family tonight." She shook her chin-length, brunette pageboy in disbelief at what she called police bumbling.

The attractive, outspoken Case interviewed Tina, who basked in the limelight and continued to bash Ken.

Ken declined comment, explaining that any further statement should come from the sheriff's office. The office, unhappy with Ken's awkward prior performance, ordered him to say no more, and it had no comment, except to report that the matter was under investigation, and the FBI had agreed to assist. Consequently, Case continually replayed Channel 14 footage quoting Ken: "We interviewed the grandfather. Everything points to a little boy lost in a snowstorm."

One of the guests on Case's show wondered who in his right mind would let a kid go off by himself in a snowstorm, especially a boy suffering from attention deficit disorder. *Case*

Law showed a clip of Detective Frank Lane saying, "The state police are considering all possibilities. We have now interviewed Mr. Clifford, the witness, but he could not provide a description of the man or a description of the vehicle seen on the highway. We, however, continue to treat the boy's disappearance as a missing person investigation."

***

A group of people who participated in the original search announced the formation of a Cody Benson Support and Search group to raise public awareness and funds. They distributed posters to Northwest law enforcement and to grocery and retail outlets. The Forest Lake Men's Club paid for and erected a billboard on the highway with Cody's picture and a telephone number.

Dottie set up a reward fund at the bank, hoping to solicit any information about the disappearance. After the national TV exposure, donations began pouring in. Lydia Blake asked Dottie to discontinue seeking funds for her proposed library. Instead, she donated all the money they had already raised to the reward fund. The pot eventually swelled past $50,000.

Ken was not pleased when he heard about Lydia's decision. It wasn't the money; he would have gladly written a check. It seemed like a slap in the face. She didn't even discuss it with him. With Lydia's library project on hold, piles of books sprouted in the house like weeds.

"Move those goddamn things to the basement," he swore after tripping over a haphazardly stacked column in the dining room. He resisted the urge to kick the volumes down the stairs. It wasn't just the books that stuck in his craw. His communication efforts with the Benson family had broken down. His superiors at the department were looking into his handling of the witness information. If that wasn't enough, people whispered about it in town—thanks to Tina Williams and the pounding from the national news media. The regulars at Dottie's stopped talking whenever Ken entered the café, and they no longer saved him the center spot at the lunch counter. They seemed polite enough, and Dottie was always happy to see him, but the little slights hurt. Ken started getting lunch from the Dairy Queen drive-up window.

"There's no concrete evidence that this kid was abducted." Ken blurted as Lydia rescued the books and set them against the wall.

"Maybe instead of a library, we can have a used book sale and donate the proceeds —" she started to say.

Ken wasn't listening. "The way people are acting in this town, you'd think I did nothing. We were shorthanded. Half the department had the flu. I was out there day and night."

"All the more reason for us to contribute to the fund," Lydia muttered. "We need to show our support, too."

"Every minute counts when a child is lost in freezing weather. There isn't time to deal with every goddamn kook that wants attention," Ken said.

Lydia took a deep breath. "Often it's the reward money that shakes things out."

"Things. Things. What things?"

"Ken, this isn't about *you*. It's about a missing little boy and a family that needs our support."

"You think I don't know that?" His face flushed purple. "Tell that to the blond air-head reporter who's trying to build a career on a tragedy." His hand rubbed the back of his neck.

"You *are* overreacting."

"Overreacting, my ass."

"Calm the hell down," she snapped. She walked out of the room like she always did to avoid arguing.

"You'd think your own wife would support you," he shouted after her. He didn't wait for an answer. He grabbed his hat and slammed the door on his way out to make his rounds.

***

The state police asked Sam Lightener to take a polygraph test. "They treated me like a criminal, asking me all those questions," he growled when Dottie came upstairs after closing the café for the evening. He'd already emptied several bottles of beer, making his angry eyes bloodshot.

"And?"

"What do you mean *and*?" His voice was thick. "And, I passed it, of course."

"Well, that should settle it then," Dottie said.

"After they disconnected me from the machine, the damn guy went out of the room. Then came back in and asked more questions like I was lying or something. He said he was givin' me one last opportunity to correct anything I already said. Then he just sat there and stared at me. Playing son-of-a-bitch games. Felt just like a dirt bag. Afterward he said I passed, like I disappointed him. I wanted to smash his face." Perspiration beaded on his damp forehead.

"It's done then."

"Done? It's not done. Never will it be done. I have to live with what's done. What I done. Done. Done. Done. What the fuck did I do? Never."

Dottie folded her arms. "You've got to get hold of yourself, Sam."

"I dream about him almost every night. He's reachin' out to me through the snow. Done. Done. Done."

"You're not gonna find a solution in a bottle."

"I never meant for this to happen. I told those officers. They kept askin' why did you send him back. I never sent him. Goddamn it! Goddamn everything!"

"Look, Sam, it was an accident. I mean, things happen. Five years ago, Freda Hansen was getting ready to serve her cherry pie at the church picnic up at the lake. She looked away for just a second. Her son drowned. Slipped out of an inner tube or somethin'. She never meant for it to happen. The church never meant for it to happen, but it did. God knows why. You've got to pull it together. If not for you, do it for me."

"Goddamn everything." Sam tipped his beer bottle to his lips. Beer dribbled down his chin. His hands shook.

"We can't go on like this, Sam. Eventually, it comes down to forgiveness."

"The hell with forgiveness," he shouted and threw the empty bottle across the room. It hit the fireplace and shattered into a dozen brown pieces just below the watercolor of Dottie's Café—a long-ago birthday gift from Christie Jenkins.

CHAPTER 13

Cally stepped up to the wide porch of the Jenkins' faded-blue, craftsman-style house on Juniper Street. She'd never met Myra. Of course, she knew Floyd from the Shell station. In fact, Floyd was the one who first mentioned it to her. "It's sure too bad about yer boy," he'd said in his soft voice as he handed her the receipt. "Myra will be callin' you." He'd tugged self-consciously on the bill of his brown baseball cap.

Cally knew that people in Forest Lake considered the Jenkins to be pillars of the community. Floyd was a deacon at the Church of Our Savior, and Myra had her hand in just about every charitable event. She'd heard that they'd lost their only daughter years ago, and that they were among the first to contribute to Cody's fund at the bank. "We have a lot in common," Myra had said over the phone.

A big, chunky woman, Myra greeted her at the front door. "I'm so glad you could come." She showed Cally into the living room. "Make yourself at home. I'll only be a minute."

Except for the white woodwork, the entire room was blue. The walls and ceiling resembled a pleasant summer sky, which the solid carpet almost matched. The darker-blue textured pattern on the sofa, loveseat, and comfortable armchair blended with the rest of the decor.

Pictures of Myra's daughter were everywhere—Christie as a young girl playing with dolls, Christie playing the piano, Christie holding a painting with a blue ribbon she won at the fair, Christie's church confirmation picture, Christie with Myra, and Christie's senior high school portrait. She was a young, fresh version of her mother, whose bloom had given way to the ravages of age and grief, but Christie's eyes seemed larger, more expressive pools of deep blue. There were no pictures of Floyd.

Watercolors blanketed the east wall. Cally was admiring them when Myra scurried in carrying a tray with a bright red teapot, two rose-flowered cups, and a plate of pink-frosted, heart-shaped ginger cookies. She set the tray on the glass coffee table. Cally removed her coat and seated herself on the sofa. Myra took the armchair.

"The stores are way ahead of us," Myra muttered. Brassy-orange dye hid most of the white spots in her hair. "We just barely finished with the New Year, and already we're into Valentine's Day." Her blue and pink flowered dress and a bulky, navy blue sweater strained around her arms. Heavy compression stockings and sensible brown oxfords helped support whatever plagued her thick legs.

Cally stared at the store-bought cookies. "Cody was born on Valentine's Day." Her cheeks flushed. She thought of the bike still waiting in Cody's room and then of the special, heart-shaped chocolate cake that she always baked for him.

"Oh, my dear, I'm so sorry. Can I get you something else? I have some Nutter Butters in the cupboard."

Cally waved her hand. "Please, no. It's okay. He would have been nine." There was the past tense again. "I mean he will be nine." She fussed with her napkin decorated with tiny hearts and took a sip of the strong, dark tea to soothe the tension squeezing her throat.

"I still celebrate Christie's birthday. Not like most people do. I mean, I take flowers to her grave and all, then Floyd and me, we light a candle."

"Lighting a candle—what a lovely way to honor her memory."

"Yes." Myra smiled broadly. She poured tea for herself and settled back into her chair, her eyes travelling from Cally's black ankle boots, to her face and back down again, where they zeroed in on her green rubber wristband that said *Hope, Courage, Faith.*

Cally sipped more warm tea and cleared her throat. "I, uh, I want to thank you for contributing to Cody's fund. That was very nice of you."

"We were happy to do it."

"You must like blue," Cally said, scanning the room, trying to keep the conversation going.

"It was Christie's favorite color," Myra said. She pointed to the watercolors. "If you look closely at her paintings, you'll see they all have wonderful skies."

"Yes. I noticed them. I especially liked the ones of the lake."

"She absolutely loved the lake. Used to take her sketch pad up there all the time."

"Your daughter certainly was talented. I understand she died tragically."

"She was murdered." Myra's melodious voice turned bitter. "Murdered," she said again as if she were spitting a seed. Her squinty, blue eyes grew cold. Like a much-played audiotape, her story started to unwind. "That dirty Indian murdered her. Lured her into his car, drove her to the lake and . . . and raped her."

"I'm so sorry. I didn't mean to make you relive the past," Cally said.

The tape inside Myra kept running. "Oh, Christie resisted all right. She was a good Christian girl. Then that dirty bastard stabbed her not once, but seventeen times."

"Oh, my God." Cally set down her cup. She wished she hadn't said anything.

"What kind of person does that? Seventeen times. Floyd had to identify the body. He still has nightmares. I hear him murmuring. I shake him and then he cries. Still cries."

"Pete cries, too. I guess we both do, but you think of men as strong pillars and then you see them crumbling. I mean I understand, but it leaves you with no one to lean on."

"Seventeen times," Myra breathed out. Her left hand rubbed her ample thigh. When the rubbing stopped, her forefinger picked at the cuticle on her thumb. "How do you live with something like that?"

Cally didn't know. Her stomach tightened. She uncrossed her legs and took a deep breath. "Pete and I don't know what happened. Did he get lost? Did someone take him? It's hell to be left hanging."

"Sometimes I'd like to stab him just so he knows how it feels."

"Floyd? You want to stab Floyd?" Cally almost choked on her cookie. She reached for her teacup to release the crumbs from her throat.

"That damn sheriff." Myra's thumb picked at the cuticles on her other fingers.

"You mean Deputy Blake?" Myra's language surprised Cally. She didn't seem like a woman who would use profanity.

"Yeah. They captured the Indian over in Curry County, and that damn half-wit cop was supposed to bring him in. Only, he let him get away. I mean seventeen times." She attacked her cuticles again.

"He just let him go?"

"The story goes that the Indian jumped him or something but Floyd and me, and a lot of folks around here, think they made it look like an escape. Blake and that Indian fella were friends—grew up with each other or some such thing. Oh, there was a big search for the Indian and an even bigger investigation of Blake. He got reprimanded and what not, but then . . . then . . . when the Indian died up there, it all got washed over." Myra's eyes narrowed. She gave Cally a knowing look. "Just the kind of thing an Indian would do—run. Come spring they found some of his pieces . . . clothing and what not." Myra dabbed her lips with her napkin. "Cougars got 'em. You know, the animals scatter the bones."

Cally clenched her teacup. That could be happening to Cody. She didn't want to go there. She set the cup down, fearing she might break it. Cally tried to get Myra back from the past, but she stayed stuck in that groove. But, how do you move on when you've lost a child? She thought about Cody every day; no, it was every minute. She saw his sweet face—thin, pale with those innocent, big brown eyes, the eyelashes—every minute she saw it. Maybe the darkness that crept in would stay, and this is what it did to you.

She was angry with Ken Blake, but she didn't want to harm him. She didn't know about his checkered past, but isn't that what you'd expect to find in a hick town like Forest Lake—an incompetent buffoon? She wanted accountability. Cody deserved that. Maybe it felt different when you knew your child was murdered. Maybe she'd end up like Myra—bitter and empty. But they didn't really know what had happened to Cody. Maybe she should just leave now. Instead, she heard herself say, "People have been very supportive, and we've been getting tons of cards. We even got one from a soldier in Iraq."

"They figure he fell into some deep gully or something," Myra went on. "Still, it's not the same. We never got justice. We never got to face him in court. That Indian never had to look me in the eye. He froze up there when that blizzard hit. That's a better death than what he deserved." Her left hand rubbed her thigh harder. Sometimes it grasped and kneaded the fabric of her flowered dress.

"That soldier heard about our story on TV and wanted to write. I mean with all he's facing over there . . . He even sent money for Cody's fund . . . I . . . Pete and I were very touched."

"I wanted to see him get the death penalty or rot in prison for what he did to my Christie. I wanted him to sit in that courtroom and squirm . . . to see the pictures of the crime scene, the blood, and my Christie lying there. She was an artist, you know. Those are her paintings on the wall." Her stony-blue eyes stared through Cally.

"Yes, you told me that," Cally said. "Cody likes to draw, too."

"Ever since she was a little girl, she loved art. There's still one of her watercolors hanging there in Dottie's Café. Maybe you seen it?"

Cally sat silent. Myra was in a conversation with herself.

"So much talent. Such great promise. She was our only child. We'll never have grandchildren." She set her teacup on the coffee table and seemed to come back to the present, as if someone pushed the recorder's pause button. "You're still young enough to have another child, but we, we, couldn't, you know."

"No. No. No. Cody's was a difficult birth. There won't be other children. I mean not of our own."

"Floyd said adopting was like buying a used car. You're just getting other people's troubles. It's harder today. Kids got more problems. I got left with nothing. *Nothing.* Christie planned on art school in the East. She could have been so much." She paused. "So much."

"I'm very sorry. Things aren't so good between Pete and me. We don't talk like we used to. I'd like to see my dad, but Pete won't hear of it. He doesn't want to see him again . . . ever."

"It takes time, honey. Losing a child takes the sap out of you. Things are never the same. There's no such thing as closure. You just have to find a way to go about life." There was blood on two of her cuticles.

"I'm still sleeping on the couch. Pete sleeps in our bed. We uh —"

"It was a long time before Floyd and I were husband and wife again, if you know what I'm sayin'."

"I mean I don't think either of us is really sleeping. Pete goes back to the mountain at least once a week—even in the snow—and calls for Cody. Sometimes I go with him. We don't know why, we just do."

We got lotsa cards, too," Myra said. "After a while, we quit opening them—just burned them in the fireplace."

Cally couldn't imagine burning the cards. She and Pete read every one—people reaching out, sharing their stories, their pain, trying to do something in small ways to help. Sometimes, late at night, she reread them and had a good cry. There probably would come a time when she no longer needed them, but not now, not when her pain was so raw. She dabbed her eyes with the crumpled napkin.

Myra stared blankly out the window where the sheared shrubs near the porch resembled cubes and lozenges waiting for spring to rescue them from their unnatural state. Cally thought she better say something. "My mother died a year ago, and Dad started drinking. We brought him out here to help him get back on his feet. Now this. And . . . and, I hear he's drinking again."

"That's one thing I can say about Floyd. He didn't turn to the bottle, but he shut down."

"The police, they asked Dad to take a polygraph."

"Floyd won't go back to the lake. Hasn't once in twenty years. If folks come to visit, he won't go. It just made me furious when I heard that Blake didn't follow up with that witness. I knew then we needed to talk."

"Sometimes I don't know what's worse, freezing to death or being with a . . . you know." Cally couldn't bring herself to say pedophile.

"If that Blake had done his job right, your dad, your husband, all of you could be right now huggin' your little boy." The blue eyes locked in a stare again. "More tea?"

"No, thank you. I need to be going."

"You gotta fight back, honey. If I was you, I'd insist the sheriff's office do a check of the volunteers who helped with your search. Especially since they're now reporting that someone saw something up there, a man strugglin' with a little boy. And, now I hear his own department is checkin' into that. I heard of a case in Washington where a guy started a fire in a hotel and then showed up to help put it out. It's how those twisted minds work. The guy that took your boy could've been right there, helping with the search."

Cally flinched at the idea that she may have brushed elbows on the mountain with someone who had actually harmed Cody. She had come expecting to be consoled. Instead, she felt like she'd been run through a blender. She yanked on her coat and struggled for the right words. "Thank you for the tea and the advice," she finally said.

Myra stood in the doorway nursing her battered cuticles with a napkin. She squinted into the light, and her eyes got that cold, faraway look. "She never would've gone off with that dirty Indian, you know. No, *never*."

Cally hurried down the porch steps and escaped into the safety of her car.

Touch the Sky

CHAPTER 14

"Shocking news tonight," Nora Case announced on her national TV program. Several pictures of Cody Benson floated across the screen as ominous music played in the background. "The cops bungle a witness tip and now—now—they discover a child molester right under their noses. Tonight we ask again where—where—is little eight-year-old Cody Benson? We want justice."

After a commercial break, Case introduced her panel of guests. "Let's go to Tina Williams, a reporter with Channel 14 News out in Oregon. Tina, weigh in on this latest development."

Tina, her blond hair styled in a sexy blunt cut, was all smiles, enjoying her time in the spotlight. Her eye makeup was flawless, her lips a new shade of crimson gloss.

"At the request of Cody's parents, the state police initiated a background check of volunteers involved in the search," Tina said. "The police found nothing. Then they checked the records of the Forest Lake Motel. They discovered the name of Len Roster. He's a registered sex offender."

"Bingo," Case blurted.

A picture of Roster flashed on the screen. He looked like anyone's next-door neighbor, reasonably attractive with a ready smile, athletic, and about thirty, with neat, close-cropped brown hair, squinty-brown eyes, and dark-framed glasses.

"A sex offender right under their noses." Case leaned in. "You'd think they would've checked this out from the get-go."

"Well, they'd been treating this as a lost child case," Tina said.

"*They*, who the heck are they?"

"Blake . . . the county," Tina stammered, taken back by Case's blunt style. "So the parents went to the state police."

Case gave her a disdainful look. "Okay, go on."

"They picked up information on Roster's vehicle, Nora, and guess what? This Roster guy drives a maroon station wagon. That's significant, because a man driving a vehicle like that was spotted in Forest Lake talking to the schoolchildren, just days before the Benson boy went missing."

"So this Roster character must be familiar with the area."

Tina looked down at her notes. "He's from Chemult, Oregon, a small town in northern Klamath County. He's now living just outside of Forest Lake in a trailer park. He works as a carpenter."

The camera flashed on a faded wooden sign that said, "Ray's Trailer Park." Then it moved along a row of older, tattletale-gray doublewides lining a narrow, potholed road. It zeroed in on a discolored turquoise-and-white trailer with a lone grocery cart standing out front next to a large green garbage can. Dilapidated latticework formed a makeshift entryway. The camera cut to an aerial view showing the distance from the trailer court to the point on Cooper's Hawk Highway where Cody disappeared.

Case introduced Kelly, one of her young, fresh-faced program researchers, who had more information on Roster. "What can you tell me, Kelly?"

"According to police and court records, Roster attended community college, majoring in physical education, but dropped out," the young woman reported. "He drifted, then got a job assisting a coach at a middle school in Roseburg, Oregon. After six months, Roster was suddenly dismissed."

"What for?" Case asked brusquely.

"We don't know," Kelly said. "He went back to Chemult. Then he hitchhiked across the country and worked at a youth camp, doing odd jobs and helping with activities. He returned to Springfield, Oregon, and began a relationship with a woman who had a ten-year-old son. Police arrested Roster after the boy told a teacher what was happening when his mother wasn't around. Roster was convicted of felony sexual abuse, did some time in prison, and was paroled. He is a registered sex offender."

"A registered sex offender; you heard it here, folks." Case cut to a distinguished looking psychologist on her panel with a white mustache and thinning hair. "Richard Stein, shed some light on this."

"He certainly fits the profile." Stein peered over his spectacles. "Predators like Roster often work in schools or youth camps, or develop a relationship with a single mother to get access to a vulnerable, lonely child."

Case replayed the sound bite featuring an unflattering shot of Ken Blake peering into the camera. "Time was of the essence. Cooper's Hawk Highway is well traveled in the ski season. There's no evidence that a child abductor was in the area."

"*No* evidence of a child molester?" Case gasped. "Ha! What's with this cop, Tina Williams?"

"He's been under scrutiny before," Tina said like a child eager to please a demanding teacher. "Twenty years ago, a man killed a young girl on the shores of Forest Lake. Blake was a transport deputy at the time. This killer was in Blake's custody when he escaped. Apparently, this man—James Fallingwater—was a boyhood friend of Blake's."

"Whoa, wait a big minute. He let a murderer escape?" Case's jaw dropped. "And he's still a cop?" She was beside herself.

"Not exactly —"

"Well, *what* exactly?" Case demanded.

Tina flushed, startled again by Case's impatient exasperation. "The department . . . they . . . uh . . . put Blake on administrative leave and conducted an investigation."

"And then what?" Now the outspoken Case looked like she'd just swallowed a hot pepper.

"He got reprimanded for not following police procedure and was reassigned to Forest Lake. They later determined that this Fallingwater guy froze to death in the wilderness. Other than that, nothing much came of it"

Case shook her head. "Unbelievable! A child is missing and we get *Mayberry R.F.D.* Thank goodness the state police are working this case," she said before the station cut to a mouthwash commercial.

After Nora Case broke the news about Len Roster on her cable TV show, local media zeroed in on the story, sparking fears and shaking the town to its roots. Forest Lake was a close-knit, conservative community whose social life centered on church, school, and family. The notion of a sex offender in their midst was as foreign to them as sunscreen to Eskimos. The part about Jim Fallingwater opened old wounds and rekindled bad memories.

People were convinced that a stranger had kidnapped Cody, and that Ken Blake wasn't doing enough to protect them. Mothers looked over their shoulders as they wheeled their grocery carts from Tillden's into the parking lot. They formed car pools, drove their children to school, and picked them up afterward. At night, they locked their doors. The hardware store sold out its supply of deadbolts in a week and ordered more. Shirley Mitchell propped a chair against her door before she headed to bed and left the hall light on. Amos Hadley took his shotgun to his small store. Folks eating breakfast at Dottie's debated what they would do if this Roster fellow ever came into the restaurant. Dottie wondered that herself as she wiped the counter and poured the coffee, especially since Sam had said he would kill him.

Ray's Trailer Park was a known trouble spot populated by transients and an assortment of lowlifes. Tenants rented the trailers instead of purchasing them, and there actually wasn't a Ray. Ray Beeler had died years ago, and the current owner, his son Ed, a big husky man with tattoos on his arms and one on his thick neck, lived in Medford. He did little to upgrade the park and only came to town to collect the rent, which fed his penchant for motorcycles. Theft at the park was rampant, although the tenants usually stole from one another. Ken went there to break up drunken brawls or to deal with domestic disputes involving live-in girlfriends. Once, he recovered Shirley Mitchell's garden gnome there.

Now people wanted Ken to shut it down and run Len Roster out of town. Ken explained that he had no authority to do that. Once a person paid his debt to society, he had rights. Yes, Roster was a person of interest, but at this point they couldn't charge him with anything. That just made folks angrier. Someone painted graffiti on the faded sign. It now said "No Perverts" in bright, awkward red letters. That brought a furious Ed Beeler to town. He replaced the sign and breathed fire and a string of profanity into Ken's face before blasting out of town on his big Harley.

Like dark clouds in the sky, the ghost of Jim Fallingwater, hung over the town. People were talking about that story again. The Portland *Oregonian* ran a sidebar on this old story, complete with the high school photo of Christie Jenkins. The article suggested that rural communities didn't have adequate protection. While some people had questioned Ken's handling of the search for Cody Benson, hearing about a past indiscretion further shattered their confidence. Myra Jenkins made copies of the *Oregonian* story on the machine at the drugstore and was out fanning flames at Dottie's, her church, Tillden's Grocery, and the barbershop. "We never got justice," she complained, her blue eyes squinting into slits. "We never did." She circulated a petition to get Ken fired.

Even the high school kids talked about it. Girls whispered in the bathroom as they lined their eyes and brushed their hair.

"That guy stabbed that woman seventeen times!"

"Rape!"

"My mom said Indians are oversexed."

"We're keeping a close eye on my little brother."

Whenever Lauren Blake came through the door, they quit talking. Some of the boys taunted a Native American sophomore by calling him "Blanket Ass."

Lauren had a crush on Robbie, a tall, lanky farm boy and football star. Suddenly his parents found more chores for him to do at home, so he spent less time in town. One Sunday evening, Lauren burst into tears after returning from a candlelight vigil at the church to honor Cody Benson, who would have celebrated his ninth birthday later that week.

"Robbie was there, but he just ignored me. Then Myra Jenkins came up to me, carrying a candle. She actually touched my hair and said, 'My Christie had lovely hair, too only . . .' She stopped just like that in mid-sentence and stared a hole in me. There was blood around her fingernails. She got some on my white blazer. She's really creepy." Lauren said she didn't want to go to school anymore.

Lydia and Ken, Janet and Jeff Parks, the parents of Katy, Lauren's best friend, and their minister, Pastor Rick, called on the high school principal. He immediately brought in counselors to talk with students, hoping to stop the hysteria. The counselors also discussed ethnic slurs at a school assembly and said the proper term for American Indians was Native Americans. The principal said any student hurling slurs at another could face expulsion.

A group of anxious grade school parents got together and signed a letter asking the sheriff to send another deputy to the Forest Lake area. The county dispatched Don Range, an affable young man with less than five years of experience on the job. To Ken, a senior deputy, with multiple duties—first responder, evidence technician, and investigator—this was the ultimate insult. Especially since Range wasn't under his direction and control but took orders from the central office.

If that wasn't enough, the regulars at Dottie's started saving the center stool at the counter for Range. Roy, who drove the tow truck at the Shell garage, picked up on Nora Case's comparison of Forest Lake with Andy Griffith and Mayberry, North Carolina. He constantly referred to Ken as Barney Fife. "Ol' Blake's gonna hafta take that bullet out of his shirt pocket and put it in his gun."

***

Night after night, Nora Case pounded away on the story. "Things just seem to be festering out there in Forest Lake, Oregon," she said. "Tonight's shocker—the parents of little Cody Benson have filed a lawsuit against the Klamath County Sheriff's Office and Deputy Ken Blake for not acting promptly regarding the possibility that Cody was abducted. Tonight we ask again, where—where—is Cody Benson, the sweet, little eight-year-old boy who disappeared while looking for a Christmas tree?"

CHAPTER 15

It all started with a rainy, windy drive up to Amos Hadley's Lake Store, where the weather was colder and the roads icy.

"What are *you* doing here?" Amos barked at Ken. "I hear they assigned a new deputy to patrol these parts. Why didn't they send t'other guy?" Ken was used to Amos's tirades, but piled onto everything else that had happened, that comment cut deep.

"Just what exactly *is* the problem, Amos?" Ken slammed his logbook on the counter and pulled off his gloves. It was midafternoon. He was tired and anxious to get back to town so he could pick up a Valentine's Day gift for Lydia.

"I guess that new fella ain't worth more than a hill of beans, if deadbeats can keep breakin' into my store."

"Amos, I don't have all day." Ken glared. A headache lingered behind his temples. This man he'd known since he was a boy had now joined the choir of his critics.

"You don't have all day, do you? Damn it to hell. Who steals peanut butter but a bunch of those goddamn liberal-ass skiers, that's who. By Jove, I carry my shotgun with me day an' night. I'm not afraid to use it, let me tell you. One of these days they're gonna be toast."

"You better watch what you do with the shotgun, Amos. People don't get the death penalty over peanut butter."

"And, if that dirtbag child-molester-sex pervert-homo sticks his head in my store, he's gonna leave without one."

"You shoot somebody, you'll get yourself sued. And you'll do time in the slammer."

"They took two of my big jars, a box of fig bars, and cleaned out my cigarettes. All my Camels. Damn it anyway."

"The folks that come here to ski the Big Bat are your customers. Most of them are good folks."

Amos wanted his pound of flesh. "It's not just any skiers. It's those dumb, liberal-ass freaks from Portland. If you ask me, everything's going to hell in a hand-basket. By God, I'd a run that sex-pervert bastard out of town and tarred and feathered his ass on the way."

"Amos, I'm here to take a report about a theft." Ken knew better than to get into a discussion with Amos about Len Roster. He took the report, shut his logbook, and headed for the door. He was glad to leave.

"You be sure and pass this theft business on to your superiors," Amos shouted after him.

Ken climbed back into his Jeep and closed the door hard. Dealing with Amos was like talking to a buzz saw, but that last comment was the ultimate insult. He had driven all that way for peanut butter, a package of fig bars, and oh yeah, some goddamn cigarettes. Shit. Screw it. Maybe he should get a real job. He had to wonder about Len Roster. Since people in town were on edge, he wondered where Roster bought his groceries these days.

Ken decided to swing by Tillden's and buy Lydia a box of valentine chocolates and a bottle of wine. There was no time to drive to Klamath Falls, and it was the best he could do in Forest Lake. The accusations, the lawsuit, the gossip, and the questioning eyes of his daughter had made things testy at home. None of this was Lydia's fault, and he wanted to make it up to her. He'd get something for Lauren, too.

He was driving by Cooper's Hawk River when he spotted them—two soaked, dirty kittens about to scramble onto the road. Ken pulled over. The kittens shivered in the cold. A third one lay dead in the frosty grass. Someone must have tried to throw them into the water. What kind of people did this?

He couldn't leave them there. The tiny kittens cried pitifully. One was solid black and the other gray-and-black-striped. Ken retrieved the empty cardboard box that he had collected for Lydia's now-defunct book project. He grabbed the paper towels he carried with him and wiped the kittens down. At least they'd be dry. "Slow down, fella," he said to the black one that started climbing up his arm. He'd have to take them home. Tomorrow he'd ask Deputy Range to drop them off at the humane society. He smirked. It would give Range something to do.

Ken picked the black kitten off his shoulder and placed it in the box he lined with the day's newspaper and more paper towels. The kitten had a goopy eye and it sneezed. Ken wiped its tiny face. The gray one cowered in a corner of the box. "You're gonna be all right," Ken assured them. He had nothing for them to eat, but then he didn't really know what they ate. At least they'd be warm and dry. He'd just got them settled in the back seat of the Jeep when he got the 10-56 report over his radio, a suicide at Dottie's Café. The doctor from the clinic was on the scene, but apparently had arrived too late.

***

Cally took the heart-shaped chocolate cake out of the oven and set it on a wire rack to cool. She was planning a memorial celebration with Pete.

While Myra Jenkins seemed bitter and at times irrational, some of what she said made sense. She was right to insist that the police check further for suspects, and Cally liked the idea of lighting a remembrance candle. She'd found a special white one at the Mercantile. She would place it next to the cake. After they lit it and said a prayer for Cody, they could even sing "Happy Birthday."

The kitchen smelled wonderful, just like old times, but it did nothing for Pete's disposition. "I don't know why you have to do that." He sneered at the cake, which now rested on a special crystal plate belonging to her mother. She'd set it next to the candle and a picture of Cody.

Sweet swirls of peanut butter icing topped the cake's luscious dark layers. Cally emptied the big jar of Jif in the fridge to make the frosting. In a strange way, it provided relief because she no longer had to stare at that jar every time she opened the refrigerator door.

"It just makes things harder," Pete grumbled when he came home. "I don't want cake. I want my son." He tossed his key ring on the kitchen counter. "This isn't the time for a goddamn celebration."

"I don't plan to ignore the birth of *my* child. We're not celebrating, we're *remembering*. He's out there somewhere, and he deserves to be remembered."

"Your child. Your child. He's my child, too." Pete's face turned beet red. "And he'd still be here if you hadn't insisted he go looking for a Christmas tree."

"I insisted? We all agreed. We thought it would help Cody. And maybe he wouldn't have needed so much help in the first place, if you'd spent more time with him."

"Oh, now it's all *my* fault. None of this would've happened if you hadn't brought your dim-witted ol' man into this house!"

"My father is an honest, hardworking, decent man."

"He's a drunk."

"He made a mistake. That's all. Welcome to the human race. That doesn't mean—"

They stopped arguing when they saw headlights and noticed a patrol car in their driveway. Cally froze. The only reason a cop car would be there was if they'd found out something about Cody. She could hear voices crackling on the police radio as Deputy Don Range got out and came to the door.

Because of the Benson's lawsuit and the kittens in his back seat, Ken had asked Range to go to the Benson home.

Cally twisted her hands. *Not on his birthday. Please God, not on his birthday.*

Pete invited the deputy into the kitchen. Range took off his hat. He looked at Cally. "I have some sad news," he said. "I'm sorry to have to tell you that your father, Sam Lightener, is deceased."

"Dead? What?"

"I'm so sorry, Mrs. Benson."

"He died? But how—"

"Suicide. He apparently hung himself over at Dottie's."

"Today is Cody's birthday." Cally's voice cracked. She glanced at Pete. He said nothing.

"I know, Mrs. Benson," Range said. He stared at the lonely cake and the picture of Cody. "I know. I understand Mr. Lightener was depressed, and had been drinking heavily. He . . . uh . . . apparently threw his belt over some pipes in the ceiling in uh . . . the apartment bathroom. Dottie came upstairs to check on him and called for help. We did everything we could. I am so, so sorry."

After Range left, Cally and Pete stood in the kitchen. She expected Pete to reach for her, but he didn't. He didn't even say he was sorry about her dad. Just nothing. When she had heard Pete crying in the trailer during those last moments on the mountain, she'd gone to him, held him, tried to fix his pain. He was her husband, yet he stood there like a pillar of cold marble, staring over her head with that expression on his face. What was in that look? *I told you so? Good riddance?* Cody was gone. Her father was dead. They were all dead. Cally looked at the cake. It seemed wrong, out of place, like a blemish on a clear face. The darkness outside seeped indoors. It felt cold, permanent, about to swallow her. "You shut Dad out," she suddenly exploded at Pete. "You shut Cody out, too. You never spent time with him."

"Calm down for Christ sakes," he yelled back.

"I hope you're satisfied." She picked up the cake and threw it at him. It narrowly missed his head. The crystal plate shattered against the wall, and the cake left a splat of chocolate and peanut butter on the plaster before crumbling to the floor on top of the shattered glass.

"Look what you've done," Pete shouted. "You broke your mother's plate."

"I broke a plate. Is that all you have to say?"

"You're a fucking mess." Pete stomped upstairs and banged the bedroom door, his feet moving heavily and rapidly overhead, shaking the ceiling. Cally slumped into a kitchen chair, put her face in her arms, and sobbed on the table. She heard Pete thud down the stairs. When she looked up, she saw he had a duffel bag in one hand. He set it down while he pulled on his jacket.

"Pete."

He jerked his house key off his key ring. "It's all yours, baby," he snapped and flung it toward her, as if everything that had happened was her fault. "I'll get my other stuff later." He slammed the door on the way out. His pickup engine revved to life before the vehicle roared down the driveway. Suddenly, it was quiet. *So quiet.* She reached for the picture of Cody and held it close to her chest.

CHAPTER 16

Investigating the Sam Lightener suicide and filing the necessary reports made it too late to get valentine presents, so Ken drove home with only the meowing kittens in a cardboard box. Lauren wiped them down while Lydia warmed some milk, which the kittens eagerly attacked with tiny pink tongues.

Ken sat at the kitchen table, nursing a Bud Light. He hadn't touched the sandwich Lydia had made for him from the roast that had long gotten cold. His mind flashed on the death scene—the empty whiskey bottle, the lifeless body, the bruising around Sam's neck, the urine smell in the room, the stunned, blank expression on Dottie's pale face—then back to the time on the mountain when he first met Sam Lightener, a scared man blinking in the falling snow, begging for help.

Lydia gave him a comforting pat on the shoulder. "It's been a rough day. You really seem beaten down."

"The last thing Cally Benson needs is a dead father." Ken's voice was husky, his throat parched. He tipped the bottle back and gulped. Beer dribbled on his chin. He wiped it away with his sleeve.

Lydia handed him a dishtowel. "Today was the little boy's birthday. I guess you knew that."

"Yeah. It's a hell of a Valentine's Day all the way around."

For a moment, they both watched Lauren sitting on the floor, cooing like a little mother and tickling the two balls of fluff that were energized by food and compassion.

"Those kitties are exactly what we needed," Lydia whispered, not wanting to distract her daughter. "They give us, especially Lauren, something else to focus on."

"I'm so sorry about our own celebration. If we just could've found that kid."

"Let it go, Ken. Let it go. None of what happened today was your fault." She kissed him softly on the neck. "You look so tired." She kneaded the tense spot between his shoulders.

Her calm touch made his blood flow again, like an icy river kissed by the sun. Lydia could always sense his feelings. "Oh, no,"was all she said when he'd first told her about Sam. She never pressed for details until he was ready. Pangs of hunger replaced the burning, nauseous feeling in his gut. The sandwich was looking good.

"I better send a card to the Bensons," Lydia said. "When the time is right, I'll call on Dottie."

Ken reached again for his beer. "We're probably the last people the Bensons want to hear from." He took a bite of his sandwich.

"All the more reason to do it," Lydia said.

The next day Lydia bought kitten food, a litter pan, a few cat toys, and a pet carrier. On President's Day, she took them to a vet in K-Falls and decided to adopt them. Lauren was ecstatic. She named the gray female, Valentina, and the black male, Velvet.

The playful kittens chased each other around the house, tumbled into each other and constantly amused the Blakes with their antics. At night, "the V kids," as Lauren called them, slept with her.

***

Dottie closed the cafe for two weeks until after the memorial at the church. People in Forest Lake couldn't remember a time when Dottie's had been closed for so long. In fact, they couldn't remember a time when anybody in Forest Lake had actually killed himself.

Cally accompanied her father's body back to Montana. After a brief funeral service there, she had him laid to rest next to her mother. Pete did not attend the memorial or the funeral.

***

Ken snapped a plastic lid over his Styrofoam coffee cup. He'd come to the K-Falls central office for an early morning debrief on Len Roster with Sargent Walt Richards, his boss, and Detective Frank Lane of the Oregon State Police. After the cafeteria cash-register clerk noticed the cat hair on his jacket and teased him about having a heavy date, he ducked into the restroom to brush it off.

Ken smiled as he headed down the hall to the small, stark debriefing room remembering how Velvet liked to climb up his pant leg and his arm, perch on his shoulder, and purr while he read the morning paper. "He's into current events," Lauren claimed with a laugh. It was good to hear that laugh.

Lane had his nose buried in the sports section. "Cheers." He lifted his own coffee cup, bearing the Starbucks logo. He pointed to a stack of files on the table. "I was tempted to start reading this stuff, but I didn't want to fuck up Richards' orderly mind."

Ken managed a thin smile. Whatever was in those files would eventually funnel its way back to the department's top brass and perhaps into the Benson's lawsuit.

Lane was okay. Slim and wiry, he was always open and friendly with Ken. Richards was another story. A big, pudgy man with a mustache, fuzzy eyebrows and large ears, he had enough arrogance to fill a room. Except for a full head of salt-and-pepper hair, he reminded Ken of Mr. Potato Head.

A somber Richards waddled in, complained about the quality of cafeteria coffee, and bemoaned the fact that he didn't have time to stop at Starbucks like Lane did. The sleepy eyes behind dark-framed glasses were deceiving. He was sharp, good at his job, and he always did his homework. He'd been on the force long enough to retire, but Central Office considered him one of its best.

Lane folded his paper and dropped it on the floor. "Life is more fun on the sports page."

Richards swallowed the last bite of a doughnut he carried, wiped his greasy hands on the napkin, and tossed it into the wastebasket. "You blue boys don't have enough to do," he grumbled and shut the door. The three of them huddled over the small table which Richards's ample, spud-like body seemed to overpower.

"So where was Roster on December 5?" Lane asked.

Ken had done the initial interview with Roster. "He said he was on his way to K-Falls to meet with the lead foreman from the development company. The meeting got cancelled because the foreman had the flu. Roster doesn't have a phone, so he didn't know the meeting was off."

"That apparently checks out, "Richards added. "There's a credit card receipt for a gas station, just outside Klamath Falls. Roster claimed he stopped there to fill up and buy food at the convenience store." Richards shifted through some paper. Ken felt a small shred of relief.

Richards shook his head. "Time-wise, he could've made it back to the Big Bat area. It woulda been tight. Doesn't make a lot of sense. Why would he do that? It's outta his way. Usually these dirtbags pass through and see an opportunity."

"Unless he was pissed about that meeting," Lane said. "When these guys get stressed, they get the urge to go out and do something sinister."

"A missed meeting? Not much of a stressor," Richards replied. "He woulda just had a nice ride."

Lane looked at Ken. "Maybe it bothered him more than we think. He's strapped for cash. He lives in a dumpy trailer park just outside of town. Right?"

"Correct," Ken said. "Didn't he take a polygraph test? Do we have the results?"

Richards pulled out the report. "Yeah, and it's got some muddy parts."

"Where's the mud?" Lane asked.

"He lied about being parked near the Forest Lake Grade School. There are some clouds around his whereabouts. When asked about the Benson boy, his answers appear truthful. When asked if he was on or near the spot where the boy went missing, his answers appear deceptive. But then we got that goddamn credit card receipt."

"Maybe he was scared shitless. That's the trouble with those tests," Lane griped. "If a guy is tired or stressed, he can skew the results."

Richards abruptly leaned forward. "Yeah, there's all of that. We'd like for him to retake the test, but now he's lawyered up."

"When Roster gets nervous, his eye starts to twitch," Ken added. "I can't remember which one." He knew that sounded lame but continued anyway. "He never made good eye contact with me, and he was always making references to God."

Richards ignored him. "We pulled all the records we could find on this guy. Got some stuff from the shrink he saw while in prison." He picked out a folder from the thick pile and tossed it in the middle of the table. He opened it and spread out photos of Roster.

Lane took a swig of coffee and stared at the borderline good looks with close-cropped brown hair and dark eyes behind chunky black plastic glasses. "He looks pretty normal, but then most of them do."

"He seemed congenial enough when I interviewed him, except for the twitching eye," Ken said. "It's too bad these guys don't have two heads or flashing eyes that would warn the kids to stay away."

"He was raised in Chemult." Richards said. "His mother died when he was thirteen. His Dad is a taciturn, hard-nosed coot, opinionated, old-school religious, detached, cold, and aloof. Never did believe his son was guilty in the Potter case. Blamed the woman. Said Lila Potter was a Jezebel and her kid a sniveling liar.

"Roster was raised to believe sex was a sin. Well, before marriage." Richards smirked. "When he was a little kid, he got caught playing doctor with a cousin. His father beat him with a belt. Other than that, there's no indication of abuse.

"Roster was quite the athlete in his small high school. Nickname: Twitch." Richards looked at Ken. "That explains the weird eye. He wasn't allowed to date, attend dances, or listen to popular music. He was in church every Sunday and at prayer meetings during the week. He attended community college, planning to major in physical education, had a C grade-point average, got a taste of drugs and alcohol. Then flunked out."

"You can see it coming, can't you?" Ken said.

Richards glared at him. He didn't like being interrupted. "As I was saying, Roster drifted for a while. Nothing new, there. Worked with his ol' man as a carpenter; then as a teacher's aide. His job was to help a middle school coach in Roseburg. After six months, they suddenly dismissed him. The records don't say why."

"Let's find out why," Lane said.

Richards' bushy eyebrows knitted into a frown. "We talked to some folks around at the time—nothing really concrete. There were rumors of inappropriate touching in the locker room. It was hushed up. The principal didn't want a scandal. He was the one that hired Roster. So that's that." He tipped his coffee cup to his lips. "Goddam battery acid," he grumbled before returning to his report.

"Roster returned to Chemult. Fought with his Dad. Yada, yada, yada. He hitchhiked across the country and worked at a youth camp helping with activities."

"Why'd he leave the camp?" Ken asked.

Richards looked over his dark-rimmed glasses. "We don't know, Blake. The camp doesn't exist anymore, but I'd venture a guess. He returned to Oregon. Took up with the Potter woman in Springfield. She was a single mom with a young son, Wayne, age ten."

"He probably glommed on to the girlfriend to get close to the boy," Ken said.

"Well, duh," Richards muttered. "Roster was arrested, fined, convicted of felony sexual abuse. Did some time in the slammer. Got paroled. He's a registered sex offender.

"Roster told his dad the woman set him up." Richards quit reading and looked up. "No parent, especially a religious one, wants to believe his kid is a sexual predator."

Ken resisted the urge to blurt, *Well duh*. He amused himself with the thought that Mr. Potato's plastic head was hollow.

"Is that it?" Lane asked.

"No, there's more. Roster was a model inmate. After the state paroled him, he moved back to the ol' man's house in Chemult and worked with him as a carpenter. Built houses. In spite of his criminal record, Roster's a good carpenter, neat, meticulous, and good at estimating costs. He moved to Forest Lake to work for a developer."

Ken provided the local angle. "Hansen, Inc. They're gonna build cabins in the lake area, supposedly starting this spring. They're also looking into the possibility of developing some kind of ski lodge on the Big Bat. Some guy Roster worked for recommended him. The guy had no idea about his record."

"In the meantime," Richards went on, "Roster's been doing handyman stuff and some farm work." He slammed the file shut. "That, my friends, is Len "Twitch" Roster's story."

"Did he violate his parole when he moved to Forest Lake? We weren't notified he was in the area," Ken said.

"He had permission from his parole officer in Klamath Falls to temporarily move for the duration of the construction project. This parole officer fella was sick a lot. Eventually took a disability retirement. They assigned a new guy, but somewhere in the process, the communication went down the tube. So no, it wasn't Roster's fault."

"Wasn't ours, either," Ken said. He knew he was being defensive.

Richards paused and gave a little snicker. "At this point Blake, we have nothing to tie him to the Benson kid. That should help you with your little personnel matter and our little lawsuit."

Ken's face flushed to the roots of his hair. The old son of a bitch always had to get his digs in. Richards had been a ten-year man when Jim Fallingwater escaped from Ken's custody. Ken knew that behind his back Richards referred to him as "Butterfingers Blake" and had openly campaigned to have Ken kicked off the force.

To Ken's relief, Lane quickly changed the subject. "What about the grandfather? He killed himself. Maybe he had a reason."

"No one believes Sam Lightener did anything to the boy," Ken said. "He passed a polygraph with flying colors. It was

Just a tragic lapse of judgment. The guy was overcome with guilt. Just a sad, sad case."

"Must be hard on the family," Lane said.

Richards nodded. "It's taken a toll. Apparently, the Bensons have split up." Lane shook his head. Ken winced.

"Keep an eye on this guy, Blake," Richards said as if lecturing a dull student. "Let Range do the routine stuff. Tail Roster's butt off. This guy smells like trouble."

Ken blushed again. He wasn't some fresh-faced cop, and he resented Richards' paternal tone. "If the town doesn't tar and feather him first. They hate child molesters almost as much as they hate developers." He tried to sound casual. "At this point, all we can conclude is that Cody Benson went missing and probably froze to death."

"Jesus, Blake." Richards' fuzzy eyebrow shot up. "I said Roster *could've* made it to the mountain on that day. His freakin' polygraph doesn't clear him on that. We don't want to be accused of fucking up again." His beady eyes burned a hole in Ken.

***

It was a beautiful day on the mountain, cold and windy but clear. The March sky was blue gray with swashes of purple and a few drifting clouds against an all-white gleaming mountain. Snow still powdered the trees that sparkled in the sunlight.

Ken sat in his Jeep cruiser in his favorite spot off Cooper's Hawk Highway, staring at the Big Bat. How quickly this placid beauty could turn treacherous.

He tried to time his trip from Klamath Falls to the Big Bat area to see whether Roster could have made it if he had been speeding. But why would someone race to the Big Bat on a cold, snowy winter day? The question gnawed at him. Maybe Roster had wanted a Christmas tree. Maybe he'd come here to clear his head, like Ken was doing now. That didn't fit. Ken had a relationship, a personal history with the Big Bat and the miles of surrounding wilderness. He'd grown up on the mountain's shoulders and climbed its craggy trails. His family had picnicked at the lake. Sometimes they'd pitched a tent and spent the night.

He'd met Sam Lightener only briefly that snowy day in December when he'd responded to the 911 call and talked with him several times later. Sam had been a salt-of-the-earth kind of guy, and Ken had liked him. Sam and Dottie would have been good for each other. Now he was dead.

The stress had taken its toll on the family. Rumors flew like spears—Pete had moved into a co-worker's house. Ken thought somebody had said the roommate was female, but Pete wasn't speaking to him anymore. When a child goes missing, the family clings to any thread that he could still be alive. That usually meant blaming someone.

Surely the lawsuit wouldn't go anywhere. There just wasn't enough concrete evidence. Of course, it could go either way once they discovered Cody's remains, depending on what they found.

The town's loss of confidence in him was the bigger problem now—not to mention the humiliation of his family. Lydia was a survivor and, over the years, had developed a tough outer shell. But Lauren struggled. She was constantly on edge. It wasn't just what the kids at school said about the past or the witness issue; it was the way she looked at him. It was different now. Something had changed.

Ken squinted at the Big Bat. Mo had tremendous respect for the mountain, calling it "Chief." All it took was a blazing campfire to get a story out of Mo. Ken could see his dark eyes flashing as he whittled. Mo said the seasons were the Chief's blankets. In spring and summer, the blanket was green; yellow and red in fall. In winter, the Chief slept beneath a white blanket. The big brown bears returned in the spring and danced around the trees. The mountain, Mo said, knew many secrets and hid them well. Somewhere under its winter blanket, the mountain had hidden Cody. Ken sensed the ghost of Jim Fallingwater floating in the thin clouds, but he could not feel Cody. If only the mountain could talk.

What would Jim's life have been like if he had lived and not fallen for Christie? The sheriff's office had dispatched Ken to take custody of Jim after his arrest near Port Orford, a fishing port on the coast. They didn't say go alone, in fact, policy required two officers to transport prisoners, but Ken had been eager to help.

He should have known. Jim had a hair-trigger temper. There was that time in high school when Melvin Dunn called Jim a "bush nigger" and threw sheep dip at him. Jim flew into a rage and almost strangled him until Ken pulled them apart. Dunn got a lecture; Jim was suspended.

Ken could still picture Jim as a young boy, laughing, beckoning him to follow him farther into the wilderness. He looked at the scar on his index finger—that long ago cut that had made them blood brothers.

What had happened that night with Christie? Whatever it was, Jim had been wrong. He had been so naïve about life. He'd been bigger than Ken and could hold his own in any fight, but Ken had always felt like his protector, especially when it came to navigating prejudices. That feeling had turned out to be his own tragic mistake.

He remembered all the charges and accusations flying around like debris during a windstorm. Ken had ended up on administrative leave and eventually got reassigned back to Forest Lake, his career shattered. Things had turned ugly, so ugly that the tension followed him home. Lydia had been pregnant. Someone had thrown a rock through their living room window and painted the words "Injun Lover" on the side of their house. Lydia couldn't sleep, hadn't been eating right, and was afraid to be home alone. They had talked about having her stay with friends in Eugene, but then something had gone terribly wrong with the pregnancy. Ken blamed Jim for the loss of that child. He'd been the loyal friend, but Jim had attacked him, gotten him in that choke hold, stolen a car, abandoned it on Cooper's Hawk Highway, and had been spotted heading for the Big Bat on foot—the only place he could go.

"See," everyone had said. "See how violent this Indian was. See. What chance did sweet Christie have that night?"

The first thing Ken had planned to do when they recaptured Jim was to make him look at a picture of that flat, cold gravestone; the second thing was to punch him in the face.

Dottie had come to their house. She was really the only one that had. She'd brought food and a small bouquet for the baby. Ken had given the baby his name, and they'd buried him—he and Lydia, their parents, the minister, and Dottie. *Kenneth Blake Jr.,* the little headstone said.

Then there was Richards, a middle-aged, hotshot special detective back then. He went around saying the department got "soft" with Ken because he'd lost his infant son. It got back to him. He knew.

Strange how the Big Bat continued to cast shadows over his life. Jim had died out there. It was only fair. His death helped quench the town's ire. Ken had gotten a second chance. Jim never had.

Maybe he should leave the force. Maybe twenty-plus years was enough in a job like this. What was it Lydia always said? He was too kind-hearted for police work. Yeah. That was it. Fuck it. He and Lydia could move when Lauren finished high school. He had spent his whole life in one little corner of the earth, in the shadow of the Big Bat.

He knew there was some talk of disciplinary action. Oh, no one said it to him directly, but it was there. He could see it in Richards' rigid scowl. During their morning meeting, he rarely made eye contact with Ken. He seemed to be talking to Lane as if Ken weren't even there. They probably wouldn't replace him with Range, but some other guy would come in; then he'd be commuting to Klamath Falls to a desk job. That would be the ultimate humiliation.

Maybe they could move to a larger community. Sometimes police officers went into security work. Maybe he could sell real estate. That's what happened to that new doctor at the clinic who moved up from California. He stole their drugs to feed his habit until the police showed up one day. His marriage fell apart, he lost his license, and the last anyone ever heard of him he was selling real estate in Eugene. When he and Lydia went there to visit friends, Ken spotted that doctor's picture on the back of a bus, smiling, with his company logo running across his chest. He looked healthy instead of pinched and thin. Ken scowled. He could picture his own face on the back of a bus.

Soon it would be time to call out the search-and-rescue crew again. If they could just find the remains, or some clue that could prove Cody had succumbed to the elements.

Mo always said that echoes bouncing off the mountain were your other self—your spirit self. Ken got out of the Jeep. "Cody Benson," he yelled at the mountain.

The mountain echoed back the last syllable, "Son, son, son."

"Captain Jack," he yelled into the sky.

"Jack, Jack, Jack," came the echo across the canyon.

"Where is Cody?" he yelled.

The echo said, "dy, dy, dy."

CHAPTER 17

On Sunday morning, Cally headed down the highway toward Dottie's Café, hardly noticing the tight spring buds or the flocks of returning birds crisscrossing in the sky. She stared straight ahead as if she were driving through a soundless, black-and-white movie.

Dottie had invited her to pick up some of her father's things and to talk. God, they needed to talk. There had been no time at the memorial. They'd both been too emotional, and then she'd left for Montana.

When she returned, she found Pete had come and taken clothing, towels, and a few pictures of Cody. She wasn't angry with him for wanting the photos. A father needed to remember his son. He didn't take the big, framed one, which still stood on the kitchen table. She was grateful for that. She had breakfast with it every morning, staring into the dark eyes and the tender, smiling lips as if they could tell her something. "Where are you, baby?" she'd ask over a bowl of shredded wheat.

Now, she slept alone in the big bed upstairs, lumbered down the stairs to the cold kitchen and brewed the morning coffee. The house felt empty, creaky, lonely, and sad. Especially, sad. After breakfast, she felt rudderless. She lacked energy to clean. There was no need to shop or to plan. Her body ached, her head always on the verge of a headache.

God bless Nora Case. She kept the quest for Cody alive. Every time her show hammered away about Cody's case, a fresh batch of cards and letters arrived. Some came from people who claimed they were psychics. They saw landfills, dumpsters, deserted houses, and shallow graves. Some volunteered to see more for a fee. None of it helped. Other people insisted they'd spotted Cody at a mall, at a convenience store two states over, in Mexico, and even in Thailand. Those she turned over to the police. At first, each bit of information was a fragment of hope; now each one stabbed at her heart.

Cally did not intend to go there, but the new sign at the entrance to Ray's Trailer Park, a striking contrast to what lay beyond it, caught her eye. It pulled on her like a magnet on steel. She turned her car down the potholed driveway. What would she say if he saw her? She was looking for a friend, or she was lost and needed directions? Would he even know who she was? She needed to see this man in person, to have the satisfaction of making him look her in the eye. She didn't know exactly why. Perhaps she would spot something that belonged to Cody. Something that hick deputy sheriff couldn't see. Something. Something. Anything.

The trailers stood in a row on small patches of gravel without a single blade of grass. Even at mid-morning, the blinds on what seemed like a group of dingy boxes remained tightly closed like still-sleeping eyes. Over-sized soft drink cups, plastic lids and forks, empty cigarette packages, and other debris lined the side of the driveway. A rotting mattress leaned against a half-built wooden fence. Green trash cans bulged with the week's refuse. Black plastic garbage bags stacked against outside walls handled the overflow. An occasional white vinyl chair, pots of withered plants, a cracked rooster lawn ornament, dime store wind chimes, and a tiny terracotta angel did little to soften this rough-edged, careless environment. A sparse grove of still leafless trees stood in the distance like a row of dark, bony skeletons.

She spotted it at the end of the driveway—the discolored turquoise-and-white trailer with decaying latticework around the front doorway, complete with the faded maroon station wagon. A smaller, blue sedan with a dent on the side squeezed in along its side. She'd seen that trailer many times on television. There was even a picture of it in the newspaper. She stopped there and sat for a moment. Now what? Maybe she should leave. Instead, she opened the door and stepped out.

Mud caked the lower portion of Roster's vehicle. The inside looked like a trash can on wheels. The dashboard was a pile of crumpled receipts, paper, and packages of Camel cigarettes. He'd taped a small calendar above the radio. The open ashtray brimmed with cigarette butts. There were several empty water bottles, pop cans, and pieces of crumpled paper on the passenger floorboard and extra clothing piled on the seat. He'd lowered the back seat to extend the cargo compartment. It contained scattered tools, a toolbox, an old blanket, a half-eaten bag of pretzels, and a clipboard. Did he live in there at times? She didn't see anything that belonged to Cody.

Cally looked over her shoulder, a little frightened by her boldness, and then lifted the trash can lid. It was full of smelly garbage, empty cans, frozen food containers, newspaper, and a few hard-liquor bottles. A coffee can by the doorway held dozens of cigarette butts.

Her heart fluttered like a scared bird trapped in a confined space. Should she go farther? It was quiet. She didn't hear a TV. Her arm stretched forward to knock on the door. She stopped. It was almost 11:00 a.m. Maybe he was still asleep. She didn't care. She tapped on the door. There was no response. She knocked again, only harder. She heard footsteps. She wanted to run, but her legs locked her in place. The door swung open, and a man stood there in his bare feet. He had short brown hair, wore glasses, and needed a shave. A distinct odor came from inside, a combination of stale tobacco and musty, dirty socks. She thought she smelled coffee. As soon as the door opened, a rumbling furnace kicked on.

"Yeah," he said. He took a long drag from his cigarette.

Cally looked directly into his bloodshot brown eyes. The lens on his glasses needed cleaning. It was him—the face she had seen on TV, only his appearance seemed normal; not like his deer-in-the-headlights mug shot. In his faded jeans and open plaid shirt over a white T-shirt, he could be anybody's neighbor on a Sunday morning.

"You sellin' something?" he asked.

This might be the man who took Cody. She forgot everything she'd planned to say. Her words tumbled out.

"I'm looking for my son."

"Your son?" He looked puzzled.

"Yes, my son, Cody."

He leaned forward and frowned. "Who?"

"Cody Benson. He's nine years old."

His face darkened. His eyes narrowed as if he heard what she said for the first time. "Hey, wait a minute. That's the kid that disappeared around here." His right eye started to twitch.

"Can you tell me—?"

"You a cop?" he interrupted.

"I'm his *mother*," she said.

He took another drag from his cigarette and blew smoke from his nose. His face flushed again. "This some kind of a trick?"

"Just tell me where he is."

"I don't know nothin' about a kid, lady." His right eye twitched rapidly, as if something festered in it.

"I have to find him—"

"How the hell . . . Like I told ya, I don't know nothin' about your kid." He gave a nervous laugh. "I told the cops all I know."

"I know *you* know something." She stared into those eyes.

"I wasn't even here then." His voice rose. "Look lady, it sure is too bad about your boy; God love him, but I don't know nothin' about him."

"You're not fooling me." Her voice broke. The words surprised her.

Roster's lips pressed hard on his cigarette. His eyes narrowed again, this time to slits. He blew out a large cloud of smoke and spit on the ground. "You don't got no right to come here, accusing me on the Lord's Day." His twitching right eye was so out of control it caused the left one to flutter.

"You know something," she insisted. "I can feel it."

"This is my home. You got no right to be here." He took a step toward her.

Cally moved back. Maybe he was going to attack. There was no one around. No one knew she was here. She heard someone move inside. *It could be her son.* "Cody!" she called.

"Who is it, Lenny?" A young woman with long, uncombed dark hair appeared in the doorway. She rubbed her eyes with one hand as if she had just gotten up. In the other, she clutched a cup of coffee. She obviously didn't wash her face before retiring; the heavy makeup around her eyes had smeared making her look like a bleary-eyed raccoon. She wore a short pink bathrobe, exposing some cleavage. The red toenails on her bare feet matched the ones on her hands. She looked at Cally, giggled, and lifted her cup as if she were making a toast. "Hey," she said.

Cally looked away. Under that robe, she wasn't wearing anything.

"I already talked with the cops," Roster said.

"Is she a cop?" the woman whispered. Roster didn't answer.

"I passed a lie detector test." His voice was loud and angry. He bounced on his heels. "Why can't you people leave me alone?" Roster backed into the trailer. "It's Sunday for Christ sake." He shut the door hard. She could hear them in there talking, he loudly, the woman murmuring. "Fuckin' dumb bitch," she heard him say.

"You haven't seen the last of me," Cally shouted back. "Bastard!"

Something inside made a crashing noise. She ran to her car. Her shaking hand tried three times before it found the car ignition. She didn't think child molesters had girlfriends.

***

"What's the matter, honey?" Dottie asked. "You're late. I was worried about you."

"I, I. . ." The room seemed to spin. She'd run up the side steps of the café to Dottie's upstairs apartment. A lone tear trickled down her cheek as if someone had wrung the last drop from a sponge. It surprised her. She didn't think she could cry anymore.

Dottie pulled her close "There. There," she said. "It's hard. I know." She patted Cally's back.

Her touch felt good. How long had it been since someone actually hugged her like that? "I stopped at that trailer park, so I could see Len Roster."

"You did what?" Dottie's jaw dropped. Without makeup, Dottie looked tired and older. At the café, she always penciled in her eyebrows and wore bright lipstick. The part on her blondish head needed touching up; her wrinkles seemed deeper.

"I wanted to see up close what a monster looks like."

159

"Oh, honey, that's a bad place. Leave those things to the police."

"I had to —"

"You're shaking like a leaf. Sit down by the fire. I just brewed a pot of coffee."

The inside of Dottie's small apartment was inviting with its large braided rug and cozy throws over the sofa and easy chair.

"I just had to, you know. I know it's him." Cally scowled at the blazing fireplace and turned away.

"Did he say anything?"

"He swore, slammed the door in my face."

"Well, that figures. You look like you seen a ghost." Dottie brought a tray containing a muffin and cinnamon roll cut into quarters, butter, jam, and some chunks of white cheddar cheese. "You need to eat something. You look peaked."

Cally hadn't eaten much at home. The food, strong coffee, and the room's bright warmth eased the headache lingering behind her temples.

They ate in silence. Finally, Dottie set down her cup. "Sam didn't bring much here, just a few clothes, his tools."

"Dad left in a hurry that night. He never did come back."

"His tools are still in his pickup. You'll need to do something about the pickup. Of course, it can stay here, but you really should do something about it."

Cally hated the sight of that pickup—a symbol of Cody's last ride. She remembered that night in December. The pickup, cold and ominous in the firelight, with the Christmas tree in the back covered with snow. Then the bonfire had gone out. Died. So had their hope. She stared at Dottie's fireplace. Now, she hated fires. She no longer made one in the kitchen woodstove. She could not bear to look at the embers or the charred, cold ashes. She had no idea what she should do with the pickup.

Dottie reached for a shoebox on the floor next to the couch. "Here's his wallet, watch, favorite belt, Sunday cufflinks, and shaving kit. I packed his clothes and gave them to the Goodwill like you wanted."

Cally opened the wallet and looked at the photo on his driver license. It actually was a good picture of him. How could he do this? She didn't need more pain. She needed him—and Cody. She picked up his watch, a gift from the trucking company when he retired. He'd been so proud of it. It was still ticking, surviving, pulsing like a heart. It seemed strange that small things like cufflinks and bigger things like pickups survived people. Houses stood years after the occupants who built them died. She wished she'd come when her father was still alive. Maybe then this would not have happened. A great lump formed in her throat. Another tear slid down her cheek.

"Just take one day at a time, honey." Dottie patted her hand. She poured more coffee. "Something ends; something begins. It's out of our control."

"I should have come here sooner, you know, to see Dad."

"Sam blamed himself. He never said a bad word about you. He was depressed. If anything, he would want you to know that he didn't send Cody back to the pickup. He said that many times. It was a mistake, a sad, tragic mistake. Then on Cody's birthday, he got up in the morning and remembered the day. He started drinking before I went down to open. Right then, you know. I was thinking this isn't any good, but I felt so sorry for him. I was going to lay the law down. Make him get some help. But I thought it was best to stay away from him, to give him some space. You know, because of the birthday. I got busy with the café. I never expected to find what I did. I didn't see that coming. Finding him that way. I can't get it out of my head." She paused for a moment. Her voice cracked. "He died alone."

Alone. That one word hit Cally hard. *Alone.* It sounded cold and austere, like a lone, giant icicle hanging from the gutter, glistening in the sunlight, breaking loose, crashing to the ground, and shattering into dozens of pieces. One of a kind. Gone. Forever. No one should die alone. What about Cody? He was out there somewhere. *Alone.*

"Dad was family," she managed to say. "He should've stayed with us."

"I think I'll see the way I found him for the rest of my life." Dottie's hand tapped the sofa arm. "He was a good man." She smiled slightly and swallowed. "I thought he was my happily ever after, but it was not to be." She reached in her pocket for a tissue and dabbed her eyes.

"We could've worked things through. I wanted to come, but Pete said no. I'm so angry at Pete. I should've come anyway. All these months, I've been treading water. Each day, I try to think about what I've accomplished or where I've been, and I don't know. I just don't know."

"Grief is like a sore that festers, honey. One day it heals, but the scar is always there. I think that's good, the scar I mean. It helps us remember. Don't be too quick to shut Pete out. Everybody needs time."

"I've heard he still goes to the mountain every weekend to look for Cody. The snow is still so bad up there. But I appreciate that." She paused and drank some coffee. "He . . . he moved in with another woman. How could he? I mean just like that. My dad is dead. Cody is missing. He finds a girlfriend. How could he think like that?"

Dottie's mouth drooped. "I heard it's someone he knew from work. Maybe he just needed a room."

As soon as Dottie said that, Cally knew that people were gossiping. That's the way it was in small towns. She hadn't known it was a coworker, and she couldn't think who it might be. Maybe that woman even came into the café. Maybe, she came with Pete. She felt a pang in her gut, a twinge of betrayal. She wanted to leave Forest Lake.

"When a child goes missing, it just rips your heart out and tears what's left in two. It's hard to hold it together," Dottie said, "let alone think straight."

"I'm living out in the country by myself. I'd like to move to Portland and get a job, but I can't leave now. I can't leave Cody behind."

"It's important to take your time. You need to go ahead and grieve. Then one day, you'll know when the time'll be right."

The pang was back. She knew Dottie meant well, trying to be comforting, but she was talking as if Cody were dead. "Myra Jenkins scares me. I don't want to become her, but I can see how that happens."

"Yeah, well, that's a whole other situation. Christie used to work for me. She wouldn't of wanted her mother to go off the deep end like that. I hear it's getting worse. Think what Cody would want for you. And, think what you'd want for Cody if you'd been the one that was gone."

There it was again, the pang and that word *gone*. It was almost as bad as *alone*. "I can't accept that Cody is dead." She almost blurted it. Dottie looked startled. "At least the Jenkins stayed together." Cally knew she was rambling. "Whenever I catch myself feeling better, I feel guilty. Why should I be happy? It feels like betrayal. We have to find Cody. I know that Roster creep knows something."

"Yes. Yes. We need answers about that." Dottie's tone was cautious.

"I certainly am not ready for a relationship. How could he?" Cally was back on Pete. "It's hardly been four months."

"Sometimes," Dottie continued, "when folks go through something tough, they never really deal with it. Don't think it through. They just get another partner. Men can take odd paths. I don't know how Pete copes with loss. Sam couldn't deal with it."

Cally jumped when the phone in Dottie's kitchen rang.

"Now what?" Dottie muttered. "People usually know to leave me alone on a Sunday." She set down her coffee cup. Her walk seemed slow and heavy. "I'm coming, I'm coming. Hold your horses. Hello. Oh. Yes, yes, she's here. Has something happened? I see." She turned toward Cally. "Honey, it's for you. It's Deputy Blake." Dottie looked tense.

Cally bolted up and grabbed the phone. "Yes . . . Hello."

"Mrs. Benson," Ken said. He paused. "I,uh,have some news. A group of wilderness trainees stumbled across the body of a young child on the Big Bat on Saturday."

Cally's grip on the receiver tightened. The *body*. Her little son was now known as the body? "You found Cody?" She needed to say his name.

"We don't have a positive identification at this point. We know the remains appear to be those of a male child. The body is, uh, not intact, as you would expect, the elements, and, uh, animals, they—"

"Cody," she said again. "The clothes. What was Cody wearing? I would know the clothes."

"We've notified your husband, and we went out to your house. Your car was spotted at Dottie's, so I took a chance and called. I wanted you to know."

"Where did you find him?"

"I'm sorry, but I'm not at liberty to say at the moment. The specific area is considered a crime scene."

She turned to Dottie, her voice tremulous, "They've found something on the mountain. A young child, a boy." Her legs felt rubbery. "They aren't sure. They need to check things out."

Cally's face turned white. Her hand cradled her forehead. Dottie took the phone.

"Yes, I'll stay with her," Dottie said into the receiver. "Yes. I understand, Ken."

"Wait, don't hang up." Cally was almost yelling, but it was too late. Dottie dropped the phone onto its cradle. "Why is he playing games? Of course, it's Cody. I'm going out there."

"No, no. Honey, listen to me. Stay here for a while, for as long as you want. He said they have to be certain. No one's allowed there. You don't want to disturb anything . . . the evidence."

"Evidence? He said they called Pete. Why didn't Pete call me? Why isn't he here?"

"Maybe he tried. Maybe he went to your house like Deputy Blake did."

"Hell with Pete. It all fits together. Damn that Roster. I'm going to kill him." Cally's stomach churned; acid crept up her throat. She couldn't breathe. She needed her Zantac. Her ears started to ring. A yellow glare clouded her vision, like someone shining a flashlight in her eyes.

"Do you want me to call the minister?" She heard Dottie's voice in the distance. "Cally? Cally? Honey!"

She could feel her knees buckle. Dottie seemed to be standing over her. A foggy darkness swallowed her.

CHAPTER 18

December 5, 2009

The boy whimpered, but could barely move. His mouth made little sucking sounds until his eyes fluttered open. A shadowy figure hovered over him. The man smelled like musty straw and had a brown face. When the stranger leaned in, the boy could see gray strands in his black hair, which was pulled back into a low hanging pony tail. Deep lines crowded his eyes. Those eyes. They were wild looking and anxious like a cornered animal.

"Are you Benny's Dad?"

"Who's Benny?" the stranger asked.

"He's my Indian friend. Sometimes we play together." He swallowed hard. "Mom says he's not real."

"Then I must be Benny's dad." He grinned. "You're talking. That's a good sign."

"Where am I?" The fire whispered hisses and made shadows on the wall. There were no windows in the odd, cluttered room. Was that a dog? He blinked, but his mind blurred and seemed to drift.

"What's your name, kid?" The man's eyes softened.

"C-Cody."

"That's a nice name."

"I'm cold." His teeth chattered.

"Just a minute." He got up and returned with a steaming cup. A big, tall man, he wore boots, faded jeans, and a heavy jacket. He squatted, put his hand behind Cody's back, and lifted him up to drink. The man had big feet. "See if you can swallow some of this. It'll warm you up."

Cody gulped the warm broth so fast he gasped and started to choke.

"Easy, easy." He wiped the boy's chin with a rag. "That's enough for now. How long has it been since you ate?"

Cody's lips parted, but made no sound. His eyes squeezed shut. His exhausted body wanted sleep.

"I'm gonna move you closer to the fire."

"Mama," Cody murmured.

CHAPTER 19

Ken swallowed two antacid tablets as he headed into the grade school auditorium. Facing those anxious little eyes seeking reassurance was tough enough, but he bristled when he learned school administrators had also invited "Range the Rookie" to the assembly. Range's presence was insult added to injury. Plus, Tina Williams, the reporter, was back in town, flashing press credentials and acting like a celebrity because she'd been on Nora Case's national TV show. He'd even seen a few teachers ask for her autograph.

Ken told the students they had not positively identified the child they'd found. He avoided using the words *body* and *remains*. "When something like this happens," he said, "we look to forensic scientists to help us." He did his best to explain in simple terms what a forensic scientist did. "They're the folks that look at things up close with microscopes and do all kinds of tests. They see things we can't see." That seemed to take. The children sat quietly. "Deputy Range and I are here this morning to give you some tips on how to stay safe until we can sort things out. Sorting through things takes time."

He'd just finished saying that when Stanley Fisher, a freckled-faced redhead raised his hand. "Will Cody's funeral be at the church?"

Ken took a deep breath. "At this point, we don't have a positive identification. In other words, we don't know who the person is."

"Who else could it be?" Martha Brudette, a studious looking little girl with glasses asked.

Before Ken could answer, Range jumped in. "Listen, we'll let everyone know as soon as we're sure. In the meantime, I'll keep an eye on the school, and if any of you kids feel uncomfortable, you can come and talk with me, okay?"

Ken was livid. What the hell kind of answer was that? He spotted Tina, notebook in hand, sitting in the front row with a smirk on her face. She must have noticed Ken's discomfort.

After counselors took over the meeting, he and Range moved outside for a brief press conference. Tina peppered Ken with questions about where they found the body. Did they question Len Roster? Could they determine the cause of death? What about clothing? How long did they think the body was there? Was it in a shallow grave or just in the bushes?

Ken declined to answer any of those questions. "I don't want to say anything at this point that would compromise the investigation."

Afterward, Tina came up to him. "Kids are a lot smarter than cops think, aren't they?" she taunted. "Why not just say what everybody knows—it's Cody Benson."

For a brief moment, they stared at each other. "We are doing everything possible to identify the child and find out who did this," Ken finally replied.

"Surely you've talked to this Roster character?"

Ken turned and started to walk away.

Tina slapped her notebook shut. "We already have overhead footage of your *secret* crime scene," she called after him. Over his shoulder, Ken saw her grilling Range, who smiled into the camera, lapping up the limelight like a hungry puppy at a bowl of milk.

Still, he was confident Range would follow Richards' instructions to keep the details of the investigation under wraps. He headed toward the drugstore to get Tylenol for his head. He just wanted to be alone.

***

Myra Jenkins shifted into high gear as soon as she heard about the discovery of a child's body under the shadows of the Big Bat. She hurried down Main Street, her stout body bent toward the sidewalk, muttering to herself. "I told Christie to stay away from that Indian. I told her. I told her. Now another one. Lord Almighty." She glanced at a cheerful bunch of daffodils and hyacinths blooming in a box in front of the hardware store, but their delicate beauty escaped her. The right shoelace on her brown oxfords was as loose as the words that tumbled from her mouth.

The cheerful morning light was not kind to Myra's orange hair, revealing a multitude of shades, the result of several different hair-color kits from the drugstore. A new perm to fluff out her thinning hair had turned out frizzy, making it look like she'd stuck her finger in an electric socket. It did nothing to soften the frown lines on her forehead that the years had deepened.

She'd gained weight, but then stress did that to her. She'd always had a penchant for those Nutter Butter cookies that she got from Tillden's Grocery. At home, she gobbled packages of them. "I just hope they got Nutter Butters in heaven," she said regularly. New rolls of doughy fat bunched around the bodice of her plain, sky-blue dress.

Myra was a woman on a mission. She carried a ream of flyers she'd created on the old portable typewriter she used to type recipes and their Christmas letter. For two days, she'd worked on the singled-spaced rambling diatribe about Deputy Sheriff Ken Blake's incompetence. "He wouldn't recognize a child molester if one stood up in his soup," she told Floyd as she typed away on a TV tray in their living room. "A little boy is dead, and nothing is being done, just like when that dirty Indian killed Christie." She reached for another Nutter Butter. Floyd aimed the remote at the TV, burying himself in a basketball game.

The flyer chastised Ken Blake for failure to follow up after a witness reported seeing a man struggling with a small boy, not knowing there was a child molester in their community, and numerous other infractions, including the bungled escape of the man who killed her daughter long ago. *It's time for the good people of Forest Lake to stand up and demand action,* she'd typed. *Enough is enough.* Blake, the flyer urged, should be fired.

Myra had "the girl at the drugstore" run off copies of her harangue on goldenrod paper. On the street, she thrust a flyer toward a rancher, who'd just come out of the hardware store clutching a bag of nails, his mind fixed on repairing fences.

"You take this and read it good," she said. "The *a* key kinda sticks and what not. That's why it isn't as black in some of the places," Myra apologized. "You can't find the stuff to clean the keys these days with everyone on computers."

The startled rancher gave her an odd look.

"A Kleenex doesn't work."

He shook his head, politely took the leaflet, and hurried off.

Pleased with herself, Myra made her way toward Dottie's for the Woman's Club luncheon. She planned to hand out flyers there, and she'd instructed Floyd to distribute them at the gas station. She would take a bunch to church on Sunday. Maybe she could leave a few over at the school or tape them to light poles. She saw a shadow in front of her and looked up. There stood the object of her contempt, Ken Blake.

"Morning, Myra," he said. She flashed her icy blue squint at him, but her eyes seemed empty and loose in her head like they weren't attached to anything. They stared through a pair of brown-framed glasses.

"You!" Myra almost spit it out. Her eyes locked on his face. She pointed her index finger at him. "You! This is the second one." There was blood around the nail of the finger she flailed in the air.

Ken's jaw tightened. Myra had done this before. Just walked up to him, stood in his way, and shrieked, "You!" He took a deep breath and glanced down at her brown oxfords and legs in dark, thick compression stockings. "Your shoelace is undone."

Myra squinted up at him and played with her earlobe, leaving a smear of blood there. She thrust a flyer toward him.

Ken hurriedly perused the contents. His lips pursed. He gritted his teeth. A child was dead, and this stupid woman was running around town, distributing trash. Disgusted, he tore the flyer into a hundred little goldenrod pieces in front of Myra's amazed face.

"I'd toss this on the street, but there's a law against leaving garbage in a public place."

"How dare you," Myra sputtered.

"And speaking of the law, there's one about libel, too. You keep this up, and you could be talking to a judge."

"Lord almighty. Who do you think you are?"

"Do you really think this is helping?"

"I'm crossing the street," Myra growled.

"If you want to be helpful, do something for the family." Ken took a step toward her.

Startled, Myra stepped on her loose shoelace and started to fall. Ken caught hold of her, although he would have loved to see her land on her big behind.

"You take your hands off me, you ninny. Don't you touch me!" She trundled across the street, clutching the flyers and brushing the places on her arms where Ken had grabbed her, as if she were warding off germs.

CHAPTER 20

December, 2009

Jim Fallingwater had not intended to be out on that cold December day, but he couldn't find a new flint striker in the last stuff Mo brought to the supply caves, only a few cigarette lighters. He'd told Mo he needed one. He knew he did because he wrote it in his notebook, but Mo's memory was dimming.

Mo had turned seventy-five that summer. He seemed thinner on his last visit in the late fall. He complained of aches, had a cough, and carried a little bottle of pills. "What will you do when I'm gone?" Mo repeatedly asked, concern etched in the brown wrinkles of his face.

"You're too stubborn to die, old man." Jim patted his back. He never told Mo about the stealing.

"I'm working on your future," Mo insisted. "I'm working on it."

Jim knew how to make a fire from dry sticks and tinder, but that could be time consuming and tricky in a damp cave, and deadly if he fell ill. He should have checked Mo's supply caves sooner. No, he needed a new flint striker, and since he didn't have one, he wanted a good supply of matches. Mo would not return until spring, and he couldn't chance a long winter without matches and plenty of them, especially since he knew the weather would be harsh. The signs were everywhere. *The raccoons have bushier tails,* he wrote in his notebook. *The bark on some trees seems thicker, and the spiders are weaving larger webs. Saw a flock of geese on my rounds today. They are leaving earlier than usual. Looks like the squirrels are storing food instead of eating it.* Jim paid close attention to messages from nature. Writing what he saw helped him remember, and writing kept him sane.

If Mo didn't bring things Jim thought he needed, he went "shopping." Stealing from the cabins around the lake was so easy. They were vacant much of the time, and city people were trusting, careless, and sometimes downright stupid. He also liked to scour empty campsites. Amos Hadley's Lake Store was more of a challenge.

It seemed like a good day to venture out on a quest for matches. It was windy, the sky overcast, but not spitting moisture. He should be able to make it to the cabin area and back again before the heavy snows came. He planned to arrive there around dusk to avoid detection. He knew he had to be careful.

"Goddammit," he muttered, after he spotted a chatty family, dressed in wool hats, boots, and bright winter clothing. They were sizing up trees. Jim had forgotten about Christmas and the tree hunters; he had no need for holiday celebrations in the wilderness. If he'd remembered, he would have taken a different route. He retreated to a clump of trees and watched from a distance with his stolen binoculars. Once the family cut their tree, they gathered around an old stump and ate snacks. It looked like they were singing. "For Christ sakes, move on," Jim grumbled in the shadows. Finally, they packed up, leaving empty food containers, pop cans, and banana peels on the ground. Seeing their trash angered him. When he got back, he would make a note about December, Christmas, and people who didn't respect nature. *Humans are the animals that need the moot help,* he would later write. *They are the only ones that have a god or need one.*

Because of the delay with the tree hunters, it was early evening when he approached the lake cabins. "Christ on a horse," he cursed after he discovered more people there. In his haste to get matches, he also forgot about the weekend which always meant more people. He crouched in the darkness, waiting for a chance. Stealing, like hunting, took patience. He surveyed his prey, noting which cabins were dark and cold and which had light coming from their windows.

Those soft, yellow rectangles permeated his brain and hung in there like a gauzy beacon he could feel but not touch. Sometimes on his stealing expeditions, he would linger and watch people through the windows. He stared as they laughed, ate, hugged one another, or danced together in close, bright places. When he did, a yearning inside gnawed at him, like a hungry beast clawing at a heavily bolted door. That was the problem. He'd always wanted in, but the doors never opened—not even when he'd lived free.

The cabin he targeted was small and had an ample supply of wood stacked under an outside porch, a good sign there'd be something inside to start it. He easily picked the lock on the flimsy back door. The downstairs was all one room with a woodstove in the center, a couch, and some easy chairs. A counter lined one wall and contained a sink and a microwave. Jim didn't know how to operate a microwave or even what it was. There was nothing in the small refrigerator, except a bottle of water, which he took. Besides a hefty supply of matches, Jim also found a couple of utility lighters, candy bars, and a small shovel. "You can't have too many shovels," he said aloud, pleased with his find. He spent the night on the cold cabin floor and left before sunrise.

To avoid discovery during daylight hours, he laid low, waiting under a hastily built crude shelter of tree branches next to a big rock. "If Mo had remembered, I wouldn't be holed up here freezing my ass off," he grumbled. He feasted on the stolen candy bars and a supply of dried venison he carried with him. How long had it been since he'd eaten a Snickers bar? He savored the candy slowly, letting the caramel and chocolate melt on his tongue. The sweetness made his mouth tingle and his eyes water. The candy tasted like the yellow light felt.

Once the gray twilight deepened, he began his trek back into the wilderness in the diffused shadows of late afternoon. It had started to snow, lightly at first, and then it got heavy, wet, and slippery. The wind picked up and blasted fat, white flakes into his face, some clumping on his eyelashes. He sought a moment of shelter under a tree, so he could wipe his eyes and pull his scarf up. He looked down. He almost tripped over it—something red in a drift near the tree. He drew his knife, approached cautiously, and brushed the snow away. The thing moved and moaned. *Good God!* It was a kid, almost frozen to death. No one was around. What was a kid doing out here all alone? He hurriedly scraped off more snow and lifted up the child. *A small boy.* If he belonged to the tree hunters, why was he so far away from them? Jim blew warm air against the kid's face. He thought he heard him whimper.

The snow seemed to be coming from every direction, whirling in the cold, biting wind that cut through his heavy jacket and the multiple layers he wore underneath. *Leave him,* the voice inside his gut said. His people are probably looking for him. He put his knife away and started to leave, but then he stopped and turned back.

He couldn't. He just couldn't.

When the tree hunters found the boy, It would be too late. Jim still had a long way to go; he needed to hurry, to stay ahead of the snowstorm. He tied the shovel to his waist, scooped the limp boy up, and held him close to his body.

"We've got to keep moving," he said as if the boy could hear. They scurried past the dark shapes of trees that bobbed in the wind, down gullies and up steep slopes.

Stopping in a snowstorm was risky; it could turn treacherous in an instant. Still, Jim paused several times under the shelter of a tree or wind-breaking cliff, unzipped his heavy jacket, and held the boy close to his warm chest. He was too big to zip inside. "Hang in there, kid. Just hang on," he said.

Jim innately sensed his way through familiar territory. He slipped and fell once, but he managed to hang on to the boy. The shovel dug into his back. "Son of a bitch," he shouted in the wind. "Hurry," he said to himself, once he was on his feet again. "We've got to hurry." The boy was getting heavier, so was the snow. Jim's arms ached. The shovel banged against his body. "Damn it, Mo," he grumbled. "Damn it to hell." He was panting but relieved when he finally disappeared into the dark womb of the earth. He maneuvered down the steep cave entrance, carefully bracing himself on the rocks. Wolf, his dog, barked happily and ran in circles, delighted to see Jim.

Like a big cat carrying its young, he set the boy on his sleeping bag. Wolf sniffed the boy and licked his face. Jim added wood to his banked fire, removed the boy's wet clothing, bundled him in one of his big wool shirts and wrapped him in a heavy blanket. Then he stuffed him inside the sleeping bag.

Shivering by the fire, he pulled off the layers of his own damp clothing, heated water for tea, fed Wolf, and swallowed some corn meal mush. The warm tea soothed his cold bones, and the food made his blood flow again. He felt warm and grateful to be alive. His anger toward Mo melted. "We've been through worse, haven't we, fella." he said to Wolf, scratching the dog's ears. Tired and exhausted, he and Wolf slept next to the boy throughout that first night to keep him warm.

The next morning, Jim kept the broth simmering near the fire, so he could give the kid a bit more when he woke up again. He prepared a meal of venison and beans for himself and sipped some of the hot broth. His body still ached from the long trek home, and he had a good-size bruise above his left buttock where he'd fallen on the shovel. While he finished his meal, he stared at the sleeping boy.

Jim had often rescued injured animals—raccoons, squirrels, numerous birds—and nursed them back to health, then set them free. Two years ago, on one of his treks back from the lake-area campground, he'd found Wolf, a scared, abandoned pup who had wandered deep into the dark forest. He was limping, starving, and neglected. What was he doing there? Jim had been as baffled to find the pup then as he was to find the boy. At first, he thought the little dog was a young wolf, but then he saw the rope around his neck and apparent cigarette burns on his back. Later, he found the deserted campsite, the empty liquor bottles, and a still smoldering campfire. The rage he'd always struggled to control surged through his body. If he'd found them, he would have killed them and dumped their bodies down some deep, remote ravine.

Jim carried the whimpering pup back to the cave, fed him, set his leg, and nursed his wounds and infected eye. Wolf grew up to be a beautiful dog with a golden-brown, grayish coat and black back, ears, and muzzle. He had a black, diamond-shaped spot in the middle of his forehead. To Jim, he resembled a wolf, but more than likely, he was some sort of German Shepherd mix.

Wolf touched Jim's soul in a way he couldn't even imagine and filled a long, festering hole in his heart. When he'd been a boy of eleven, his father had shot his dog, Trigger, a black lab-cocker spaniel mix. The ol' man had come home drunk, confused, and disoriented and was having DTs. He thought the dog was some vicious animal about to attack. Jim struggled with his father, trying to protect Trigger, but the ol' man shoved him out of the way and shot the dog in the backyard. Then he'd just stood there and laughed.

Laughed. As if it didn't matter.

Jim had screamed at his father and pummeled him with his small fists, but he was no match for the big, drunken lout who had beaten Jim with a board, leaving a deep, bleeding gash on his forehead. Trigger had been the only thing in that house that had ever loved him. Jim ran away and spent several scary nights in the cold, damp woods. He vowed to get revenge, to kill the son of a bitch—bash his face so bad, he'd never laugh again. Jim didn't have to keep his vow. The next year, the wasted drunk died of a heart attack. Jim hadn't shed a tear. In fact, he'd been glad. The ol' bastard was out of his life forever, but he'd left his son with a smoldering rage that nothing could tamp down.

Wolf gave Jim unconditional love, a sense of purpose, a reason to get up in the morning, and constantly entertained him with his young-dog antics. "You big clown," he laughed after Wolf snatched one of his boots and ran around the cave with Jim in hot pursuit. Jim spent hours training him and relying on his keen sense of smell for hunting and protection. They ate together; they slept together. *Somehow, they know it when you've helped them,* Jim wrote in his notebook. *We're both strays who have found each other. Wolf is an amazing gift. The Creator must have wanted it this way.*

He never told Mo about his "shopping" trips, or that he kept Wolf. He did tell Mo he had found an abandoned puppy, but lied about where he found him. "Get rid of the dog," Mo ordered. "It's too risky. He could give us away. Sometimes you have to be cruel to survive."

The kid was different. The kid wasn't a pet. Once the boy recovered, he could talk. Then what? It would all be over. Blake would remember. He would piece it together and come looking for him. Mo would be furious. No, it would crush him. He'd be arrested for aiding a fugitive and spend his final days alone in some dark prison. After *all* he had done for Jim. He should've left the kid under that tree and let nature take its course. You just couldn't ask a kid to keep his mouth shut. He was a kid, for Christ sakes. He grabbed his notebook and began writing. *You have to be cruel to survive.* Then he drew a line through it. Maybe he could drug the kid with those magic mushrooms he discovered in the woods. No. No. No. He needed to think. *Think. Think. Think.* Writing always helped him see solutions when there was no one there to listen. *Mo, I am so sorry. You should have let me die.*

Jim would have a long time to think. A ferocious blizzard hit, and it refused to let up. The wind howled, screeched, and blew for days while Jim, Wolf, and the boy huddled like hibernating bears deep inside the earth, insulated by rock and a thick quilt of snow, not knowing that miles away, hundreds of searchers and two grieving parents had left the mountain with heavy hearts.

Jean Rover

CHAPTER 21

The Forest Lake Woman's Club didn't meet about much anymore except lunch. They used to organize the big, annual rummage sale over at the church and use the earnings to sponsor the high school mother-and-daughter tea.

Over the years, club membership had dropped off, not because of competing interests but because its members had simply passed away. Now it was just Dorothea Hart, Harriet Cole, Myrtle Mason, Carol Leach, Helen Billings, and Myra Jenkins. Age spots speckled their swollen-knuckled hands and news about grandchildren, great-grandchildren, various ailments, and people they knew who'd died sprinkled their talk. Dorothea, a plain woman pushing eighty with moles on her chin and several long, dark hairs on her legs, was the president. After everyone else had taken a turn, the presidency had reverted to her and pretty much stayed there. Myrtle was the treasurer.

Dorothea usually waited for everyone to arrive in the back room of Dottie's Café. Over lunch, she called the meeting to order and asked for the treasurer's report. They had $195 in the bank after donating $500 to the Cody Benson Fund. Myrtle always reported on the interest their account earned, which wasn't much these days.

Today was different. Myrtle was down with a cold, and Myra just burst into the room claiming Deputy Blake tried to attack her. "He grabbed my handout and tried to push me to the ground." She distributed copies of the bright goldenrod flyer to each of the women.

"You can't be serious," said Harriet, a short, squat woman whose bright lipstick accented her prune lips. "I've known Ken Blake since he was a little boy." Over the years, the women had learned to take Myra like they took their salt and caffeine—sparingly.

Myra managed a tear. "He did. He did. He grabbed me right here, on my shoulder. He was going to throw me to the ground, but I got away."

Dorothea's voice was measured. "Let's see this flyer." She used the reading glasses that always hung around her wrinkled neck to peruse Myra's missive.

"He tore it up right in front of me and tossed it in the street," Myra claimed.

The women, between sips of salty tomato soup and bites of sandwiches, slowly read Myra's flyer.

Helen, comfortable in elastic waistband jeans and a denim jacket broke the silence. "I can see why he'd be upset with you. This whole thing is such a mess."

"He pushed me and threatened me," Myra insisted.

Dorothea looked over her glasses directly at Myra. "If he did that, honey, you should report it. You really should."

Carol set down her egg salad sandwich. "I guess that Benson woman fainted when she got the news. You know, about the body. Fainted right upstairs here at Dottie's. We saw the ambulance coming back from church."

Helen tore open her bag of potato chips. "I think we should send a wreath to the funeral. We got the money."

Dorothea, who always followed procedure, responded testily, "Myrtle's down with a cold. We can't make a decision like that without her."

Helen pursed her lips, miffed at Dorothea's blunt answer. "So the whole world has to stand still? Who gets a cold in the spring, anyway? Not good with Easter coming up."

Carol reached for her water glass that contained a wedge of lemon. "My daughter says the police was over at the grade school this morning, and that nice new officer keeps patrolling around when the kids come and go. They warned the high school, too."

"This is just terrible," Harriet said. "I don't know the Bensons, but I guess the husband moved out of the house and didn't waste any time shacking up with a lady friend."

Eyebrows jumped up.

Carol squeezed her lemon wedge so hard a squirt shot across the table and almost hit Harriet. "Can that be true?" she gasped.

Nothing fazed Harriet. "I heard it at the drugstore. Went in there to buy some liniment. Alma Bradshaw told me. She should know. She said he was in there buying condoms."

The room got silent. They all looked at one another, as if wondering what Alma passed on about them.

Carol cringed, her face an uncomfortable red. She worried that Alma might be telling the whole town that she bought hemorrhoid cream. Her buttocks tightened. She anxiously changed the subject. "In all the years I've lived here, they never did find a body on the mountain. Oh, some skiers got hurt, but they never died."

Myra wadded her napkin. Her face turned purple. "You're forgettin' about my Christie!" she shrieked. "I've been telling people all these years that we're vunnerable. Vunnerable."

The women's eyes shifted away from Myra, hoping to prevent another long diatribe on the Christie tragedy. It's not that they didn't care. They were all mothers, and they understood how tragic it was to lose a child. Dorothea had lost a son in Vietnam. Helen's son-in-law died of a heart attack at a young age. Harriet lost a grandchild. No group was more caring and supportive than they were when Myra lost Christie. But over the years, Myra had gotten stuck in a rut, and their patience had worn thin.

Dorothea reached over and patted Myra's shoulder. "Carol wasn't living here then, honey. When a child dies, it takes a toll on the family. I know that."

"Now the cops are attacking the people," Myra sputtered. "We have to do something, or none of us is safe."

"What's happened to our small town?" Harriet asked. "It doesn't feel safe anymore. We all might as well move to San Francisco."

Carol nodded. "Why is it taking so long to identify that little boy?"

"Haven't you ever come across a dead deer or a dead possum on the road?" Dorothea asked. "When you find remains, it's not a pretty sight."

"When Blake got that tip of some man struggling with a boy," Myra blurted, "he should have checked into it."

"Calm down, honey. Drink some water," Dorothea said.

"The grandfather hung himself you know," Helen pointed out. "Well, who lets a youngster go wandering off by himself."

Harriet's blue-veined hand flailed the air. "A murder. A suicide. A child molester living over there in the trailer park right under our noses." Her voice rose. "We haven't had such bad news since that boy drowned several years ago. What was his name?" No one could remember.

"Christie! Don't forget my Christie."

"I meant lately, Myra," Harriet said.

Myra slammed her hand down on the table. "Maybe we wouldn't be talking about a body here if that Blake had done the right thing. We need to remember he let that dirty Indian get away."

The women exchanged glances, not sure what to do about Myra.

Carol said, "I guess they're really watching that molester. He don't dare show his face in this town."

"It's just a matter of time before they slap the handcuffs on him," Harriet added. "The FBI has been out there, grilling him. Heard that from Alma, too. Her boy went to school with the Benson child, and he's really upset."

Carol leaned into the table. "That reporter girl is back in town. I seen her on the TV. You can't miss her on the street, all those fancy clothes and that makeup. Maybe we should ask her what's up. Sometimes she eats here at Dottie's."

Dottie came into the room carrying a carafe of decaf. "More coffee, ladies?" She looked at Myra. "Can I bring you something for your hands? Your cuticles look mighty raw."

"He pushed me."

"Who pushed you?" Dottie asked.

"That Deputy Blake. He accosted me."

"Goodness!" Dottie said. Dorothea handed her a goldenrod flyer.

Myra's mind was twenty years away. "I told her. I told her. You know I told her. You be careful of that Indian."

"Take a deep breath, Myra," Dottie said. She squinted and held the flyer at arm's length to read it. "Harrumph!" she muttered after she finished. She set it down and looked at the women like a teacher who just returned to the classroom and caught her pupils shooting spit wads. "I think it's time for dessert." She took her pencil from behind her ear and a pad from her apron. The women knew by the set of her jaw the flyer conversation was over.

Myra gave Dottie her vacant, blue-eyed stare. "You don't happen to have some Nutter Butters, do you?"

Touch the Sky

CHAPTER 22

Winter 1989

Mo never expected Jim to survive the harsh mountain winter of 1989. Not even if he managed to find the two caves Mo camped in during extended absences when, as Happy Face said, he was "out by the Big Bat playing Indian." The caves, located far from the areas the campers and skiers used, had fire pits and some wood, along with food rations, tools, a sleeping bag, blankets, traps, fishing, and hunting gear.

Mo knew he had taught Jim well, but even so, the '89 Blizzard was one of the worst to hit the area. Jim never had to fend for himself in the wilderness. Maybe in the frenzy of escape, he'd injured himself. Maybe his body lay in some dark gully. Maybe—while he pondered Jim's chances of survival, a more tormenting thought crept in: *How could this young man I loved and practically raised have done such a thing?*

Happy Face always took Jim's side. "We don't know about that girl. We don't know what she did to our boy." Her hands clenched into fists. "We just don't know."

Mo waved his arm to silence her. "I warned him. I told him that temper of his would come back to bite him in the ass. When a sheep dog turns mean and starts killing, it's no good, no good."

Happy Face knew the ranchers always shot the dog. "You tease. You dangle meat. What do you expect?" She never used the word *murder*.

"Just a goddamned, hot-headed fool. He should've stayed with his own kind."

Happy Face rubbed her temples. "He was a good boy."

Mo's neck flushed red. He didn't answer. He went out to his place of solace—the backyard shed—and whittled late into the night, his heart aching.

***

The police scoured the mountain wilderness, looking for this killer whose crime had jolted the quiet, sleepy town unaccustomed to violence and ill equipped to handle its outrage. Confusion muddled clear thinking. How could this have happened? All the players were homegrown, and the beautiful victim was the daughter of honest, law-abiding citizens. Church people.

Folks in Forest Lake stuck together, lived close to the earth, worked hard, cared, and prayed. Like thunder shaking a dark sky, an answer emerged: The killer wasn't like them. He was different. That had to be it. Carl, a weathered-faced rancher, said it first. "You never know when a wild animal is gonna turn on you. It's best to let them Indians stay out where they belong. Don't be bringing 'em home."

The people, struggling with their emotions, pounced on Ken Blake. They accused him of letting his Indian friend get away, and they shunned Mo and Happy Face. After receiving death threats, she and Mo stayed away from town, buying supplies in Klamath Falls.

Only Dottie Johnston visited the grieving couple. She knocked on the door of their small house one morning with a basket of warm buttermilk muffins. "I can't say I understand how this all came down," she said shaking her head, her face pale, her eyes red-rimmed with dark circles underneath. "He was always nice to me, and Christie had so much goin' for her." Dottie pulled the carved wooden bird from her pocket and held it out to Happy Face. "Jim gave me this one time. I thought you might like to have it."

Happy Face took it with both hands and pressed it to her wet cheek.

Even though a shaken Ken pleaded with Mo to help search for Jim, he refused. What would he do if they found him? Watch the police shackle him? Maybe even shoot him, if he didn't surrender? And Mo knew Jim wouldn't surrender. No, it was better for him to go back to nature on his own terms, to die on the mountain.

***

Spring 1990

After the heavy winter snows started to melt, Mo took an early spring trek deep into the still, chilly wilderness near the area of his caves—the one place Jim could go. Mo's best hope was to recover Jim's remains and have a private funeral. On a whim, he gave the signal only Jim would know—the sound of a coyote in distress, four short yelps and a high-pitched howl. He paused to listen; then repeated the signal several times.

Nothing.

Still, howling like a wild animal grieving over the loss of its young provided a cathartic release for his bottled-up anguish. "Goodbye!" he screamed. Swallowing tears, he looked toward the heavens and gave one final, loud coyote cry. The wail came from his whole body, echoing his pain through the deep forest and into the primal stillness.

What was that?

His ears perked up. He howled the signal again. Mingled in the wind and a few falling snowflakes came a weak reply. Mo rushed toward the sound, which seemed to come from the direction of the larger cave. There he found Jim, steadying himself against the rocky cave entrance, haggard, feverish, and shivering in the cold.

Like a lost child, Jim's thin arms reached for Mo. They clung to each other, and they both wept.

"Let me die," Jim begged.

"My son," Mo said.

"I deserve to die."

"No. Goddamn you. No." His fished a pack of cigarettes from his pocket, lit one, and took a long pull. He handed it to Jim. Mo's eyes narrowed. "No," he said again. "No, we need to think."

Mo returned with food, first-aid supplies, warm clothes, and camping gear. He nursed Jim back to health, and he eventually helped him move to a different, more secluded cave that was big enough for Jim to stand in.

For Jim, it was enough. Whenever that ugly night by the lake with Christie seeped into his mind, he shuddered in disbelief. He clung to the wilderness for solace, mourning for the person he once was; he had no desire to start a new life elsewhere.

Like a cougar, Mo was solitary, cunning, and always aware of possible danger. He took Jim's clothing, made tears like animal claws would make and scattered pieces of it many miles away from Jim's actual location, so hunters would find them. He even tossed in the aching tooth Jim had extracted earlier and had him cut himself to add blood. Then Mo used his reputation as a seasoned mountaineer to help fuel the idea that Jim Fallingwater died on the frozen shoulders of the Big Bat and that animals had gnawed his bones and scattered his remains in the deep underbrush, making any recovery impossible. Mo never told Happy Face, who liked to talk, that he'd found Jim.

During his spring, summer, and early fall treks to the Big Bat, Mo continually packed in food and other supplies. To avoid suspicion, he stocked up during the winter by shopping in

Medford, Ashland, or Grants Pass, hiding his cache in the backyard shed—a place Happy Face never frequented. Sometimes he drove across the California border. Mo never went directly to the caves. He took his time bobbing and weaving along the paths the animals made. He taught Jim to do the same thing. It took longer, but because the animals had already beaten down trails, using them left no trace of human presence.

Whenever Mo approached the area near Jim's cave, he gave the coyote signal. His heart sang when he heard a reply. Then he'd go to one of his supply caves, move the rocks covering the entrance and wait.

To avoid detection, the always-cautious Mo had Jim come to him and never set foot inside Jim's cave. Jim could tell his location by the signal. Mo made four short yelps for the smaller cave, one mile to the east, and five yelps for the larger one, a mile in the opposite direction. When Jim arrived, they'd hug, eat, and talk for hours. Mo told him about Forest Lake and the world. Sometimes he wrapped his supplies in newspapers, which Jim kept and read.

Besides food, over the years Mo provided Jim with medical supplies, sleeping bags, backpacks, blankets, snow shoes, dark-colored outdoor gear, clothes, wool hats, a can opener, camping utensils, fishing gear, hunting knives, carving knives, candles, soap, toothbrushes, a washtub, flint strikers, waterproof matches, cigarette lighters, lanterns, axes, saws, shovels, hammers, and nails.

Jim stored the rations of flour, cornmeal, rice, and dried beans in metal containers that Mo supplied and used them sparingly. He saved tin cans and reused the metal by cutting off the ends and pounding several flat sheets together to make a reflector that, when placed near the fire, gave off more heat and light. Mo occasionally brought surprises like popcorn, coffee, tea, and Jim's favorite—cigarettes.

Mo also packed in writing materials, a few used handbooks on wilderness survival, plant and bird identification, paperbacks on Native American tribes, and a deck of cards. Jim read the books several times, skipping parts that didn't interest him. He would rather work with his hands, carving or repairing things. Sometimes, though, he would read aloud just to make sure his voice worked.

While Mo was a lifeline and the items he provided not only made life on the mountain easier but also possible, Jim, out of necessity, became an experienced survivalist. Mo taught him bow hunting, using a compound bow complete with pulleys, cables, and a scope sight. He also showed him how to set traps to catch smaller prey.

During the good weather months, Jim fished, hunted fowl and deer, picked berries, and learned how to preserve food by drying it. He cut and stored wood to ensure he had adequate fuel to make it through harsh winters.

The entrance to Jim's cave angled down into the earth about twenty feet. He made a "stairway" of strategically placed rocks to avoid falling. When he first moved in, Mo had helped him build a fire pit near the bottom of the entryway on the left side. He dug two holes into the ground, a larger one for the firewood and smaller one to supply air, causing the fire to burn from the top downward. He lined the bottom of the pit with rock. The unique pit created a hotter fire that required less wood and produced little or no visible smoke. The natural temperature inside the main cave hovered at forty-two degrees. The constant fire provided warmth and helped combat the moisture.

There were two big boulder-size rocks inside the cave. The bigger one made a nice table. Jim sat on the smaller one. On the right side, there was another cave room—essentially a long, narrow lava tube—which Jim used to store wood, tools, and supplies. It actually provided another exit to the outside where he dug a latrine under the shelter of trees and rocks.

During the dark soul of winter, the moist, cellar-like cave was Jim's bunker. He hibernated like a bear and felt like a mole for about six months before venturing out. On those long winter days, Jim did repairs and chopped kindling. At night, he sat by the fire and carved animals and Indian faces out of wood he collected especially for that purpose. He also made several wooden flutes, which he played as flames from the fire danced and cast shadows on the cave wall. He assembled a drum, too, from deer hide and a hollowed-out tree stump, but he favored the flutes.

In the summer, he moved outside and lived a few feet from his cave in a well-hidden shelter made of sticks, leaves, and pine branches. He camped in the fresh air as long as possible. A spring, which flowed in a nearby gully, provided water in the good weather. Socked in during the winter, he melted snow.

Jim had never been much of a writer. Whenever he'd had to write something in school, it had been like nailing jelly to a tree. Alone in the wilderness, though, he started making notes on scraps of paper about the weather, things to repair, or supplies he needed. Soon, his sentences got longer and his notes more detailed. He called his solitary life in the wild the Great Silence. The more he wrote about it, even with short, choppy sentences, the better he felt. It helped him focus, relieved his anxiety, and gave him someone to talk to, even if it was just himself.

CHAPTER 23

The fragrant smell of the big daphne bush wafted through the basement window of the church, filling the room with the hope of spring. Lauren Blake was there with her best friend, Katy Parks, for their monthly youth group meeting. Lauren looked especially pretty that Sunday evening, wearing a red sweater that set off her blond hair and high coloring.

While teenagers fidgeted in rows of gray metal chairs, Pastor Rick Knox, a short, chubby man with frameless glasses and a bald head, gave a brief devotion and ended with a special thank you to the youth group for its successful food drive. "Your good work answered the prayers of many hungry people. We can always count on God to help us when things get tough." He held a Bible close to his chest and looked at the ceiling.

Karen Emery, who moved to Forest Lake from Iowa two years before, played an awkward *Rock of Ages* on her accordion. Pastor Rick's wife, Rachel, announced the dates for the group's annual beach trip and asked for volunteers to help serve at the congregational potluck the following Sunday.

Katy's mother, Janet, and even Myra Jenkins, were among the churchwomen who came to chaperone, announce the games, and help with refreshments. Tonight they set out frosted cupcakes, nuts, an assortment of cheeses and crackers, Rachel Knox's soft, chewy oatmeal cookies, and Myra's red Jell-O, topped with a thick layer of whipped cream.

Janet Parks brought her special punch bowl, the one used at her wedding in this very same church so long ago. "You might as well take it," her husband had said. "It's just been sitting in that box in the garage, collecting dust."

Life in Forest Lake didn't present many opportunities to use a fancy punch bowl with its tiny matching cups. Ever since his mother had died, Jeff Parks had been adamant about using things. "You can't take stuff with you," he said. He reached into the cupboard for Janet's best relish dish and filled it with olives for their Sunday dinner.

Janet took the bowl out of its box, washed and carefully dried it. Now, filled with pink punch, matching ice cubes, and thin slices of lemon floating on top, it gleamed on the table.

Lauren and Katy watched a shuffleboard match between Nadine, a short, pudgy eighth grader, and Donnie Knox, Pastor Rick's son. Donnie, a small wiry boy with an impish grin and his mother's red hair, was in Lauren's class at the high school. He wasn't athletic, but he was well liked, smart, and made up for his lack of brawn by being the class clown. The other boys called him P.K. or The Shrimp. Donnie didn't take much of anything seriously except reading and chess. Most of the jocks and farm boys in Forest Lake couldn't begin to get their minds around chess. But Donnie traveled to Eugene several times a year to play in tournaments, and he always came home with a trophy.

"Robbie is still ignoring me," Lauren complained to Katy as they watched Donnie go down to defeat, roll on the floor, and pretend to be devastated. Tall, dark-haired Robbie hung out on the other side of the room with a group of boys. "I wonder if he's figuring to go on the beach trip."

"Maybe you just need to invite him over," Katy whispered. "Why don't you challenge him to a game of shuffleboard?" Her deep brown, almost black eyes looked at Lauren and then in Robbie's direction as if to nudge her on.

Lauren seriously considered it, but then Donnie's mother announced that they would play Brown Shoe Bingo, a game in which each person is given a bingo card with a list of characteristics such as "has on brown shoes," "has the darkest eyes," "is wearing some shade of green," "has a strange pet." The goal was to find someone else in the group with that quality and write his or her name next to it. The first person to complete the card and shout "Bingo!" would win a special leather bookmark.

Lauren went up to Robbie. "I believe you have the darkest eyes," she lied. She knew Katy's eyes were darker.

His lips tightened into an uneasy grin. "Are you sure? I would have picked your friend, Katy." He looked away.

Lauren's face turned as red as her sweater. "Um, let me see your socks. We're also supposed to find the person with the weirdest socks."

"You picked the wrong guy. You should check out Donnie." He pointed across the room. Someone had already discovered Donnie, who held his pant legs up to reveal red Easter socks covered with silly white bunnies.

"Are you planning to go on the beach trip?" Lauren asked, determined to engage him. "It sounds like it will be a lot of fun." Before Robbie could answer, Mrs. Knox shouted, "Time's up." She awarded the bookmark to Blaine, a small thin girl with acne.

Janet Parks clapped her hands. "Kids, let's eat." She gestured toward the food on a long folding banquet table covered with a white tablecloth.

"I struck out with Robbie," Lauren complained to Katy as they got in line. Her usually pert mouth drooped.

"The night's still young. In the meantime, let's smother your sorrows with a cupcake."

Lauren reached for a paper plate. "Oh, Mrs. Knox brought those delicious oatmeal cookies again."

"I don't need a whole cupcake," Katy said. "Sweet things give me zits. Let's split one."

Lauren laughed. "Which one do you want—chocolate with nuts and chips or the white one with a mound of pink frosting?"

"Let's get the chocolate one," Katy said. She was about to reach for it when the lights went off.

"What going on?" Lauren wondered. "It's pitch black."

"Let's everybody neck," shouted Donnie who stood directly behind them.

"We've apparently blown a fuse," Pastor Rick announced. "Someone plugged the coffee maker into the same outlet as the microwave. I gotta get to the fuse box. Does anybody have a flashlight?"

Myra Jenkins inched her way toward the girls carrying a large white candle, her eyes as cold as blue ice. She stared at Lauren's bright blond curls. "Your hair is so pretty in the candlelight," she said. Lauren instinctively took a step back remembering how Myra had touched her hair before with her bloodied fingers.

"Hey, watch it!" Donnie said to Lauren. "You're standing on my foot."

In the darkness, Myra suddenly lunged forward and shoved the candle toward Lauren's blond hair.

Lauren tossed her paper plate in the air. "Help me!" she screamed. "My hair is on fire!"

"Is this a joke?" Donnie asked.

Katy grabbed the bowl of pink punch and doused Lauren's hair. The heavy bowl slipped from her hands, hit the floor, and cracked into pieces.

Myra was coming at Lauren with the candle again. This time she aimed the flame at her clothes.

"No!" screamed Katy, blocking her. She grabbed at Myra's big body, but Myra pushed her away. Katy crashed into Donnie and they both fell to the floor.

Robbie, a three-year varsity football player, leaped toward the candlelight. He butted Myra in the stomach and tackled her to the floor. Myra's heavy body, tumbling like a pillar, hit the table overturning it. The platter of cupcakes went flying along with the nuts, crackers, cheese, and oatmeal cookies. The bowl of Jell-O slid off, spilling its contents which sat on the floor in a quiet, thick red puddle.

"Get the candle!" someone screamed. It had flown through the air and landed next to a filmy curtain. "Oh, my God!" The gauzy drape burst into flames. Janet Parks came running from the kitchen with the coffee urn and dumped its contents on the drape, dousing the fire.

Several other boys, hearing Robbie struggling to hold Myra down, trampled over cupcakes and cookies and piled on top. A heap of teenaged boys, legs and arms sticking out everywhere buried Myra's large body. "Get off me. Get off me!" she screamed. The church basement smelled like a good party gone wrong.

"Rick! Rick!" Rachel yelled.

Suddenly, the lights came on. Katy sat on the floor holding Lauren, who was crying and moaning. She had burns on the left side of her face. Her hair was wilted and sticky. A piece of sliced lemon stuck to the back of her head.

Pastor Rick, returning from the fuse box in the hallway, saw the overturned table, food splattered all over the floor, a pile of kids on top of Myra, and a group of girls huddled together in a corner crying. "What the . . . Mother of God," he cried.

Janet Parks pointed toward Myra. "She tried to set that child's hair on fire. I called 911."

***

Ken Blake rushed through the door. "What's going on? We got a call that a . . . Oh, no!" He hurried over to Lauren, now cradled by a parent, while another woman nursed her face with a cold, wet cloth.

"Mrs. Jenkins tried to set her hair on fire," Katy screamed. She pointed to the mountain of boys on top of a squirming Myra.

"Daddy," Lauren cried.

"Good God. Call an ambulance," Ken shouted, kneeling beside his daughter. She had a red, festering spot on the left side of her cheek that spread up to her temple and into a patch of frizzy hair.

"It's on its way," Janet Parks said. "I'll stay with Lauren, Ken. You better get those kids off Myra."

Ken rushed over to the mound of humanity on top of Myra. "Okay, everybody off," Ken ordered. One-by-one, the boys rolled off her.

A dazed Myra, her brown-framed glasses broken on the floor, sat up, brushing herself off. "What's wrong with you people?" she screamed. "Why did you attack me?"

Ken grabbed Myra's hands and handcuffed them behind her back.

"What the hell are you doing?" she shouted. "I'm not a criminal. Don't you touch me, you idiot! It was an accident. Those ruffians attacked *me*."

"No, they didn't, Mr. Blake," Katy said. "I saw the whole thing." She pointed at Myra. "You tried to burn Lauren's hair. When that didn't work, you tried to torch her sweater."

"You're hurting me," Myra blubbered. "Get away from me!" A mashed chocolate cupcake stuck to her wide back.

Deputy Don Range arrived at the church just as a fire engine pulled into the parking lot.

"Does she have to go to jail?" asked Pastor Rick. "She obviously needs help."

"We need to book her on assault," Range said. "The judge can decide her mental condition." Ken heaved a sigh and returned to his daughter's side.

"You need to come with me now," Range said to Myra. "Ohhh,"he groaned, noticing a wet spot growing around Myra's backside.

"Help me!" Myra shouted. "Somebody help me." Her heavy legs banged against the floor, like a child having a tantrum.

Pastor Rick knelt down and put his arm around her. "Calm down, Myra. I'm coming with you. Nobody's going to hurt you."

"My Christie," Myra cried. "Why does he get to have his daughter, and I can't have mine?"

"Deputy Blake never harmed Christie," Pastor Rick said.

"We never got justice. We never did. That dirty Indian!"

"Sweetheart," Pastor Rick said, his voice gentle. "We just have to leave it in God's hands. I'm going with you. No one will hurt you. We'll pray to Jesus on the way." He turned toward the door. "Somebody call Floyd!" he shouted. "Please, somebody call Floyd." He looked at Myra. The woman who had done so much for the church was unraveling before his eyes. He had tried so hard to counsel her over the years, only to have it come to this. "Floyd is on his way," he told her. "I just know he's on his way."

Pastor Rick helped Myra up. The wet spot on the back of her dress was even bigger. They walked slowly with Deputy Range to his patrol car.

The ambulance attendants placed Lauren on a stretcher, a piece of white gauze covered the left side of her face. "She's going to be all right," a paramedic assured Ken. "We've given her pain medication. The burns aren't severe, but she'll probably want to get a haircut. She's a lucky girl."

Ken bent over his daughter. "You're still beautiful," he whispered, "even with your sticky hair. Everything is going to be okay, honey." He kissed her forehead above her swollen left eye. "They need to take you to the hospital and check you over, then Mom and I'll come and take you home."

"I'll ride with her, Mr. Blake." Robbie said.

Lauren's eyes widened. Then she smiled.

"Thanks, Robbie. Her mother is on the way. As soon as I wrap things up here, I'll be along." He watched Robbie hold Lauren's hand as they wheeled her out to the waiting ambulance.

Katy stood to one side with a group of friends, watching, biting her index finger. Ken walked over and hugged her. "Thank you. You saved her life."

"She going to be okay?" she asked teary-eyed.

"Yes, thanks to you." He turned to the other girls. "You kids look after Katy, now." He pulled out his logbook and approached Rachel Knox, who waved him aside.

"We can't let these children just go home. Not after all this," she blurted. "Come on, kids, let's gather over here and try to calm down. We'll have the closing prayer."

Donnie retrieved a cupcake from the floor and was about to take a bite. "Don't eat that. God knows what's on it," Janet Parks scolded, standing over the pieces of her shattered punch bowl with a broom and dustpan. Donnie dropped the cupcake.

"Good Lord, Donnie, you're standing in a Jell-O slick."

Karen Emery was playing an even more awkward *Rock of Ages* on her accordion while a grim Rachel Knox flapped her left hand like a robot encouraging the group to sing.

"Go join the others," Janet ordered, "and sing."

"At least no one died in this wreck," Donnie muttered, walking toward the group, his sneakers squeaking, leaving a trail of sticky red footprints on the floor.

CHAPTER 24

The sign above the heavy glass door of Bradshaw's pharmacy simply said **DRUG STORE** in big white letters against a pinkish-red background. Just walking through the entrance of the plain, two-story building and hearing the bell jingle put Cally on edge. She especially wanted to avoid Alma, Artie Bradshaw's mother—a thick woman with large breasts—who never seemed to have enough to do and was always too eager to gossip. People in Forest Lake called her the walking newspaper.

Inside, Cally lurked behind rows of dark, round vitamin bottles lined up like miniature soldiers in flat white helmets. "Hiding out" had almost become second nature. Well-meaning people who touched her arm and said they were sorry for her loss made her stiffen and ache. With all the publicity about Cody, it was hard to be anonymous in Forest Lake, but she was too drained, too exhausted to drive somewhere else to get her prescriptions filled. She picked up a bottle of B vitamins whose soft gels promised energy and immediately set it down.

Cally passed a bin of stuffed animals—chicks and rabbits holding carrots. The candy aisle brimmed with Easter baskets and packages of rainbow-colored candy eggs, chocolate bunnies, marshmallow Peeps, and Reese's peanut butter cups, Cody's favorite. It suddenly dawned on her why people were leaving fluffy bunnies in front of the grade school to honor Cody. She had totally forgotten about Easter. Holidays no longer meant anything. Last year at this time, she would have fixed a basket for her son. That was before—everything she thought about centered on that date—*December 5.* She now divided her life into things and events that happened before Cody disappeared, and things that happened afterward. This morning she started to toss a magazine, looked at the date, and realized she'd read it when he was still at home. She left it on the coffee table. The purse she'd bought when the handle on her old one gave way was an "after" item.

She had come to fill prescriptions for Xanax and something new to help her sleep. The little, pink football-shaped sleeping pills her doctor ordered following her fainting spell hadn't helped. After spending several restless nights staring at the dark ceiling, she jerked the lid off the bottle, dumped the pills into the toilet, and flushed them into the swirling bowels of the house. She'd resisted the urge to crack open the bottle of gin she knew was in the cupboard. She didn't want to become her father, but now she could almost understand why he drank.

She was moving to the rear of the drugstore to drop off her prescriptions when she stopped. Alma Bradshaw, wearing a flowered shirt and brown polyester pants, stood next to an older woman with a cane who complained that the arches she bought for her shoes hurt her feet.

"Folks can't return things they already used," Alma squawked. "Once you've worn orthotics, it's just not sanitary."

"Well, I can't use 'em," the woman snapped. "I'm not made outa money. My feet hurt, and I got a bunion. I can't even wear heels no more, not even to church on Sundays."

"We have some nice foam inserts that might work for you," Alma said.

Cally could see Alma's head with her brown tortoise-shell glasses and short, blond hair, floating above the aisle as she led the woman to another part of the store. The black-and-white linoleum floor creaked beneath their feet. "Did you hear what happened to Myra over at the church?" Alma asked in a serious voice. She didn't wait for an answer. "Wowee," she blurted. Cally tried to listen, but the two women moved away.

Cally dropped her prescriptions into the flat wooden box with a sign that said **PRESCRIPTIONS IN. RING THE BELL, IF YOU NEED TO TALK TO THE PHARMACIST.** It was next to the one labeled **PRESCRIPTIONS OUT. PLEASE PAY AT THE REGISTER.** No wonder Alma had time on her hands.

She decided to hide out in the makeup aisle until her prescriptions were ready. There, she stared at the rows of lipsticks, mascara, and false eyelashes that looked like some kind of insect. Who wears blue eye shadow—especially in Forest Lake? She glanced in the mirror on the cosmetic counter. She no longer bothered with makeup. Dark circles cradled her swollen-and-bloodshot eyes. Her hair was pulled straight back into a ponytail. She looked pale, tense, and years older. Nothing could help this.

She'd talked with the sheriff's office again this morning. They'd asked what Cody had been wearing. How many times did they have to ask her? Her words poured into the receiver, rote, like a memorized poem for school. Why didn't they read their records? Did they just want to hear her talk? Were they toying with her? They told her they would call as soon as they identified the remains, but in a town the size of Forest Lake, who else—

She fingered a display of twenty-four-hour kissable lip stain. That ever-present chill inched up her spine. She didn't feel kissable. How could Pete get interested in someone else at a time like this? She barely had the energy to scrub the toilet, let alone carry her plate to the dishwasher. Sometimes she ached for those warm, cheery pancake mornings. Pete had always made a nice fire and had the coffee ready. He'd sneak up behind her and nuzzle her neck. She had felt so protected—that all seemed long ago. Where was he now? What was he thinking? Did he ever think about her? She knew he still went to the mountain and searched.

She needed toothpaste, but she couldn't decide which one to buy. Pete had always liked the one with fluoride or was it with brightener? Cody had wanted the one with red stripes, something that tasted good, he said. Her precious little boy. He'd even drawn a picture of Santa at the North Pole, brushing his teeth with candy-striped toothpaste. What an imagination. It made no difference now. Pete wasn't there. Cody was gone. Everything was upside down. She had a continual headache, and her body ached. One horrendous December day had turned her home into a cold, empty house, and her life into a nightmare.

The older woman's cane tapped the tile floor and the bell on the door jingled as she went out. No one else, except Alma, was in the store now. She looked at the box of Crest in her hand. What was next for her? Soon the police would announce what everybody already knew. Then what? Decisions—about leaving Forest Lake, finding a job, saying good-bye, getting a divorce. Every time her mind tried to go there, a tremendous wave of fatigue swept over her.

She sensed someone's eyes on her back. Alma, she shuddered, had found her. She turned slowly. There he stood—big, pudgy Artie Bradshaw with his chubby, red cheeks and freckled face.

The bully.

But something was different. That smirky grin that seemed permanently pasted on was upside down. She had always wanted to shake him for tormenting Cody, but today she saw something else in that cheerless face. Fear maybe?

"I was at the assembly at school," he sputtered. "The sheriff was there. He said they found a . . . a body."

His comments caught her off guard. "Yes. We're waiting for—" How exactly did you explain to a child that some eerie men in lab coats were trying to identify pieces of your son?

"I took his hat," Artie blubbered. "Called him stuff. I, I shoved him in the janitor's closet that time. I never meant for anything bad to happen."

"What? You shoved him into a closet?" The bullying had been worse than she'd imagined. "Why, Artie? Why did you do those things?" She tightened her grip on the box of toothpaste. She could feel burning in her stomach. She wanted to slap him.

Artie's face crumpled. "I . . . I don't know," he stammered. His body cringed like a dog expecting a blow.

"He's upset," a booming man's voice said. There stood big Burt Bradshaw, Artie's father. "How ya doin'?" He handed Cally a small white paper bag containing her prescriptions. "Have you . . . uh . . . heard anything? I mean about the bod—"

"No," she interrupted and looked away.

"Artie can't sleep. We're keeping him out of school for a while." He pointed to the bag he just handed her. "You pay at the register."

"I know." So Artie was upset. What did they think it felt like to be her?

"We decided he should stay with us at the drugstore. If there are child killers runnin' loose out there, well, we want our Artie to be safe."

Cally looked at the father and then at Artie—a pampered, chubby boy, standing next to his overfed, bald father, who looked like a giant sausage with a mustache. That wasn't right, either. Artie was a child. A young boy, like Cody. Somebody's son. Alive. Somehow, he had made a connection between his behavior and Cody's disappearance. He seemed scared, sorry even.

The chill returned to her spine. It wasn't just grief. It was guilt, too. Why had she let Cody go that day? Why had she trusted her father to keep an eye on a boy she knew had trouble focusing? Look what guilt had done to her father. Anger, hate, blame. Isn't that what took Pete down and destroyed her marriage?

"Artie," she said, her throat dry, her voice like gravel. "I really appreciate your telling me how you feel about things that happened." Artie burst into tears, his chubby shoulders heaving.

"There. There." His father put his arm around Artie's back. He looked at Cally. "Pastor Rick has been over a couple of times."

Cally moved forward, kneeled down and hugged Artie, his wet face on her shoulder. "Just promise me you won't do that anymore . . . bully . . . tease other children."

Burt Bradshaw cleared his throat "Now looky here. Artie's not to blame—boys will be boys."

"No one's blaming him."

"I'm just sayin'."

Cally lifted Artie's double chin, forcing him to look directly at her. "Promise me." Artie's head went up and down. "I know Cody would not want you to be sad."

"He wouldn't?" He wiped his nose on his sleeve.

"Of course, not."

"The other kids say, I . . . I made him run away." His head dropped to his chest.

Is that what people were saying? Her lips tightened. "Cody *did not* run away," she said firmly. It was an honest response. She never for one minute believed Cody ran off. "Something happened out there. We still don't know what."

"I said a prayer for him at church," Artie sniffed.

Cally squeezed his hand. "That was nice of you. Now, let me see you smile."

Artie managed a grin. She patted his back.

"Thank you," Burt Bradshaw said. "Thank you, Mrs.—"He paused, looked embarrassed and stretched out his plump hand.

"Benson," Cally said, realizing that Burt Bradshaw couldn't even remember her name. "It's Benson." She shook his hand anyway.

CHAPTER 25

The talk at Dottie's was all about Myra's big melt-down, but a late afternoon announcement on Wednesday eclipsed her fall from grace. The Josephine and Klamath County sheriffs' offices held a joint press conference regarding the remains found on the Big Bat.

The press, including Tina Williams, once again gathered in Forest Lake like a flock of returning geese descending on a spring pond. Tina, dressed in a red jacket, her blond hair blowing in the wind, her bright lips serious, gave her report to the TV cameras. She stood on the gravel shoulder of Cooper's Hawk Highway, a shot of the Big Bat in the background.

"The Oregon State Medical Examiner's office has confirmed that the remains found about two miles in from here in a shallow grave are those of seven-year-old Randy Wilkes of Grants Pass. Cause of death: homicide."

A shot of rusty haired, blue-eyed Randy playing with his dog flashed on the screen. He had a splatter of freckles on his nose and a front tooth missing from his grin. He looked like anyone's son, dressed in jeans and a striped T-shirt.

"A group of wilderness survival trainees stumbled on the remains near the Big Bat Mountain," she said as the camera panned a rugged area and cut to file footage of an overhead shot of the police recovery team.

"Randy Wilkes has been missing since November of last year." Tina pushed back the hair a gust of wind blew into her face. "This is the little boy who got off his school bus in a rural area south of Grants Pass, Oregon and disappeared into thin air. He was last seen waving to his friends and walking down the country road toward his home. The place where he went missing is almost four hours away from the area near the Big Bat where the body was found." A map showing the geographical distance appeared on the screen.

"At the press conference, police said trauma to the skull area indicates his death resulted from a gunshot wound to the head. Because the body was not intact, they cannot determine if the boy was molested. The Wilkes family issued a statement thanking all those who helped search for their son, but they declined to be interviewed." The camera cut to a close-up of a sad-looking green farmhouse with the blinds tightly closed. A lonely black-and-white dog on the porch barked. The camera zoomed to a hand-written note pinned on the screen door that said, *Please respect our privacy during this difficult time. Thank you.*

"The body was found close to the area where another little boy, Cody Benson, disappeared around Christmas time. Local police have always maintained that Cody Benson got lost in a snowstorm while looking for a Christmas tree with his grand-father and froze to death."

The camera cut away to scenes of the snowy December rescue efforts and to unflattering and spliced file footage of Ken Blake squinting, "Everything so far has indicated Cody succumbed to the cold. There's no evidence that a child abductor was in the area."

The discolored turquoise-and-white trailer in Ray's Trailer Park filled the screen, followed by a close-up of Len Roster. "State police subsequently learned a registered sex offender lives in the area. At this point, Roster is not a suspect in either case, but is considered a person of interest."

The camera shifted to Tina's interview with a retired forensic psychologist in Portland. "In my opinion," he said, "this latest discovery changes everything. The Wilkes boy goes missing in November and then almost a month later, Cody Benson comes up missing. The fact that Randy's body was found close to the area where Cody disappeared suggests to me there's a child killer on the loose."

Back on the edge of the mountain, the wind rippled Tina's clothing. She looked straight at the camera. "Tina Williams reporting live from Forest Lake, Oregon."

Detectives from the Josephine County Sheriff's Office grilled Len Roster but left tight-lipped, saying only that Roster was not, at this point, a suspect in the Randy Wilkes case. Almost everyone else in town had already condemned him. Things got so bad Roster's father again stepped forward to bankroll a lawyer.

***

While most people in Forest Lake expressed concern about Lauren Blake, Ken knew some of the influential old-timers blamed him for Myra's condition. Several of Myra's church friends had asked the Blakes to drop charges against Myra, but they refused.

"They're not going to sweep this one under the rug," Lydia said. "I know Myra needs help, but she attacked our child and could have disfigured her for life. Lauren will never feel safe if that woman is out running loose on the streets."

"Hell," Ken agreed, "she could've killed her."

Nevertheless, Velma Wright, a tall, upright woman from the church with a long face, square jaw, and short, stiff gray hair that looked like a Brillo pad, called on Lydia. She carefully carried her famous lemon-coconut cake topped with creamy, white frosting sprinkled with shredded coconut. Her recipe was a well-guarded secret, and the cake always won blue ribbons at the fair. If Velma presented someone with one of her cakes, it was equivalent to receiving the crown jewel. Once, when the church wasn't available for her quilt show, she asked the principal to let her use the high school cafeteria. He'd repeatedly refused to open the school until she personally called on him armed with her special cake. Once he saw it, he caved like a stack of cards. People said Velma's cakes could stop an earthquake.

Velma proudly placed her precious concoction on the center of Lydia's kitchen table and eagerly accepted her offer of coffee. After stirring in cream and sugar, inquiring about Lauren, and exchanging a few pleasantries, she confidently turned the conversation to Myra. "She's had a lot of grief in her life with her own daughter and all. Still, she's managed to do a lot for the church and the school. So has Floyd."

Lydia felt her body stiffen.

"In Forest Lake," Velma said, "Myra is an institution." She paused, cleared her throat, and looked right at Lydia. "If you forgive others, our heavenly father will also forgive you."

Lydia smiled and sipped her coffee. She took a deep breath, set down her cup, and crossed her arms. "Listen, before forgiveness comes accountability," she said as if scolding one of her sixth-grade students, "not to mention common sense. This woman was about to set fire to a child. Who does that?"

"Of course, it was an accident," Velma insisted. "She tripped. She didn't mean —"

"There are plenty of witnesses that say otherwise." Lydia looked straight into Velma's startled face. She pushed back her chair. "I certainly don't hate Myra. Myra is sick in the head. I get that. She needs help, and a court session with a judge will ensure that she gets it." She stood up and straightened her blouse, indicating their visit was over.

Velma hastily checked her watch and claimed she was late for some meeting. Lydia handed her the cake. Velma looked like she just swallowed a gold fish whole, and it was still gasping for air in her throat. No one had ever pushed aside her prized cake. "Oh, you can keep it," she sputtered.

"No, thank you. My daughter has nightmares," Lydia said. "She wakes up screaming, thinking the house is on fire. Cake is not going to fix that."

"You did the right thing," Ken said when he heard the story. "I'm proud of you." But just thinking about that luscious coconut covered cake made his mouth water. His eyes turned mischievous. "But gee, I would have kept that cake." He smacked his lips.

Lydia playfully swatted him on the head. "It may have been laced with poison. Do I look like Snow White?"

***

"Sorry to hear about your daughter," said Sergeant Walt Richards. He, Ken, and Detective Frank Lane huddled in gloomy Conference Room B to discuss the latest developments. The acidy cafeteria coffee they sipped matched the mood in the room. Richards had not brought doughnut holes, a sign he was especially serious.

"Lauren will probably have some scarring near the hairline," Ken said. "She's a lucky girl. Fortunately, she had a fast-thinking friend. We've taken her out of school, and she's working with a counselor."

"I guess that older lady just lost it, huh?" asked Lane.

"Myra's been transferred to a mental health facility in Klamath Falls until her trial date," Ken explained. "Floyd and Pastor Rick visit her regularly. I guess Dottie's been over there. This is someone who's done a lot for the community but just couldn't get over the death of her daughter."

"As you recall," Richards said, his face level, looking at Ken, "Mrs. Jenkins' daughter was *murdered*. Her killer never had to face the music, thanks to you."

Ken ran his hand across his forehead. "There was evidence that he froze to—"

"Nothin' that would give the poor woman closure."

Why did Richards always have to be a butt? It was a cheap shot considering what happened to Lauren.

Lane took a sip from his Styrofoam cup. "God bless Dottie. She's got a heart of gold. And, her coffee is a hell of a lot better. God, this stuff tastes like tobacco juice. If I didn't already have a wife, I'd marry her."

Ken was grateful to Lane for changing the subject. "Dottie's got a few years on you," he said, happy to avoid Richards's sour face.

Lane chuckled. "I'd marry her anyway. She'd take care of me for the rest of my life."

Richards, like a shark smelling blood was not about to back off. "Yeah, and now with the Wilkes homicide, the Bensons' lawyer is all over us like white on rice. And I heard the Wilkes family thinks that witness report of a man struggling with a little boy could've been the someone who snagged Randy." He swallowed some coffee and grimaced. "If this job doesn't kill me, this damn coffee will. That's the thing about a good doughnut. It covers the taste of rotten coffee."

Lane gave Richards a half smile and shook his head. "One dead child, another missing, a suicide, and an assault—this must be the year from hell for Forest Lake."

Ken nodded. "A lot of the folks are boiling over. They want the trailer park shut down. Some of the business people are worried that folks aren't going to bring their families to the lake this summer. Deputy Range is spending his time patrolling around the schools. We may need more backup."

Richards wasn't listening. Instead, he opened his large file folder and flipped through pages. "The polygraph we gave Roster about the Benson case was inconclusive. He appeared to be telling the truth when he said he didn't know the Benson kid, but muddy when asked about his whereabouts. His lawyer won't let him take another one."

"How did he do with the Wilkes kid?" Ken asked.

"He wasn't asked about that case during the test."

"He wasn't?" Ken was incredulous. "Why wasn't he?"

"At that time, Blake, we didn't think the two cases were related." Richards looked down, indicating he knew that was sloppy work.

It felt good to have his boss on the defensive. Ken happily skewered Richards like a juicy steak on the barbeque grill. "Well, it just makes sense. Two kids go missing in Southern Oregon; you'd think Roster would have been asked about that."

Lane seemed amused. He gave Richards a sideways glance. Richards's face reddened. His chubby fingers tilted his coffee cup.

"We're about to organize a search team to look for Cody's remains," Ken continued. "If we can find him, it may be the piece that finishes the puzzle."

"Does Roster have an alibi in the Wilkes case?" Lane looked at Richards. "Did anybody ask him?"

Richards bristled. His hand rubbed the side of his nose. "Detectives from Josephine County and the FBI have been all over his ass on that. According to all accounts, his father claims Roster was working with him doing carpentry work on that day. He says there was no reason his son needed to be in the Grants Pass area."

"Doesn't mean he wasn't," said Ken.

Lane tapped his fingers on the table. "Hmm, if what the old man says is true, then who killed Randy Wilkes, and what was this person doing up at the Big Bat?"

Richards's bushy eyebrows knitted together. "I'd say it's someone familiar with the area. Very familiar."

***

Ed Beeler, the owner of Ray's Trailer Park, roared into town again, this time on his big black Harley. Someone had defaced the new trailer park sign with black spray paint. It made him so angry that he gave Len Roster and his girlfriend thirty days' notice. "Just get the hell out," he sneered.

Roster's right eye twitched out of control. He pleaded for more time. He didn't have a job. Once Hansen Inc., the development firm, learned about his background, it withdrew the job offer. For Roster, it meant going back to Chemult and moving in with his father, who wouldn't allow the girlfriend in the house. With all the publicity, Roster's handyman and farm-laborer jobs had dried up.

There was other vandalism at the trailer park. Someone tampered with the sewer hookups, causing a major stink. Beeler got a stiff warning from the health department, and it cost several thousand dollars to repair. His home address and telephone number mysteriously appeared on the community bulletin board. Shortly afterward, he received death threats. So did Len Roster.

Beeler was fed up. Breathing fire, he stomped into Dottie's Café at the height of the lunch hour, wearing black leather boots and faded jeans that almost slid off his slim rear end. His muscular arms jutted out of a sleeveless gray sweatshirt. A tattoo of a skull and bones graced his right bicep; on his left, a squirrel on a motorcycle, smoking a cigarette. He stood in front of the counter with his legs spread apart and his arms crossed.

"I got something to say, and I figure this is the best way to get it out. I gave that bastard, Roster, notice," his loud voice boomed. Coffee mugs returned to tables, forks quit clinking against dishes. "Now I gotta bike shop to run over in Medford, so I don't wanna hear nothing from any of you no more. You send me death threats, ruin my property, or deface my sign again, I'm gonna come lookin' for you. When I find you, I'm gonna cram the damn sign up your ass." He stomped out of the café, cranked up his big Harley, and roared out of town.

Jean Rover

CHAPTER 26

December 2009

The fierce wind blew snow in every direction. The screeching
sounds of the blizzard frightened Cody. The dim cave smelled
earthy, like soft mud, making him think of the dark, moist
basement at Brittany's house. He huddled in his jacket close to
the fire and sipped warm broth, his big eyes searching the
man's face every time a blast of wind howled. At first, the tall
stranger with the black, wild-looking eyes seemed as scary as
the weather. His brown face had deep lines starting at the eyes and
continuing down the unkempt stubble on his high cheekbones.
Except for his big feet and long hair, the man dressed like the
ranchers Cody'd seen in town.

"Where are we, Ben?" he finally asked, convinced Jim was
Benny's dad.

"We're here, kid." He took a long drag off his cigarette.

"Where's here?"

"Out in the wild."

"By the mountain?"

"Yeah."

"Oh."

The continual darkness in the cave made it hard for Cody
to tell when it was nighttime, except that's when Ben made the

main meal. The food tasted funny, not like anything he'd had at home, but he was hungry. He knew from the movies he'd seen that Indians hunted buffalo and other wild things, that they cooked over fires in front of teepees. He didn't think they lived in caves.

After they ate, they sat around the fire while the strange man smoked cigarettes and whittled. Sometimes he played soothing melodies on a wooden stick.

***

Jim played his flute until the kid, as he called Cody, got tired and crawled into the sleeping bag. He liked to watch him sleep by the firelight. How delicate he was with his small, white body and those big chocolate eyes, like two mint patties dominating his thin face. Jim couldn't remember being that small. When he was younger, he'd dreamed of having a son. He hadn't dreamed about anything for a long, long time.

Jim and Wolf slept next to the boy to keep him warm and calm. Sometimes his little hand came out from under the heavy blankets and reached. The delicate, uncertain fingers grasped Jim's sleeve and hung on until deep sleep released them.

Days passed, and then weeks. The boy shadowed Jim as he did chores, just like Wolf had as a puppy. He seemed to understand that the mountain weather was treacherous and that they'd have to stay inside for a long time, but he fretted whenever Jim left the cave with a bucket to dispose of their waste in the latrine outside or took a pan to gather snow for water.

"What if a big, mean bear gets in here?" His lower lip trembled.

Jim pulled on his heavy parka and rain chaps. "He won't. The bears are all asleep."

Cody's uneasy eyes looked down at the ground, as if he feared Jim planned to abandon him. "I want to go home." He looked like he might cry.

"Listen, kid, Wolf'll stay with you. Stay close to him until I get back," Jim cautioned. "I won't be long. You're gonna be okay."

Except for the few visits with Mo, Jim led a life of silence. He only talked to Wolf or himself. He wasn't used to the kid's constant chatter and insatiable curiosity.

"My mom and dad are probably mad."

"I don't think so."

"I bet they are."

"You're safe here."

"Miss Brackston is going to pull my ears."

"Who's Miss Brackston?"

"My teacher. She eats nails." Cody made a face.

Jim chuckled. "I'll write a note for you, kid."

Jim regularly stoked the fire, and he added more wood from the ready supply he kept covered under a tarp in the side cave. He let the boy help carry the kindling he'd chopped into the main cave and stack it next to the fire to keep it dry.

"Never let the fire go out," Jim warned.

Cody's big eyes watched Jim carve Indian faces by the fire at night. "How can you carve faces you never saw, Ben?" He picked up the shavings, tossed them into the warm fire, and watched them burn.

"It's all upstairs," Jim said, pointing to his head.

He let Cody play with some of his smaller carvings—the coyotes, the bears, and the rabbits. Cody made up stories about their lives in the forest and had them talking to one another. Jim listened to his prattle, amused. The kid had quite an imagination.

Cody looked up from his play. "Did you have a tribe?"

"Modoc."

"I never heard of them."

"Most folks haven't."

"I'd be an Apache," Cody said, holding up a small bear.

"Why?"

"They lived in teepees and had horses."

"You don't get to choose your family, kid."

"Where are they?"

"Who?"

"Your tribe."

"They're out there. All around us . . . in spirit."

Cody glanced at the cave entrance. "Will they hurt us?"

"No."

"Why do you live in a cave?"

"The rent's cheap." Jim continued carving.

Jim could see that Wolf captivated Cody, and the dog basked in the extra attention. The boy liked to feed Wolf by hand, watching the morsels of food disappear behind the sloppy pink tongue and big teeth. He never tired of tossing a twig in the cave, and he squealed and clapped his hands when Wolf brought it back to him. He found an old towel, and the two played tug-of-war. Sometimes, Wolf jerked the towel away and ran around the cave. When Cody caught up with him, Wolf licked his face and nibbled at his ears.

"I wanted a dog, but Dad wouldn't let me," he said, his big brown eyes sad. He threw his arms around Wolf's neck. The dog seemed to comfort him.

He told Jim he'd gone with his grandfather to get a Christmas tree. "Then I went back to get candy, but I woke up here. Grandpa is mad at me. Artie Bradshaw picks on me. He said I play with girls."

"Do you?"

"Just Brittany. She's my best friend."

"I see." He didn't really. As a child, Jim had never played with girls. Ken Blake had been his only friend.

"Artie stole my hat. One time he threw rocks at me. So I kicked him."

Jim couldn't picture the kid in a fight with some young thug. Not this boy. He didn't look like the husky farm boys he grew up with. Jim was big. He could always hold his own and more. Boys who fought with him usually regretted it. The only way they could get even was by name-calling behind his back.

"The teacher called my mom."

"Look kid, there's no Artie out here and if there was, I'd take care of him." He lit another cigarette.

As a boy, Jim had faced his share of abusive treatment, but he always felt it had more to do with the color of his skin and being poor. Having an alcoholic father pounding on him hadn't helped, either.

He remembered the baseball game in Red Carson's pasture. Red, freckle-faced with orange hair, thought it was funny to pitch a rotten egg when it was Jim's turn at bat. After the stinking egg splattered down Jim's T-shirt, Red rolled on the ground laughing. He didn't think it was so funny when Jim got a hold of him and dragged him not once, but twice through a couple of fresh cow pies. Red ran howling to his house. Then Mrs. Carson came out as mad as hell, swinging her broom. "You savage," she yelled, chasing him down the road. Apparently, Red got cow shit all over her clean bathroom.

Cody was getting restless. "Can Wolf and I go outside?" he asked several times.

"It's too risky, kid."

"Even for a little while?"

"There's tons of snow blowing around out there."

"Is it Christmas yet?"

Jim hadn't even thought about Christmas. Out in the wild, one day just melted into another. Christmas had never been much at his house. His father had usually been drunk. There hadn't been any money for presents or special food. His mother just lit a candle, sewed him a new shirt, and called it good.

"I need to get home for Christmas."

"Not gonna happen."

Cody's shoulders drooped. "You can't ride a bike in a cave anyway."

"What?"

"A bike. I wanted a bike for Christmas."

The wind howled outside. Cody's big, sad eyes touched a spot in Jim's heart. That night he made a stew out of dried venison and beans. Later, as a treat, he popped popcorn in his black skillet over the fire. Thanks to Mo.

Cody laughed as the popcorn lifted the lid off the pan. He'd never seen popcorn made that way. "We have an electric popcorn maker."

"There are no outlets in a cave, kid."

"Where do you get popcorn out here?"

"From a popcorn tree."

Cody gave him a skeptical look. "Corn grows on stalks."

"Sometimes I go shopping." Jim chuckled. This kid is smart.

"Is there a store nearby?"

"No. I walk lotsa miles when the weather is good."

"Why don't you have a horse?"

"No place to keep 'em."

"There's a store on the way to the lake," Cody said. "You could go there."

"Good ol' Amos Hadley." Jim's eyes sparkled.

"Do you know Mr. Hadley?"

"I'm one of his *best* customers." He smirked and quickly changed the subject. "Listen, do you wanna hear a story?"

"I guess."

Jim brought out the big drum he'd made and struck it several times. "My people believe the drum beat is Mother Earth's heart," he said. He took the striker, a firm stick whose end he'd covered with hide, and placed it in Cody's small hand.

He showed Cody how to strike a single beat, as he made enchanting sounds of nature flow from the flute.

"Play another one, Ben!" Cody begged. He loved beating the drum. Sometimes he threw in extra beats and giggled when Jim gave him a sideways look.

"I'll bet Artie can't play a drum. I'll bet he never lived in a cave, either." He gave Wolf a proud hug. "Can I keep Wolf?"

"He's ours, kid."

Cody leaned his head against Wolf's furry, warm body. Jim told him the story of the drum.

"A long, long time ago when the Creator was making the earth . . . you heard of him?"

"God."

Okay. God. You know him, right?"

"He lives in our church."

"Well, the Creator had just finished makin' the sky, rivers, mountains, and just about everything else when he heard a loud noise. He listened carefully. Then he made the oceans, deep lakes, and all the animals. Finally, he got down to folks. When he finished, there was that loud noise again." Jim struck the drum hard. Cody jumped. Wolf barked. "Well, the noise got louder, see, until it was right in front of the Creator's face. Ka-boom! Just like that." He struck the drum again. "Well, the Creator about shi . . . uh . . . jumped outa his boots."

Cody clapped his hands. "God doesn't wear boots. Well, maybe you can't see them because he wears a long robe."

Jim grinned. He deepened his voice. "'Who are you?'" asked the Creator. The pitch of Jim's voice got higher. "'I am the spirit of the drum.'" He struck the drum several more times. "'I am the heartbeat of Mother Earth, here to accompany the singing of all peoples who sing from their hearts.' From that day on, the drum accompanied singing everywhere."

Cody smiled. "Drums can't talk."

"Sure they can. You have to listen close. Now you sing. Sing from your heart." Jim played *Jingle Bells* on his wooden flute. Cody's face brightened. The boy sang softly as his small arm pounded out the beat on the drum. "No, no," Jim interrupted. "Sing louder, so the Creator can hear." The little boy took a breath and raised his voice to sing the words again. "Good. Good. That time I could hear your heart."

"Play it again, Ben." Cody laughed. Jim played another round with Cody belting out the words and beating on the drum.

"Tell me another story, Ben," Cody begged, but Jim could see the kid's eyes starting to droop.

"In a minute," Jim said. He picked up the drum and its striker and put it away. When he returned with more wood for the fire, he found Cody had fallen asleep against Wolf's side.

Jim carried the boy to the sleeping bag and tucked him in. He wrapped the heavy blankets around him. He wasn't all that sure, tomorrow could actually be Christmas. Even it wasn't, it was close enough for the kid. Christmas for Christ's sake. What did he have to give a kid? Then he remembered his flutes. He had carved several over the years, sitting near the fire in the stillness of long winter nights. He picked out an earlier one. He had learned much since he carved that small one, but it was good enough for the kid. The kid would like it.

The wind whistled and blew thick snow, bending trees in the forest and crashing limbs to the ground while the middle-aged, half-wild man and a tender sprout of a boy had made music by the firelight.

Miles away a distraught father in a cold living room stared out of a black window. The gusting wind whined in the darkness blending with a mother's sobs, as she lay awake in her bedroom, watching the stark branches tap the window. Down the hall, a shiny, new bike stood. Alone.

***

The next morning, Jim reheated the venison stew and made cornbread over the fire in his iron skillet.

"At home we have pancakes," Cody said. "And peanut butter." He mentioned peanut butter several times.

After they ate, Jim gave him the flute. Cody loved the haunting sounds he could make. He laughed at the way Wolf perked his ears when he blew into it. Jim spent much of the day teaching him how to move his fingers over the holes. "Don't play notes," he said. "Play emotions." Cody learned quickly. That night sitting by the fire, they made music together.

"Can I take my flute to bed with me?"

"Sure, kid."

While Cody settled into his sleeping bag, Jim promised another story. One that Mo had told him when he was a boy.

"Many, many years ago, there was this young brave, see. He was about your age. Well, the brave was out playing in the woods." Jim looked at Cody to see whether he was paying attention.

Cody giggled. "I'm a brave, too, aren't I, Ben?"

"Sure kid. See, the brave was supposed to be diggin' roots, but instead he fooled around. Soon he tired out, fell asleep under a tree. A big red-and-black woodpecker with a long beak flew in. He was huntin' for some tasty bugs to eat, so he hammered holes in a hollow tree branch. *Tatta tat tat. Tatta tat tat.* How could the young brave sleep with that silly bird making all that racket? *Tatta tatta tat. Tatta ratta boom peck peck tat.*"

Cody laughed when Jim made the bird sounds. "You're a funny bird."

"Aw, come on. I do a good bird."

Cody held his small hand over his mouth. Giggles escaped through his fingers. "No you don't."

"Anyway, the young brave tossed a rock, shooing the bird. *Ka-pow.*"

"Did he hurt the bird?"

"Naw, birds are smarter than people. So, it was getting' cold, see. A strong wind blew through the tree. When it gusted through the hollow branch, it made wonderful sounds. Like this." Jim lifted the flute to his lips, making wind-like music. "Soon the brave fell fast asleep. When he got up the next morning, he cut the hollow branch and blew into it." Jim's flute warbled like a bird. "The singing branch made beautiful music, so the brave took it home. At first, his ma was pissed because he didn't bring any roots."

"Pissed," Cody repeated and giggled. He couldn't say bad words at home. "She was pissed."

"Really pissed. So when his ol' lady heard that music, it made her happy. Soon, everyone was happy. And, that's how the flute came to be. Well, that's what people say."

Jim glanced at Cody. The boy's eyes fluttered, then closed tightly, his little chest rising and falling. The small hand still clasped his wooden flute. His own little brave had fallen asleep. "Merry Christmas, kid," he said to the sleeping boy. He couldn't remember the last time he'd uttered those words.

CHAPTER 27

January 2010

Weeks in the damp cave took a toll on Cody. He hardly touched the bland, dried venison and fish that made up most of their meals. Finally, he pushed it away. "I don't want it," he said. "My stomach hurts." The following morning, his face flushed, his throat burned, and his nose started to drip. For the next few days, he coughed incessantly and hardly kept anything down. Jim moved him close to the fire and treated his fever with a wet cloth. He sat with him throughout the night, insisting Cody drink warm water to stay hydrated. He made a tea for him out of dried berries to which he added a crushed aspirin, the only medication he had. He hoped it was the right thing.

He worried that the kid had lost too much weight. When he started to improve, Jim fed him from his supply of canned goods, rationing the food as best he could, but the stash steadily dwindled. Mo had brought in some extra supplies in the late fall, but Jim hadn't planned to tap them until spring. The unpredictable weather made it risky, but over the last two days, it had settled a bit. If he were to make a trek to the supply cave, he needed to do it now.

"Don't leave me," Cody cried when Jim told him he planned to go shopping.

"Look, kid, Wolf will stay here with you. Keep the fire going." He showed Cody how to drop pieces of wood into the fire pit. He went over it several times and moved a stack of chopped wood nearby. "That's all there is to it. Okay?"

"I want to go."

"It's too dangerous, kid. You still have a cough. You don't want a setback."

Jim bundled up in the heavy winter coat he'd "borrowed" from Hadley's Lake Store, pulled on his rain gear, and slung a large backpack over his shoulders. He tied the small shovel onto his waist. When he reached for his hunting bow, Cody jumped to his feet.

"Why are you taking that?"

"Just in case."

"You meet a robber?"

"Might be a chance for some fresh meat. You never know what's out there."

"Are you coming back?" Cody's large eyes looked like two frightened, dark saucers.

"Sure, kid."

"You promise?" Cody threw his arms around Jim's waist and hung on. It surprised him. He patted the kid's skinny shoulders, pried his hands loose, and squatted so he could peer into his peaked face.

"I'll be back before dinnertime. I'm just gonna shop for a few things. There's extra food in the skillet. You can heat stuff over the fire when you're hungry. Whatever you do, stay put. Don't let the fire go out. Stay with Wolf until I return."

***

Navigating the big icy drifts was slow and tough. Sometimes his feet sunk a foot down into cold snow. Once he dropped into a bank up to his hips but extricated himself. It took several hours to slog to the far supply cave, which was hard to find in the white terrain. After he spotted the familiar crooked tree with the gnarled bark, he took a deep breath. Ten more feet to the right, and he'd be there. He counted each step aloud. When he approached the location of the cave entrance, he used the shovel to dig down through the snow and wrestled with the rocks blocking the narrow opening. He pushed his way inside and collapsed on the floor, sweaty and wet. His throat burned from breathing frigid air. He rubbed his eyes and blinked continually until they adjusted to the darkness. The cave ceiling was low, so he pawed the floor until he found Mo's old lantern. He groped for the matches in his pocket, lit the lantern, and held it up. Things inside hadn't been disturbed. He rested on the old, musty blanket Mo used on visits, wiped his hands on his wet pants, and slowly ate pieces of dried venison and a biscuit he carried with him. He swallowed carefully, wishing he had something warm to drink.

The lantern cast shadowy shapes on the cave walls. Sometimes he felt like a damn mole going from one dark hole to the next. If someone had told him years ago that his life would turn out this way, he would've killed himself. When he was young, he yearned for a real home. It didn't need to be fancy or in a great location, just a comfortable house with a bunch of folks who'd be happy to see him. In his upside-down world, he no longer desired to be around people. They usually made him mad, and he couldn't trust himself when they did that.

His life had always been remote. It was out there, all right, but it wouldn't let him in, like those little water globes they had in the Mercantile around Christmas time. A happy scene inside a glass bubble accompanied by music, but you couldn't touch it. Not really. Now he had to worry about the kid. Keeping him had been a mistake, a big one that probably wasn't going to end well. His tired body wanted to linger, but he needed to work fast.

He scooped up cans of soup, tuna, chicken, corned beef and peaches. Mo had also packed in a couple of small cans of coffee, a few bars of soap, and some razor blades. God bless Mo. He checked a metal container and found a five-pound bag of rice secured in several plastic freezer bags. They'd have to be super careful with the canned food. He had enough dried venison, fish, and berries to hold them until a break in the weather would let him hunt and set his traps.

His heart sank when he poked his head out of the cave. The cement-colored sky spit icy sleet. He thought about waiting it out, but realized that was too risky. If he stayed holed up in his sheltered cocoon, he'd have to spend the night. The weather might be worse in the morning. Wolf'd be okay. He'd fed him good before he left, and he was trained to relieve himself in the place Jim had prepared in the far end of the side cave. But the kid was another story. The kid would probably panic, and God knows what then. He pushed the rocks back over the cave entrance and shoveled snow over them.

His full backpack weighed him down, making the trip back slow and strenuous. He pulled the hood of his jacket over his wool hat and covered his face with his muffler. *Speed up*, he coached himself. *Keep going. Walk. Walk. Walk.* The sleet morphed into thick flakes; the wind drove into him, gusted, stirred up fallen snow, and blew it into his face. He walked with his eyes nearly blinded.

His breath came hard and fast. Getting out in this stuff for a few cans of food seemed foolhardy. He wasn't getting any younger. Don't panic, he told himself. *Think.* It seemed like he'd been walking for hours. He fought off the idea to stop and rest. *Keep going.* He stumbled down a small ravine and stopped to get his bearings. Shivers shook his body. Had he been walking in a circle? He brushed the crusted snow off his clothing and wrapped the blanket he carried over his head and backpack. He was glad he'd thought to bring it. Stop again, and he'd freeze to death.

He lumbered on for some time, but when the sky darkened, he knew he'd have to hole up. Somewhere. He could hardly see as it was. It would be insane to keep going once it got dark. Then his shoulder hit something. His numb hands felt it and his mind remembered—a boulder like the one near his cave entrance. Was it real or was his mind tricking him? He touched it again. No, he was right. He was closer that he thought. When the whirling snow thinned, he could see a familiar shadow in the distance— the rock ledge around the opening to the cave. He thought he heard Wolf bark. Had the dog detected him? That was barking wasn't it? That had to be coming from the cave. A pang of fear welled in his gut. "Kid! Are you okay?" he called, but the wind and snow muffled his rusted voice.

In a final burst of energy, he scrambled forward, finally reaching the cave entrance. It instantly felt warmer. He staggered down the rocky steps. The cave seemed dimmer, but then he was tired, cold, and his eyelids were red and swollen. Wolf rushed to greet him, licking the snow from his gloved hands, his tail wagging. Jim pulled off the snow-crusted blanket from his shoulders and tossed it down.

"Ben!" Cody cried. "You're back."

Jim blinked several times while his eyes adjusted. He could see the reason the cave appeared dim. The kid had let the fire burn down to a low flame. He saw why. Cody had taken his journal, ripped out some pages and had been so absorbed with drawing that he forgot about adding wood. Jim dropped his backpack of supplies and pushed Cody aside.

"What the hell are you doing?" he yelled, his throat still raw from breathing cold air. "Didn't I tell you to keep the fire going?"

Cody hung his head. "I put some wood on it," he said.

"Look at you, you're shivering. Who said you could take my things?" Jim shouted. Cody's face turned white. His lip trembled.

Jim pulled off his stiff gloves and hurriedly got some dry kindling, stoked the embers, and tossed on more wood.

Cody retreated to the sleeping bag, sat down, and whimpered, his little shoulders shaking with each sob. Wolf plopped down beside him, licking tears from his face.

The low flames hungrily devoured the new kindling, bursting into a robust fire. At least Jim didn't have to start it from scratch. He took some water from the bucket and heated it in an open kettle. When the water started to boil, he threw in coffee grounds—his reward for bracing the elements. He poured two cups.

"Here," he said to Cody, handing him a cup. "Drink this. It'll warm you up."

"I want to go home," Cody sniffed. "I don't like it here." He took a sip of the bitter coffee and spat. He wiped his wet face on his sleeve. His shoulders slumped. Wolf whined and nudged Cody's arm.

Jim said nothing. The hot coffee burned his sore throat but sent waves of warmth through his bones. He opened a can of vegetable soup and heated it over the fire. There were still some biscuits left from the day before.

"Get over here by the fire before you freeze to death," Jim ordered. Cody obeyed but crouched there, his head bent like a turtle about to retract into its shell. Wolf followed him.

Jim filled his own empty coffee cup with soup. "Here, I'll trade you," he said, taking Cody's untouched cup.

Jim gave Wolf a hefty serving of dried venison, which he gobbled fast. He followed that up with a fresh bone from the stash he kept in the cold side cave.

He and the boy ate silently. Wolf, oblivious to the tension, plopped down by Cody and happily gnawed.

As soon as the warm coffee and soup soothed Jim's nerves, he could think. A sad boy with a dog. He relived those awful moments with his angry, crazed ol' man and instantly felt guilty. What was the big deal? He made it back without a scratch; the kid and Wolf were okay. There was no harm done. Jim picked up his notebook and the loose pages. He looked at the sketches Cody had drawn. He knew that was what really sparked his anger. The drawings were excellent. There were several sketches of his mother, Wolf, things in the cave, and oh, Jesus God, a fairly good rendering of himself, right down to the jagged white scar on his forehead, the souvenir from his father's beating. The kid could not only talk about where he'd been but also draw pictures for cops like Blake.

He sucked in a deep breath. "Look, kid. Out here it's hard to come by things. We need to hang onto everything we got."

Cody's shoulders drooped, his face sullen. He slowly dunked a biscuit in his soup.

"Out here, we don't know how long it will be before we have a chance to get more stuff. Understand?"

Cody nodded. "Uh-huh."

"We don't. We really don't. Always ask before you take somethin'. I'm not mad at you, kid. I'm just wore out. I just want us to survive. Understand?"

"I make everybody mad. I don't know why."

"I used to make people mad, too."

"You did?"

"Some of 'em are still mad at me."

"Why?"

"You're not bad, kid. You're just a young brave with a lot to learn."

"Am I still a brave?"

"Sure. Yeah. You made a mistake, but you gotta keep trying. Otherwise, the wild will swallow you up, and it won't be pretty."

"I'm sorry, Ben." He got up and buried his face on Jim's shoulder and cried.

Jim patted Cody's bony shoulders. It felt awkward. He was not used to being touched. His voice cracked. "Sometimes braves trip up, stumble around, but they're still braves as long as they get up and keep tryin'." What the hell did he know about taking care of a kid anyway? He should not have brought him here. But what was he supposed to do, let him die? "I didn't mean to yell. I'm just tired and cold. I want you to keep drawing, kid. Don't ever stop. Okay?"

"Okay."

"Life out here is treacherous, so you have to listen to me. Listen to everything I say, okay?"

"Yeah."

He tore some pages from the back of his notebook and handed them to Cody. He ripped off the label from the empty soup can. "Here you can draw on the back of this, too." That night, while Cody lay sleeping, Jim sat writing in his journal, too exhausted to sleep. The biting wind outside howled. Another fierce storm had rolled in. Jim knew he had made it back just in time. He watched the boy dozing next to Wolf. Had the kid just taken some blank pages from his notebook or had he read parts of it—especially the parts where Jim wondered what to do with him? He couldn't be sure.

How is this going to end? That fear gnawed at his gut. The kid was bright. He watched everything Jim did, constantly pestering him with questions. Where were they? When would the weather change? When could he go home? Where was the "store?" When could they go outside? If they did, would he run away? He said he didn't like it here. The big eyes were innocent, but the kid was dumb like a fox.

Who would believe that a fugitive, a murderer, a thief, oh yeah, and a rapist, just happened to find a boy? How do you get a kid back to where he belongs without losing your own life? *What if you couldn't?*

He remembered a blurry story from the past. He'd been sitting on a stool in Dottie's Café about to dive into his favorite breakfast of ham and eggs. One of the guys had started talking about Vietnam. Mack was his name. He had a body like a truck and ate like one. Yeah, that was the guy. The one that was always telling war stories over the mile-high stack of pancakes and three eggs he devoured every morning. He was a vet or somethin'.

It was a story about a platoon leader who led his men through enemy territory. *"This officer guy heard a rustle in the bushes. Viet Cong, he thought. So, he leveled his rifle approaching cautiously."* Mack had raised his arms to form an imaginary gun. *"When he got close enough, he saw it was a little girl. He grabbed the squirmin' girl around the waist. He couldn't let her go because if he did, she'd go 'n tell the villagers what she'd seen. Once she revealed their location, it woulda brought an ambush and sure death for his men. He was responsible for them. They depended on him. They couldn't take her with 'em either. I mean you can't have a kid in the middle of a firefight. So he did the only thing he could do — he quietly slit her throat."*

Christ. As soon as Mack'd said that Jim had *quit* cutting his ham. His hands instinctively rose to his own throat.

Mack had smirked. *"I'm tellin' ya war is hell."* He'd chewed and jabbed the air with his fork. *"Look, he didn't have no other choice. I'm tellin' ya it was all about survival."*

Survival.

Jim's wild eyes stared at the sleeping boy. He couldn't relate to that story back then, but he could now. He saw Mo's dark, beady eyes and that chilling look when he told him he'd found a puppy in the woods. "You're not fooling me. Stay away from the campers and get rid of the dog. You get us discovered, and I'll slit your throat. Sometimes you have to be cruel to survive."

How could he win the kid's loyalty, and how could he be sure? *Life is easier when you're alone. Kids are harder than dogs*, he wrote. When he finished writing, he hid the notebook in a place the kid would never find.

Touch the Sky

CHAPTER 28

Six weeks later

Jim shuddered, crouching in the snow behind dense underbrush. How had they found him? A throng of officers in dark helmets and vests surrounded his hiding place like a swarm of yellow jackets, their assault rifles pointed, itchy fingers on triggers. There was no chance to surrender. One loud crack and a bullet hit his leg. He felt the searing, hot pain in his thigh. He tried to run, but both legs went numb.

They must have loosed their dogs. He could hear them panting, barking, getting closer and closer. In the foggy distance came those familiar screams and he saw the blood. All that blood mingling with the red hair that smelled like lilacs. He jerked up in panic, moaning, sweating, breathing hard.

Wolf stood over him barking.

"Ben, what is it?" cried Cody.

"I'm hit!" Jim grunted.

Cody shook his arm. "Where? What hit you?"

He saw the light from the low-burning fire, the cave, the frightened boy's soulful eyes; Wolf pacing, agitated.

"It's okay kid," his breath was still coming hard. "I . . . I just had a bad dream."

Cody jumped up and ran to the water bucket, returning with a dripping dipper. He held it to Jim's lips and steadied his trembling hands. Once Jim could grasp it, Cody grabbed a cloth, dipped it in the bucket, and began wiping Jim's brow.

The coolness brought Jim's world into focus. "Thanks, buddy." He patted Cody's thin shoulder.

He watched as the boy brought wood for the fire and stoked it like a pint-size version of himself.

Jim hadn't had the dream for a long time. Maybe the screeching wind that sounded like a woman screaming in the distance had brought it on, or maybe the feeling of being lost in that storm weeks ago still lingered inside.

"Everything's okay. We're all okay," Cody said.

The kid, Jim thought. The kid. He's even starting to sound like me.

***

Jim Fallingwater was twenty-four years old when he murdered Christie Jenkins. There was no delicate way to put it. He was a murderer. He did it. He'd snuffed out a life in a fit of anger. It happened the weekend after he bought a secondhand TV at the thrift store, so he could watch football. He thought his life was beginning. He should have known that was too much to ask.

Jim had grown up to be a big kid. He was over six feet and weighed 220 pounds. People said he had the biggest feet in the county. He lived with his parents and one sister, Mavis, in a small, drafty house they rented in town. His father worked at the D&R Sawmill until heavy drinking cost him his job. After that, he did odd jobs whenever he bothered to look for them. One Saturday afternoon, he had crawled under the house to rescue Mavis's kitty and died of a heart attack. Twelve-year-old Jim never shed a tear. He was glad. Relieved even, because he no longer had to think about killing the bastard.

Jim knew he was different, and it turned him into a quiet, reclusive kid. Ken Blake was his only friend. Their friendship took off that windy day in the park when a bunch of mostly eleven-year-olds gathered to play football. As they picked sides, Jim stood there, his unkempt hair greasy, his jeans soiled, wanting to join in, but no one chose him.

Big Eddie Reed, a farm kid, who was going on thirteen, sneered. "Get lost, Tonto. You stink, an yer ol' man's a drunk." Jim didn't budge. Eddie took a step closer, opened his fly, placed his hand on his hips, and peed right in front of Jim, as if he were a fire hydrant.

Like a bull ready to charge, Jim clenched his fists and glared at Eddie. Out of the corner of his eye, he saw Ken coming toward him. He thought he would have to fight both of them.

"Hey, Fallingwater," Ken called. Jim turned toward him. Ken grinned and tossed him the ball. "You gonna stand there or play?"

"Yeah, sure," Jim said and ran to join Ken's team. Once the game got going, Jim, a natural athlete, tackled big Eddie again and again, but the best part of that was rubbing Eddie's face in the muddy grass when he got the chance. After Eddie's team lost, he left the park blubbering that the bush nigger didn't play fair.

"Aw, he's just a sore head," Ken said. He gave Jim a high five. "Football's your thing."

Jim looked at the ground and smiled shyly. "Yeah," he said. "Yeah."

Still, poverty and his father's drinking binges took a toll on Jim's fragile self-esteem. When his old man came home drunk, he knocked his mother around, and Jim, too. Once to avoid a beating, Jim snuck out and ran to Ken's house. Ken's mother, Addie, was surprised to find him hiding in Ken's bedroom. She made him toasted cheese sandwiches, insisted he take a bath in their tub, and let him sleep there whenever he was too scared to go home.

After Jim's father died, Dottie talked Tillie Tillden into giving Edna, Jim's mother, a job checking groceries. Jim was proud to have his mother working at Tillden's, because she rubbed elbows with just about everyone in town. "Your gym teacher always buys sardines," she told him and, "Mr. Johnson, the plumber, hides his six-pack under the bread in case he runs into the preacher." Edna's job didn't last long, but then nothing in Jim's life ever did. Some people complained that she talked too much, made mistakes on their bills, and they didn't particularly like her handling their food.

"I know you think I should help, and I'm tryin' to," Tillie told Dottie, "but for Christ sakes, I'm losin' customers. A store ain't nothin' without customers." Soon Edna disappeared from the cash register, ending up in the back room where she did inventory. After that, she came in at night and did janitorial work. It didn't bring in enough to pay the bills, so she also scrubbed floors and toilets at Bradshaw's Drugstore and over at the school on weekends. When Mavis turned eighteen, she got a job cleaning houses in Klamath Falls, then ran off with the meter reader, never to be heard from again.

Jim first met Mo at Ken's house. Mo'd stopped by to give Addie Blake some trout he'd snagged on a fishing trip. Addie invited him in and sat Jim next to Mo at her kitchen table. "I think you share the same ancestors," she said while serving apple pie and vanilla ice cream.

Mo took an instant liking to Jim. He told him stories about Captain Jack, the legendary Modoc chief, and about the beliefs and customs of his tribe. He took him hunting and fishing. It worked out well for Ken, too, because he got to go along. Mo taught Jim survival skills and introduced him to woodcarving, which became Jim's special gift. Mo could carve just about anything out of wood, but Jim was better at it than Mo.

Even though Jim was a big kid, people in Forest Lake hardly noticed him, until he made the high school football team and began scoring touchdowns. The coach had to special-order his shoes. His four years on the football team were the best in his life. He lettered his first year and graduated with four green stripes on his blue varsity sweater with a big FL on the side.

The town emptied and shops closed early for those Friday-night home games so people could pack the bleachers and cheer for the Forest Lake Raiders. Sometimes Jim, clutching the ball, glanced toward the bleachers and saw the crowd on their feet, arms jabbing the air, "Go, Go, Go," they screamed and "Whoohaw!" when he crossed the finish line. The small squad of cheerleaders bounced around chanting, "Hit 'em again. Hit 'em again. Harder. Harder." They leaped in the air, spread their legs, and hugged one another when they landed.

Off the homecoming field, life was different. Jim only went to one dance. After scoring a winning touchdown, he entered the cafeteria that night feeling like a hero, but none of the girls flirted with him. He stood there, watching couples gyrating to "Slip Slidin' Away" and "Night Fever." Then he realized he didn't know how to dance. Embarrassed, he retreated to a dark corner. After a while, he worked his way up to the food table where he downed four cupcakes, practically emptied a bowl of corn curls, and swallowed two cans of Coke. Soon the crotchety, bent algebra teacher, Miss Crafton, doing overtime as chaperone, glowered at him with a face that would easily be at home on Mount Rushmore. "Get away from there," she hissed, as if she had a pickle up her ass. He slipped out into the cool air and never went to another dance.

While Jim was deft at football, his big problem was his temper. If someone from the other team slammed into him the wrong way, he erupted like a volcano and retaliated. His hair-trigger temper almost got him kicked off the team, except that the coach knew he needed him if the Raiders were going to make it to state. It wasn't just the adrenaline on the football field that could light his fuse. His anger surfaced at other times, too. Once a kid at school tossed sheep dip in his face. Jim exploded, almost killing him. He would have, too, if Ken hadn't pulled him off. Ken always said Jim's anger problem resulted from an abusive father.

"You'd better keep a lid on that temper of yours, or you'll end up on the outside looking in," Mo chastised, his small dark eyes flecked with anger.

Jim clenched his jaw and gritted his teeth. "We're already on the outside," he said bitterly.

"You blow it, don't come crying to me," Mo scolded.

"How much farther out can we be?"

"You better keep a lid on that trap of yours, too." Mo had the last word. He always did.

An all-star in football, Jim didn't excel in school. After he graduated and the cheering stopped, there wasn't much left for him. Like his father, he went to work at the sawmill and lived at home with Edna until she died two years later of an infected gallbladder. They didn't have money to pay a doctor or the undertaker. Dottie saw to it that Jim's mother got a decent burial. Jim gave Dottie a beautiful carving of a song sparrow perched on a branch for her birthday.

Ken went off to college in the valley. After he graduated, he became a police officer, completed police academy requirements, and took a job in Klamath Falls. Jim rented a small room above the hardware store. It came with a table, two chairs, a sofa bed, a hot plate, a mini refrigerator, and a dinky bathroom. It was his first real home. He saved his money, bought a second-hand, red pickup, and spent hours polishing it.

"You'd think he bought a Cadillac," Mo told Happy Face.

"At least he knows how to take care of things," she said.

On weekdays Jim ate breakfast at Dottie's Café along with other sawmill workers, ranchers, and truck drivers. It was at Dottie's that he met Christie Jenkins, a pretty red-haired waitress. She was the seventeen-year-old daughter of Myra and Floyd Jenkins. Myra had her hand in everything—the church sewing circle, the Woman's Club, and activities at the school. Floyd not only ran the Shell station but also was a deacon at the church. For years, Myra taught Sunday School.

Jim loved to watch Christie fill his thermos with coffee and to sneak peeks down her low-cut blouses and clinging sweaters. Whenever she walked away, he watched her buttocks move like two compact loaves under the tight black skirt she always wore. She so captivated him, he sometimes let his breakfast get cold. Her creamy, flawless complexion reminded him of the delicate, peach-colored blossoms on the rhododendron bush in front of the high school. Whenever she passed by, she left a scent of lilacs in the air; he'd never seen such blue eyes. He dreamed about rubbing his cheek in that long, bright hair, and more. Christie made him so dizzy that he once walked right into a table.

"Don't you go gettin' no ideas about that one," an old-timer cautioned. "Her momma gonna cut your nuts off. She ain't gonna let her daughter end up being no squaw."

Christie loved flirting with all the men and the big tips it brought. She knew Jim was a former high school football star and interested in sports, so she always had something to say about the latest game, even though she never watched one. "How about those Dolphins?" she would say. "Do you think the Beavs will beat the Ducks?"

Jim sputtered as he struggled to find the right words for a cool response. Usually, it was only, "Yeah, they did good." Then he looked down at his coffee mug wondering why his tongue stiffened whenever Christie asked him something.

Christie was a talented watercolorist, and Dottie happily displayed her paintings of Forest Lake and the Big Bat on the walls of the café. When Christie sold her first painting to an older couple who'd been visiting the lake, the regulars chipped in and toasted her with a bottle of wine they'd bought at Tillden's. Jim slipped her a small wooden box decorated with a beautiful carved iris on top. He loved her art, and she admired his carvings. She told him he should try his hand at larger wood sculptures. Jim read a lot more into her attention than she ever intended.

Christie's real interest was Bill Janes who came down from Portland during the summers to work on his uncle's ranch. He was studying pharmacy at Oregon State in Corvallis. Bill's father was an executive with some timber-exporting company. Bill ate lunch at the café when he was in town getting supplies or driving the truck. Because he came in with the lunch crowd, Jim was not there to see Christie fawn over Bill, or the way they groped in his pickup behind the restaurant, Bill's hands all over her. In the fall, he went back to college to finish his senior year. Christie told Dottie she was going to ride the Greyhound bus to Corvallis sometime to see Bill and go to a football game. Maybe they would get together again in December.

Jim didn't have a lot of experience with women. The fact was, he didn't have any, so he didn't recognize the tart in Christie. It was the first time in his life he'd been in love. Christie wanted to take pictures for her watercolor paintings, so Jim took her hiking in the wilderness up on the Big Bat.

After that, Jim invited Christie to a movie at the grange hall because the town didn't actually have a theater and she wanted to see *When Harry Met Sally*. Afterward, they drove to the lake to stare at the big moon hanging over the glistening water. "It's so beautiful here," she said. "It's like being in a painting." She laid her soft cheek against his face, and then she kissed him right on the mouth. Startled, Jim responded like a big moose in heat. It was more than he ever expected. She let him kiss her again and again and to rub his face in her soft red hair. Soon, she was tugging at his clothes. They made love in the front seat of that rickety pickup. Convinced she loved him, Jim was dead set on marrying her.

Once they pulled their clothes back on, they sat holding hands in the moonlight. Jim kissed Christie again. He never wanted to let her go. "I've got my eye on a little spread," he told her, "five acres far out of town, out in the open spaces where you can hear the coyotes howl and walk free."

He drew her closer. "I've always wanted a family. A real one. Let's do this forever. Let's get married."

"You can't be serious." She laughed.

"I love you."

"Mother would never hear of it. She wants me to go to art school on the East Coast, but we don't have the money right now."

"You're goin' away to school?"

"Mother says maybe when Gram dies. Besides, I'm going to marry Bill Janes."

"Bill Janes? The guy that works summers on his uncle's place?" Jim remembered Bill. He was a tall, nice-enough-looking guy with curly brown hair and a ruddy face. Other than that, he was a pure dude. All thumbs. Jim had helped Janes get his pickup running when it had stalled on the highway. Janes knew nothing about fixing engines. His hands were white with clean fingernails and no calluses. "Shouldn't we call somebody?" he'd said when Jim pulled open the hood and started tinkering.

"Bill's my ticket out of this town . . . this place . . . this dump. I'm not going to spend my life waiting tables, and I'm not waiting for an old lady to die to start my life. Bill graduates in June. Then we're moving to San Francisco, where the women wear dresses, men wear suits, and they drink wine. All the time."

Jim's whole body went numb. They had just made love. Once you did that with a woman for Christ sakes, you married her.

"Forest Lake is the armpit of the state when it comes to living. I mean real living — things to do, nightlife, the theatre, fine art," Christie said. "You can't even buy a post-card in Forest Lake."

"You . . . you're engaged?"

The next thing he knew, she was laughing again. "Well not quite, but I'm working on it. Just reeling Billy Boy in before he knows what hit him." Her right hand wound an imaginary reel. "Bill's daddy is rich."

He could see the red lips, the white teeth. Laughing. "We just made love. You did that, all the while knowing you were gonna marry another man?"

"Look, we had sex. Not love."

"What are you doing out here with me?"

"Seriously? You mean . . . you thought. You big dope. Oh, that's a scream."

"But —"

"Mother doesn't even know I'm here. She thinks I'm at the church helping sort through junk for the rummage sale. She'd shit a freakin' brick if she knew I was out with you."

Jim had never heard a woman talk that way, say those words, and she was laughing.

Laughing.

He could feel the rage building. His hands started to shake, his chest wanted to explode. He took a deep breath and another deeper one trying to stop it.

She slapped her thigh. "All the time you were doing that to me, I was pretending you were Bill. You're such a fool."

If she had just stopped. If she hadn't said those words. *Fool. Pretending he was Bill.* Was everybody laughing at him? All the pain he'd ever felt surged through his body. His fingers gripped the hunting knife he'd always carried in the side door pocket of the truck. Everything went white. He flew at her. He remembered slashing her and hearing the screams. She'd managed to get out of the pickup he thought, but he couldn't be sure whether she'd gotten out on her own or whether he'd pushed her. He'd panicked and driven off.

He didn't remember much more about that night, just the white, blinding anger. He'd killed her, and it was wrong. He'd done it and he couldn't unravel it. They'd said a lot of the wounds were superficial, but the fatal one hit Christie's carotid artery in the neck.

He was arrested at the coast, sitting in his pickup, watching the sun burn off the fog, smelling the salt air, listening to the seagulls. What had he done? All the time he had his pickup, he'd never driven to the coast. How big the world was, and he'd never driven around in it.

Two patrol cars surrounded him, the lights flashing. He hadn't resisted. That was the last he ever saw of his red truck. Then there were the TV cameras, the lights, and someone shouting, "Did you kill Christie Jenkins?" He covered his face.

It wasn't long before Ken, now a transport cop, showed up to bring him back to the county jail. He was glad to see him, but Ken seemed distant, in cop mode. A lot of the rest was a blur. Ken was talking to him, trying to explain crimes of passion, how he'd probably still have to do some time. "It all depends on the jury," he said, sitting there in his clean, unsullied uniform. Then he started talking about Lydia and said they were expecting a baby. Jim felt dirty. He couldn't breathe. His head ached. He clenched his fists. Did Ken think he was stupid? Didn't he hear the charges—aggravated murder, assault, rape? The jury? The Jenkins were big shots in town. He was an Indian. Oregon had the death penalty. Forest Lake was a redneck town. Would anybody believe the sex with a seventeen-year-old was consensual? What friggin' planet was Ken on?

"We're blood brothers," Ken kept saying. "Remember that? Remember. I'll do everything I can to help." He slapped Jim's shoulder. Talking and talking. Did he think Jim was a fool, too? A *fool*. A big dumb dope. Was he just *pretending*?

On the ride back, Jim convinced him that he was sick, about to pass out, had chest pains. Ken stopped the cruiser and rushed to the back to aid him, pumping his chest with his hands. *Ken was so friggin' easy.*

"Let me die," Jim begged. "I want to die." He moaned. His eyes fluttered. *So easy.*

Ken undid the handcuffs and continued pumping. Jim went limp. "Hang on buddy, I'll radio for help. Just hang on."

In that one horrific moment with Christie, Jim's world shattered. He remembered the ocean. He could hear the waves crashing in his head. He never had a chance to touch them. He never would. His rage exploded. He sprang up, getting Ken in a chokehold, squeezing and shaking him hard until his body crumpled and fell back like a loose sack of grain on a flatbed truck.

Jim found the key to undo the leg irons. Then he ran, not knowing, not caring, whether he'd killed Ken, too. He stole a car. Abandoned it. Stole another one and drove and drove. Abandoned it and ran some more to the only place that seemed safe—Big Bat Mountain.

People were scary. They measured you by who you knew, what you did, what you had, fancy cars, big houses, money. Of the money, for the money, by the money. *Bill's daddy is rich, isn't that what Christie had said that night? Laughing.*

He'd gone from a small, dingy apartment to a cave. Animals always had a reason for attacking you, and they never laughed at you for loving them. Of course, he was sorry. He was sorry every friggin,' waking day. What the hell good was sorry? It didn't change a goddamn thing.

Touch the Sky

CHAPTER 29

February 14, 2009

Jim clambered down into the cave exhausted, but happy to feel the warmth from the fire and to see his strange little family intact. He had survived another reckless trek in the dead, cold winter to Amos Hadley's Lake Store. "Hot damn," he chortled, slapping his thigh and carefully removing his snow-covered backpack from his aching shoulders. "I made it."

Wolf gleefully licked at the snow on his rain pants, barking and wagging his tail, his eyes bright, panting contently waiting for Jim to scratch his ears. Cody helped him out of his wet clothing. The boy had hot water ready and a stew of beans and rice bubbled in a pot. A wave of primal pleasure surged deep in Jim's body, a feeling one gets after coming in from cold danger to welcoming faces, a warm fire, and safe abode that says you're home. Home. Finally.

Cody's small chest puffed with pride. "I kept the fire going, and I just threw on some extra wood."

"You done good, kid. You done good," Jim croaked, his vocal cords still chilled. He held the cup of heated water to warm his hands, and then took slow sips.

"Whoops. Easy," Cody said when Jim set the cup down, coughing. Cody scooped beans and rice into a tin bowl. He handed it to Jim. "When you're ready."

Jim grinned. He's doing it again, taking care of me. He rubbed his thighs vigorously to warm his legs. Then he burst out laughing. What cuss words would Mo mutter if he knew Jim had risked discovery and losing his life to get peanut butter for a little kid's birthday? Peanut butter for Christ's sake.

Cody had been sad, almost on the verge of tears. He'd huddled in a little ball, not wanting to talk, but Jim had finally nudged it out of him. He'd said he had dreamed about his mom and the cake she always baked on his birthday, which fell on Valentine's Day—a heart-shaped, chocolate cake with peanut butter frosting.

"It seemed so real. I could almost taste it, but then I woke up." His voice quivered, his eyes mournful. "How much longer do we have to stay here?"

Jim took Cody up to the cave entrance to show him the drifts of snow and to let him feel the gusting winds. Afterward, the boy was glad to get back to the fire.

Away from home, there was no school, no bedtime, no Miss Brackston, no Artie Bradshaw. Cody seemed to love the stories Jim told him about his people and that mystical trickster, Coyote, but Jim knew he deeply missed his family, and that he was eager to tell his friends all about living like an Indian in a cave with Benny's dad. He especially wanted to tell Artie.

Cody invited Jim to live in one of their upstairs bedrooms. "We have a TV and a computer in our living room. You can bring your drum, but you wouldn't want to play it around Grandpa and Dad. They're okay, but sometimes they get grumpy."

Jim couldn't begin to understand why anyone would be excited about having a computer, which made Cody giggle.

"Mom's a good cook. She's fun as long as you keep your room clean and don't cause trouble at school."

Jim forced a smile. If the kid only realized how impossible all that was.

***

It was foolish to make a trek in February, Jim realized, but the kid had made so much progress. At first, it was hard to get the boy focused, but once Jim let him do things and praised him, he seemed to take off. Cody learned to tend the fire, target-practice in the cave with the small bow Jim had made for him, feed Wolf, cook food, and entertain himself by drawing, especially drawing. He even developed a taste for black coffee whenever Jim made it and the other strange, bland foods he prepared. Over the past few weeks, the kid had put some flesh on his bones. His face seemed fuller and less pale.

Still, when Jim prepared to go "shopping," Cody hunched over, hugging his arms. "Why do you have to go?" His voice was shaky, like he feared something awful would happen.

"You're a good brave. You'll be fine."

"But what if you get lost or something out there gets you?"

"When you're part of the wild, you don't fear it. Understand?" Cody didn't respond, so Jim knelt down and lifted his hanging head. "Look kid, if you get scared about somethin' just close your eyes real tight." He took the boy's hand and placed it against his small chest. "And go to this special place inside. That way you can still talk to me when I'm away. Think real hard, and answers will come. C'mon, you try it."

Cody placed his hand over his heart and closed his eyes so tight he wrinkled his nose. They suddenly opened with a giggle.

"There, see. Now, you take good care of Wolf."

***

Jim broke into the Lake Store in the dead of night to get peanut butter. Peanut butter for crying out loud. He arrived frozen, panting, and out of breath, but managed to pry open a back storage-room window. The store smelled like stale coffee. It felt warm and cozy, because Amos always banked the fire in his wood stove. Jim chuckled when he saw the big padlocks Amos had added to the doors. Fortunately, Amos was a forgetful skinflint—too tight to add an alarm system, too neglectful to bolt down the storage-room window.

In the darkness, Jim's gloved hands snatched a tuna sandwich from the cooler and washed it down with a small carton of milk. Like an animal, always on the alert, he constantly listened and glanced around the room while he ate. The snow on his boots left a puddle on the wooden floor. He snickered, knowing it would make Amos's blood boil. He could see the old man's face, glowering red as a lobster. He grabbed some bags of pretzels and nuts to eat on the long trek back.

He loaded several jars of peanut butter into his backpack. Jelly went with peanut butter he knew, but he didn't see any in the back of the store. Amos kept a small light burning toward the front near the large windows, but Jim was careful to stay out of its beam. Instead of jelly, he grabbed several packages of fig bars. He helped himself to cigarettes, a flashlight, and some batteries. He was going for the chocolate candy, but he thought he heard a noise that sounded like someone coming, so he stuffed what he had in his backpack and left in a hurry.

***

"Why are you laughing, Ben?"

"Because it's your birthday. Look here, I've got something for you." He opened his backpack.

"Peanut butter! Peanut butter!" Cody danced around. He opened the lid and stuck in a finger. He and Wolf ran in circles. "We got peanut butter," he shouted as if he just discovered a pot of gold.

"Happy Birthday, kid."

"Can I give Wolf some, Ben?"

"It's your birthday. Do what you want."

He stuck his finger in the jar of Jif and held it out. Wolf's face brightened. He licked it eagerly, wagged his tail and nudged his dark muzzle against the jar wanting more.

"He likes it!" Cody giggled

"You're spoiling him," Jim laughed.

"He got the crunchy kind. It's my favorite!" Cody told Wolf.

A happy accident, Jim thought.

Jim played a tired Happy Birthday on his flute, and the little boy, the fugitive man, and the stray dog sat around the campfire scarfing down crunchy peanut butter spread on fig bars like starving Israelites discovering manna in the desert.

"When we get back home, you can see my room," Cody said, licking his fingers. "My Grandpa needs a friend, someone to hang out with, so he doesn't make Dad mad. Can Wolf sleep with me in my room?"

Jim drew a deep breath. A chilling pang hit the pit of his stomach. It was time to change the subject. "Look, kid, we need to talk."

"What, Ben? What is it?"

Jim held out his hand and showed him the faint crossed scar on his forefinger. "When two braves care about each other, they become blood brothers. Do you know about blood brothers?"

"Kinda."

"Blood brothers are loyal, see. They . . . uh . . . always take care of each other, no matter what. Understand?"

"Yeah."

"We make a little nick in each of our fingers and mingle our blood. Is that something you want to do?"

"Yeah." Cody's dark eyes turned serious.

"Are you sure?"

"I'm a brave." He grinned.

In reality, Jim didn't know a lot about blood-brother ceremonies—in fact, he knew nothing—but he hoped it would work. It was better than the grim alternative. He didn't even think Modocs ever did such a thing, but when he and Ken Blake were around thirteen, they saw an old black-and-white movie in which an Indian and a white man become blood brothers. He couldn't even remember which movie, or who starred in it, but they'd seen it down at the Grange Hall where the kids went on Saturday afternoons. On the next trek with Mo, they'd snuck off into the heavy underbrush, did the thing, smoked cigarettes Jim had stolen from Tillden's, and were darn proud of it.

Mo chuckled when he heard about their ceremony but ended up scolding them for playing with knives. He screwed up his nose. "What's that I smell on your clothes?" He gave them his sideways dark glare that always meant trouble. The boys, eyes downcast and innocent, shrugged their shoulders. Mo shook his finger. "If I ever catch you smoking cigarettes out here, I'll hang you by your ears over Cooper's Hawk River. You start a fire here, and there won't even be that much to hang once I get through with you."

***

They needed some kind of ceremony, so Jim piled more wood on the fire, making it brighter. He reached for his flute and began playing melodious sounds while Cody beat out the rhythm on the big drum.

Afterward, Cody closed his eyes and screwed up his face when Jim made a quick, small cut in Cody's forefinger. He placed it against a similar one he made on his middle finger.

"Are you okay?" Jim asked. He winced at the oozing blood from Cody's small finger. The boy's hands were so delicate, white, and trusting, compared with Jim's thick brown ones with their swollen joints, calloused by years of hard work in the wilderness.

"Yeah." Cody opened his dark eyes. The eyes were different now, almost solemn. They no longer belonged to that scared, uncertain boy he'd carried in from the cold.

They held the fingers together briefly.

"Now the blood in my veins runs through the blood in yours," Jim said. "We are one. We are family." Cody smiled. He hugged Jim, who sat there like a fallen tree. He still didn't know how to react to Cody's bursts of affection.

"Your Indian name is Wolf Boy, and I'm Captain Jack," he said, his voice serious. Some tribes, Jim knew, painted the faces of the young men when they received their Indian names, but he wasn't well versed in Native rituals. Then an idea came to him. He grabbed a piece of charcoal wood, rubbed his finger against it and smeared a dark line under each of Cody's eyes, like football players did to protect themselves from the sun's glare. He made the same marks on his own face.

Cody was delighted. "Can Wolf be our blood brother, too?"

"He already is. Dogs come with pure hearts. They're born that way. Only people need oaths." After a pause, he added "and laws. Look, I have something else for you. Close your eyes." Jim reached into his pocket and pulled out a carving that looked exactly like Wolf right down to the dark diamond in the middle of his forehead. "Now open."

"Wolf, it's you!" Cody cried. "I can carry you in my pocket. Thank you, Ben."

"Now, Wolf Boy, you have a dog of your own—a totem that will stay with you and guard you."

"I'm an Indian, a real brave." Cody told Wolf that several times. "We need to pray," he suddenly announced.

"What?"

"We need to thank God for making us brothers."

"Oh, listen, kid." Jim had no idea about how to pray.

"Mom says we should always give thanks when something good happens."

Jim hadn't thought about God in such a long time. Maybe he never did, but then why should he? God had never been there for him. Why would someone's God want to hear from him? He was a murderer, a thief, and a liar.

"Come on, I'll show you," Cody said. "We do it in church on Sundays." He pulled on Jim's hand as he got down. The big, awkward man and the little boy knelt on the rocky, damp cave floor. Cody folded his small hands and closed his eyes. Jim's wild eyes remained open; he clasped his hands.

"Thank you, God, for making us brothers and taking care of us," Cody said. "Now, you say something, too."

Jim struggled for the right words. "Uh, thank you for us. Yeah, that's it," he finally said.

"Amen," said Cody, jumping up. He whooped like the brave he thought he was while he and Wolf played hide-and-seek around the rocks in the cave.

Jim shook his head, smiling to himself. His body ached; middle age was catching up with him. He needed to sleep; his eyelids were at half-mast. He lit a cigarette and took a long drag. There was nothing like the strong taste of an unfiltered Camel to take the edge off a long day. He watched the happy boy chasing the dog and whooping. Life was crazy, sideways like a thick, foggy cloud sometimes choking you and sometimes letting a little sun in. God, he'd never seen anyone so happy to be an Indian.

CHAPTER 30

May 2009

As the days became longer, the ground started to thaw. Melting snow and ice trickled down the mountain feeding the lake and causing Cooper's Hawk River to swell. In town, people welcomed the return of light, happily reset their clocks, and smiled more. Soon, the cries of happy children playing outside lasted well past the dinner hour.

On the Big Bat, retreating snow again transformed the slopes near the summit into a shape that resembled giant wings. Still, spring unrolled at a slower pace at higher elevations. Even in May, the sky spit snow, and sleet mingled in a chilling wind. Nevertheless, Jim judged it safe enough to allow the boy to venture out with him and Wolf to check his traps. Cody eagerly skipped around the cave, anticipating his first real excursion into the wilderness. Except for quick trips to get spring water, he'd been holed up for six months.

Once outside, he twirled about, turned his face skyward, and let the sparse flakes land on his cheeks. Wolf trotted ahead, sniffing everything, and occasionally leaving the trail in pursuit of a startled squirrel. Cody dashed after him. Jim laughed when he joined Wolf for a roll in the snow.

"C'mon," he finally said. "We're out here for business." His traps, however, were not that productive. He'd only snared a marmot which Jim released. "We don't need it. Out here, take only what you'll use." He wrinkled his nose. "Besides, they taste like rodents."

"Guh." Cody's jaw dropped. "You ate rats?"

"There was a time I was so hungry, I ate anything that moved."

***

Back at the cave, Cody shook off icy flakes and pulled off the layers of warm clothing. He ran his hand through his dark hair that now hung in an uneven pageboy to his shoulders. His nose and cheeks were pink. He kindled the fire, layered on more wood, and filled the pot with water, so they could warm up.

Jim rubbed his hands over the heat. The kid was a quick study. He seemed to focus and tend to survival issues instead of worrying about himself. He'd also started to fill out and was a bit taller. Jim had let the button out around the waist of the kid's pants, but they fit snug around the hips and were threadbare due to the washing and wringing Jim did while Cody, bundled in Jim's long wool shirt and coat, waited for them to dry over the fire.

Jim sighed happily. "You did good out there." He carefully measured the coffee grounds to preserve his scarce supply and tossed them into the boiling water. "Good ol' hobo coffee," he said, sniffing the fragrant aroma coming from the steam. "Ain't nothing like it."

Grinning, Cody wiped Wolf's wet coat and feet with a towel. "You did good, boy," he said mimicking Jim. Wolf vigorously wagged his tail and panted, his mouth open, as if smiling.

Weeks ago, Jim had bagged a deer and a few rabbits. He'd refrigerated the meat in deep snow and covered the place with rocks to keep scavengers away. Now he warmed leftover rabbit stew and served it with yesterday's cold biscuits. Wolf had a dinner of venison and entertained himself by gnawing on a bone.

"I'll have to go shoppin' and get you some new duds," Jim said between bites looking at Cody's tight, faded jeans.

Cody sat up straight, eager for another adventure. "Can I go with you, Ben?"

"Naw, not yet. It's still too risky weather-wise."

"I can handle it. I did okay today, didn't I?"

"Yeah, you sure did." He patted Cody's head. "But it's a way longer trip. Too chancy. Even in spring, the weather up here can change on a dime."

"I want to go, Ben." Cody protested. "I could help, I could —what's that?" A strange eerie sound came from somewhere in the distance. Cody's eyes got big.

Wolf barked. The fur between his shoulders stood straight up.

"Shhh," Jim ordered. "Quiet, Wolf."

They heard it again—four short yelps and a high-pitched howl. The sound of a coyote in distress.

Mo.

Jim jumped up. "It's . . . uh . . . sounds like a coyote." He pulled on his outdoor gear. They heard the call again. Wolf paced and growled like he wanted to get at something.

"Stay," Jim commanded. He looked at Cody. "It could be a whole pack of them," he lied. "They probably smelled the meat I stashed in the snow. This could be dangerous. I'm gonna check it out. You stay here and keep an eye on Wolf. He'd be defenseless against a bunch of coyotes." He reached for his bow to convince Cody.

Cody put his arms around Wolf. "You stay with me, boy." Wolf's sloppy tongue licked his face.

Jim shuffled out of the cave. The sleeting snow had stopped, but the biting, cold wind hung on. He didn't want Mo to come too close. When he was a safe distance away, he returned the coyote call and listened. Four short yelps. That meant Mo would be at the smaller supply cave. He broke into a run.

Mo, bundled up in a heavy, hooded jacket, leaning on a walking stick, waited for him under a pine tree. He had already removed the rocks covering the cave entrance.

Jim rushed to embrace him. "Hey, fella, you okay?"

Mo's small dark eyes were anxious. "Leave it. Leave it." He waved Jim away, his breath coming in raspy gasps. He jerked the lid off a small, amber bottle, popped a tiny pill in his mouth and took a sip of water from a plastic water bottle.

"What's that for?" Jim asked.

"Gives me energy." He waved his hands again, indicating he didn't want to talk about it.

"You look drained. Let's go inside the cave and make a fire, so you can rest and get warm. Have a bite to eat. Did you bring coffee?"

"You have to go." Mo's face darkened, his breath making little cloud spurts in the cold air. He reached into his pocket and pulled out a cigarette.

"Go where?"

"Away from here. Leave the mountain."

"What?" Jim's mouth dropped. "You're not making sense. Let's go inside, make a fire."

Mo lit the cigarette and took a long drag. "Relax," he said, and handed it to Jim.

"I hope you brought more of these." Jim sucked the smoke into his mouth, inhaled deeply, and breathed the smoke out of his nose. He felt that first sensuous puff right down to his boots.

Mo gripped the handle of his walking stick. "They found a body on the mountain. A small boy."

"What? A body. Are you sure? He died on the mountain?"

"He was kidnapped. Murdered."

"Murdered? A boy from Forest Lake?"

"No, from around Grants Pass."

"That far? Murdered! Here on the Big Bat? Why?"

"He got grabbed when he got off his school bus."

"How'd he get here?"

"They don't know. He was shot."

"Somebody shot a kid?"

Mo pointed his finger to his temple. "In the head."

"Jesus. God. Was it an accident?"

"No. Murder, I said. No. They're looking for the killer, a pedophile."

"A what?"

"Sex. Someone that has sex with a kid."

"Jesus H. Christ."

"You have to go."

"Go? Why me? I never did nothin'. You don't think I—"

"No. No. Not you. Listen to me. Another little boy is missing."

"Another one!"

"Benson boy. He's somewhere around the Big Bat. Believed dead. He's the second one."

The kid, Jim thought. He's talking about the kid.

"They want me to help with the search. They're gonna scour the mountain. A Forest Lake boy. They'll stop at nothing. They'll come looking for the remains. If they find you—you have to leave."

"Leave. I can't just leave. What the hell are you thinking?"

"You must go."

"Go where?" He wondered whether the kid had told him the truth about how he got to the mountain. Had he really gotten lost in the snow or had he escaped from something worse?

"I contacted a relative in Oklahoma with our tribe. You will go there."

"Oklahoma! You're nuts."

"Listen to me." He jabbed his walking stick at the ground. He was breathing hard again.

"That's clear across the country. Get in the cave. You need to rest. Clear your head."

Mo grabbed Jim's chin and pulled his face toward him. "Remember the story I told you about our people. A long time ago, they chained them together and forced them to go to eastern Oklahoma. Some of my relatives are still there. Go there. Mention me. They will hide you."

"And just how in the hell am I supposed to get there, catch a bus at the next tree? Get real." He snorted a laugh. "Did you bring a flint striker? I need a flint striker."

"No more flint strikers. You *have* to go."

"No. I'm not leavin'."

"Listen to me. You must get to Tule Lake across the California border."

"You're mad." He tossed down the cigarette butt.

"Many Mexicans and skin people live there."

"Skin people?"

"People of color. No one will look for you there. Here's the address to a house." He handed Jim a piece of paper. "Ask for Frank Blaze. He will get you to Oklahoma."

"No!" Jim's hand rubbed the side of his face. "Man, I've got a lot of things I need to get done here before the next winter rolls around."

"Your life here is done." Mo drank more water from the bottle and took a deep breath. "Done." Even in the cold, his forehead seemed moist. "I put clothes in the cave for you, so you'll look like a Mexican farm worker. Cut your hair. Wear the dark glasses and hat I brought. There's a backpack, some food to carry, and money. Here's a map."

Jim looked at the map and then threw it down. "Tule Lake! That's miles from here."

"You go on foot. Maybe takes two, three days. Take food with you. Sleep in the woods at night if you have to. You know how. You know that much. You must go fast."

"Fast? What—"

"Fast."

"Live with people after all these years? Have you been drinkin' something besides water? I couldn't trust myself to be around people no more." Jim took what he wanted and had no need for money. Leave the mountain. It was his home. He couldn't abandon Wolf. What would he do with the kid? Two things he wouldn't be discussing with Mo.

"You got to leave!" Mo's dark eyes flamed. His voice rose. "I'm old and sick. I can't supply you no more."

"I can make it on my own. I've learned a lot, being out here all these years."

"You're stupid if you think you can make it in the wild on your own. No help? Hah." His laugh was weak. "Don't kid yourself. You'll die here. You have to go. Now."

"You don't understand old man. You just don't understand."

Mo threw up his hands. "I've done all I can do." His small eyes watered.

Jim had not seen Mo so emotional since he found him near death years ago. "Maybe it's a good thing I should die here."

"My son," Mo said. "You can go now or spend the rest of your life in a cell or worse. Your life now is in your hands, alone." He hugged Jim, stood back, and patted his shoulder.

"What are you sayin'?"

"I won't see you again."

"What the hell is in those pills of yours, huh? Stay here overnight and rest."

Mo picked up his backpack. "I have done my best for you. Now it is done." His face turned mellow, like a person at a funeral finally accepting the death of a friend.

"I can't just leave. This *is* my life."

"Good-bye," Mo said. He turned swiftly and walked away, leaning on his walking stick, his movements unsteady.

"Mo, wait. Stay here awhile." Jim called. "Let's at least eat together . . . have another cigarette."

"No time," Mo muttered. "Go see Happy Face." He didn't look back; he kept walking, leaving Jim standing there, his head spinning.

"Come back!" Jim yelled, but Mo disappeared into the woods.

Murder. Kidnap. Sex with a kid. A dead boy. Who the hell does that? If I'm caught, they'll blame me. Is that worse? I'm already a murderer and a so-called rapist. I can't let the kid just go. He'll talk. And, what would he say? He's just a kid. And Wolf? He'd die in the wilderness. He's a stray. We're both strays. Used to the wild. Maybe I could take the kid with me, but then there'd be questions. Isn't there something about taking a kid across state lines? Wouldn't that be kidnapping? Mo already told this Frank Blaze about me. What to expect. That didn't include a kid.

Saving the kid was a mistake, but then the cops think he's already dead. He needs new clothes, clothes that can't be traced. What to do? What to do? He just leaves. Walks off and says he won't be seeing me again. Dead to me. Just like that.

The sky darkened and started to throw sleet again. Jim breathed in the cold flakes. Tears welled in his eyes. He hadn't cried since that time twenty years ago. Running. Running. Sitting there in that dark cave, realizing what he'd done, and that he couldn't fix it.

This is where it all began. And now ended? Abandoned. All over again. Alone. How could he just leave like that? Shows up, says this is the last time he'd see me. Just like that over some cock'n bull story. Throws me away. Dumps me like garbage.

Jim's throat tightened, his stomach burned, and a wave of nausea crept from his gut to his throat. He threw up by the edge of the cave. He wiped his mouth on his sleeve. Like a lit fuse connecting with gunpowder, the rage inside him exploded. He smashed his hunting bow against a rock repeatedly; cables snapped, and pulleys flew until nothing but a few pulverized pieces remained. "Son of a bitch," he screamed into the emptiness. "Son of a fuckin'bitch."

CHAPTER 31

A search party of twenty-five set up a base camp along Cooper's Hawk Highway near the area where Cody had gone missing. The party included Ken Blake, county search-and-rescue deputies, forest service employees, members of the Cody Benson Search and Support Group, and other volunteers.

Dottie donated sandwiches and coffee for the search crew and drove Cally to the site. "I'll be prayin' for you honey, and I know Sam is looking' down on us. If it gets to be too much, you just give me a call." She hugged Cally warmly and patted her back before leaving.

Cally stayed at the base camp inside a trailer, courtesy of the search team. She didn't join their efforts because she didn't really want to find Cody out there, not that way. Even if they did find him, it wouldn't be over. There would still be those haunting questions. What had really happened to him? Why hadn't they rescued him in time? *Why did she let him go?*

Pete, who had moved to Medford, did not come. Instead, he left a message on Cally's answering machine, saying he'd become extremely emotional about the idea of finding Cody's remains. "I'm seeing a therapist to help me process it all. I . . .

uh . . . personally contacted the police and asked them to notify me immediately if they find any trace of my son."

His son? Cally felt like she'd been kicked in the stomach. She had so hoped that he would come so they could talk maybe even reconcile. That evening she slipped his photo from the silver frame next to her bed. In the morning, she ran it through the paper shredder.

Tina Williams and a camera crew came to the site for a short segment. "Searchers are here looking for Cody Benson, the nine-year-old Forest Lake boy who disappeared while searching for a Christmas tree six months ago." She stood in front of a picturesque view of the Big Bat, her blond hair blowing in the wind. "The search for Cody was one of the largest in the county. It ended when blizzard conditions forced searchers out of the Big Bat Wilderness area." She paused and frowned. "Just a few weeks ago, the body of seven-year-old Randy Wilkes was discovered a few miles from here. Investigators are working to determine if there's a connection between these two cases."

Tina sought an interview with Ken, but on Richards' orders, he declined. That left Tina with a spokesperson from the Search and Support Group who didn't have much to say, and an earlier interview with Cally, which was replayed on the nightly news.

"I'm not expecting a miracle," Cally had said, "but I hope and pray that we'll at least get some answers." She had been recovering from a cold that had left her eyes bloodshot, her nostrils red, and her voice scratchy. "If they don't find him out there, then where is he?"

"Do you think your son is alive?" Tina asked.

"In my heart, absolutely. I don't think he got lost. I think they, the police bungled it. Something happened." She choked back tears.

Tina reminded viewers that a witness had spotted a man struggling with a small boy, but authorities had failed to follow up on that lead. Her blue eyes narrowed. "Deputy Ken Blake, coordinator for this massive search, declined to speak with us. Tina Williams, reporting live from Forest Lake, Oregon."

***

Inside the trailer, Cally struggled with shortness of breath, chest pain, and a dry, tightening throat—symptoms she had come to recognize as panic attacks. She fought them off by taking Xanax and breathing into a paper bag. The search site brought back memories of the day Cody had gone missing—thick falling snow, the blazing bonfire burning throughout the night, her father crying, Pete's anguish, his throat raw from continually calling for their son. She thought about Cody every day. Sometimes at night, she saw him standing at the foot of her bed, a small bright-eyed, ghostlike figure, smiling at her. She even talked to him. It seemed like yesterday that he had been warm, alive, and spreading peanut butter on just about everything. She missed his drawings and the wild, imaginative stories that came with them. They should have gotten him the dog he wanted so much.

***

Half the search team combed the area where Cody and Sam had looked for Christmas trees. Ken was convinced Cody's remains couldn't be too far from where he'd last been spotted. The other half trekked in the area where they'd found Randy Wilkes's body. Four days later, when the first group made a wider sweep of the area, they indeed found a body.

It was Mo.

He'd died of an apparent heart attack and exposure.

***

That night, Ken lay in bed, his hands cupping his head, unable to sleep. "No wonder I couldn't get a hold of Mo. I talked with him shortly after we called off the search last year," he told

Lydia. "I asked for his help. I never intended that he go out there looking on his own."

Lydia set the book she was reading on the nightstand. "He was a good man. He had a soft spot for kids. Too bad he didn't have a son of his own. There was Jim, but that just ended all wrong."

"He knew the area like the back of his hand. I thought the ol' fool could work with us. Give us some good pointers."

She adjusted her pillows. "Maybe he wanted to do it his way. He was always a loner. Some folks just don't know what time it is, when it comes to what they can do anymore." She turned toward Ken. "Here, sit up, let me massage your shoulders. Try to get some sleep. You're making yourself depressed."

***

Dottie and Ken wanted Mo to have a proper funeral. "He's an ol' timer in this town," she said. "A regular fixture, like the flag pole that sets in front of the school. He kept to himself, but he had a good heart."

Ken thought they should cremate the body and spread Mo's ashes in the Big Bat Wilderness, but Dottie insisted they bury him next to Happy Face. Ken didn't argue with Dottie. Nobody did. Since Mo never set foot inside a church but loved the outdoors, they settled on a graveside service. They picked out a modest coffin, a headstone, and split the cost.

On a sunny but cold spring day, the Blakes, Dottie, and a few members of the search party gathered at the little cemetery north of town to honor the man they believed died searching for Cody Benson. A few other grateful members of the community slipped in. Cally came, too, to show her appreciation, but she stood at a safe distance from the Blakes and made no effort to speak to them.

Pastor Rick, hatless in his gray suit and black overcoat, conducted the brief service. He cleared his throat. "I don't know a lot about Mo, but I would like to read a passage from Psalms." He pulled on his reading glasses and opened his big Bible.

"*The Lord is my shepherd; I shall not want. He maketh me to lie down in green pastures; he leadeth me beside the still waters.*" Pastor Rick licked his lips as if he could taste the words he read. He adjusted his glasses. Periodically, he looked up at the sky. "The images of nature in this passage remind me so much of this man, known to most of us as just *Mo*. I didn't know him well." Pastor Rick cleared his throat. "He never set foot in our church."

Ken looked down at his feet. "How many times does he have to say that?" he whispered to Lydia. Her spine stiffened. She glared at the minister.

"But whenever I saw him in town," he continued, "he always had a warm smile on his face." He squinted to find his place and read, "*Surely, goodness and mercy shall follow me all the days of my life, and I will dwell in the house of the Lord forever.* He lived a quiet, simple life, close to nature. It's fitting that he died on the mountain. May he rest in peace, and may God grant his final wish to find our precious little boy—Cody Benson. Amen."

"Amen," said the group. They seemed to be waiting for him to say more. Instead, Pastor Rick closed his Bible and took off his glasses. He cleared his throat again and stood there as if he didn't know how to end the service. Dottie stepped forward and invited everyone to come to the café for some hot vegetable soup. Pastor Rick let out a big sigh. "Yes, yes. Let's have soup." She slipped him an envelope with a hundred-dollar bill.

Ken didn't linger. He was on duty, he and Lydia needed to get back to the school. Cally hung back to avoid the Blakes. As people got into their cars, two men in coveralls lowered the casket.

***

"That was awfully brief," Lydia said on their way home. She clutched her handbag. "And he never once mentioned Mo's last name. He must've had one."

Ken smiled. "He eventually went by White. Jim said his last name was Whitefeather, but it changed every time ol' Mo told a story. Once he claimed it was Whitecloud. Then he said it was Whitewing." He shot an amused glance at Lydia, who looked perplexed.

"So why did he settle on White, then?"

"One day, Happy Face explained taxes and Social Security to him. Then she laid down the law. She said it's not White this, not White that. It's White. Period." Ken laughed.

Lydia stared straight ahead. "Well, Pastor Rick could have said a prayer or something about his woodcarving. Mo did beautiful work. He had a special talent for that."

"He probably didn't know. I guess we should have told him. He was kind of reluctant to do the service since Mo never went to church."

"Are you kidding me?"

"He said it was hard for him to pray over nonbelievers."

"Well, he probably did that a lot of times and didn't know it. Just because someone sits in a pew . . . doesn't mean . . . who knows what's in a person's heart? I don't know what Mo believed, do you?"

"I suspect the good pastor's feelings had more to do with the Jenkins, you know, Myra, and Mo's connection to Jim Fallingwater. The Jenkins did a lot for the church."

"Mo was not responsible for what Jim did." Lydia's face always flushed when she was irritated. "And he never caused Myra to go over the edge. She did that to herself. What a hypocrite. It reminds me of that time he was all in a snit after the Tilldens decided to open the grocery store on Sundays to accommodate the tourists. He got over it in a hurry when they threatened to quit contributing to the building fund. Sheesh."

"Dottie read him the riot act over Mo," Ken chuckled. "You know Dottie. Once she got through with him, he was probably begging to pray over a dead raccoon."

Lydia laughed. Ken reached over and squeezed her knee. She genuinely cared about people, and she had a good, broad mind. Thank God for that.

He dropped Lydia off at the grade school and headed up Cooper's Hawk Highway toward the mountain to that special spot. A huge cloud hung in the blue sky like a gigantic swirl of cotton over the mountain's snowy cap. Ken thought the odd-shaped cloud was nature's way of honoring Mo. He stepped out of his Jeep cruiser and took a deep breath. *Who knows, maybe Mo's last name really was Whitecloud.*

Ken hated funerals. When he and Lydia had walked to their car, he'd looked over his shoulder and seen the small bulldozer pushing a pile of dirt over the grave. *They put you in the cold ground and dump dirt on you. Then the world is done with you.* He wished now he hadn't looked. His stomach gnawed at him. He couldn't switch off his thoughts. *You live a life with all its difficulties. In the end, people gather over you and try to sum you up, but they struggle because they couldn't really know.* He had been close to Mo as a boy, but he never felt like he knew him. Mo had always been elusive. No—*enigmatic* was a better word. He could never tell what had been going on behind those small, dark eyes and that smile. Sometimes his childlike talk had meandered, but the guy could look right through you. He'd known what you were thinking before you did.

Dottie was right. Mo had a good heart. He'd taken Jim under his wing, and Ken had gone along. It had been one of the best times of his life. Jim Fallingwater. Mo had done so much for him, given him a chance, and in the end, Jim had blown it. A short, ruined life.

Ken's last link to that era was now dead. Perhaps he could put it all to rest. How ironic that both of them had died on the Big Bat, their spirits out there mingling in the brisk wind. So much had happened in the past six months—two adults dead, two young boys gone, his daughter recovering from a senseless act. Things you never thought would happen in a small town. After four days of searching, there still was no trace of Cody. Maybe he was wrong. Maybe Cody wasn't on the mountain.

"Captain Jack," Ken shouted impulsively to the spirit world.

Jack, Jack, Jack, the mountain echoed.

"Mo is gone."

Gone, Gone, the words bounced back.

He took a beaded bracelet from his pocket. Mo had made it for him and one just like it for Jim when they were young boys. He'd kept it all these years in the back of Lydia's jewelry box. He fingered the beads in his hand and then tossed it over the cliff. "This belongs with you. Rest in peace, buddy," he said. "We're gonna find that boy for you."

CHAPTER 32

Len Roster's right eye twitched so severely, it made the left one flutter chaotically in weird harmony. Even with his glasses, he could hardly see the road. He took a long, slow drag off his non-filtered Camel cigarette to savor the full effect of the tobacco, but it did nothing to calm him. His shaking hands gripped the wheel.

I need a joint, but you can't get one in a place like Forest Lake. You hafta drive all the way out to Bender's, hang out in a smoky, dark corner, and wait for that weird Smitty. Then you couldn't trust the guy.

He flicked an inch of ashes into the ashtray already brimming with butts. *Why the hell couldn't Trula ever empty the thing? Damn lazy broad. Just sits on her butt and watches the tube.*

"Shut up! Quit crying!" he yelled through a cloud of smoke at the little blond boy in the front seat. "I'm taking you to your Ma, for Christ sakes." His shouting did no good. The child bawled.

Why can't they leave me alone? All those damn people gnawing on me. I tried. I honest-to-God tried, even had a job lined up, but all those damn do-gooders pointed fingers at me. Made me lose it. It wasn't my fault.

Then that bastard landlord came buzzin' in from Medford, or wherever the hell he's from, on that big friggin' Harley, and ordered us out. Me and Trula paid the rent on that poor excuse of a tin box. Where the hell are we supposed to go?

He checked the rearview mirror and stepped on the gas. So far, so good. He was the only one driving up the highway. "Look, there's nothin' left for me now," he said to the child fidgeting in the seat, as if he could make him understand, "except to go back to Chemult and live with the ol' man. Home. What a raging joke. The house is a dump, filled with junk." Roster's voice got louder. He slapped the steering wheel. "As soon as I set a foot in the door, the ol' fart will foam at the mouth and start yapping fire and brimstone. I'd rather die."

The child's eyes widened. "Mama," he wailed.

"Can't bring Trula there. The ol' man won't have it. God, I need Trula."

The little boy howled and pummeled his small legs against the seat. Roster's hand came off the wheel and slammed against the dashboard. "Knock it off!" he yelled, "or, I'll hogtie ya."

He didn't know where it came from, that strange electricity that moved through his body. It'd surged again that day he'd parked in front of the Forest Lake Grade school and asked those young boys for directions. He'd tried to relieve it by smoking pot and looking at his collection of kid pornography that he hid behind a wall in the trailer. It didn't help much. Nothing helped. And pot cost money. Lots of it. The times with Trula didn't stop that deep ache. He needed her though, but it was only with boys, young boys, that it really felt like love.

The image of Trula, leaning against the door of their trailer, shot through his mind. "I'm leaving," she'd said, lids flicking nervously over gray eyes. "I can't take it anymore. Every time I go into town, they give me those evil looks." They'd let the air out of her tires, and someone fingered the words "White

Trash" on the side door of her dirty car. She picked at the black, chipped polish on her fingernails. "I'm afraid. I'm very afraid."

And the ol' man, preachin' at me all the time. Hell and damnation. Hell and damnation. All the time saying I'm gonna burn in hell. I couldn't help how things turned out. I tried. God knows, I tried. God made me, too. Those friggin' high-and-mighty people. They took my job, my house, my woman. What the hell do they expect? Ha. Who knows what they do in their bedrooms?

He passed farmhouses with barns and field after field dotted with grazing cows. Soon signs of civilization slipped away. The highway steepened and narrowed, causing the car to chug. He shifted to a lower gear. "C'mon baby. Easy. Easy."

I always hafta grab what I need. It's the only way to calm the throbbing inside me. I never meant to kill that Randy, but I couldn't get through to him. That damn kid bit me. I loved that kid. I really did. Hell, Trula wanted to move in. Something had to give.

A yellow sign warned of approaching curves. Roster laughed his silly, feckless laugh and took another long drag off his Camel. There were all those times no one knew about and never would.

Cops are stupid. So goddammed stupid. None of the others told except that one. What was his name? Wayne. That's it. That stupid freckle-faced little chub. I was just trying to show him some love, and he enjoyed it. I know he did.

He crammed the cigarette butt into the ashtray. With his right hand, he worked another one out of the pack, clenched it firmly between his lips, lit up, and took several long pulls.

The trick is to reel 'em in. Let them tag along. Listen. Then hook 'em like a fish. That Wilkes kid shoulda never bit me. He tried to run, too. Why? Fed him. Gave him a place to sleep. Randy Dandy. I loved the kid. That's why I kept his belt and that one shoe in the wall there with his pictures. All I have to do is touch 'em, and those rousing feelings come back.

He rounded a curve, almost losing control. "Shit," he said and eased his foot off the accelerator. *It's not enough now. Don't work like before. Why couldn't they get off my back? I need to get this friggin' tension out of my body. Just get it out, so I can think. If only this damn kid would shut up. He's a young one, but I didn't have no choice.*

He wouldn't be taking this kid back to the trailer like before, but he wasn't planning on keeping him. There wasn't time. He just needed to get to the Big Bat and afterward head off to Nevada. Roster checked his mirror again and glimpsed a huge truck coming up fast on his rear. That wasn't good. Truck drivers riding high up could get a good look into a car. He sped up and pulled off to the side until the truck rumbled by with the driver looking straight ahead.

Phew. When I get to Arizona, I'm gonna have myself a hamburger and a big bunch of fries. And a strawberry milkshake. After I find a place to stay, I'll contact Trula. I can work her like putty. At least she promised to bring my things.

He pulled back onto the highway, watching his speed and trying to steady his driving. He was getting close to the mountain now, driving into a heavily forested area, trees running by the car windows on both sides.

He gave his little passenger a baleful smile and clenched his teeth. The child was leaning sideways, trying to wiggle his way out of the seatbelt. Roster jerked him upright in the seat. The car swerved. The child cowered and continued to cry.

"I said, knock it off!"

The stupid little kid wandered toward the vending machines by the doors, trying to get a gumball. You could always depend on a kid to wander. Ha. Plunked in a quarter, gave the kid the treat. Told him there were more in the car and just led him out the door like a blind sheep. Why the hell doesn't he shut up? I need a joint, if I just had a joint, I could calm these damn jitters. "Shut up! Shut up! Shut up!"

Four-year-old Jason Atwater of Klamath Falls and his mother were shopping at the SavCo grocery store. She chatted up the checker while bagging her groceries, quibbling about the discount she was supposed to get on coffee and telling the cashier what a good deal they had on cereal. She'd bought five boxes for ten dollars. "Jason just loves cereal, especially the sugar charms, don't you Jason?" She thought Jason was by her side, but when she turned to him, he was gone. At first, she thought he might have disappeared down one of the aisles, playing with that little red plastic airplane he had. A store employee in a green apron checked aisles and the restrooms. No Jason.

Witnesses remembered seeing a little boy by the vending machines, but that was all. A heavyset, blond woman said she saw a young child in the parking lot with his father. She didn't remember seeing a vehicle.

"It couldn't be Jason's father," the distraught mother cried, "his father lives in Minnesota."

After they found the red plastic airplane on the asphalt, the store manager dialed 911. The mother gripped the little red toy and sobbed. An officer came to the store. Minutes later, police issued an Amber Alert:

> *We have just received this important information regarding an abducted child in Klamath County. The Klamath County Sheriff's Office is looking for a child who was last seen at the SaveCo Grocery store and is believed to be in danger. The child's name is Jason Atwater. He is four years old with blond hair and blue eyes. He is wearing a red jacket and brown pants. Authorities say the child may be in the company of an adult male. If you have any information on the whereabouts of this child, please contact the Klamath County Sheriff's Office or the Oregon State Police.*

***

A middle-aged couple driving toward Medford spotted a maroon station wagon speeding and moving erratically on the highway. When they heard the scary buzzing sound announcing the Amber Alert on their car radio, they contacted police. They could not see inside the vehicle, they said, but it seemed suspicious, like maybe the driver was struggling with someone or something. The alert was updated:

> *… Authorities say the child may be in the company of an adult male, and they may be traveling in a maroon station wagon that was last seen heading toward Medford. If you have any information about this child, please contact the Klamath County Sheriff's Office or the Oregon State Police.*

***

When Ken heard the updated radio report, he thought of one person, *Roster*. He sped to Ray's Trailer Park, down the potholed driveway until he came to the faded turquoise-and-white trailer. The maroon station wagon was not there. He knocked. No answer. "Police! Open up!" he shouted. Nothing. A dog barked off in the distance. He hurried to the back, but no one came to that door, either. All the blinds were drawn. When he returned to the front, a small group of tenants had gathered on the other side of the driveway. Six blank faces stared at him.

"Have you seen the guy that lives here?" Ken shouted.

The group looked stunned. "No," a scruffy man in a white T-shirt and black pants said. He took a long drag from his cigarette and blew smoke. "Last I heard he got kicked outta here."

Ken turned back to the trailer. He raised his leg and kicked the door with all his might. Someone in the small crowd gasped. A fat woman in a worn, pink bathrobe asked, "Do you think there's gonna be shooting?" The flimsy door sprung. Inside, a heavy smell of tobacco lingered in the air. Kitchen cabinet doors gaped open. A cereal box stood on the counter next to a rotting banana peel. In the corner, a wastebasket brimmed with empty beer cans. A drip-drip-drip sound came from a leaky faucet in the small bathroom. A stack of two suitcases sat on the couch next to a pile of dirty laundry. A row of packed cardboard boxes lined the wall. *He's coming back*, Ken thought. *He's getting ready to move, but he's coming back.*

He hurried to his Jeep cruiser. His radio crackled. Someone had spotted the maroon station wagon heading back toward Forest Lake. *That figures.* The police planned to set up a roadblock on the highway. All units were ordered to assist.

Ken had a gut feeling, something inside that he couldn't explain. He disregarded the order to help with the roadblock and instead headed toward the Big Bat. If he was wrong, he'd probably be chewed out royally, maybe disciplined. What the heck, he'd already entered a residence without a search warrant. Maybe they'd fire him, but he didn't care. *A child's life is at stake.* If that wasn't reason enough, maybe he should get into another line of work.

***

Jim Fallingwater took one final trek to the lake area to find clothes for Cody. He needed to make sure the kid wasn't wearing anything that could be identified. He surveyed the vacant cabins to see what people stored on their back porches—toys, baseball bats, Frisbees, and smaller bikes meant kids stayed there. It took two break-ins to get what he wanted. He snagged a pair of jeans, a couple of shirts, a sweater, a jacket, and even some underwear. The clothes might be a little big, but they would do. He also found a jar of peanuts and a tin of coffee.

Smug about his loot, he headed back. He still struggled to make sense of what Mo had said. Sometimes he thought the ol' guy was coming unhinged, but then again, Mo had never lied to him. *Never.* He wished their meeting wasn't so rushed. He had a thousand questions he wanted to ask.

What was that?

He halted. Sounds like a kid crying? He jumped off the trail, ducked down behind some brush, and waited. He never expected to meet anyone out here in the middle of the week. There they are, coming up the trail—a father and his little boy. The kid's bawling. The man is pulling him along.

"Quit that blubbering. Why can't you shut up?" Roster grabbed Jason around the waist, picked him up roughly, and shook him.

A chill swept up Jim's back. Can this be a father and son? Something's wrong. The kid isn't dressed right for a trek into the wild—light jacket, no hat or boots, just tennis shoes covered with wet mud. He remembered what Mo said about the man who grabbed kids for sex. In the shadows, Jim followed them for some time. He watched so intently, his big foot stepped on a fallen branch and it snapped.

Roster pulled out a gun and shoved the boy down. He turned and looked. After his body made a full revolution, he grabbed the sobbing little boy and held him in front, like a shield.

"Who's there?" Roster shouted. His right eye twitched out of control. Sometimes it seemed like his whole face twitched. He listened. He looked. Except for the wailing kid, there was only silence.

Roster set the boy down, jerked a cigarette from his pocket. His hand shook as he lit it. He took two long drags. He started walking again, gun still drawn, pulling the child along.

"Mama," Jason cried, tears ran down his apple cheeks. His clothes were all muddy. He'd wet his pants.

Jim eyed Roster's gun. He remembered what Mo had said. *They found the body of a boy. He'd been shot in the head.*

The child dragged his feet, trying to sit. Roster jerked him up. "You little shit, you've gone an' pissed your pants." He slapped him on the back of the head. Jason fell to the ground. "You want more, I'll give you more. Now shut up!"

When Roster struck Jason, something cracked like lightning inside Jim. For a moment, he saw a vision of his own father holding a gun, standing over his dog that lay bleeding in the grass. That white, blinding rage exploded. He sprang from the bushes, his big body crashing against Roster's. The cigarette flew from Roster's mouth. Jim gripped his wrist, knocking the gun from his hand. Roster was no match for this large, feral man, who now had him in a chokehold and squeezed with his big hands until he lost consciousness and crumpled like a rag doll. Jim was shaking and breathing hard.

The terrified boy screamed. Jim knelt in front of him. "Look, kid, don't cry." It didn't help. "Okay, cry," Jim muttered. "I don't blame you. I'd cry, too." He grabbed Jason and held him close to his chest while he bounded back toward the highway. When he got there, he saw a small blue Ford with a dent on the side parked on the shoulder. No one was around. The kid kept screaming. Jim couldn't be sure if this was the man's car, but it didn't matter. The doors were unlocked. Someone would come along and find a little boy. It was the best he could do.

"Sorry, little one." He put the boy in the back seat and locked the doors, just as a police cruiser approached with its lights flashing. "Oh, Jesus." He bounded back to the forest, like a deer running from a mountain lion.

Ken spotted the parked car and saw a man dart from it into the woods. He pulled up behind the Ford, jumped out, and drew his Glock ready to pursue.

But wait.

Someone was looking at him through the back window. *There's a little boy inside.* He approached the car cautiously.

Where was the maroon station wagon? Where was Roster? Someone might be hiding inside, but then he'd seen a man running from this car.

Blond hair, red jacket, brown pants, about four years old. *It's the missing child.* He appeared to be in there alone. Startled by a gunshot coming from the woods, Ken crouched down and waited. No more shots. He got up slowly, broke the front window with his sap baton and pulled up the lock. He reached in and unlocked the back door. "Hi Jason," he said. "It's all right. I'm a police officer, and I'm going to take you home." He holstered his gun, scooped up little Jason, who clung to him.

"Mama," he sobbed.

"It's okay, Jason." Ken patted his back as he carried him to the cruiser. He readied his gun again, radioed headquarters, called for backup, and asked them to send an ambulance. He tried to quiet the child. "Don't cry, little Jason. Mommy's coming." Using the boy's name calmed him a bit.

Snot from Jason's nose dribbled into his mouth. Ken reached for a handful of Kleenex and began wiping the boy's face. He didn't have a stuffed animal or much of anything else in the cruiser that was suitable to entertain a child. He remembered the roll of cherry Life Savers stowed in the glove compartment. "How would you like a piece of candy?" Jason watched him warily with his big blue eyes. "It's okay, Jason. Mommy's coming," Ken repeated.

Hesitantly, Jason took the candy. He pointed his index finger. "Bad man taked me. I want Mama."

"It's okay, now." Ken unpinned his shiny badge and handed it to the boy. "Here you hold this. No one will hurt you." He tweaked the little boy's nose. Jason looked up and gave a half smile.

***

Roster lay sprawled on the ground next to his gun, glasses, and baseball cap. He was unconscious but still breathing. Jim towered over him, his breath coming in quick gasps from running hard. He didn't have a lot of time. Those cops had spotted him. They'd be here any minute. His eyes focused on the gun. Then he remembered. *This dirtbag looked right at me once I jumped him. I can't chance it.*

Jim picked up the gun with his gloved hands and wrapped Roster's fingers around the butt and trigger. He stared at Roster's peaceful face, half lying in the mud. For a brief moment, an image of his father floated through his mind. Smirking. Laughing. Lunging at him, hand raised to strike. Jim pointed the gun at Roster's temple and squeezed the trigger. As soon as he did, the torment he felt drifted away.

***

Ken wanted to pursue Roster or whoever that man was, but he knew that wouldn't be wise. There could be more than one person involved. And why the gunshot? No, his first responsibility was to the child.

***

Jim leaned over the body, calmly ripped two buttons from Roster's coat, pulled the pack of Camel cigarettes from the pocket, and sprang into the dense woods.

CHAPTER 33

A leathery-faced rancher at Bartley's Feed Store wrote out a check for the sacks of alfalfa hay pellets stacked on his pickup bed. He scratched his head. "This is just crazy. It used to be more steers than people died around here." He hooked his thumbs behind the straps of bib overalls. "Now it's t'other way round."

Ed Bartley shook his head. "You can't get no answers from a dead man. That's for sure." He stuffed the check in the register.

***

"It's a terrible time for us," Millie Harbaugh, a cook at the school, declared in the waiting room at the clinic. She had come to get more pills for her high blood pressure, which was growing higher by the minute. She smoothed the navy blue and pink floral print skirt over her thick legs. "My grandkids were supposed to come for the summer. Now we just don't know." She pulled the gold wrapper from a piece of butterscotch candy she always carried in her pocket and popped the hard disc into her mouth. "We just don't know," she said again as the sweetness filled her mouth and the candy clicked against her dentures.

***

Even though little Jason Atwater was rescued and Roster was dead, the schoolchildren were restless, some even scared. Their parents wondered how much freedom to give them during the summer. Teachers and counselors agreed that some positive activity would help. And so, on a sunny Friday afternoon in late May, a crowd of over one-hundred came to Delaney Park, a small patch of grass with a swing set, slide, and baseball diamond, to attend a ceremony honoring Cody Benson.

Ken and Lydia Blake came. So did Dottie Johnson, along with Deputy Don Range and State Police Detective Frank Lane. Jason Atwater's mother drove from Klamath Falls with the boy's father, who flew in from Minnesota. They stood next to the Blakes. The Tilldens and the Bradshaws left their stores in the hands of hired help so they could come. Dorothea Hart, Harriet Cole, and Carol Leach from the Forest Lake Woman's Club arrived in Dorothea's green Comet. Carol managed to steer her friends away from the Bradshaws. She still worried that Alma was telling people about her buying the hemorrhoid cream.

Cally overhead Dorothea Hart say that Myra Jenkins was still in a mental health facility in Klamath Falls. She didn't know when she'd be released, if ever. Floyd, she said, was living alone in the old house, and he'd lost a lot of weight. "He's just wearin' himself out trying to get over there to Klamath Falls and still run that gas station."

Velma Wright arrived with an aluminum TV tray and one of her famous lemon coconut cakes which she beamed over as if she'd just given birth. She set up under a tree, her confection perched on a pedestal-style cake plate with a glass dome. To raise more funds for the Cody Benson reward fund, she sold five-dollar raffle tickets from the fat roll she'd bought at the Mercantile. To help sales, she removed the glass dome, so the creamy white frosting gleamed in the sunshine, sending out the mouth-watering aroma of sugar and fat. Soon a long line formed for a chance at the cake. Velma placed the money she collected in a green Tupperware container.

When Tina Williams and her cameraman showed up to shoot some background footage, people turned their heads and stopped talking. Fortunately, just as she arrived, the high school band started playing. They kicked off the ceremony with a blaring rendition of "Nearer my God to Thee."

Once they finished, Pastor Rick stepped up to the microphone on a small platform the high school shop class had hastily constructed for the occasion. "There's always a silver lining," he said, "even in the darkest hours." He fumbled his notes. "There's always a silver lining," he said again. His hand touched the center of his dark-framed glasses. He looked up. "I'd like to recognize Cally Benson, Cody's mother. She's been a strong pillar through all of this." He asked her to come forward. It took him two tries to pin a corsage of red-and-white carnations on her jacket. He chuckled. "My wife's better at these kinds of things." There was a low hum of laugher from the crowd. When he finally succeeded to a burst of applause, he offered Cally a seat on a white plastic chair next to the platform.

"And where is Deputy Ken Blake?" he asked. Ken raised his arm. "Deputy Blake's quick thinking saved a little boy's life. God was speaking to him. He followed his heart, and we have little Jason Atwater home, safe and happy with his parents. You're a hero, Ken Blake."

The crowd applauded. Ken flushed, managed a smile, and waved again from the crowd. Mr. Atwater, who was standing next to him, patted him on the back. Mrs. Atwater shook his hand with both of hers. Lydia looked on proudly. Dottie winked at him. Frank Lane punched him on the shoulder. Cally took a deep breath, stared straight ahead, and did not applaud.

Ken didn't expect any recognition. He didn't consider himself a hero, and hearing it made him uncomfortable. But at least he was back in the town's good graces. The guys down at Dottie's were saving the center seat for him at lunch again. Even Floyd Jenkins managed a half smile when he stopped in at the Shell Station. He knew the Bensons didn't think of him as a hero, and that deep-down, Floyd probably didn't either. No, it wasn't over yet, and it wouldn't be until he had some answers about Cody.

Pastor Rick recognized Jason's parents. "Thank you for coming all this way. Our—"

He stopped and smiled nervously as the crowd drowned him out with applause for the Atwaters. "As I was saying, our little town of Forest Lake has been brought to its knees and to the depths of despair over the recent months. Lives have been lost—precious Randy Wilkes, Sam Lightener, Cody's grandfather, and old Mo, a man with a good heart. Even so, we still hold out hope for Cody Andrew Benson. Try as we may, we can't be everywhere. That's God's job, and we pray that he will bring Cody home to us soon."

He urged the crowd to take a moment for a silent prayer to remember those who had passed and, in their own way, to pray for Cody's safe return. After an appropriate time, he lifted his head and asked the group to join him saying the Lord's Prayer. When they finished, he said "Amen and Amen." He paused and looked at his notes. Then he nodded to Miss Brackston, Cody's teacher.

Miss Brackston, wearing the familiar denim skirt and brown leather boots, stood up from her plastic chair on the other side of the platform, her rosy nose pointing up. She led the children in Cody's class to some risers and lined them up. Miss Brackston's right arm made wide swings in the air while the children sang an energetic "You'll Never Walk Alone." Cally could see Brittany singing with all her heart and pudgy, red-cheeked Artie Bradshaw fidgeting in the back row, struggling to remember the words.

"Oh, that was wonderful," Pastor Rick said when they finished. "Just wonderful. Thank you, Miss Brackston and children. Thank you so much." He cleared his throat. "We don't always understand why things happen, but one thing I do know — God has Randy Wilkes in His arms. We pray that He will bring Cody Benson home, and that He will keep all our youngsters safe." He nodded again toward Miss Brackston.

She signaled for the children to follow her to a bank of tethered balloons. Some men from the fire department helped her distribute handfuls. "On the count of three," Miss Brackston said. "One, two, three release!" Hundreds of red and white balloons filled the air. Brittany clapped her hands and waved as the balloons floated toward the blue sky.

Cally choked back tears watching the wind carry the last few balloons over the trees. The children had done their best — everyone had. But their efforts could not quell the despair that lingered deep inside. Nothing would soothe her bruised heart until she could once-and-for-all hold Cody in her arms again. After the vigil, people came up one by one to offer hugs or shake her hand. She still felt empty.

Out of the corner of her eye, she saw Deputy Range laughing and gloating because he'd won Velma's prize cake, and groups of people hovering around Deputy Blake and the Atwaters. It hurt. Of course, she was happy for the Atwaters, but she couldn't help it. They had their son, she didn't. And that Ken Blake. He may have rescued that little boy, but he'd failed Cody.

The crowd finally thinned. Cally stood in the tiny park alone — with so many memories. She had brought Cody here when he was little and pushed him in those very swings. He'd fed part of his lunch to a curious squirrel and gotten a bee sting on his nose because he'd watched it too closely.

A white balloon trailed on the ground and sailed in her direction. She tried to toss it in the air, but it refused to go. For some reason it wouldn't float like the others. She picked up the lonely, abandoned balloon. "I guess you're just different," she said and hugged it tightly to her chest. It pressed against the pin that held her corsage. The sudden pop made her jump. She looked at the shattered white latex in her hand, one minute it was here, and the next it was gone, just like Cody and her life. In that instant, her heart told her what she already knew. She had to leave Forest Lake. The ceremony was over. Everything was over. Oh, the police assured her they were planning to search portions of the heavy terrain again, but Cody wasn't on the mountain. He couldn't be. She felt powerless. And alone, so alone. She needed to restart her life. Somehow. She did not want to become another Myra Jenkins, hanging onto the past, until little by little it devoured her. She bent to pick up her purse when she felt a tug on her sweater. She turned to see Artie Bradshaw standing there holding a bouquet of bright, yellow flowers.

"These are for you." He hung his head.

"Thank you, Artie." Cally bent over and kissed him on his ruddy cheek. He looked up at her, grinned sheepishly, and scampered back to his parents who waited for him. They smiled and nodded. Alma even waved.

They're a family, Cally thought. Quirky maybe, but still a *family.* Something she no longer had. It was time to go.

***

The police had snared the maroon station wagon speeding back to Forest Lake during the highway roadblock. The driver was Trula Davis, Len Roster's girlfriend. Now, she fidgeted in the interview room, twisting the ends of her long, dark hair. She nervously pushed away the jagged bangs that hung over her eyebrows. She had a thin, heart-shaped face and a silver bead lip piercing on the left side. A tattoo of six dark dots peeked from her bangs and continued down her left cheek. Her perfume smelled overly sweet. It mingled with the strong odor of tobacco on her clothes, making her scent stale and cheap. Her gray eyes, heavily made up with black mascara smeared on the upper and lower lids, surveyed Walt Richards, Frank Lane, and Ken Blake. She looked like a scared raccoon.

Roster had asked her to drive to Medford to pick up a package, she said, and to fill up on gas at a certain Chevron station on the way back. "I had no idea what Lenny was off doing." Her hand played with a pack of Camel cigarettes. Richards had told her she couldn't smoke in the interview room. "Lenny said he was going to find a new place for us to live. Then I was to pack up the station wagon with our stuff and join him."

The police had confiscated the package she'd picked up. Inside they uncovered Randy Wilkes' belt, his shoe, and Roster's collection of pornography. Apparently, that special package was Roster's way of ensuring he could keep those items.

The stop at a busy gas station, police speculated, was to produce a receipt for an alibi. That way Roster could claim he was in Medford when little Jason went missing. Trula knew nothing about Randy Wilkes. She and Roster had not been living together then. When Randy had become too difficult for Roster, police suspected, he got rid of him and invited Trula to share his trailer.

Trula said she met Lenny while working at Bender's, the bar out on the highway. She could offer no details about Cody Benson. "His mother did come to our place that one time, asking about him." Lenny, she said, did not ask her to run any "errands" on or around December 5 when Cody went missing. Roster claimed he had gone to Klamath Falls on that date for an interview, which he said he didn't know had been cancelled because there wasn't a phone in the trailer. He had produced a gas receipt from the same Chevron station.

"Maybe he had someone else do the run?" Ken asked. "Maybe he had an accomplice."

Trula shook her head. She didn't know. "I can't get my mind around all this stuff you're sayin' about Lenny. He was a really sweet guy. We were both going to get heart tattoos. We hadn't decided where." She giggled and then realized she was the only one laughing. "I mean I don't know what I'm gonna do now that he's gone." She picked up the pack of Camel cigarettes. "These were Lenny's favorites," she said. "Is it okay if I smoke now?"

"Take it outside," Richards growled. He watched Trula saunter out of the room in her short skirt.

"I just don't get it." He held his face in his hands.

"You mean about the Benson kid?" Lane wondered.

"I mean why the lip piercing and that tramp stamp? She's not a half-bad looking gal."

Lane shot a glance at Ken. They both stared at Richards.

"They can ditch the lip gadget, but those tattoos. They don't ever come off." He shook his head.

***

Jason Atwater was too young to be of help to the investigation. Len Roster's father, Lyle, a big, stocky man with stooped shoulders, a shock of white hair, and a bulbous, red nose, was about as helpful as a glass of ice water in a blizzard. "Len was a good Christian boy," he claimed, when the police drove to his home outside Chemult to interview him. "He was raised in a good family. He woulda never done the things you all are sayin'. Somebody set him up."

"Did he have any guy friends?" Ken asked.

"Just what are you implying?" Lyle snorted.

"Someone who may have influenced him, or maybe helped him?" Ken said. "I mean, you just said he was set up."

"He was livin' with that little bar fly. I knew that would come to no good." Lyle rambled on. "He killed himself because of that whole rotten town, that incestuous den of iniquity was pickin' on him like a swarm of locusts. The Bible says you're not supposed to take your life. It's not what God wants." He spit on the ground. "He was my son," he said sadly. "My wife died. He was all I had. I did the best I could."

CHAPTER 34

On Monday following the ceremony for Cody, Cally braced herself for the long drive to southeast Portland for a weeklong visit with the Gaiser family.

Cally hadn't heard from Ellen, her high school friend, in years. "I didn't even know you were in Oregon until I read about your missing son in the paper. I am so sorry," Ellen had said in a telephone call. She also sent a thoughtful sympathy card after Cally's father died, with this added note: *We'd love to see you. If there's ever anything we can do to help you, just give us a call.* Cally had finally reached out.

***

The Gaiser home was a tiny but neat, white bungalow in a modest neighborhood with a patch of grass in the front that sloped down to the sidewalk, a detached garage, and a small, fenced backyard.

A stay-at-home mom, Ellen had put on weight, and her once bright chestnut hair sported a few gray strands. But she still had those inviting blue eyes and that natural, cheery smile that had earned her the "Most Friendly" designation in the "Senior Personalities" section of their high school yearbook.

Her husband, Jerry, with thinning, curly brown hair and glasses, was a short man who carried his weight in his stomach. Ellen's son, Justin, a pint-size version of his dad, had just turned thirteen. Jerry proudly introduced him as an honor student who played clarinet in the band and had earned a spot on the softball team. The two constantly talked sports and tossed softballs in the backyard, things Pete had never done with Cody

The little girl, Sally, was in the first grade. She had light brown hair and her mother's blue eyes. Jerry tucked her in at night and read her bedtime stories. They displayed Sally's awkward crayon artwork all over the bulletin board in their cramped but cheery kitchen. Photographs of family outings and the kids' accomplishments covered three sides of the fridge. The only thing tacked on Cally's refrigerator was the grocery list.

The Gaisers treated their dog, Max, a lovable golden retriever, like a family member. At night, he slept in Justin's room. When Cally sat on the living room sofa, Max laid his chin on her knee and looked at her with two dark eyes, as if he could feel her pain. Once she patted his head, he settled down by her feet. She wished they'd gotten Cody a dog. The children adored Max, and he had such a calming effect on everyone.

Over a dinner of meatloaf, mashed potatoes, and green beans, they talked about the good ol' days in Montana. After the children were excused, Cally told them about her troubled marriage and her desire to leave Forest Lake. "Of course, I'd need to find a job and a place to stay. My degree from Bozeman State was in liberal arts, so I don't have a lot of job skills. What I really want to do, well eventually, is to return to college and finish requirements to teach grade school."

Ellen brightened. "Oh, honey, that's an admirable goal."

Jerry thought so, too. A high school math teacher, he said he knew someone who worked downtown at the Portland State University Library. "I just talked with Rena today. She was trying to fill some position. I'm not sure what." After a dessert of applesauce and homemade oatmeal cookies, he made a phone call.

Ellen assured her that she could stay with them for as long as she needed, but Cally knew that wouldn't be a good idea; there was barely enough room in that small house for her now.

"Oh, you're so kind, but if I'm going to do this, I need to stand on my own two feet." An image of Myra Jenkins's cold, empty stare floated in front of her.

Things happened fast. By Wednesday, Cally had interviewed for a temporary library assistant position. Late that afternoon, Rena called the house and offered her the job, saying there was a good possibility it could become a permanent one. The salary was modest, Rena explained, but if—and when—she became a full-time employee, she could attend classes at the university at a lower rate. The one catch—they wanted her to start as soon as possible.

On Thursday, Cally ventured downtown again to sign some papers and pick up a new employee packet. She stopped in at the PSU library to look around. The curved library building with its multi-levels and banks of glass windows looked like a huge cruise ship. Students of all ages studied there and browsed what seemed like thousands of books. The student body alone was fifty times bigger than the population of the city of Forest Lake.

Earlier, the gray sky had puddled rain on the brick walkways. Now they glistened as if wrapped in cellophane. Tall buildings with their rows of boxy windows loomed overhead like concrete giants. In the city, everything—the traffic, cabs, buses—pulsed. Even the air, redolent with gasoline fumes, sweet pastries, and coffee, seemed exciting. Women wearing heels, makeup, and jewelry, and men in business suits all rushed about, constantly checking their cell phones. The younger crowd brushed by in their own world, hooked up to earphones. Back home, out in the hinterlands, a person could drive all day and only meet a couple of cars. But here, under the pearl-gray light, she felt anonymous, free, comforted. People didn't grow quiet and stare at her like they did in Forest Lake, as if they expected her to explode or worse.

The events of the past few months had made her feel tired and old. Now, did she dare say it, she felt alive, searching, hopeful … and *guilty*. It had always seemed wrong to feel anything while her only child was missing, perhaps being tortured or maybe even dead.

That afternoon she found a small studio apartment in Southeast Portland, next to the bus line and six blocks away from the MAX light rail system. The prior tenant, the landlord said, was a college student. The apartment wasn't much, just a single room with a brownish-gray carpet, neutral walls, and a separate bathroom. Its kitchen was a counter and some cabinets along one wall. The bathroom had a tub with a shower, a pedestal sink, and a medicine cabinet with a mirrored door. A dripping sink faucet left a brown stain by the drain. Everything in it needed a good scrubbing. She cautiously opened the cabinet door. Tacked on the inside was a piece of yellowing paper with a typewritten quote:

> *Become the sky.*
> *Take an axe to the prison wall.*
> *Escape.*
> *Walk out like someone suddenly born into*
> *color.*
> *Do it now.*
>
> *--Rumi*

She pulled it loose, folded it, and put it in her purse. *Escape. Walk out.* She made a deposit and signed the tenant agreement, which instantly gave her a sense of relief. Now she had her own special place. She'd bring her sewing machine and make it cozy.

Outside, the cleansing rain had stopped, and the gray light brightened.

Back at the Gaiser house, she slept on a small folding bed in a corner of their finished basement. The bed stood next to an older, scuffed dresser. A round mirror with a chip near the top hung on the wall above it. That was helpful because the house had only one bathroom. Cally used a wobbly metal rack that stood next to the dresser to hang the few clothes she'd brought. There was a portable space heater and an extra wool blanket. Despite the lumpy bed that squeaked whenever she turned and the furnace rumbling throughout the night, after four days of whirlwind events, she easily fell into a deep sleep.

***

On Friday morning, Cally rose early. She was combing her hair when Sally wandered in. She sat on the bed, hugging Bailey, a worn, brown stuffed bear with one eye, and watched Cally apply eyeliner and lipstick.

"And how are you today?" Cally said cheerfully. She straightened her shoulders and glanced into the mirror, pleased with the face looking back.

"Grandma always sleeps down here," Sally said. "When she comes, we have ice cream."

Cally smiled. "That's very nice. Does Grandma come often?"

"Sometimes." She swung her small legs.

Cally blotted her lips with a tissue. "You must look forward to her visits."

"She doesn't wear lipstick."

"Oh, well, Grandmas don't have to. What's your favorite ice cream?"

The little girl continued to stare. "Mommy said we're not supposed to ask you anything about your lost boy." She clutched her stuffed animal. "Is that why you look sad?"

Cally's mouth dropped. She glanced back at the mirror and then down at Sally. Before she could answer, the little girl jumped off the bed and darted upstairs.

***

"It will be so nice to have you up here," Ellen said as Cally prepared to leave. "We can go shopping together, hit all those flea markets, and catch up on old times. I'll finally have someone to go with me to the symphony. Jerry's not much on those things."

Cally couldn't remember the last time she'd been to a concert or had bought anything for herself. "I can't thank you enough." She gave Ellen a warm hug.

"Don't mention it. When you get ready to move some of the bigger stuff like beds and sofas, just let us know. Jerry and I will pack a lunch and come down there with a U-Haul trailer."

Cally settled in her car, turned, and waved through the opened window. When she did, she saw Sally peeking at her from behind her mother's skirt. When their eyes met, the little girl ducked back.

***

As she drove away, she pulled the Rumi quote from her purse and laid it on the passenger seat of her car for inspiration. *Become the sky.* By the time she reached her driveway in Forest Lake, she had memorized it.

At home, Cally made endless lists and spent Saturday morning packing. Brown cardboard boxes sprouted up throughout the house, like ugly weeds in the spring grass. For her first week in Portland, she would take clothes, her inflatable bed, a few personal items, cooking utensils, and some groceries. In time, she'd have to contact Pete about his stuff, but she couldn't go there now. At least Pete still sent her money and paid the mortgage. Once settled in Portland, she'd ask around, find a lawyer, and file for a divorce. They would have to sell the house and the property. She'd eventually need to rent some kind of storage unit.

She stood in the doorway of Cody's room, staring out the window into the leafy branches of the big oak tree — the tree he used to climb to watch the ants. What an imagination he had. She remembered the story he'd told her about the rabbit that lived under the tool shed in their garden. Sunny the Bunny, he'd called him and described him in detail. Cally had even gone out to give Cody some lettuce for Sunny before she'd realized he wasn't real. Her eyes got moist.

She'd intended to leave things in Cody's room as they were until he returned. Now it didn't matter. She would take the big picture of Cody from the kitchen, a few of his drawings, some Harry Potter books, the stuffed bear with the dog collar that still sat on his Christmas bike, the little clay bowl he had made for her at school for Mother's Day, and his baby-picture album.

She'd take some of his clothes, too, the ones that still bore his scent, so she could hug them in weak moments. Like now. She picked up Cody's denim jacket that hung over a chair and buried her face in it. Was she doing the right thing? *"Become the sky . . . Escape. Do it now."* Yes. Yes.

She had just sat down to a quick lunch of canned tomato soup, crackers, and cheese when the telephone rang, causing her to jump. "Hello," she said cautiously.

"Mrs. Benson, this is Deputy Ken Blake."

"Yes?"

"The search team has recovered a hatchet very similar to the one we believe Cody carried on the day he went missing."

The news hit Cally like a bullet. "Are you sure?"

"It was found near the area where your father and Cody had looked for Christmas trees but farther in, uh, more, I'd say, to the east. We're sending it to the lab for further analysis. I just wanted you to know."

Cally gripped the phone. She couldn't speak.

"Mrs. Benson?"

"Yes. I'm here."

"I'll let you know when we get the lab results. In the meantime, I want to assure you that we are continuing our search for Cody, especially in the area where they found the hatchet. We're hopeful that we're getting close."

"Yes, okay. Thank you." After she hung up, her shaking hands poured the soup down the drain.

The hatchet made the eleven o'clock news as the latest development in the Cody Benson Case. Tina Williams had called earlier for a quote, but Cally let the call go to the answering machine. Now in her bathrobe, pale and trembling, she watched the broadcast in her dark living room. A picture of her smiling son flashed on the screen. She instinctively reached over to pat Max on the head, but he wasn't there. The newscasters cut to footage of Cody's recent vigil and a close-up of Cally, sitting by the platform in the plastic chair, wearing her corsage of white and red carnations. The corsage still rested on the kitchen counter wilting like her soul.

To complete her segment, Tina had an interview with a local forensic scientist who said that the police would probably have the hatchet examined for DNA evidence. "It's not likely that they'll find any of the boy's DNA on it or anybody else's for that matter. This is an object that's been out in the harsh weather all these months. But the fact that the police say it's the same type as the one Cody carried and was found in the general area where he'd been lends credence to the theory that the boy wandered off and probably froze to death."

She gritted her teeth and aimed the remote at his head. "Shut up. Why don't you just shut up," she yelled as the scientist dissolved into the blank, dark screen. "He's not dead."

Cody could have gotten lost, or he may just have dropped the hatchet as he made his way back to the highway. Was he on the mountain or somewhere else? The searchers had found no other trace of him, but if his remains might be there, she couldn't move to Portland. Not now. On the other hand, she wanted to believe he was still alive. *What to do? What to do?* She spent a sleepless night on the couch. The stacks of cardboard boxes loomed in the shadows like ghosts. By Sunday morning, the infusion of life that had filled her body in Portland had evaporated. She awoke feeling tired and drained, like a leaking, old bucket.

She took a hot shower, but it left her numb. Her stomach burned. Her mouth felt swollen. She couldn't eat. And she couldn't remember exactly what Blake had said. She thought it was something about being hopeful. *Hopeful. What did he mean by that? Was that about finding Cody or vindicating himself?*

She paced back and forth. The library expected her on Monday. Portland was over three hundred miles away, a six-hour drive. She had impressed the interview team as someone who was mature and reliable, but what about Cody? They didn't know about her son. Maybe she could make them understand. She reached for the phone; then stopped. It was Sunday. What if they did find him and she wasn't here? *I can't just go. I can't. I can't.*

She needed to talk to someone. That should be Pete, the father of her son, who used to be her rock. Surely the police had contacted him. Now, when things got tough—long, drawn out tough—Pete disappeared like a scared rabbit down a hole. He probably was still in bed or making coffee for his girlfriend.

Cally's sour stomach worsened; waves of nausea engulfed her. She rushed to the bathroom for a dry heave over the toilet. She wiped her mouth with tissue paper. While staring at the swirling toilet water, the answer came to her: Dottie Johnson.

CHAPTER 35

Cally trudged up the steps to Dottie's apartment. A wooden sign with a bright yellow daisy painted on the side said "WELCOME." She raised her hand to knock and then thought better of it. She had no right to walk in on this woman. The door suddenly opened. Dottie stood there, still in her light-blue bathrobe, blinking in the morning light. She'd combed her hair but wore no makeup. "I thought I heard someone comin' up the stairs." She reached out, grabbed Cally's arm, and pulled her in.

Once inside, Dottie snapped off the television set. "I was just thinkin' about you. I suppose you know you're on the news again?"

"I know. My phone's been ringing off the hook. I . . . I had to get out of there." Cally rubbed her red-rimmed eyes and pushed back bits of dark hair that had escaped from her messy clump of a ponytail. Dottie's apartment seemed warm and homey compared with the upheaval she'd left. The smell of freshly brewed coffee beckoned.

"Please, sit down," Dottie said. She handed her a cup of hot coffee and the warmed bagel with cream cheese she'd prepared for herself.

"Oh, no, no." Cally put up her hand to refuse it. "Please, no. I just needed to talk. I'm so sorry to bother you. It's just that . . . I think I'm losing it. I can't eat."

"Yes, you can," Dottie insisted. "I won't take no for an answer. You're gonna make yourself sick. Now you listen to me, little bites, little sips." Dottie went into her kitchen and returned with her own mug of coffee and a blueberry muffin. She kicked off her slippers and curled up in the big armchair. "I make a hell of a cup of coffee, if I say so myself. She looked intently at Cally, said no more but listened quietly while pent-up words tumbled out of Cally's mouth like winter wheat escaping from a hole in a grain sack.

"I was so certain about Portland. For a moment there, I thought I could do it. I thought I could actually leave . . . escape." She pulled off a piece of the bagel with her fingers and chewed. "Now I don't know. I just don't know. I feel guilty leaving if he's there, his body ..." She choked on that last word. She lifted the cup to her lips as if she could wash that word down.

"Well, I'll tell you," Dottie said once Cally had stopped. "I've been through lots in my life. Three marriages. Two divorces. My share of deaths. Whenever I get to these crossroads, I ask myself, what would my loved ones want me to do? Do you really think Cody or your dad want you stay here and fester? And what if it'd been you, the one that was lost or worse. Would you want Cody to stop his life?"

"No, of course not," Cally said politely. She'd heard all this before. Maybe coming here was a mistake.

"I think you absolutely must go. It's the right thing."

"You do?"

"Without question. You know your dad, Sam, was a good man, and he set out to do somethin' decent. But he made one mistake, a tragic one. That one thing wasn't all of who he was.

He just couldn't let go of what happened. Look how it ended for him. And Pete, he only saw the part of Sam that lost Cody. That *one* thing. Look what that did to your marriage. Ken Blake is a good man, too. Even good men make mistakes sometimes."

Cally's body stiffened. Dad. Pete. And Blake. A good man? That idiot. She dug her fingernails into her arm, leaving little half-moon indentions. She remembered Myra's story about Christie Jenkins. "That Blake made a whopping blunder before we ever got here. How many chances does one man get?"

"I know there's lots of bad feelings there," Dottie continued. "The way I see it, he believed Cody was out there in the freezin' cold and wanted to get to him in time. Maybe he should've paid more attention to what that witness told him. Who knows?" Her eyebrows arched. "But the second time around, he sure got it right. Saved a little boy's life." She pulled the paper wrapping from her muffin and broke it in half. "Folks are mighty proud of him."

"I'm glad that turned out well for the Atwaters," Cally said halfheartedly. Of course, she was; she'd even sent them a note. But she *still* had a missing child. And Dottie would believe those things about Blake, she'd spent her whole life in Forest Lake. "I'd expect this town to defend Blake," she continued. "That's the way small towns are. The people go around scratching each other's back. It's different in Portland." As soon as she said that, she wished she hadn't. She'd only been in Portland for a few days. She could see the surprise in Dottie's face. What was she thinking? Dottie had done so much for her. "Oh, I didn't mean —"

Dottie licked her fingers and wiped them on her paper napkin. "That's just your pain talkin,' honey. What I'm tryin' to say is God sees the whole heart, not just the broken parts. We all need fixin,' one way or another. But seein' the whole of a person like that is what makes forgiveness possible. Don't get all wrapped up in bitterness. It'll just take you down, and you know what? At the end of the day, it won't buy you a sack of groceries. You go."

"On the surface, I get what you're saying. It's just that deep down—"

"You get on with your life." Dottie looked directly at Cally. Her eyes narrowed. It almost sounded like an order.

"I mean, if they find Cody, I'll need to be here to take care of things."

"Tell yourself whatever you have to, so you can take that first step. You'll never be sorry you did. Now you take Myra." She shot a glance at the watercolor of the café that Christie had painted so many years ago. "What happened to her daughter was an awful thing. Poor Myra, it left her as bitter as day-old coffee. But that bitterness is what got her stuck in the past, until one day she tried to set a young girl's hair on fire. Just a horrible thing. She detested a killer, and then set out to become one. Don't you think Ken Blake loves his daughter as much as she loved hers and as much as you loved Cody?"

Cally sat quietly. She jiggled her foot. Her face reddened. Dottie had spoken of Cody using the past tense. That continued to stab at her, even though she sometimes did it herself. She hadn't thought of Ken Blake as a father, just some stupid, bungling small town cop.

"You feel Cody whether he's here physically or not. Mothers do that. Just tuck him in a special corner of your heart and take him with you. When you let go, you don't forget. It just gets that big rock off your back. You don't have to choose, honey. Not really."

"I do feel sorry for the Blake girl."

"They say the ordeal left a scar on her face that the doctors can fix, but who knows what else Myra scarred. I mean inside."

"I never thought Myra was that far gone. A little strange, maybe, but I really thought she just wanted to help me."

"I doubt that she ever gets out of that so-called care facility." Dottie paused and frowned. "Floyd's the one I feel sorry for. He's got to get up every mornin', go down to the gas station, then come back to that sorry, dark house. Poor guy, he never had a chance. He just sort of went along with all her ways." Dottie waved her hand in the air as if she was pushing Myra out of her thoughts, so she could continue worrying about Cally. "For your first week, don't make a big production out of it. Just take a few things, your toothbrush, a change of clothes, your deodorant."

"Well, I better take that for everyone's sake." They both laughed.

"You know what I'm sayin,' your overnight bag. Do it step-by-step. Stayin' here won't change a damn thing. They're either gonna find your boy out there, or not. What can you do about it?"

Cally shrugged. She shook her head. Since the day Cody had gone missing, she'd felt powerless.

"I'll be here for you, and I know a lot of other people will, too. We'll watch your place. Take care of things on this end. I'll send out Squeak if any heavy things need to be done."

"Squeak?"

"He's my new handyman. Whenever he moves, his right knee makes a cracking sound. The guys all call him Squeak."

It was the second time Dottie had made Cally laugh. It definitely helped. So did the coffee and eating the bagel. It made her feel stronger. The stress started lifting from her body like dense fog yielding to the sun's warmth.

"Well, I'll tell you, he can't hammer a nail as straight as Sam could. But he does pretty good, and you can set your clock by him. Do whatever you need to do to make your peace about leaving Cody. Light a candle, say a prayer, or whatever it takes to get the job done. Then get on with it."

Cally stood up and carried her cup and dish into Dottie's kitchen.

"You can still get to Portland by dinnertime, honey."

Cally reached out and hugged her tightly. "Thank you for everything."

"You betcha. Now you go, honey. Reach for the sky, and when you get to that big, shinin' city, you call me. That way I'll know you made it there all right."

CHAPTER 36

Grocery-store flowers always seemed to come with wilted leaves and slimy stems, but Tillden's was the only store in Forest Lake open on Sunday. Cally settled on a cello-wrapped bunch of yellow roses and another cluster of multicolor daisies that reminded her of those artificial-looking daffodils children dipped in dye. She stooped to pull them from the buckets in the floral aisle.

"I see you're trying to rush summer."

Cally spotted the familiar brown boots and followed them up the denim skirt to see Miss Brackston standing there with an empty cart and a grin on her bright red lips. Her heart sank. She stood up clutching her flowers, forcing a smile. "How are you, Miss Brackston? I've been meaning to thank you for the wonderful job the children did at Cody's remembrance service. That was very nice."

"My kids are eager for summer. Of course, there's lots of concern about Cody, I mean, too." Her small, rosy nose pointed toward the ceiling.

Cally wondered how it held up her heavy, dark-rimmed glasses.

Miss Brackston's face turned glum. "Do you know any more? I mean I heard they found a hatchet." She stared at Cally's bouquets as if they were for a funeral.

"No. No, I do not. Just that they found something."

"I guess that pretty much cinches it. I mean about him being lost up there."

Miss Brackston's lips formed that smug smile Cally always hated. "Not for me it doesn't." Her shoulders tightened.

"I always thought it was a shame that he couldn't have gotten some help sooner, you know, with the attention disorder."

Cally wanted to slap her. She imagined whopping the woman with the flowers so thoroughly that it left her with daisies sticking out of her mouth. Instead she blurted, "Cody was bullied at your school, and you did *nothing* about it."

Miss Brackston's face flushed. She gripped the handle of her empty cart, her mouth agape. Cally spun around and walked rapidly to the checkout counter. Over her shoulder, she could see the woman slowly push her cart toward the wine aisle. Once out of the store, Cally dashed to her car.

She sped along Cooper's Hawk Highway to the Big Bat wilderness area and didn't stop until she reached the same pullout where her father had parked his pickup and where Cody had last walked. Once she made her peace, as Dottie called it, she would go home, pack a few things and begin her new life in Portland. She'd lost her son, her dad, she bit her lip, and her marriage. Dottie was right. She needed to go.

It was a sunny morning on the mountain, but cold and windy with patches of snow at the lower elevation. A few fluffy, white clouds lingered in the bright-blue sky, so unlike the pearl gray of the valley. At first she thought she'd lay the flowers in the pullout, but then decided the crisp wind might blow them back out to the highway where passing cars would mash them. No, she wanted to leave them somewhere special.

Months ago, heavy snow had covered this very spot. That first time everything was so emotional. She'd always grieved in the background, confined to one trailer or another. Today, she would walk, touch, and feel the places where Cody had been.

She took slow, cautious steps and made frequent stops, searching for a special place, one she might find again, a sort of memorial. The clumps of white pine were full and beautiful. No wonder her dad had come here to get a Christmas tree. She glommed onto a branch as if she were shaking someone's hand and touched the bough of the needles to her face. If trees could only talk. She walked farther, carefully stepping over fallen branches and wind-blown debris. *Don't go too far, you still have to drive to Portland.* The terrain got steeper, but she continued.

She stood for a while, thinking about what Dottie had said about God and how he sees the whole heart. She shouldn't have come down on Miss Brackston, but that woman represented everything she hated about Forest Lake—limited, small-minded, petty, hypocritical, conventional. It made her want to strike back. A teacher should be more caring.

Could she ever forgive Pete? Pete had walked this very spot in deep, cold snow, calling out for Cody until his voice got hoarse, and he came down with pneumonia. Pete had cried in the trailer that night they both knew the search was over. He loved their son. Did he still love her? Her dad had tried hard to be a good grandfather. Why couldn't Pete see that? They could've made it work. They *all* could have worked it out.

Soon she came to what seemed like a narrow trail leading uphill. It looked like the kind animals make. She didn't think hikers came in here. The trail led her to a wooded area where the underbrush was heavier. It felt colder. She pulled her wool hat down around her ears, thankful for her jeans, boots, sweater, and warm jacket.

What if she stumbled on something of Cody's—a piece of clothing, a boot? Sometimes mothers could do that. They had that inner sense and all those intuitive feelings. What would she do? The thought made her shudder. She stopped again and looked around. For some reason, she sensed somebody was watching her. When she and Ellen had been kids, they used to play a game. They would stare at someone's back because a teacher had told them that if they stared long enough, the person would feel it. In church, instead of listening to the sermon, they'd focused hard on old Mr. Thorvaldsen whose speckled bald head hung toward his chest as he dozed in the pew. They'd giggled when he suddenly jerked up and looked around.

How silly to feel that out here. Maybe it was because she was alone. Cold. Broken. Helpless. No, she definitely heard something moving in the thick underbrush. Maybe it was a squirrel or a rabbit. She listened again. It sounded more like footsteps. A deer perhaps? The steps seemed more measured, cautious even. *Is someone out here? Afraid she'd find something?* Hadn't the search team been through here dozens of times? But there was some speculation in the newspaper that Roster had an accomplice. It was something Blake had said in an interview. Something about the man he saw running from the car—that he didn't look exactly like Roster. Could it be that Trula woman Roster lived with or someone else? No one knew she was out here. She had told absolutely no one. Dottie had said make your peace. She didn't say go to the Big Bat wilderness and wander around in it all alone.

"Who's there?" she called. The footsteps stopped. The tall pines creaked in the wind. Did she know where she was? Things all looked the same out here. Getting lost would be easy, especially for a little boy. Snow, she knew, would make it even harder. *She thought she heard something again.* Her heart raced under her sweater. She pulled out her cell phone, but it went to roaming. There was no connection. Maybe she should turn back. *No. No, she'd come all this way on a mission for Cody. Nothing, no one could stop her now.* She gripped her flowers and walked quickly until she came to a little meadow-like clearing. To the left, she spotted a weathered, gray-brown stump with a craggy back where some large tree had broken off. Moss clung to its sides. She set down her purse and laid the flowers on the stump, wishing she'd brought a candle, but then with the wind, it probably would be difficult to light. She looked up through the tall trees at the blue sky, then turned and glanced around. Except for the wind, it was still. She no longer heard the footsteps.

Her shrine seemed so forlorn. At the beginning of this venture, she'd been on a purposeful mission. Now there was nothing, just a lonely stump with flowers on it. In time, the flowers would wilt. She needed to leave something more permanent. She unfastened the chain of her necklace with the heart-shaped pendant Pete had given her years ago. Why she still wore it, she didn't know. They had celebrated Cody's birthday, and then he'd said, "And here's something for my other valentine." They'd kissed. Later, they'd made love. What had happened to them?

Her eyes misted. She didn't think she could cry anymore, but a tear spilled down her cheek. "Cody," she said looking at the flowers on the stump. "I'm not leaving you, honey, and I'll come back. I promise."

The wilderness, nature, was so immense. What chance did a little boy have out here? Maybe he had died all alone in the cold. If he had, and his body was somewhere, wouldn't his spirit linger here, too? She believed that. She looked up again at the blue sky. Maybe Cody was looking down on her. Maybe those noises—those footsteps—she'd heard were his spirit, trying to signal his presence. She'd heard stories like that, where the phone always rang at the same time, but nobody was there. Or where doors in rooms eerily opened and closed on their own. "Cody!" she yelled at the top of her lungs, just as Pete had on that cold, windy December day.

What was that? It wasn't footsteps, but something in the wind. It sounded like "*mmmm.*"

"Cody!" *There it was again.* A weird echo? Is someone in distress? A hurt animal? Maybe it was a cat, a big cat. Were there cougars out here? A mountain lion? Were they the same thing?

"Cody!" she screamed. Now, it sounded like "*maaaaa.*" Beyond the little clearing, the trail ended. Whatever those sounds were, they were coming from the wooded area in the distance. She ran toward the trees, following the sound, moving uphill, deeper into the dark forest. "Cody," she called, and then listened.

Oh, god. She remembered she left her purse back at that stump. It contained her cell phone, her wallet, credit cards, and oh, Jesus, the car keys. A chill swept over her body like that time years ago when Cody was small and she realized she had lost her wallet in town. Fortunately, someone had turned it in at the drugstore. *Go back and get your purse. Now. Before it's too late.*

What was that in the distance, waving in the wind? Was it a low-slung branch from a tree, or a small bush, just a dark shadow? The light streaming through the trees partially blinded her. Oh, my gosh, whatever it was it was coming closer wasn't it? It wasn't an animal. It looked like a child, a young girl with shoulder-length, dark hair. Why was she waving? Cally waved back. "Hello," she called. There's a child out here all alone, a child who needs help. That was a child wasn't it, in dark clothing? If only someone had helped Cody.

She picked up speed, trying to run uphill, but it was difficult with all the broken-off branches strewn on the ground. Her boot caught on one. Pulling it free, she lost her footing and fell. Her left knee hit a small rock. "Damn," she muttered. She scrambled to her feet; pain shot through her leg. She stood on one foot, rubbing her knee. She looked up. The little girl was still there. She was coming closer, her arms outstretched. Cally wiped her hands on her jeans. Could it be a — it looks like — but it couldn't be. Finally, she was close enough to see them—those two big chocolate eyes.

"Cody!" she screamed.

"Mom!" he answered as clear as a bell.

"Oh, my God, Cody."

The boy rushed into her arms. "Mom!" He buried his face in her shoulder.

Was this really her child, or was she having a weird out-of-body experience? How many times before had she thought she'd seen his shadowy figure in a dream, standing at the end of her bed? This child looked bigger, fuller. Cody had short hair. She squatted and gripped his face with both her hands. No, he looks different in a way, older, sadder maybe, but no those are his eyes. That's his face. She pinched his cheek. He's real.

"Cody, for God's sake."

"Why are you crying, Mom?"

"I'm just so glad to see you. Are you okay?"

"I was scared."

"Of course, you were scared." She looked over her shoulder to see if anyone else was there. "It's okay, son. It's okay. God, it's okay."

"I didn't know if I could find it."

"Find what?"

"The highway."

"Oh, Cody, let's go home before I wake up."

He looked puzzled. "I can't go yet."

"What?"

"I've got to wait for Ben."

"Is he the man that took you? Where is he? I'll kill him."

The boy shook his head and held his hand up as if to defend himself. "No, Mom. It's Benny's dad."

"Who?"

"Benny's dad."

"Your Indian friend, Benny?"

"We were going shopping."

"Shopping?"

"I told him he could live with us."

"It's okay, Cody. It's okay, son." Something's wrong with his mind, but they said that happens. He's traumatized, been held captive. God knows what that bastard did to him. Children can't leap from one world to another just like that. *Stay calm. Think.*

"We'll come back and look for him—your friend." Cody seemed agitated. He tried to pull away. She wasn't about to let him go.

"No. No. Let's just be calm. Calm down, baby." She knelt down again, pushed the long hair back from his forehead, and looked into his eyes.

"He told me to wait on the big rock back there."

"Who, who told you that?"

"He went back for Wolf."

"What? There's a wolf out here?"

"Wolf, our dog. He said to wait until the sun got past the big trees and then walk to the highway. He would meet me there. I didn't know if I could find it. I was scared."

"Oh, Cody, I can't tell you how much I've missed that imagination of yours. Oh, my god. Cody. It's you. It's really you."

"I need to go back to the cave."

"Cave? What cave?"

"That's where Wolf is. I have to go." He tried to loosen himself from her grip.

"No, don't go. Don't go." She hung onto him and scanned the woods again to check for strangers. No one was there. "Where did you come from?"

"Is Grandpa mad at me? I lost his hatchet."

Oh, my god, of course he doesn't know. "Nobody's mad, Cody. Nobody's mad, honey. Let me look at you."

"I can't leave yet."

"Listen, Cody. Listen, sweetheart. We'll drive down to the Lake Store and . . . remember the Lake Store?"

"Yeah."

"Well, uh, we'll get sandwiches, one for you and one for your friend, Benny."

"Ben. Benny's dad."

"Right. Okay. Benny's dad. Then we'll come back and wait for him by the highway. And, uh, the dog. Okay?"

"Dad won't let Wolf stay."

"Yes he will, Cody," she insisted. "Yes, he will. The dog can stay. Don't worry. Dad won't care." So much had changed. So much. Cally placed her right arm around Cody's shoulder and grabbed his arm tightly with her left hand. She still had that feeling. Someone else *is* out here. A kid doesn't just show up in the wilderness. Especially one that's been missing for months. Someone brought him here. That monster is watching us, lurking somewhere. He'd want to silence Cody, to keep him from talking. Maybe he'd found her purse and her car keys. Maybe he already took off in her car. She was defenseless. *But she knew one thing, she would fight to the death if anyone tried to take her child again.*

"Hurry, Cody, Ben could already be down at the highway, waiting for us."

"Okay."

"You don't want him to miss you, do you?"

"No."

"Let's walk fast, son. And, we'll get something for the dog to eat, too. What was his name?"

"Wolf."

"Okay, for Wolf, too."

She found her purse just as she left it by the stump. Her knee ached, but she kept up the brisk pace. Once back in the car, Cally locked the doors and stepped on the gas. She whipped out her cell phone. She glanced at her son. He looked so different. He needed a bath and a good haircut. Where had he gotten those baggy clothes?

Farther down Cooper's Hawk Highway, her phone picked up a signal. "I'm going to pull over and place an order, so the food would be waiting for us," she told Cody. Once she stepped out of the car, she dialed 911 and asked for help, then hopped back in and continued to drive as the dispatcher advised. "Three sandwiches coming up," she said, all the time keeping the phone pressed to her ear. "One they say is peanut butter."

Cody didn't respond. He just sat there. He closed his eyes tight and wrinkled his nose. Cally drove faster. *What if all this is a dream? What if I'm just a crazed, grieving mother having another panic attack? What if help arrives, and I'm the only one in the car? I could end up in the same facility as Myra Jenkins. What if none of this is real?*

But it was.

Ken Blake and Don Range, in separate cruisers, an ambulance, and a state police car met them just as they were nearing the Lake Store.

Amos Hadley stepped out of his store, awestruck, as the caravan of flashing lights from the cruisers and the ambulance passed by. He shook his head. "Will ya look at that? All them cops, but they're never around when I need 'em." As he drove by, Ken flashed a thumbs-up sign. Amos just stood there with his mouth open. The police escorted the ambulance with Cody and Cally inside all the way to the hospital in Klamath Falls.

***

Jim stood over the cheerless stump, staring at the flowers and the golden necklace. He felt empty, like the day he'd watched Mo, old and broken, hobble away. People who'd cared about him, forever gone. He had intended to keep an eye on the kid, to follow, to make sure he made it to the highway in time to meet that maintenance crew he knew passed by there around noon. He never expected the mother—that had to be her. She looked just like the pictures the kid drew, but she was an even luckier solution. *The kid was safe.* He bent down, picked up the bouquet of yellow roses, and broke one off. He scooped up Cally's necklace, fingered the heart for a moment, and dropped it in his pocket. He had to scramble and fast. They'd be coming for him.

CHAPTER 37

"**BENSON BOY FOUND**," screamed banner headlines on newspapers across the state. Reporters and television crews poured into Klamath Falls, frantically competing for footage, photos, and an interview, but Cally and Cody remained secluded in the hospital with a police guard at the door. The Klamath County Sheriff finally called a press conference, flanked by Walt Richards and Ken Blake. They confirmed Cody was alive and in good condition. Blake explained how he was found, but declined to say more. The family, he said, needed privacy.

"Can you tell us how you think the boy got to the area where he was found?" Tina Williams of Channel 14 News shouted.

"We can't comment on that," the Sheriff answered. "We're continuing to investigate."

"Is Cody injured in any way?" Tina persisted.

"The boy is in good condition. Now, I'm sorry we have to go," the Sheriff said. "This is an ongoing investigation."

Tina stood her ground. "Do you have any idea who Roster's accomplice is?"

"Thank you all for coming," Richards said. He nudged Ken, and they walked away from the microphones. Richards and the Sheriff lingered to talk with some city officials. Ken headed for his cruiser.

"Yo, Blake." He heard someone call. He turned. There was Tina, blond hair askew, eyes fluttering, with a microphone in hand, and an unhappy cameraman in tow. "Do you think someone in the family was involved?"

"What?"

"Well, the father doesn't seem to be around much. Do you think he was involved?"

Ken laughed. "You must be desperate for a story, but you'll just have to wait like the rest of us." Tina's mouth puckered. He could tell he touched a nerve. That made him happy.

Her eyes narrowed. Like a cat, she pounced. "So how does it feel to know you were wrong—that the kid wasn't lost, but abducted?"

"I'm—we're pleased he's back with his family." He managed a pleasant smile.

Tina moved closer, a smirk on her face. "Don't you wish you'd acted sooner on the abduction and saved the kid from abuse?" She thrust her microphone toward his face.

Ken, used to Tina's tricks, took a deep breath and held his smile. She was after a sound bite. "Cody is alive and well. Let's celebrate that." He got into his cruiser and slammed the door. "Stupid bitch," he muttered to himself. He could see Tina's lips moving in his rearview mirror. He sped off.

***

"Shocking news tonight!" Nora Case exclaimed on her evening TV program. "Cody Benson, the nine-year old Oregon boy who's been missing for six months, has been found." The camera showed file footage of Cody, the unflattering image of Cally sitting in the plastic chair at Cody's remembrance, and the search team combing the Big Bat wilderness area.

"Things are sure hoppin' out there in Oregon. Let's go now to Tina Williams from our West Coast affiliate. She's on the scene in Klamath Falls." Case said. "Weigh in, Tina."

"Nora, we don't know much at this point." She stood on the steps of the hospital. "But the mother apparently went to the Big Bat wilderness area to place flowers on the spot where Cody went missing. Voila! She finds her child."

"He was standing right there?"

"No, apparently she decided to walk farther into the forest and—"

"Do they know how he got there?" Case interrupted; her voice tinged with impatience.

"If they do, they're not saying. Everybody is being tight-lipped about this whole situation."

"Well, Roster, the perp, killed himself, so there must have been someone else involved."

"It certainly looks that way, Nora. Len Roster committed suicide two weeks ago. Then someone left the Benson boy in the wilderness all alone, almost in the same place he first went missing. He and his mother are now here at the hospital." She turned and pointed to the glass doors. "That's about all they're saying. They aren't offering any theories."

"Pop the champagne corks," Case said. She looked directly into the camera. Her previous impatience dissipated, and her voice filled with emotion. "Thank God this little boy is safe and apparently well. This certainly gives any parent of a missing child hope. We'll definitely be following this story."

***

Cody sat up in the hospital bed. The small room swelled with flowers, balloons, and stuffed animals sent by well-wishers. Dottie Johnson sent him a big jar of Jif peanut butter, tied up in a yellow ribbon. The makers of Jif, the J.M. Smucker Company of Orville, Ohio, offered to send Cody and his family to Disneyland.

He had just finished a hamburger and fries-drowned-in-ketchup lunch when Dr. Morgan showed up for a follow-up examination. Afterward, the doctor asked Cally to step outside.

"I looked at all the reports. The boy is in fine shape physically. Now, we just have to deal with the psychological part of it."

"He seems okay." Cally smiled. "Does that mean he wasn't —" She couldn't bring herself to say *molested*.

"It doesn't appear that Cody was sexually abused, but in cases like this, we don't know what or how else the pervert pleasured himself—what he required of the boy."

"Oh." Cally wilted. She felt that old anxiety coming back.

"That's the next mountain we have to climb. We need to determine the extent and degree of Cody's trauma."

"How can I help him?"

"Give him time. Don't question him. Don't expect him to be the little boy you remember, at least not yet. It could take weeks or months, maybe longer, to be sure he's emotionally stable. I'm referring you to a psychiatrist, a Dr. Milton Halfan. He's really good with kids."

"Can I take him home? Get him out of this atmosphere."

"I'll release him once Dr. Halfan talks with him. And I think the police will want to have a say in where you all go next."

Cally stiffened. It wasn't over yet.

After Dr. Morgan left, the young redheaded nurse came in with a black-and-white stuffed bear.

"We're going to have to get you another room, just to hold all this stuff," she teased.

Cody giggled. Cally was still trying to process what Dr. Morgan had said. What was she thinking? Of course, it wasn't over. There was still a long way to go.

"You have a visitor," the nurse said.

Cally turned around, ready to do battle with a reporter.

"Dad!" Cody shouted. Pete rushed past Cally to his son's bed. He threw his arms around him and cried softly into his son's small chest. He lifted his head. "Let me look at you. Just let me look at you," he kept repeating.

Cally touched his shoulder. Pete looked thinner and a bit haggard, as if he had little sleep. "Here, have a seat." She offered the only chair in the room.

"Oh, no, no. That's all right." He turned toward her. Cally started to lift her arms, expecting him to give her a hug, too, but Pete just reached for a handful of tissue from the box on Cody's bed stand and blew his nose.

"Hey, buddy, you need a haircut," he said, looking at Cody's long hair, which he wore in a ponytail.

"No!" Cody cried and looked at Cally. "Don't let them cut my hair."

"It's okay, Cody," Cally said. "No one is going to cut your hair. I promise."

Pete frowned. He looked perplexed.

"Don't upset him," she said calmly. "He likes his hair that way, so Dr. Halfan says we're going to let it be." She gave Pete a knowing look.

"Sure, sure," he managed to say.

Cally moved closer to Pete and whispered, "They say he's okay. Uh, physically." In that close moment, she picked up his familiar scent, although it seemed mixed with some new cologne or maybe aftershave. She lingered next to him.

"I know. I've talked with the doctors and the police."

"Oh." She felt a stab in her stomach, as if she'd just been left out of something.

"Wait," he said to Cody. "I have something for you."

He turned, stepped outside the door, and came back in with a squirming, yellow puppy.

"A dog!" Cody shouted. Pete lifted the chubby puppy over the bed rail and placed it next to Cody.

"The hospital said it was okay to bring it," Pete said to Cally. "He's a golden retriever," he said to Cody.

Cody threw his arms around the puppy while it eagerly licked his face. "Is it mine? Is it really mine?"

"Of course," Pete said. "He's all yours."

Cally forced a smile. "You'll have to think of a name." She tried to sound pleasant. Inside, her stomach churned. Why hadn't Pete consulted with her first? Why did this have to be *his* gift and not *theirs*? She looked at Cody's happy face. Getting Cody a dog was absolutely the right thing to do. If Pete had not done that, she would have. Actually, it was sweet of him.

"How have you been?" Pete finally asked.

"Stressed." She looked toward the doorway. She could see a young, petite woman with brown, shoulder-length hair and bangs standing there, her pretty face smiling, her eyes teary. She must have been holding the dog until Pete retrieved it. She noticed something else, too—the woman was wearing a maternity smock. She turned toward Pete, her back straight as a broomstick. "Don't you want to invite your friend in?"

CHAPTER 38

Walt Richards tore open the box of chocolate-iced doughnuts covered with candy sprinkles. He shoved it to the center of the table in the small, windowless conference room. "Help yourself," he said to Ken and Detective Frank Lane. "I delivered the stuff, but I'm not gonna serve it." Richards hung his jacket on the hook behind the door and plopped his ample body down in a straight-back chair.

Lane poured coffee from the carafe into three paper cups. "That seems so redundant."

"What does?" asked Ken.

"That they put those candy things on top of the chocolate icing."

"Jeez, Lane." Ken hated doughnuts They always gave him heartburn and the sweet, yeasty smell permeating the small room made him yearn for an open window.

Richards didn't look up. He reached for a donut and began thumbing through his thick file, rattling off facts.

"According to the medical report, the Benson boy is in fine physical shape and apparently was well cared for. Dr. Milton Halfan, the psychiatrist treating Cody, says the boy told him about a bearlike man, but the kid has severe memory lapses. His teachers say he always had a vivid imagination that included imaginary friends." Richards ran his thick finger down the page. "The psychiatrist agrees with that assessment. The boy may suffer from attention deficit. Dr. Halfan believes it will be some time before Cody actually remembers what happened, if he ever does."

Ken leaned forward. "Did Cody say who brought him back to the Big Bat?"

"No. When asked about that, he said he was going shopping."

"Shopping?" Ken's eyebrows rose in disbelief. He sipped his coffee.

"That's what the transcript says here, Blake. I'm not making this stuff up." He took a big bite of his doughnut, chewed and washed it down with coffee.

"Where's he been all this time?" Lane wondered.

"His mother said he mentioned a cave. Cody also told Dr. Halfan he was kept in a cave, but then he said it was a house, then a teepee, then he lived in the trees, and then he doesn't remember. When asked who took care of him he says it was Ben or Benny. Mrs. Benson said Benny is an imaginary Indian friend that began appearing when the kid was about four years old."

"Cripe." Lane helped himself to a doughnut. "Sounds like this kid's a mess." He offered the box to Ken. There were smears of chocolate on the lid.

Ken raised his hands to wave it away. "Was he sexually abused?"

"According to the medical report, there are no physical signs of it, but that doesn't exclude oral sex or other things a pervert dirtbag may have required him to do. His counselors say not to push him, to give him time."

"So, we don't know how he ended up in the wilderness after Roster had been dead for two weeks?" Ken asked.

"Not yet. This kid has been through a lot. First, he wandered away from Grandpa in the snow and probably made it to the highway. Then Roster abducts him, but we don't know what went on from there. After six months, he's left again in the wilderness and told to find his way down to the highway. He finally gets back to his mother only to learn his grandfather is dead and his parents are no longer together. I spoke with Dr. Halfan several times. Cody feels sad, empty, and tearful. They are still working on that and probably will for some time in the future. Halfan says kids blame themselves for what happens to the family."

Lane shook his head. "These things take their toll. I've seen that happen so many times before. It's just a damn shame."

"The clothes Cody wore were stolen from the lake cabins," Richards continued. "Someone took good care of him, except for the hair. They never bothered to cut his hair."

"They?" Lane finished his doughnut and wiped his hands on a napkin. He brushed candy sprinkles from the table.

"Well, Roster is dead, and two weeks later the Benson kid shows up. There musta been some accomplice. I'm not saying that person abducted the boy, but he or she may have had custody of him. Then when Roster ended up dead, there's the problem of what to do with him."

Ken fixed his eyes on Richards. "Maybe Roster didn't have anything to do with the Benson case."

"Here are the facts, Blake." Richards was on his second doughnut. "Roster abducts Jason Atwater, leaves him in the car and for some reason shoots himself out there. Maybe it finally dawned on him what a son of a bitch he really was. Anyway, there are two buttons missing from his jacket. Two weeks later, Cody's mother finds him on the mountain. He has Roster's buttons in his pants pocket. Connect the dots. We definitely know there's a connection to Roster."

"Were there prints on the buttons?" Lane asked.

"Just Roster's. Cody also had this in the pocket of his jacket." Richards took an object out of a small paper sack and placed the little carved version of Wolf on the table.

Ken picked it up and turned it over examining it in his hand. "Did it have prints?"

"Only Cody's."

"How do you know the stolen clothes came from the cabins?" Lane asked.

"We think Roster stole the clothes a few days before he shot himself."

"We think?"

Some colored sugar sprinkles stuck to Richards' mustache. "Well, for the most part, they're unsoiled. The lake cabins were unoccupied, but we talked to one owner who said his family was at their cabin the week before Roster offed himself, and the clothes were there then."

"Any witnesses, other than the mother, the day Cody was found?" Ken inquired.

"His mother saw nobody, and there was no other vehicle at the turn out when she arrived or when she left. Mrs. Benson said she thought she heard footsteps in the heavy underbrush near where she eventually found Cody, but she never saw anyone. She's pretty convinced, though, that someone was there, and that he was watching her."

"That person could have come after she arrived," Ken pointed out.

"Yeah, but the kid was already there when Mrs. Benson went for her hike, and he was farther in."

"What about our friend Trula?" Lane asked.

"We've thoroughly grilled Trula. She agreed to and passed a polygraph. She has no idea. In fact, she's flabbergasted. And remember, she didn't know about Randy Wilkes, either. Roster may have had a lover, someone on the side that he never told her about."

Lane took a deep breath. "He liked little boys. Maybe he had a gay lover. Maybe the gay lover wanted a son. Maybe this gay lover was Native American."

"At this point, we just don't know." Richards made a small burp behind his napkin.

"Hmmm," Ken said. "There's something about this case that doesn't add up. We've been all over that area and other parts with a fine-tooth comb. We don't find a trace of the boy. Then he shows up in the same location."

"You think?" Richards looked over his glasses at Ken as if he needed a dunce cap. "There's a helluva-lot about this case that doesn't make sense, Blake. I've had people out checking the spot where Cody surfaced, and we got zip. I've had people talking with the gay folks in and around K-Falls, but no one ever remembers seeing Roster alone or with a partner."

"That fella I saw running from the blue car that day we recovered Jason Atwater—he seemed bigger, and I thought I saw a ponytail hanging down in the back. When I squatted by the car, there were footprints, big footprints. Bigger feet than Roster had."

Richards' voice was curt. "Are you *sure*, Blake?"

"It happened fast, but I'm convinced the man was bigger."

"Do we have shots or casts of those footprints?" Lane asked.

Ken shook his head. "After police, the ambulance, and everyone else showed up to assist little Jason and deal with Roster's body, they pretty much tramped out that evidence."

"What about prints on Trula's car?" Lane asked.

"Just hers and Roster's," Richards said.

Ken kept turning the wooden dog in his hand. "Jim Fallingwater," he suddenly said.

"Who?" Lane asked.

"This carved dog. It's the kind of thing Jim Fallingwater used to make. Could Jim Fallingwater still be out there?" He looked at Richards and then at Lane.

"Oh, you mean that old case," Lane said.

"You gotta be kidding." Richards's bushy eyebrow shot up. "Christ, after how many years, and how many man-killing blizzards, and you'd have us believe that Fallingwater, or his ghost, is still walkin' around out there in the wilderness? Come on."

"He was a big man. He had big feet. He carved things like this." Ken held up the little carved dog. "I've seen Jim run hundreds of times on the football field. Now that I think about it, the guy running loped like him."

"Blake, you better have a doughnut." Richards pushed the box toward Ken.

Ken ignored the gesture. "I even have some of his work." He set the little dog down on the table. "He could be the Indian Cody seems to think he was with. He would fit the description of a bearlike man more than Roster does."

"You're dreaming, Blake." Richards's eyes were laughing. "Dr. Halfan thinks Roster and Ben or Benny's dad are the same person. He thinks Cody lapsed into his imaginary world to cope with what was happening to him. He said it's typical of sexually abused children. They latch on to a false reality and use it as a defense mechanism. In this case, an imaginary childhood friend gets transformed into an adult who protects him."

"Well, I'd like to talk with the boy," Ken insisted.

Richards frowned. "Look, we know there's a connection to Roster because of the buttons. Fallingwater. Ha! Jesus Christ. How long ago was that? Twenty years? Cougars don't even last that long up there. Fallingwater. Who the hell's gonna believe that?"

"Where would Roster get a carved dog like this?" Ken thrust the little dog toward Richards. His brush-off angered him.

"Roster was a thief," Richards shot back. "He probably stole that, too. There are a lot of Native Americans that know how to carve stuff."

"We never found Fallingwater," Ken insisted. "Not really. Just pieces of —"

Richards cleared his throat of doughnut crumbs. His angry voiced boomed. "Blake, sometimes I don't know what you've been smoking."

"I'd still like to talk with the boy."

"Yeah, well, you're not exactly one of the Benson's favorite people. They suspected someone abducted Cody, and it turns out they were right. They—"

"What have you got to lose?" Lane interrupted. "I don't mean about this Fallingwater character, but talking to the boy directly might plug some holes."

CHAPTER 39

Cally agreed to a meeting with Cody, provided she, his psychiatrist, and counselor were present. Richards reserved a small, comfortable meeting room at the central office. It had two brown leather couches, a matching chair, and a round oak coffee table in the center. A picture of the Oregon coast hung on the wall.

At Dr. Halfan's request, Richards and Blake wore slacks and sweaters to keep things informal. Once Mary Storitz, Cody's counselor arrived, Dr. Halfan, a tall, trim man with dark eyebrows, white hair, and a high forehead, conducted a preliminary meeting on how to proceed with Cody. "What we want is gentle questioning. Don't press for details if he gets uncomfortable. If I see that happening, I'll interrupt. Children who have been abused resort to dissociation as a defense mechanism. These children often go away in their mind and take on different identities. Some even create a whole imaginary world."

"We certainly understand," Richards said.

"Dissociation is a crucial survival mechanism for children like Cody. Right now, for example, he thinks he's an Indian boy."

"You just jump right in there, Dr. Halfan, whenever you have to. Right, Blake?"

"Absolutely."

Dr. Halfan smiled at Cally. "Okay, Mrs. Benson. Please bring Cody in."

"Hi, Cody," Dr. Halfan smiled at the boy. Cody looked wary. He had on jeans and a dark green sweatshirt, a gift from his classmates that said *Forest Lake*. He still wore his long hair tied back in a ponytail. "Come and sit over here with Mary and me." Cody obediently sat between the two. "These gentlemen are police officers, Cody, and they want to ask you some questions," Dr. Halfan continued. "You didn't do anything wrong, we're just trying to understand what happened to you. Is that okay?"

"Okay," said Cody. He clenched his hands. His right foot jiggled.

"You probably know Officer Blake. I know he's come to your school numerous times to talk about safety."

Cody nodded. He glanced at the big, pudgy Richards and folded his arms in front of his chest.

Mary Storitz, a tall, pleasant woman with short, straight apricot hair, reached for the pitcher of ice water on the coffee table and poured a glass. "Would you like some water, Cody?" She had a soft, calm voice.

"I want coffee," Cody said.

"Coffee?" Mary shot a glance at Cally.

"He likes black coffee," Cally said, a bit embarrassed. "They must have . . . I mean he asks for it. Dr. Morgan says he can have it. He must have had it while, uh, he was away."

Richards jumped up and returned with a cup of coffee and a peanut butter cookie wrapped in a napkin. He squatted in front of Cody. "I heard you liked peanut butter." He handed him the cookie. "This coffee is from the cafeteria." His big face turned kind. "Sorry, it isn't Starbucks. Most people don't like the cafeteria stuff." Richards smiled and his voice softened. "If you don't like it, you don't have to drink it."

He'd turned into a big teddy bear, someone Ken didn't recognize. *He's good. He's very good at his job*

Cody gripped the cup with both hands and took a long sip. He didn't flinch.

"What do you say, Cody," Cally said.

"Thank you."

"You're very welcome," Richards said. He took his seat beside Ken.

"Let's start out easy," Ken began. "Why don't you tell me your full name?"

"Wolf Boy," Cody blurted, his face serious. He took a bite of the cookie and another sip of his coffee.

"Cody, honey," Cally said calmly. "This is for real. Please tell Deputy Blake your real name."

"Cody Andrew Benson."

"And how old are you?"

"Nine."

"I know you went to the Big Bat area with your grandfather to get a Christmas tree. What happened after that?"

Cody looked pained. He set the cookie down. "We didn't getta tree."

"Don't worry about the tree," Dr. Halfan said. "Can you tell us how you got separated from your Grandpa?"

"Um, I started to go back to the pickup. Then I got real cold."

"Then what happened?" Ken asked.

"I fell asleep."

"Where did you wake up?"

"In his house."

"Do you remember where the house was?"

"No."

"Did he give you something that made you tired? That made you fall asleep?"

Cody shrugged his shoulders. "I don't remember."

"We've got a big transcript on all that, Blake," Richards whispered. "You can read all that."

"I think this belongs to you," Ken said. He held out the carved wooden dog.

"Totem!" Cody cried. He held out his hand. "Mom, this is Wolf. The dog I told you about."

Ken looked at the outstretched right hand and noticed the scar on Cody's forefinger. The same kind of scar he had on his own finger.

"Where did you get this dog?" Ken asked.

"He gave it to me."

"Who gave it to you?"

"The man I was with."

"Where did he get it?"

"I don't know."

"Can I see your hand?"

Cody thrust out his left hand.

Ken smiled. "No, the other one."

Cody paused. He gave Ken a cautious look and then offered his right hand palm down in a little fist.

Ken took his hand, turned it palm up, and pried open the fingers. "That scar you have on your finger there. What is that?"

Cody shrugged his shoulders, as if he were in trouble in school. He looked at his mother.

"Let me see," she said. "I never noticed it before." Cody pulled his hand away.

"See, I have one like that, too." Ken said. "Only mine's a bit faded. Can you see it there?" He showed Cody the faint crossed scar on his forefinger.

"Uh-huh."

"How'd you get your scar?"

Cody closed his eyes tight and then opened them. He rocked. back and forth. "I always had it." In the background, Cally signaled no by slightly shaking her head

"I got mine when I was a kid," Blake said. "Me and a friend, Jim, we became blood brothers. Do you know about that?"

Cody's shoulder muscles tightened. He closed his eyes again. When he opened them, he said, "I hurt my hand one time."

Ken paused to see if he would say more.

Cody looked down at the carved dog and remembered the words: *Now you have a dog of your own, a totem that will stay with you, guard you.* "Dogs have pure hearts," he said.

Cally smiled.

"That's right," said Mary.

"I have a dog, a real one."

"His dad got him a puppy," Cally said.

"How nice," Mary said. "How very, very nice."

Cody swung his legs. He glanced at the floor.

Richards checked his watch and cleared his throat. "Let's move it along, Blake."

Cody clenched his wooden dog. He looked uneasy.

Ken cleared his throat and pulled out a large manila envelope. "I have some photos here I'd like you to look at, Cody." He laid three photos mounted under a plastic sheet on the coffee table. The sheet contained a picture of Roster, an unknown man who scowled under an unkempt bunch of blond hair, and an old file copy of a younger Jim Fallingwater with short hair, staring at the camera. "I'd like you to look at these photos and see if one of them is the man who took care of you. Can you do that?"

Cody jiggled his leg. His dark eyes searched the faces in the room.

"You don't need to be afraid, Cody," Dr. Halfan said in his reassuring voice. He put his arm around the boy's shoulders. "No one is going to hurt you. We just won't let that happen. Okay?"

"Okay." Cody stared at the photographs. His eyes lingered on the picture of Jim; his small shoulders trembled.

"Do you recognize that man?" Ken asked.

Cody looked up, his large, dark eyes serious. "Whad'd he do?"

Ken looked at Dr. Halfan. "It's okay?"

Dr. Halfan nodded.

"A long time ago, he did a bad thing. He killed a woman," Ken said. "He was never found."

"Oh." Cody squirmed in his seat and looked down.

"We need you to identify the man you were with, okay?" Ken said.

"Okay."

"Take your time, son."

Cody looked at his mother. She nodded. "Go ahead dear. You can tell these nice men the truth."

***

They were all looking at him. Cody swallowed hard and took another drink of the black coffee. He knew who Len Roster was. He'd seen his picture on TV and in the newspapers that were all over the house. He was a bad man, and he was dead. But that other picture in there looked like Ben, only younger. He knew it had to be, since he had that same scar on his forehead. He knew that face so well, because he had drawn it so many times in the notebooks Ben had given him. It wasn't true. Ben wouldn't hurt anybody.

"The truth, honey, just tell the truth," he heard his mother say again somewhere in the foggy distance.

Cody clutched the wooden dog close to his chest. He closed his eyes tight and wrinkled his nose. In his mind, he saw that brown face and those wild eyes that turned kind when they looked at him, the big hands whittling by the flickering fire, Wolf licking his face. He remembered how Ben went out in the snow to bring him peanut butter for his birthday, and the ceremony that night with Captain Jack. He remembered everything, especially those words: *You can still talk to me when I'm away. If you're scared, just close your eyes and think real hard. Answers will come.*

"Are you okay?" Mary asked, noticing Cody's closed eyes and scrunched-up face. "He does that a lot," she whispered to Dr. Halfan who nodded in agreement.

Cody opened his eyes. "That's him," he said. "He's the one." His small finger reached forward and touched Roster's picture.

***

After the meeting, when everyone had gone, Richards slapped Ken on the back. "Well, that settles that," he said with a big, smug smile on his face. "Case closed."

It didn't end there. Every time they were in a meeting together, Richards managed to slip in a wise crack. "You busted any ghosts lately?" he'd suddenly ask in front of everybody.

"Have a doughnut, Blake, it cures delusions."

Still, Ken refused to let it go. *It didn't make sense. I saw a large man running from the car, a man who left big footprints in the mud; the kid shows up with a wooden dog that looks like the stuff Jim used to carve, he has the same scar on his finger that I do, and the kid is fixated on some imaginary Indian he calls Ben.*

Ken drove out to the Big Bat and looked for more evidence on his own. There were caves out there, and Fallingwater knew where they were. He did manage to locate some of the lava tubes he and Jim had played in as kids, but other than that he found nothing, just the wind and the gray-green silence.

On his way back to town he spotted Wade Hickman, an old rancher, parked along the side of Cooper's Hawk Highway. Wade frequently came up to the Big Bat area to cut timber to make his own fence posts. His hefty load had come undone; logs were scattered over the highway. Ken stopped to give him a hand.

"Wade, you need to get a new truck. This one's a bucket of bolts."

Wade bit down on his pipe. He wore a black-and-red checked mackinaw and a red cap over his wispy white hair. "There's still a lot of juice in this ol' baby. That's the trouble with you young fellers. All you think about is buy, buy, buy. Hell, I don't even own a credit card."

Ken helped him load the posts and tighten the cables around them. "Now don't let these blamed things fall off again, or I'm gonna have to write you a ticket."

"The hell you will." Wade narrowed his eyes.

"Looks like you got enough posts here to fence in all of Forest Lake."

"Been comin' up here the past two months, finally decided to take my load out. I cut 'em, then like to cure 'em before I haul 'em home and treat 'em."

"So, you seen anybody up here. Any strangers?"

"You talkin' about that boy that was missin'? I guess they found 'im."

"Yeah, just trying to tie up loose ends."

"Well, I ain't seen nobody except a couple of moose and some dang Mexican feller walkin' along the highway with his dog. They're takin' over everything, you know."

"The moose?"

"I mean them Mexican fellers. More and more of them are comin' here, takin' jobs. We need more guards at the border. Now there's a problem."

Five years later

That summer Ken and Lydia went to Ashland on vacation to see Shakespeare's *Twelfth Night*. The next morning Lydia wanted to shop, so Ken decided to kill some time in a local coffee shop. After he got his coffee, he noticed Pete Benson sitting at a small table all by himself.

"I thought that was you," Pete said. He stood up and shook Ken's hand.

"I needed a place to hang out while Lydia spends down our bank account," Ken laughed.

"Have a seat."

"And how is Cody? I think about him a lot."

"He's doing really well. Really well. He lives with his mother in Portland. He's in a gifted learning program."

"I always thought he was a bright kid."

"He's very into Native American art and culture. Adjusted like a bandit. All the kid needed was a challenge. When he got that, all that other crap about hyperactivity, acting out or whatever the hell they said it was just went away. Turns out, he was just bored."

"So you all live in Portland now?" Ken noticed the wedding ring on his finger.

"No, not quite. Cally and the boy do. No, I still live in Medford. Cally finished her teaching degree. She's going to law school at night. I've, uh, remarried and I . . . we have a little girl."

Ken didn't know what to say. Congratulations seemed wrong. He just said, "I see."

"Cody's coming down in July. He's a teenager now, fourteen years old. Can you believe that?"

"They grow up fast. Lauren just finished college. She's going to be a teacher, like her mother."

Pete nodded. "They sure do. We're going camping. Just me, the kid, and Jack."

"Jack?"

"The dog I gave him. A golden retriever, he named him Jack. Captain Jack."

"Captain Jack," Ken repeated, his eyes widened. "The Modoc Indian chief."

"I guess. Like I said, Cody is very into Native American studies. Can't get enough of it, wants to study anthropology and art when he goes to college. He's already talking college, can you believe that? And, he loves that dog. Getting him that dog, that's the one thing I did right."

***

Ken told nobody, not even Lydia, but he returned to the remote wilderness area several times, looking for signs of Jim. He even left notes in secret places, hoping Jim would find them.

"The boy is okay," he scribbled. "You did the right thing." But there never was any sign of Jim or anybody else for that matter. Nothing. Absolutely nothing. The weather faded and withered the notes. The wind blew the pieces into obscurity. With Roster dead, there were no more thefts reported at the Lake Store and very few in the Lake cabins. "That," said Lydia, "ought to convince you."

Maybe Richards was right. He had been jousting at windmills. After one last trek in the Big Bat wilderness area, Ken drove to that special place out by the canyon. He got out of his Jeep and drank in the fresh air.

"Captain Jack," he yelled, "wherever you are."

"Are, are, are," came the echo.

"Peace," Ken yelled.

"Peace, peace," bounced off the mountain. Except for the birds chirping in the trees, there was just stillness, a passing cloud, and the Big Bat gleaming in the distance keeping its secrets.

ACKNOWLEDGMENTS

Writing a novel is a special journey but equally special are the people who offered helpful advice along the way. I'd like to thank Lois Rosen for her helpful suggestions, and encouragement and Jane Fernandez, Dawn Smith, Cathy Ingalls, Margo Hampton, Sandy McDow, and the Thursday Night Group for top notch critiques and for being tireless beta readers. Thanks also to Yvette and Don Baker, Corky, Max, Counter, Harley, Buddy, and Leo just for being there and to Smidge, Princess, Shanti, B.C., and sweet little Tara for your love and inspiration. There's a little bit of all of us in this work.

And for those who think a young boy unwittingly let a murderer walk free, don't—as some person famously said—believe everything that you think. Watch for the sequel, "Ready or Not," coming soon in which a grown up Cody goes looking for the man who not only saved his life but changed it forever.

ABOUT THE AUTHOR

Jean Rover's short fiction has received awards or recognition from *Writer's Digest, Short Story America,* Willamette Writers, and Oregon Writers Colony. Her work has appeared in various literary magazines and anthologies, including the *Saturday Evening Post's* Great American Fiction Contest Anthology. Other stories were performed at Liars' League events in London, England and Portland, Oregon. She has also authored a chapbook, *Beneath the Boughs Unseen,* featuring holiday stories about society's invisible people. She lives and writes in Oregon's lush Willamette Valley.